Lynn Duffy is originally from South East London but now lives in the picturesque county of Kent, also known as the 'Garden of England!' Lynn has many hobbies, one of which is singing in a choir. Lynn believes she has inherited her sense of humour from her family, in particular, her late grandmother, Lilian. She hopes this comes across in this her first-ever novel. They say love makes the world go round, and Lynn grew up in a house filled with love and laughter.

To all my family and friends, I wouldn't be who I am today without your love and support.

Lynn Duffy

TAKE 2 IN TUSCANY

AUSTIN MACAULEY PUBLISHERS™

LONDON * CAMBRIDGE * NEW YORK * SHARJAH

A CIP catalogue record for this title is available from the British Library.

ISBN 9781528916929 (Paperback)
ISBN 9781528961721 (ePub e-book)

www.austinmacauley.com

First Published 2022
Austin Macauley Publishers Ltd®
1 Canada Square
Canary Wharf
London
E14 5AA

Thank you to everyone who has helped me to believe in myself.
(Some of the proceeds from this novel will be donated to Great Ormond Street
Children's Hospital.)

Chapter 1

The day had not started too well for Sarah Carrington. As soon as she had got up that morning, she'd stubbed her big toe on the bottom of her bed which had made her yelp, and then had been horrified to see a tiny, but nevertheless, bright red spot which was positively glowing on her chin. She hadn't had one like that since she was a teenager. She would have to use plenty of concealer on that baby! After a rushed breakfast, she eventually left the house in a taxi, only to find that the 8.50 train to Charing Cross had been cancelled. Apparently, this was due to a donkey on the line. *Just when you think you've heard every excuse possible*, Sarah thought, she would definitely have to go on the internet later on!

When she finally arrived for her hair appointment, Frederick, her usual hairdresser, was off sick! Surely the day couldn't get any worse. Ellie, the new stylist, had been duly assigned to do her hair in Frederick's absence, ably assisted by Jean-Paul. Given that she had turned up late, they had been very accommodating. As a precaution, she'd sent her friend Annabel a text warning her that she was running late. Thankfully, by the time she'd left the salon, her nightmare mane of hair had been smoothed and tamed into soft waves. So-Hair had been Sarah's hairdressers since she had been in her early teens. In fact, it had been Annabel who had first discovered this little gem whilst working as an office junior for a large advertising agency. It was tucked away in a little back street in Soho. Sarah had never found any other hairdresser, who could control her thick head of hair, like Frederick. Although, to give credit where it was due, Jean-Paul and Ellie had actually done a brilliant job for her that day.

Luckily, she was out of the hairdresser's at a reasonable time and her fortune had changed, as she had managed to catch a taxi, practically straight away. As usual, the traffic in London was horrendous, but finally her cab drew up outside Claridge's. The driver was an interesting man, who had told her he was from the East End of London. "Third generation," he'd said proudly. However, he was rather talkative and had spent most of the time banging on about some big demonstration that was taking place the following day. It would cause chaos with the traffic, which he wasn't too happy about and understandably so. Selfishly, she was glad that she had chosen to come up to London that day and thus avoiding the dreaded demonstration. She paid the driver his fare and as she was in a happy mood, she added a rather generous tip.

He gave her a broad smile and winked at her. "Ta love. Have a nice day."

"I will, thank you." Sarah had a spring in her step, as she almost glided into the foyer of Claridge's and, as always, she instantly began to feel more relaxed. It had certainly been a hectic morning, but nothing was going to spoil the rest of her day. The doorman had given Sarah an admiring glance, but typically, she hadn't noticed. She couldn't see any sign of Annabel as yet, so she made a quick visit to the ladies' to powder her nose before meeting up with her friend. On the whole she thought she'd scrubbed up okay in her pink Vintage dress, which, her mother had once commented, "made her look youthful," and she knew it showed off her trim waist. Jean-Pierre had kindly allowed Sarah to get changed in his flat above the shop and she'd even received a wolf whistle from him and had laughed when he'd told her she looked "hot".

Sarah came out of the ladies' and immediately caught sight of Annabel. You couldn't really miss her, with her shiny, bright red hair and even though she was only 5'1", she always stood out from the crowd. She had a vibrant personality and dressed accordingly, in her trademark black leather biker jacket, and knee-high boots over skinny jeans. Although clearly not a natural red head, she did, however, have a fiery nature and generally had a short fuse. It was her way or the highway!

Annabel had quickly noticed Sarah and walked over to her. "Oh there you are babe," she said, kissing Sarah on both cheeks. "You made good time then, as I thought you were going to be late!" Sarah had no time to reply, before Annabel said, "Right, follow me; I feel the lure of a Cocktail coming on!" Sarah shrugged her shoulders and did as she was told. Annabel, as usual, was in charge and she followed her friend into the Cocktail lounge, where she quickly hopped up onto a barstool. She ordered two Archers' Woo Woos. The barman began mixing and shaking their cocktails with all the expertise of someone who had been doing it for years. Both women watched him avidly as he poured the red liquid concoction into two long-stemmed glasses, without spilling a single drop. You could tell he loved the attention he was receiving and he'd flirted with them just a little, but without going over the top. Sarah noticed that Annabel was enjoying his attention too, as she smiled and gave him one of her come-hither looks. She was, after all, the original Flirty Gertie! "Oh thank you kind Sir," Annabel said, taking a long sip of her drink.

The barman smiled at them in a friendly manner, "My pleasure, ladies." Annabel had been looking forward to this moment all morning.

"God it's been manic at work, but now I have the rest of the day to devote totally to you, Sarah."

"Thank you, I am deeply honoured."

"Well, so you should be," Annabel said, smiling at her bestie.

"Now why don't you try your cocktail?"

"Okay, Miss Bossy Boots," and Sarah took a small sip, although she wasn't usually much of a drinker.

"Isn't that delicious and refreshing?" Annabel enquired.

"Not bad I guess and it's very fruity, isn't it."

"Never mind the fruitiness, it's the vodka content that really matters."

"You know alcohol always goes straight to my head."

"That's because you don't drink nearly enough of it. Anyway," Annabel said mischievously, "you're so much more fun when you've had a drink and by the way, you look fabulous! Did Frederick do your hair today?"

"No he didn't actually. The poor guy is poorly with some flu bug. Ellie and Jean-Paul did it for me."

"It took two to do your hair?"

"What can I say, it's not easy taming my mane. Anyway, it was a case of having to, because as you know, I was running late, so it put them behind a bit."

"Well, it looks amazing."

"Thank you. I've also got some gossip for you!"

"Ooh, spill the beans," Annabel said, taking another sip of her cocktail.

"Well, Jean-Paul told me that he and Frederick are getting married in December, just before Christmas and we're both invited."

"Wow about time I'd say and it's certainly one wedding I don't want to miss."

"Me neither, in fact I'd pay good money to go," Sarah quipped, "and there's bound to be some way over the top frou frou."

Annabel smiled and said, "Yes no doubt about that, and I for one want a front row seat! Of course, more than likely there will be a few dramas and fireworks before the big day. When those two fall out, you can cut the atmosphere in that salon with a pair of scissors." Both women laughed.

"Still it's good news and something to look forward to, Annabel."

"Yes and I can hardly wait. Right, let's finish off our devilishly delicious cocktails and that's not easy for me to say right now, trust me! I'm ravenous." Annabel downed her cocktail swiftly and looked at Sarah, who felt obliged to do the same and finished hers off as well. She just hoped she didn't regret it later.

They were met by the Maître d who checked their reservation before they were shown to their table, which was right in the middle of the beautiful and decadent restaurant. Claridge's was a favourite place for them to meet up for lunch and where they had shared some special occasions over the years. The food was fabulous and the surroundings of the Art Deco Restaurant were opulent and classy but, at the same time, warm and inviting. Both women had a fondness for that particular era. It somehow gave it an intimate and cosy atmosphere.

The waiter greeted them warmly. After recommending the Dover Sole, he took their order and quickly disappeared. He was friendly towards them, recognising that he had seen them several times before. Both women were certainly easy on the eye and the blonde one, in particular, had a cracking pair of legs. Still he had to concentrate on the job in hand. That's what he was paid to do.

He was an ambitious young man who had every intention of working his way up to the top at Claridge's, just as his grandfather had done before him.

"So, Sarah, come on, tell your Auntie Annabel how are you feeling?"

Sarah took an intake of breath, before saying, "You could say not ecstatic, but at least I am a free woman now that I have finally and I repeat *finally*, got my Decree Absolute."

"About bloody time I'd say."

"Yes, our divorce has been a rather drawn-out affair, hasn't it."

"That's putting it mildly and so typical of Richard to drag his heels."

"Well, you know it's been a complete nightmare for me, but somehow I still feel a bit of a failure, Annabel."

"How can you say that, Sarah. Don't be ridiculous, the only failure, disappointment, whatever you want to call him, is Richard, or Mr Perfect as he thought he was!"

Sarah sighed. "Yes, I know but after nearly 18 years of marriage, you do actually begin to think it's for keeps. I did love him once you know, warts and all. Do you remember when we first saw him down in Brighton?"

Annabel laughed. "Yeah, of course I do. How can I ever forget that, it's ingrained on my brain? Our first holiday together, just the two of us. We were sweet seventeen and as innocent and pure as the driven snow," Annabel said reflectively.

"Yes, we certainly were, but we also thought ourselves to be so very grown up, didn't we?"

"Yes, that's true, and what about that grotty little bed and breakfast place where we stayed. God, it was a bit of a fleapit and that woman was so irritating. She was a right old dragon Sarah and treated us as if we were a pair of ten-year-olds, what with all her rules and regulations."

Annabel looked somewhat more serious when she said to Sarah, "Your life changed that day, Sarah, as we stood waiting at the bus stop. Richard pulled up in that flashy red sports car of his and offered us a lift, well you really!"

"I know and we had our skimpy little shorts on, which we'd made from our jeans."

"Sarah, it's no wonder Richard stopped, as your shorts were even skimpier than mine and your legs go on forever."

Sarah protested, "No they were not, were they?"

"Yes they were!" Annabel said emphatically, "Anyhow, I felt a complete idiot in that 'Kiss Me Quick' hat and Richard looked so sophisticated."

"Yes I can see why you fell for him, Sarah, as he was a proper charmer back then and he swept you right off your feet. He definitely only had eyes for you back then, for sure!"

"Did I ever tell you that he could also be very imaginative in the bedroom?"

"Hold it there, sister, you're making me blush!"

"Just saying," Sarah said laughing. "Anyway, please, you blush, huh don't make me laugh," Sarah continued. "It was you who taught me all about the birds and the bees," she blurted out, rather more loudly than she'd intended. A couple of the diners who were sitting near them turned around and looked in their direction. "Whoops, I knew I shouldn't have downed that Woo Woo."

"Oh it's good to see you let yourself go for once, Sarah."

"You know, I did wonder if we'd had children, would things have been different."

"Oh, stop it please, don't beat yourself up," Annabel said, giving Sarah's hand a gentle squeeze, sensing her friend was feeling emotional. She would have liked to have given her a hug, but it would only draw even more attention to themselves from the other diners in the restaurant.

The waiter brought over a silver ice bucket which shone as it caught the light from the crystal chandeliers in the restaurant and placed it down alongside Annabel. Sarah looked at Annabel and said, "What are you up to? That's a very expensive bottle of champagne! You shouldn't have!"

"You deserve a treat. Only the best for you today." The waiter popped the cork and poured them each a glass of bubbling champagne. Annabel stared at the waiter as he departed. "Wow, Check him out, he's so handsome, isn't he? And he has a fabulously tight butt."

"Yes he is and you're right he does, and you say that every time you see him, but he is still way too young for you. He'd probably think you were a cougar."

"Well he'd be right then wouldn't he?"

"Yes that's true," and Sarah shook her head and said, "you are incorrigible," and they both laughed. "Anyway, Sarah, this is a pivotal moment in your life and I know that today isn't necessarily a celebration, but this is where your life begins," and she paused briefly, before saying, "again!" She raised her champagne glass into the air, "To new beginnings."

"I'll drink to that, Annabel," and they clinked their glasses together. "I hope you're right."

"Come on where is your faith, I'm always right, aren't I?"

Sarah raised her eyebrows at her friend. "Let's say sometimes you're right Annabel."

"Anyway, you should have received a medal for staying with that man for as long as you did." Sarah had a large sip of her champagne, which warmed her throat as it went down. She was enjoying it until a rather loud hiccup escaped, which totally took her by surprise. "Oopsy," Sarah said placing her hand over her mouth and with her face turning bright red said. "Excuse me, Annabel."

Annabel tutted and said in a mocking tone, "I simply cannot take you anywhere, can I, Sarah." They smiled at one another and then as they were apt to do, got a fit of the giggles, but given where they were, they soon managed to control their laughter! "Maybe I shouldn't have any more!"

"Nonsense, simply take smaller sips."

"Hold on a tick, Sarah, I just need to pop to the loo."

Sarah became rather self-conscious sitting in the restaurant without Annabel to talk to, but a group of women who were sat on the other side of the restaurant caught her attention. They were all clearly having fun and just a tad on the noisy side. One of them was heavily pregnant and looked as if she was ready to pop at any moment.

She had noticed her before, as she had made frequent visits to the loo, accompanied by one of her friends, who all had a nervous and concerned look on their faces! Sarah thought it would make a great story, baby born in the dining room at Claridge's, but definitely, not for the poor mother!

Annabel returned to the table and sat back down. "That's better. Now, Sarah, have you got any ideas on what you're going to do next?"

"No, not yet. The trouble is, Annabel, I'm bored now. The business was my life and I put my heart and soul into it."

"More than that, Sarah, you were the driving force within it. It was you who had the business acumen and creativity, not Richard! All he had was a load of old flannel and I guess a certain amount of charm."

"Thanks, Annabel. But now I do need to find myself a job and soon. Something completely different. I really do love my afternoons at The Bake Stop. I have fifteen in my cake decorating class at the moment. I have one lovely lady who is a real character, Peggy, and she has us all in stitches with her tales of when she ran a stall in Camden market. However, in the long term, this just isn't enough to occupy me completely."

Annabel wrinkled her nose. "It all sounds way too twee for me, darling, but it has been good for you I must say!"

"Yes it has, but I am actually in danger of turning into a couch potato. Watching way too much daytime telly and if I'm not careful, I will end up joining my mother's Friday lunch club."

Annabel rolled her eyes as she said, "I would never let that happen to you, babe. Hey, have you ever thought about giving speed dating a try? Now that's an experience I can tell you. It's fun," Annabel continued, but noticed the disgust on Sarah's face. "No, honestly, it really is, as long as you don't take it too seriously. Of course you meet quite a lot of frogs along the way, but there are a few princes out there still too!"

"NO, Annabel, that's definitely not for me!"

"So how do you think Richard will cope with the business without you, Sarah?"

"Well, he has his Sue Ling now, doesn't he, so I'm sure he will be perfectly okay. All those trips to South East Asia, telling me how good he was at driving a hard bargain."

"Um, I have a feeling, Sarah, that his hard bargain will end up costing him a lot of money one day. Thankfully, in a lower tone Annabel said, and what he found the easiest to do of course, was screwing the arse off of her. What is it they say, there is no fool like an old fool!"

"She is a manipulating little cow, Annabel, and if I was him, I would sleep with one eye open from now on. They deserve one another!"

"Are you sure he didn't meet her whilst out in Thailand, in some shady little nightclub, where she was pushing out ping pong balls, from well you know where!"

"Annabel, please, remember where you are! Anyway, you know he didn't. Actually, it might have made it a lot easier for me if he had somehow. She is a respectable business woman, who also happens to be young and beautiful."

"You're being way too generous, Sarah, as usual."

"Well, Sue Ling appears to have it all and now she has Richard."

"Yes, you see, there is always a downside to everything isn't there?"

"You're outrageous, Annabel."

"Not outrageous, I'm just being bloody honest. You're way too good for Richard. You always were, Sarah, and for the record by the way, you're gorgeous too, so stop fishing for compliments."

"I wasn't honestly." Sarah thought how lucky she was to have such a supportive friend as Annabel. She always knew how to lift her spirits. "Why don't you start your own business up? You're a trained chef for goodness' sake!"

"Oh, I'm not sure. Maybe it's something I could think about doing in the future. I'm just not ready for anything like that right now."

"Well, look, if you like, why don't I give Sam a ring, she may have something that might suit you. She has some high-profile clients on her books."

"What do you think?"

"Yes I suppose there would be no harm in checking it out, thanks. I must say as much as I love my mother, it's weird living with her. I also find it strange having to let someone know where I will be 24/7. Then there's her smoking."

"Oh Dotty Diva is lovely, Sarah, she's a real trooper and her stories about when she was a tiller girl, are absolutely hilarious. She should definitely write a book."

"Oh God, Annabel, don't you ever give her any ideas for goodness' sake. Let's remember how she earned her Diva title!"

"Yes, but she totally owns that title, Sarah, and anyhow it's a lot easier than trying to pronounce her surname, Dotty Doherty. What a mouthful," Annabel quipped.

"Yeah, you're right, Sarah, laughed and I have to give her credit, as she can still do those high kicks and what with her yoga, she's very fit and flexible."

The waiter brought over their dessert, of Buttermilk Panna Cotta, with red cherries and shortbread. It looked fabulous and the cherries were so perfect, they didn't look real. The chef had created a piece of art on a plate. It was a shame to spoil it really. "This looks extremely fattening," Sarah commented.

"Oh it's only now and again. Come on let's live dangerously at least for now!"

"Yes you're right," Sarah said tucking into her dessert.

"Dare I ask how you and Liam are doing?"

"Please can we not talk about Liam today? We never see eye to eye when his name comes up. I'll just say, we're still seeing each other. Anyhow, today is all about you." Sarah hoped everything was all right between them. Annabel was extremely guarded when his name was mentioned. Still reluctantly she had to agree with Annabel that this wouldn't be a good time to challenge her friend about him. "Okay, we will talk another time. Annabel, thank you for being such a good friend to me. You know how much I love you, don't you."

"'Course I do silly." Their lunch had been a rather lengthy and relaxing affair, but eventually it was time to say their goodbyes. They hugged one another. "Thanks, Annabel, you're a star."

"My pleasure, babe. I will call you later, after I have spoken to Sam."

"Thank you and take care."

"You too."

Sarah splashed out on yet another cab to Charing Cross Station, the buses were always full at that particular time of day and she wasn't overly keen on the underground.

The traffic had been slow yet again and with minutes to spare, she had only just managed to catch her train. She had ran, albeit not overly elegantly, down the platform as quickly as she could and by the time she took her seat, she was out of breath and panting slightly. A city gent in a pinstripe suit, with a ruddy complexion peered at her from over his newspaper and was ogling her. She glared back at him and his head very quickly disappeared behind his newspaper once more. When her breathing eventually returned to normal, she felt tired, but relaxed. It had been a good lunch. However, Sarah was still a little concerned about Annabel. She personally believed Liam to be bad news and it was highly unlikely that he would ever leave his wife and family. But, Annabel was in love with him and therefore any criticism of him fell on deaf ears.

Annabel had been her best friend since they were eleven years old. They were polar opposites. Annabel was a born leader and had enough confidence for the both of them. She really didn't care what people thought about her either, which Sarah really admired about her friend. They had only ever fallen out once at school, whilst in the Sixth form. Andy Springate was a blonde, blue-eyed Adonis and both of them had had a major crush on him. Much to their surprise, it was Moira Simpson, a quiet studious girl in their class, who had eventually snatched him away from right under their very noses. They certainly hadn't seen that one coming!

Sarah knew she had to make some changes in her life. She couldn't vegetate at her mother's forever. It simply wasn't an option and she was worried that she may end up falling out with her and she wouldn't want that to happen. The train pulled into Sarah's station and she alighted and as there were no taxis outside, she decided not to wait and walked home. It was a fair distance, but it was still light and the air warm. After all the food and drink she'd consumed earlier, the exercise would be good for her. If nothing else, it may clear her head, which she had to admit was thudding somewhat! She'd only ever had a head similar to this before and that was uncannily on her hen night!

Sarah was just about to put her key into the front door when her mum opened it. "Oh there you are, Sarah."

"Yes, the wanderer returns, Mum."

"Annabel just rang for you. She wants you to call her back. She's been trying to ring you on your mobile, but didn't get any answer!"

"Oh crikes, I think it's on silent. Thanks, Mum. How are you?"

"I'm fine thanks, I went to yoga this morning. You really ought to take it up, Sarah."

"Maybe, Mum, although I'm quite happy with my Pilates." Sarah slumped down onto the sofa, kicking off her now rather uncomfortable nude shoes as she did so.

"Well aren't you going to call Annabel?"

"In a minute, Mum." Dotty noticed that her daughter looked tired, but didn't want to say anything.

"Righty ho. I'm about to make a cuppa, would you like one love," Dotty said walking towards the kitchen. "Yes please. Have you been smoking again, Mum?"

"Yes and what of it, after all this is my home."

"I know, Mum, so you keep telling me."

"Blooming heck, I even had all the windows open too. With that nose of yours, have you ever thought about becoming a sniffer dog."

"Very funny, Mum. Sorry, but you know what I'm like."

"Yes I'm certainly finding out." Sarah laughed. *Here we go again.* Her mother's smoking was something they argued about constantly. However, Dotty had remonstrated that at almost 72, she wasn't giving it up any time soon.

Sarah rang Annabel and she answered almost immediately. "Oh thank goodness, Sarah. I've been trying to ring you for ages."

"Yes sorry, I had my mobile on silent. To be honest, I had a little catnap on the journey home."

"I don't blame you. You were hitting the champers a bit hard and you're not used to it are you!"

"I know, not like me at all."

"Anyway, I've spoken to Sam and you're in luck. There's a job that you may be interested in."

"Go on."

"She's just received a new instruction to find a Personal Assistant for none other than Steve Fountain, he's a well-known film director. You've heard of him, haven't you."

"Yes I have actually."

"So this should be right up your street. It would be a wonderful opportunity, Sarah, as you're a proper film buff."

"Yes I am, but—"

"No buts, you told me earlier you want to make some major changes in your life."

"Yes I suppose I do."

"This sounds fabulous. Think of all the travelling you would do when he's on location."

"I don't know what to say, Annabel."

"Please say you will think about it at least and give Sam a call. She cannot sit on this one for too long. Apparently Steve Fountain needs someone urgently. Basically if you're interested, Sam will put you forward as being an ideal candidate!"

"But I don't have any real experience in that field."

"Oh don't worry about that, just go for it, please!" Sarah took down Sam's number and promised Annabel she would get in touch with her. Sarah, however, didn't feel anywhere near as enthusiastic about it all as Annabel did.

Sarah acknowledged that she had certainly overdone it with the champagne earlier, but at last she also did feel free from her past and a lot calmer than she had in ages. Of course, this again could be down to the champagne. Thankfully, all the raw emotions she'd once had were now dissipating and today had been full of more highs than lows and she was grateful. She would definitely give Sam a call, she at least owed Annabel that much. Along with her family, Annabel had always been her stalwart and she would not have got through her divorce without her best friend. Sarah also noticed she had another missed call from her solicitor. It was too late to call her back now. Tomorrow would have to do. Hopefully it would be about a completion date on the apartment she was buying in Whitstable.

Dotty, meanwhile, was in the kitchen. She was naturally still concerned about her daughter. She could tell that the Absolute on her divorce coming through had been bitter sweet for her. Sarah had been through so much and it had saddened Dotty to see her daughter so unhappy. On the day that Sarah had found out about Richard's affair and he'd walked out on her, Dotty immediately went to comfort her daughter, who had been in bits. She had sobbed from somewhere deep within her soul and Dotty would never forget it and she would never ever forgive Richard. Thankfully, she was almost back to her old self now. That swine Richard had put Sarah through the ringer and hung her out to dry.

When she had brought him home for the first time, Dotty had thought he was an arrogant young man. Sarah was only 17 and Richard was almost 22. She hadn't approved, right from the start. However, her late husband, Jeffrey, had told her to give him the benefit of the doubt, as it was clear that Sarah was potty about him. Dotty hoped that her lovely daughter would eventually find someone more deserving of her one day. Thank goodness things had been smoother with her son, Tony. He'd met Megan at Durham University and they were now married and had three daughters, and as far as she was aware, they were still happily married. In fact, Megan was more like another daughter to her.

Dotty picked up the tea tray and took it through to the lounge as breezily as she could muster. "Here you are," Dotty said passing Sarah her tea. "Are you okay, love?"

"I think I have had way too much champagne at lunch time, Mum."

"You little devil."

"I know but Annabel insisted on treating me today. I quite enjoyed it actually."

"Oh she's a lovely girl, I'm very fond of her, as you know. Here have a fondant fancy, that will soak up some of the alcohol."

"Thanks, Mum, I think I will."

"So what did Annabel want then?"

"Annabel's friend Sam runs an employment agency in London, and she has a job which they seem to think would be ideal for me."

"What kind of a job?"

"I would be working as a Personal Assistant."

"That sounds a bit fancy."

"Not really but it would be working for a film director no less."

"Oh yes, what's his name?"

"Steve Fountain."

"Oh. Now that name rings a bell."

"Does it?"

"Yes, I know. I think he's the son of Eddie Fountain. He used to be a TV and film producer years ago. I knew him quite well back in the day and met him loads of times, when we did Sunday Night at the Palladium. Yes Eddie, now that brings back fond memories." The twinkle in her mother's eyes didn't escape Sarah's notice. "Those were the days."

"Oh, Mum, tell me you didn't, did you."

"You cheeky girl."

"There have only ever been two men in my life and one of those was your dad."

"Who was the other one, Mum? That's on an 'as and when need to know basis', young lady. Maybe you'll read all about it in me memoirs one day." Sarah raised her eyebrows. Her mother was impossible sometimes. "Well to be honest, I did have a little dalliance with Eddie, but it didn't go too far, really. I was only a slip of a girl back then and he was after all a married man and believe it or not, I do have some scruples."

"Phew, thank goodness for that."

"Anyway, his wife was a bit snooty, American she was. I never actually met her properly like, but I saw her a few times with him. By all accounts she was a formidable woman, if ever there was one. She came from a moneyed background and she definitely wore the trousers. I guess Eddie knew what side his bread was buttered on of course. Still there are two sides to every story. He certainly loved the ladies though, for sure. Everyone knew that. I heard he divorced her eventually. Oh sorry, love. Me and my big mouth."

"Don't worry, Mum. God, I'm not that sensitive. Anyway, I'm single and ready to mingle now." Dotty looked at her daughter more closely.

"Are you really?"

"No, of course not, but I am single and Annabel thought I ought to give speed dating a try."

"Oh lord you're not going to do it, are you, love?"

"No, of course not and I actually couldn't think of anything worse! Right, I'm off to bed; it's an early night for me, Mum," Sarah said stifling a yawn and kissed her mother goodnight, who rather unexpectedly said night love.

"Sleep tight and don't let the bed bugs bite." Her mother hadn't said that to her since she was a little girl. Sarah laughed.

"Hey, Mum, I said I was single, not reverting back to my childhood!"

"I know, I know, I'm just feeling a bit emotional."

Sarah kissed her mother once more. "Night, Mum, and I'm perfectly okay honestly." As she went up the stairs, Sarah decided it was now or never and she would give Sam a call, before she had a chance to change her mind.

Sam had been pleased to hear from her. She'd told Sarah, that if she was really interested in the position, then she would make contact with Steve Fountain's Management Team and all Sarah had to do, was send her CV through to her, as soon as possible. Sarah briefly mulled it over and thought what had she to lose. She would just have to wait now and see if Sam arranged an interview for her. She got her CV up on her laptop to email to Sam and hesitated briefly before sending it off. Right it's done now she thought as she ran herself a hot bath and added a generous amount of bubble bath.

She laid back fully in the bath and soaked herself for a good half an hour, before she got out, dried herself off and put on her PJs. She was feeling really relaxed. She knew with some certainty, that if she got an interview and was lucky enough to be offered this job working for Steve Fountain, then she would accept it. She had to do something with her life and she couldn't go on feeling sorry for herself any more. Annabel was right about one thing, today would definitely be a new beginning. She realised that Richard had always been controlling and had known exactly how to manipulate her. He had once been her weakness. Thankfully, he wasn't any longer and never would be again. He was out of her life and suddenly it felt good as she was now ready to move on. With that she jumped into bed with the full intention of reading her book, but she couldn't keep her eyes open past the first page and it wasn't long before she went out like a light.

Chapter 2

Sarah checked herself out in front of her full-length mirror and for once, a much more confident woman stared back at her. She did, in fact, feel more like her old self and certainly more optimistic about her future. After several changes of outfits, Sarah opted to wear a smart black pencil skirt and a cream silk blouse, with her newly acquired and expensive black leather jacket, which was so soft to the touch. It had been an impulse buy, but at the time she'd told herself that she deserved a treat. In her opinion, she didn't really think this interview would necessitate a full-on corporate look. She looked at her reflection in the mirror once more and thought she looked just right for an interview and a killer pair of heels would finish it all off perfectly. Anyway, it would have to do for now, because Sarah didn't have time to change again. Luckily, for once, her hair had behaved itself and after extensive straightening, it looked sleek and shiny. Surprisingly she felt calm at this precise moment and didn't feel nervous in the slightest about her interview! She took her shoes off and put on a little pair of pumps to wear up to London and placed her high-heeled shoes into an oversized black handbag, which thankfully were fashionable.

Dotty was sat at the kitchen table eating her breakfast. "Well, Mum, how do I look?" Dotty stood up.

"Oh, Sarah, you look totes amaze."

"Oh, Mum, you watch far too much television."

"You know me. You can take the girl out of Essex." Sarah interrupted her mother.

"Yes, Mum, I think I know how that one goes."

"Well I'm the original Essex bird, born and bred in Chigwell I was."

"You certainly are, Mum. Anyway, I'd best be off. I don't want to miss my train."

"Go knock him dead love. He'd be lucky to have you working for him," her mother said warmly. "You look gorgeous."

"Thanks, Mum, but I think you're a tad biased."

"You know with them legs and your height, you could easily have been a model, or a dancer."

"Yes, but let's not go there again, Mum," Sarah said looking at her mother, slightly exasperated. "I really do have to go now," she said as she kissed and hugged her mother briefly and almost made it to the front door, when her mother stopped her in her tracks.

"Hold on, Sarah, you cannot leave without this."

"Without what, Mum?" Dotty went over to the sideboard and rummaged quickly through its drawers.

"Ah here it is."

"What are you doing now?"

"It's my lucky rabbit's foot. It always used to work for me when I was a dancer. I got every audition I went for." Dotty placed the once white, shabby rabbit's foot into the palm of her daughter's hand. Sarah just smiled at her. "You know you are mad, don't you?"

"Me mad never, but just take it for luck. Humour me!"

"Of course I will."

"Take care, love."

"I'll try."

"I love you mad woman."

"Love you too," and with that Sarah was on her way.

Sarah arrived at the swanky-looking Kensington offices, with time to spare, before her interview. It was clearly a new build and therefore had a very contemporary look, which consisted mainly of glass and boy did it sparkle in the mid-day sunshine. She had been told by Sam that Steve Fountain's offices were on the eleventh floor and made her way to the lift. She wasn't keen on using lifts, but even less keen on walking up eleven flights of stairs, today of all days. The lift stopped at the eleventh floor and she waited anxiously for the lift doors to open and then walked towards a door, which led into the reception area of Steve Fountain's offices. Sarah looked out across at the stunning views of Kensington Gardens in the distance. This was a haven away from the hectic rush of London life. Sarah was still taking in the spectacular view, when the receptionist called out rather loudly. "Can I help you?" She looked slightly peeved, but smiled at Sarah nevertheless.

"I am sorry, I was miles away. I am Sarah Carrington. I have an appointment with Maxine Hargrave."

"Would you just sign in and then take a seat please?" Sarah did as she was asked and sat herself down.

She picked up a magazine and flicked through its pages, not paying too much attention to its content. She still felt incredibly calm, after all it wouldn't be the end of the world if she didn't get this job. Or was that just bravado. She had to admit to herself that her pride may be dented. She was naturally curious about Steve Fountain and wondered if she would get to meet him today.

A petite woman whose blonde hair was tied up in a ponytail, hurried into the reception, looking somewhat harassed. "Hello, Sarah, I'm Maxine Hargrave, pleased to meet you. I'm so sorry to have kept you waiting. It's been one of those days!"

"No worries."

"Would you like to come through?"

"Yes, of course." Sarah followed Maxine into a large office, where a huge desk took centre stage. It was tastefully decorated with two rather expensive looking leather sofas and modern artwork around its walls. "Do take a seat Sarah."

"Thank you. Steve was hoping to join us today, but he is stuck in a meeting in Manchester at the moment."

There was a light tap on the door and a young man entered the room, and Sarah couldn't fail to notice how handsome he was, with just a hint of stubble. He was immaculately dressed in a well-cut suit and had dark shoulder-length hair. He looked to Sarah to be a metro-male, as he was so well groomed, not a hair out of place and in total contrast to Maxine, who appeared to be shabby chic in a short floaty floral dress, worn over black leggings and a cutesy little pink cardigan.

"Ah there you are, James, come and join us. Let me introduce you to Sarah Carrington."

James shook her hand, "Pleased to meet you," he said before sitting down next to Maxine. He was American and by the sound of his accent, from New York. "Right, just to let you know, Sarah, James and I are both part of Steve's management team and he has entrusted us with the task of interviewing you today. Firstly we'd like to thank you for coming at such short notice, Maxine said flicking through Sarah's CV. I see that you have come highly recommended by Sam at the Agency and I must say, your CV is very impressive. The fact that you've run your own business and a successful one at that speaks volumes. So my first question is, what interests you about becoming a Personal Assistant?"

Sarah hesitated briefly. "Well, to be candid, I am newly divorced." Sarah hadn't intended to mention anything about her personal life, but she felt relaxed and anyway, that was in the past now and this job, if she got it would be part of her future. "My ex-husband and I used to run a business together. Obviously we couldn't remain working together in the company and in the end it was easier for me to sell my half of the business to him." Sarah wasn't about to tell them how much of a wrench it had been for her to let go of their business.

"So are you looking to give something new a try now?" Maxine asked her.

"Yes, a challenge if you like and I am a massive film buff, as my dad used to be a projectionist at the Odeon Cinema in Leicester Square. I've seen hundreds of films, mostly for free and we've got loads of home cine films."

"If it's a challenge you're looking for, I think Steve will certainly deliver on that front," Maxine said as she smiled at James. "He is a wonderful guy, but he can be extremely demanding. How would you describe him, James?"

"Demanding and a right pain in the ass." James apologised to Sarah, "I'm sorry to be so crass but you know I'm just being honest."

Sarah smiled, "That's okay, anyway, I wouldn't want you to oversell him to me."

"In fairness, Sarah," Maxine said, "he does have a heart of gold, but he is a perfectionist and will accept nothing less from any of his team."

"I have come across a fair few awkward people in my time, so I don't think it will phase me at all."

"How would you feel about travel? I take it you have an up-to-date passport and a clean Driving Licence?"

"Yes I do on both counts."

"Steve does spend his time between here and in LA and of course overseas when he's shooting a film. You of course would be expected to accompany him whilst he's on location and occasionally when he is in LA. You will be expected to be there for him round the clock! Naturally, you will get some time off!"

"Nothing you've said has put me off and it all sounds very exciting and as I am used to travelling extensively, when I ran my own business I am comfortable about living out of a suitcase."

Maxine looked at Sarah directly. "Steve will require someone who will be 100% committed to him. You would have to stand up to him occasionally and it can be manic and full on pressure sometimes. The days are long when on location and not everything always goes according to plan. Do you think you could handle that?"

Sarah wanted to be totally honest with them both. "I believe I can and if I didn't I wouldn't be sitting here right now." Sarah hoped she hadn't come across as too arrogant, but she was no shrivelling violet either, not where work was concerned anyhow. "He needs organising, otherwise everything goes belly up."

"Don't worry on that score. I am so organised, I think my mother would say that I invented the word!"

"Is there anything you would like to ask us?"

"No I don't think so, the salary seems more than generous." In truth, the salary was way off what she drew when running her own business, but then again she wouldn't expect it to be. "Oh don't worry James said, you will earn every penny." Sarah just loved his accent and he was also rather charming and very easy on the eye. Maxine glanced at James and then asked Sarah to step outside.

Maxine took her back to the reception area. "Would you like a cup of tea or coffee?"

"Yes please a cup of tea thank you."

"I'll get that organised for you and we will see you shortly." Sarah wondered what on earth she'd said during her interview. At this precise moment, it was all one big blur. Still it was done now, no going back as they say. A young lad who looked extremely shy, smiled at her nervously as he brought over a small tray with tea and biscuits on it and she thanked him. She was ready for something to drink, as her mouth had suddenly gone very dry. She had forgotten what it was like to be interviewed. It was much harder than she'd remembered.

She was much more used to selling her business than herself. It was tough. She had to admit Maxine and James had been very easy to get along with.

As she drank the last of her tea, James popped his head around the door. Hi Sarah, can you come back in now. Sarah stood up and thought to herself here we go then. She sat down opposite her two interviewers once more. Maxine smiled in James' direction. "Well we have had a little discussion and we are both in agreement, that you would be perfect for this job. We both like you and we need someone, like yesterday! Obviously you haven't had the experience, but we both felt that your passion and enthusiasm would be enough. If you don't mind me saying. The fact that you're a bit more mature will be a good thing."

James interjected and said, "And more importantly you won't take any of Steve's shit, sorry that just slipped out! I feel sure you will be able to handle him. What about you Sarah, would you be interested in joining our band of merry men and women? Of course if you need more time to mull it over, we would understand!"

As if on automatic pilot, Sarah replied. "No, you bet, I accept. Nothing you've said, James, has put me off."

Maxine looked at James. "I think we have found Steve's new Personal Assistant." James and Maxine smiled and looked somewhat relieved. "The next question is when can you start?" Maxine enquired. "Steve needs someone like yesterday, as we said."

Sarah hesitated briefly, before saying once again, without much thought, "By the end of the month." This would give her just under two weeks, but what the heck. She wanted this job. "It should be enough time for me to sort myself out," she told them sounding more confident than she felt. "Well," Maxine continued, "I will get the necessary paperwork sorted at our end and I will of course liaise with you. I think it would be good for you to meet up with Steve before you start, what do you think?"

"Yes that would be great."

"Okay I will see what I can arrange and be in touch." Maxine and James both shook her hand and with the pleasantries over with, Sarah took her leave.

Sarah walked out of the office in a complete daze as she waited for the lift and when the doors opened, two men were inside, deep in conversation. They barely glanced in her direction and carried on, with what appeared to be a slightly heated discussion. Sarah quickly recognised one of them to be, none other than Steve Fountain. He was taller than she'd expected, but she didn't feel comfortable looking across at them, so began to fiddle with her mobile phone. Manchester indeed, he clearly had more important things to do than to see her, but she wasn't overly offended.

As the lift reached the ground floor, she exited it rapidly and was relieved to be back outside in the fresh air and sunshine. She was surprised with herself now, after accepting the job so readily. She was, however, excited at the prospect of what lie ahead. She gave Annabel a ring, but her secretary had said she was on another call and Sarah left a message to call her back. She went into the nearest coffee house and ordered herself a cappuccino and sat down. She realised she ought to ring Sam too and let her know how the interview went. Sam was extremely pleased for Sarah and no doubt her Agency would be getting a big fat fee. Her mobile phone rang and it was Annabel. "Hi, Sarah, how did you get on?"

"Hi ya, let's say you are talking to the new Personal Assistant to Steve Fountain."

"Oh well done, hun. Look whilst you're up here do you fancy meeting up for a drink later."

"I guess I could be persuaded."

"Great I could do with a girlie chat." Sarah sensed there maybe something wrong as Annabel didn't sound her usual bubbly self. "OK, where shall we meet."

"There's a new wine and cocktail bar in Covent Garden, called Blue Print. I will try and get there for as close to 6 as I can and make some excuse; otherwise, I'll be here until 8 like usual."

"Your boss works you far too hard."

"You could be right. I need to have a word with Liam and tell him what you said."

"Bet you don't."

"Oh you know me too well."

"Anyhow that's not a problem, Annabel, I can do a bit of retail therapy, before we meet up. I'm thinking that I should really get myself a whole new wardrobe. Out with the old and in with the new."

"You might need to get some bikinis for when you go out to LA."

"I'm not sure about that, as I will be there primarily to work."

"Yes but you will get some free time too. You lucky so and so. I'm quite jealous you know. Anyhow I'd better get cracking because if I don't, I definitely won't get out of the office before six. See you later."

"Yes, bye, Annabel."

Sarah knew she should speak to her mother and let her know how things had gone during her interview, but she would rather tell her the news face to face. Dotty may think she was rather hasty in accepting this new job. She quickly sent her a text to say that the interview had gone well. She had also told her not to wait up, as she was meeting up with Annabel. She finished off her coffee and had a quick read of the Daily Mail, she loved a bit of gossip.

Sarah did contemplate on what her mother might have to say about the decision she'd made. She could possibly think that Sarah should have discussed it all with her first. One thing she was certain of though, Dotty would never stand in her way and would be pleased for her. Sarah took a leisurely look around the shops, but had only been tempted to purchase some new underwear from Victoria's Secret. Underwear, like shoes and handbags were her passion, and she had drawers full of them. Every bit was colour co-ordinated and each bra had matching knickers. By now her feet were killing her. She'd been a complete idiot for not putting her pumps back on. Vanity had prevailed and now she regretted it big time. She would definitely change into them before she went back home. She glanced at her watch and thought it was time to make her way to Covent Garden to meet up with Annabel.

It was late when Sarah eventually arrived home that evening and she was surprised to see her mother was still up. Dotty had insisted she'd been watching a late night film. Oh yes Sarah said not believing her mother for one minute. "Are you sure, Mum?"

"Oh all right, it's curiosity that's what has kept me up."

"Didn't that kill the cat?"

"So they say! Anyway, I know you better than you think! If my hunch is correct, you have accepted that job. Am I right?"

"Crikey do you have a crystal ball, Mum?"

"No, I don't need one love. But for some reason, I was suspicious the minute I received that text from you. It got me thinking that there was more to it than maybe meets the eye!"

"Sorry, Mum. I just wanted to tell you in person and that's why I sent you the text. You don't mind, do you?"

"Of course not. If you think this is what you really want to do, then I couldn't be happier for you, you know that. I only ever want what is best for you love."

Dotty hoped her daughter hadn't noticed her bottom lip quiver, ever so slightly. She was really going to miss her daughter. Yes they argued, but at the same time they were best pals. Dotty however had always known it would be a temporary arrangement. She would soon adjust. She would have to! Pulling herself together she said. "When an opportunity like this comes along, then you should grab it with both hands Sarah, especially after what you've been through."

"Oh thanks, Mum, I knew you'd be okay about it."

"So tell me more?"

"Well I didn't actually get to meet Steve Fountain, but I met James and Maxine, who are part of his management team. I must say they were both very nice and friendly. They must have liked me, as they offered me the job there and then. Of course I was naturally very flattered and found myself accepting it, without any hesitation actually. But I am excited, albeit a little bit apprehensive."

"You'll be fine love. The world's your oyster. You'll be like a little fledgling bird, leaving its nest for the very first time. You will simply spread your wings and soar."

"Oh, don't go all poetic on me, Mum." Dotty laughed.

"Well you get my gist."

"I do, Mum."

"So how's Annabel."

"Oh she's fine very busy at work. Her firm is working on a major project for a very well-known department store. I think it has the Royal seal of approval!"

"Oh yes."

"It's all top secret until the deal has been signed on the dotted line. Marketing can be crazy sometimes and very competitive, but Annabel clearly thrives on it all."

Sarah didn't want to divulge to Dotty that Annabel had been a bit down in the dumps that night. The Blue Print cocktail bar had been a very lively place, but even after a couple of cocktails, they didn't lift Annabel's spirits, which wasn't like her one bit. Sarah was a little concerned about her friend and thought she may have been pushing herself a bit too hard at work.

Annabel had unusually let her guard down for once, which she didn't normally do and had told Sarah that she was having serious doubts about her relationship with Liam. Sarah had been totally surprised to hear her say that. Normally, she either said nothing, or sang his praises for some reason. Apparently she was even considering ending it all with him. She was growing tired of the clandestine lifestyle she was leading. Worst of all, she'd said that being with Liam, made her feel bad about herself. Sarah knew that certainly wasn't right, or good for her. It would however have been futile to offer her any advice. All she could do was listen to her friend and she would always support Annabel, on whatever decision she eventually made. Sarah had known her long enough to know when to stay quiet and tonight had been one of those occasions. She could also be rather fickle and in all likelihood by the morning, she would have changed her mind completely.

Chapter 3

The time was passing by rather quicker than Sarah would have liked it to, before her departure. She'd spent most of it getting everything in place, which included sorting out essential matters that had to be dealt with before leaving In particular her finances and the apartment in Whitstable. Her mother had been so supportive and appeared to be as enthusiastic as Sarah was about her future job.

Today would be her last day at The Bake Stop, and a surprise party had been planned, for one very special lady! Having left the house early, she had been busy ever, since, running errands before finally pulling up in the car park at the rear of The Bake Stop. In her opinion, Biddenford was one of the prettiest villages in Kent. Attractive cottages were dotted around its green with a good mix of shops, with two very popular pubs, which both served excellent food. Cricket was played on the village green throughout the summer, most Sundays. Sarah considered herself to be very fortunate to have been brought up in such a lovely part of the country.

It was still relatively early, but the shop was lively and full of customers and Sarah gave a quick wave to Iris, who was rather busy serving a customer as she made her way up the stairs. It was going to be a busy morning with all the preparations for Peggy's birthday party and she was really looking forward to surprising her. She had a real soft spot for Peggy, who was a warm and generous lady. Having been widowed at a young age, she'd brought up her four children, practically single-handed and had so much spirit and determination, which she herself admired greatly. Peggy still cycled everywhere on her rusty old red bike with its basket and a loud bell, which she used constantly. She said it kept her fit and you couldn't argue with that! Sarah was especially pleased with the way Peggy's cake had turned out too. It was as close as she could get to Camden Market, with fondant icing and sugar paste.

Sarah made her way back down to her car to collect some of the food, which she'd prepared earlier and this time as she returned to the shop, Iris called out to her, "Morning, Sarah."

"Morning, Iris, how are you?"

"Fine thank you. We've been very busy this morning. It always is on Fridays. How did the cake turn out then?"

"Pretty darn good even if I do say so myself. You are coming up later, aren't you?"

"Oh yes, wouldn't miss it! Sue is going to cover the shop for me this afternoon. The girls are going to miss you, you know."

"I will miss them too. It's been a real privilege to share my craft with them all and I have to say, I have loved every minute of it!"

"If you need a hand later, Sarah, just give me a shout and keep your mobile handy, as I will text you as soon as Peggy arrives!"

"Will do, thanks."

"Oh and before you leave today, Dave and I wondered if you would like to have a quick drink with us to send you on your way."

"Yes, of course, I will." Another customer came into the shop, so Sarah made her exit back up the stairs, which were quite steep and narrow, and made the large cool box which she was carrying, rather awkward for her. Sarah took her time, as she didn't want to disturb any of the dainty little sandwiches and pastries which she had made and wrapped securely in foil. Everyone would bring a contribution with them today for the surprise celebration. It would be a nice way to celebrate Peggy's 80th birthday and it would give Sarah the opportunity of saying a fond farewell to everyone. It had been agreed that a traditional 'Afternoon Tea' would be something Peggy would enjoy the most. As well as the sandwiches and pastries, a variety of home-made cakes and scones were being baked, hopefully there would be lashings of clotted cream.

Sarah had built up such a rapport with everyone in her class, but more importantly it had given her a purpose these past months. Also her passion and enthusiasm for cooking and baking had returned. As a teenager it had been her ambition to own a restaurant one day, once she had finished catering college. That, of course, had been before she had met and married Richard. She would now have to store the new state of the art kitchen gadgets, which she had purchased at her mother's house. Hopefully, she would put them all to good use again one day!

Sarah made what she hoped would be her last journey to the car. This time she bumped into Tracy and Sophie, who both had their hands full. "Morning, girls, go straight up, I'm just getting the cake out and then I will join you. Oh by the way, have you got the balloons, Tracy?"

"Yes I have, so I hope you have got plenty of puff!"

"So do I," Sarah replied as she smiled at them. Sarah had bonded with everyone in her class, but in particular with Sophie and Tracy.

They were certainly an eclectic bunch of women, who ranged from young mothers with children of school age, to a retired Head Teacher and a Bank Manager, right up to Peggy, who was the eldest. The three women worked tirelessly before the others joined them. Everyone and everything was now in place. They were just waiting for the birthday girl to arrive.

Balloons and bunting had been put up all around the room. Vases full of rich pink roses had been placed on the tables, which looked stunning. Beautiful fine bone chinaware, which had been hired, set it off perfectly, giving it a sophisticated shabby chic look. Everyone had made a big effort and all of the cakes and pastries looked delicious. Sarah's mobile buzzed, at last their guest of honour had arrived!

They waited in silence for Peggy to walk in and as soon as she entered the room, they all shouted out, "Surprise!" Peggy did indeed look genuinely surprised.

"Oh my goodness, it's not often that I am speechless, but I am right now." Jenny promptly gave Peggy a glass of champagne. "Ooh lovely, ta Jen." It didn't take long for Peggy to enter into the spirit as she said, "Come on, girls, let's get this party started."

With the eating and drinking well under way, Sarah and Sophie discreetly disappeared into the kitchen. "Peggy will love your cake, Sarah, it's amazing."

"Do you think so?"

"Yes, of course, she will."

"Thanks Sophie, I'd forgotten how much I loved doing all of this." Sarah was always critical of her own work, but trusted Sophie's opinion. Sophie lit the candles and Sarah carefully carried the cake through to where the others were all waiting and on cue they began to sing 'Happy Birthday'.

Peggy was just as excited as any child, as she blew out her candles in one go. Naturally, they hadn't put 80 candles on the cake, but enough to warrant plenty of puff to blow them all out! She then made her wish. "Oh I'm having such a wonderful time today she said looking down at her cake. And this takes me right back to my youth. Oh yes, I can still remember it." A ripple of laughter filled the room. "Thank you all so much for making my birthday so special. Sarah, the cake is fantastic; it's a real masterpiece. Is that me behind the fruit and veg stall?"

"Yes, Peggy," Sarah answered. "Blimey it looks a bit like me too, back in the day before me hair turned grey! Is that me, Dad." Peggy caught her breath and her voice cracked slightly. "Oh how did you manage that?"

"Oh I did a little research, Peggy, and your daughter sent me a lovely photograph of you both."

Peggy hugged Sarah and then said, "It's a shame to cut into it really."

"Don't worry, Peggy, I will take some photographs for you!"

"Oh thank you, Iris, that would be lovely."

With the party nearly over, Sarah and a few of the women were clearing up in the kitchen. Sarah was just about to put the leftover cake away, back into its box, when Sophie asked her if she could lend a hand with some of the chairs. "Yes, of course," Sarah said, placing down the tea towel which she was still holding. This time it was she who got the surprise, as Peggy presented her with a huge bouquet of gorgeous brightly coloured pink and orange flowers.

"This is a big thank you for all you have done for us. Giving up your time and sharing your knowledge with us all. We wish you every happiness in the future love." Sarah kissed Peggy on the cheek.

"Oh goodness now I am the one who is speechless! Anyhow it's me who should be thanking you, because I have enjoyed every minute of it. You've all helped me, more than you'll ever know."

"Anyone got a tissue?" Sophie quickly put some into her hand, before placing her arm around Sarah and giving her a gentle squeeze. Sarah really appreciated their thoughtfulness. She certainly hadn't expected that.

Once everyone had gone, Iris turned to Sarah and said, "Well, I think you can safely say that Peggy thoroughly enjoyed her party, Sarah. It was definitely a success."

"Thank goodness for that. Right I had better take this last box down to the car."

"Do you need a hand?"

"No that's all right thank you, Iris."

"Don't forget to pop in to see us before you go, Dave and I want to have a little chat with you."

"Will do, see you in a tick." Sarah was a little curious as to what this little chat could be about and stopped to take a moment to glance around the room, before she left. She became slightly emotional about everything that she had achieved there, and then closed the door for the last time. It had certainly been the best ever experience for her in a long time and it had most definitely been instrumental in getting some of her mojo back.

She put the box into the boot of her car and as she returned to the shop, Dave was waiting to let her back in. By now they had closed the shop for the day. "Come through, Sarah." She followed Dave into the back room, as Iris brought through a pot of tea for them. Dave pulled a face at his wife. "I thought we were going to have a toast, Iris? You need a proper drink for that surely!"

"Well, you can, Dave, but Sarah's driving and she's asked for tea."

"You don't mind if I help myself to a beer do you girls?"

"Fine by me," Sarah replied. Iris looked at her husband, "go on then."

"So how's your mum?"

"She's fine, thank you."

"I guess she's going to miss you when you leave isn't she?"

"Oh, of course, she will and I will miss her too, but you know my mum, she has so many friends."

"Yes, she does and she is game for anything."

"Don't remind me," Sarah said with a whimsical look.

"It's been lovely to be back home for a while and it's going to be strange when I do leave. Anyway, I will be back from time to time."

"Your new job sounds fascinating."

"Well, it's certainly different from anything I have ever done, that's for sure!" Dave came back with a beer in his hand. "Well obviously Dave and I wish you all the luck for the future, don't we, Dave?"

"We most certainly do."

"Now as you know Dave and I have our Villa in Portugal, which we get to use on high days and holidays. Unfortunately, we don't get out there nearly as much as we would like to."

"Come on, Iris, get to the point, Sarah hasn't got all day," Dave said interrupting his wife.

"Well the thing is, Dave and I are thinking about selling up, within the next year to eighteen months. We would like to retire and spend six months of the year in Portugal. Iris hesitated briefly. We know you've taken on your new job, but we would like to offer you first refusal, on The Bake Stop."

Sarah was shocked. "Oh that's so kind of you and I am really flattered. But I am not a master baker."

"We know that, Sarah, but you have mentioned before that you would like to start up your own business again, in the future. All we're saying is to give it some thought. There are all kinds of possibilities which you could think about. You've got a while yet before we pack it all in and obviously you have your new job."

"I cannot imagine you two not being here running this place."

"Neither can we really, but to be honest with you, we're both looking forward to taking life a bit easier and soaking up some sun in Portugal. Of course, we would be back here in the village the other half of the year. Please say you will give it some thought. Obviously, no rush and no pressure."

"Thanks. I certainly will. Anyhow I'd best be on my way now," Sarah said finishing off the last of her tea. "Thank you so much for allowing me to hold the classes here. I've had a brilliant time and I feel that I have benefited from it as well."

"Our pleasure love," Iris said as she and Dave walked her to the door and she kissed them both, whilst they stood on the step and waved her goodbye.

Sarah waved back at them before she pulled off and her eyes smarted as she realised just how much she would miss everyone at The Bake Stop. What was wrong with her? However, without Dave and Iris' help, she would never have got her classes off the ground. They were such a lovely couple. Maybe in the future she would give the news which they had just imparted some thought.

She certainly wasn't in the mood for digesting anything like that at the moment. For now, she wanted to focus totally on her new job and nothing else, except to maybe soak up some LA sunshine, or was that being overly presumptuous!

Chapter 4

"Hurry up, Sarah, you know what your brother is like if we are late. Anyway, it's a beautiful day and I don't want to miss a moment of it."

"Okay, I will be with you in a minute, Mum. See you outside then and by the way I've got the wine."

"I will just get Betsy out of the garage." *Oh no*, Sarah thought. Betsy was a 1960 Mark II Jaguar XK150 which had once belonged to her late father. Betsy was only brought out on high days and holidays. The trouble was, her mother treated it with kid gloves and wouldn't drive her much over 30 miles an hour. No wonder she was chivvying her up to get on their way. Not wanting to wind up her mother more than necessary, Sarah quickly finished off applying her make-up and grabbed her bag. She went over to the fridge and took out the fresh berry pavlova she'd made earlier. A favourite with her nieces. As she closed the front door, her mother was reversing out of the garage gingerly, as usual. She stopped the car. "I thought it would be nice to give Betsy a little run."

"Shut the garage door, will you, love." Sarah did as she was asked, placing her Pavlova carefully onto the back seat, before doing so. Once in the car, Sarah thought it would be wise to check whether they had enough petrol to get them to their destination. Sarah had a quick glance at the petrol gauge and fortunately it was practically full.

On one occasion, when they'd gone out for a little spin as Dotty liked to call it into the country, Betsy had run out of petrol. It had happened miles away from a garage. Fortunately for them, her brother Tony had been at home and had come to their rescue with petrol cans. It was always nostalgic to go out in her dad's old car. Betsy had been her father's pride and joy and as always when she thought about him, she caught her breath and felt a pang of sadness. She still missed him and although her mother didn't say much, she knew she missed him terribly too. As they drove along the country lanes, Betsy's engine purred like a pussycat. She was regularly serviced, just the same as when her dad had been around. Her dad used to spend hours working on her. You could see your reflection clearly in its bright red shiny paintwork. In fact, her mother used to joke that she was the third person in their marriage, as he'd spent more time with Betsy than he had with her.

Tony was mowing his lawn as they pulled up, but as soon as he saw them, he stopped what he was doing and came over to greet them. "Oh I see why you're late now," he laughed and looked across at Sarah. "Did Mum manage to drive Betsy over 20 mph, Sis?"

"Well, I think we may have just crept up to 28 mph," Sarah said teasingly.

They both loved to wind their mother up! "Enough you two. I have to drive her with respect. Dad would never forgive me if I thrashed Betsy."

"There's not much chance of that, Mum," Sarah said sharing a smile with her brother. "I'd love to give the old girl a good run for you, Mum, blow out some of the cobwebs."

"Of course you can, son, but you had better not thrash her."

"I won't, I would probably feel the wrath of Dad from up above if I did." Dotty laughed that's for sure. Of course she said more seriously, "One day she will be yours, but not yet, son." Sarah noticed her brother looked a little disappointed, as he couldn't wait to get his hands on Betsy. However she knew, that Tony would respect their mother's wishes and wait patiently. She just wasn't ready to part with her yet! Sarah passed the Pavlova to her brother, whilst she grabbed the wine and took it inside to the kitchen, where she found Megan busy at the sink washing lettuce. Sarah noticed her two youngest nieces, Mya and Sacha were outside playing on their trampoline. "Lovely to see you, Megan, how are you?" Sarah said hugging her sister-in-law.

"I'm okay thanks, what about you?"

"Fine thanks. No Amee today, or is she upstairs on her iPhone chatting to one of her friends as usual?"

Megan stopped what she was doing. "No, you'll never guess, she's only gone and got herself a boyfriend."

"What my little Amee!"

"Yes, your little Amee, my daughter, the stroppy teenager!"

"So what's he like?"

"He seems very nice and his name is Jack. He is in the 6th Form at Amee's school."

"So what does Tony think about it all?"

"Um, you can imagine, he's a bit overly protective. It's all a little bit terrifying Sarah."

"Yes but you have to let her grow up."

"I agree with you, but can you tell that to your brother. Anyway, Amee is besotted with him, so if Tony has any views, he'd best keep them to himself."

"Don't worry Megan, Amee is a sensible girl."

"Yes I guess so, but as you know, she never ever confides in me."

"You probably want her to remain your little girl forever. This is just the beginning and you will have to find a balance."

Megan laughed, "Yes, you're right, of course. I will let you know when it finds us."

"This new job of yours sounds interesting."

"I hope so, but instead of giving out the orders I will have to take them."

"I wouldn't mind swapping with you. You certainly deserve some good luck, Sarah."

"Thanks, Megan." Dotty and Tony came into the kitchen and joined them.

"What you going to have to drink then, Mum."

"My usual, of course, a G and T, ice and a slice."

"Coming up, madam, but you're only going to get the T as in tonic because you're driving."

"Spoilsport."

"Dad would never approve of you drinking and driving."

"I know, son, I was just testing you for goodness sake!"

"So what are you two having to drink girls?"

"My usual, Tony," Megan replied. "One red wine coming up and what about you, Sarah?"

"I'm okay for a minute thanks."

"Are you sure?" he said handing his mother and Megan's drinks to them.

"Yes, I'm sure."

"Right, I have a job for you, walk this way and you can come and help me in the garden to get this BBQ under way."

"Oh, no peace for the wicked then."

"Too right, we've been slaving away hard at it all morning haven't we Megan."

"Well I have Tony, but you will have to remind me what it is that you have been doing." Tony scratched his head.

41

"Well, I cleaned up the BBQ, didn't I?"

"Yes and that's about it." Tony laughed. "Well you know I am useless in the kitchen."

"That's true Megan replied. Anyway, you had better get that Pavlova into the fridge please, before the cream on it turns to cream cheese in this heat."

"Right, that's all done now. Here take hold of these will you," Tony said passing some chicken and sausages from the fridge to Sarah.

"Of course, boss." Tony put his arm around his sister as they walked down towards the end of the garden. Mya and Sacha both waved at Sarah as they merrily bounced up and down on their trampoline. "Hi, girls, I've made you a Pavlova."

"Oh yummy," Sacha replied.

Mya said, "Awesome!" as she popped her head out through the gap in the net.

"Are you coming on the trampoline, Auntie Sarah?"

"Maybe later, your daddy has conned me into helping him with the BBQ."

"Okay, we're starving aren't we, Sacha."

"Yes hurry up, Daddy."

"You will just have to be patient girls."

"Oh look at that charcoal, it's perfect," Tony bragged. "It couldn't be any better," he exclaimed. "Here stick these sausages on James Martin," Sarah quipped. "So, sis, do you think you're ready for this job with the infamous Steve Fountain?"

"As ready as I ever will be. It's so far removed from anything I have ever done before."

"Well, I happen to think it will be great for you and what about when you jet off to LA. All that lovely sunshine, it will do you good. I'm well jealous."

"It's going to be a challenge and a good one, well at least I hope so. Actually I'm not sure how much time I will be spending in LA Tony."

"But what a wonderful opportunity."

"Yes, of course, it will be. Apparently he's a bit high maintenance and it will be long hours, especially when on location."

"You'll be more than capable, Sis."

"Yeah, nothing that I cannot handle."

"Sounds to me like it is all coming together for you at last Sarah."

"Yes seems like it! Also I have a completion date on my apartment and the Letting Agents have now found a nice couple who want to rent it from me."

"What are they like?" Tony asked.

"I haven't met them as yet, but apparently they're a retired couple who have lived in London all their lives. They love Whitstable and have been going down there at the weekends for years. Anyhow, they're going to rent the apartment from me for a while, before deciding on whether or not to buy a property."

"I'm sure it will be a very good investment for you."

"I hope so, Tony. It has a lovely view overlooking the sea. On a good day with the sun shining and a sparkling sea, it feels like you're in the Mediterranean from the balcony."

Tony laughed. "That's if you don't get a glimpse of the Isle of Sheppey in the background."

Sarah smiled as she said reflectively, "Looking back, Tony, we did have some great times down there with Mum and Dad when we were kids, didn't we?"

"The best. I think we all have a soft spot for it."

Sarah looked more serious as she said, "Mum's going to be okay when I move out, isn't she, Tony?"

"You know Mum, she'll be fine, Sis."

"I know we do clash sometimes, but she's been so supportive of me. So have you and Megan. In my dark times Tony I couldn't even get out of bed."

Tony gave her hug. "Don't, Sarah, that's all in the past now and it's the future you should be thinking about."

"You have so much to look forward to."

"Thanks, Tony. I guess I am just worried that Mum has got used to me being around."

"Oh come on, Mum will be fine. Her social life is better than anyone else's I know."

"Yes I know you're right."

"Hey what about Mum and her 'rumpy-pumpy moment' with Eddie Fountain then."

"Oh my God, did she tell you about him?"

"No, but she told Megan."

"Tony, please don't even joke about it. I go hot and cold just at the mere mention of it. She assured me it was nothing serious. Can you imagine if Steve

Fountain found out that my mother once had a fling with his father, whilst married to his mother."

"Oh you know Dotty. She's probably exaggerating. If you want my opinion, all that happened was, that he probably just pinched her bum and chatted her up a bit. Mum loves to hype things up and embellish the truth. It makes her life sound far more exciting than it actually is or was. It's part of her charm."

"I'm not so sure, Tony, you didn't see the twinkle in Mum's eyes when she told me."

"Oh don't worry, it all happened yonks ago now."

"Yeah that's true! Tell you what though, Sis, she's still a darn attractive woman, for…"

Sarah stopped him mid-flow, "Oh don't you say for her age, she will kill you. Actually you're probably right," and they both laughed. "Anyway, Tony, I just hope that Mum doesn't get too carried away at Steve Fountain's Charity Garden Party tomorrow."

"Oh she'll be okay and can behave when she has to! Anyway, how come you got an invite to this flashy event then?"

"I'm not sure and I was really surprised, but also delighted. It may be because, after the initial interview, I was asked to go back up to London again, because Steve Fountain wasn't present at my first interview. But, then when I arrived, a rather embarrassed Maxine explained that he had got called away yet again, to another urgent meeting. She was very kind and took me out to lunch and afterwards, I met up with some of the team."

"Did I tell you at my first interview, as I was leaving, I actually got in the lift with him. I'd been told he was in Manchester, at another alleged meeting. Of course, he didn't know who I was, but looking back, I do feel a little miffed about it now."

"Oh don't take it personal, Sarah, there must have been a very good reason for it!"

"Yes like he couldn't care less whether he met me or not! Anyway, it will be nice to finally meet up with him tomorrow. I did think about taking Annabel with me, but then I thought about how much Mum would enjoy it. She was over the moon when I asked her to come with me and she can hardly wait."

"Tony, I don't want to be harsh, but I do hope she doesn't embarrass me."

"What on earth do you mean," Tony said teasing his sister, with a wry look on his face.

"Oh you know exactly what I mean. How about the time when we took her for Afternoon Tea at the Ritz on her 65th birthday and later Mum had one too many cocktails in the bar. She then came out of the ladies' loo with her dress tucked inside her tights."

"Oh that embarrassing moment. Yes I do remember, how could I ever forget it! We all laughed so much, but at the same time we were mortified, but the best bit was that Mum was so far gone she couldn't have cared less."

"That's our mum for you, Tony."

"Yes, she's definitely a one off, Sarah, but we wouldn't have her any other way would we?"

"No that's for sure."

They had all spent a lovely fun filled family day together on one of the hottest days of the year so far. June had always been Sarah's favourite month. Mya and Sacha had even managed to persuade her to have a go on the trampoline. After a few simple moves, Sarah had found her stride. She'd been quite proficient at it, as a young girl. Her young nieces had certainly been impressed. Sarah had been disappointed not to meet Amee's boyfriend. She loved all three of her nieces, but there was a special bond between herself and Amee. She'd always been able to confide in Sarah and even more so since becoming a teenager. It was such a shame, because she and Megan constantly argued and fell out. Not so long ago, there had been a huge rumpus, when Amee went behind her parents' back and got her belly button pierced. Sarah had always tried to be the voice of reason, but she had struggled to defend her decision on that one. Anyhow, it had become badly infected and she'd had it removed.

Whenever Amee chose to confide in her, Sarah, was careful to keep what she'd told her in complete confidence. Megan, bless her, was gracious enough to be grateful that her daughter had someone else to turn to. After all, most teenage girls go to war with their parents and particularly with their mothers. Sarah and Dotty had certainly had plenty of battles whilst she herself was growing up.

Sarah had taken what she hoped would be some good photographs of all the family that day. She'd used her trusty Cannon camera, which had been a present from her dad on her 21st birthday, and, for a change, she would do them in black and white, which she occasionally preferred to do. Sarah and her dad had both shared a love of photography.

Sarah and Dotty had made the decision to leave her brother's house at a respectable time, not wanting to stay out too late. It was going to be another hectic day for them both at the garden party. Sarah was looking forward to it, and, although excited, she had butterflies in her tummy about the prospect of finally meeting up with Steve Fountain.

What if he didn't like her? More to the point, what if she didn't like him!

As a treat for her mother, Sarah had organised a beauty therapist to come around early the following morning to do their hair and make-up. She wanted to make sure that they both looked good for the day ahead and she knew how much her mother would enjoy a full pampering, as she would herself.

Chapter 5

Dotty was beginning to get very excited as their chauffeur driven car turned into a gated area and drove up the drive. "That house looks impressive, doesn't it," Dotty remarked as the car came to a halt.

"It certainly does, Mum." George, the chauffeur dutifully helped Sarah out of the car first, followed by Dotty, who appeared to take rather longer than was necessary, whilst holding on to George's hand.

"Well, ladies, here you are and do have a fabulous time."

Sarah thanked George, "Yes, thank you, George."

"You're a star," her mother said, giving George one of her warmest of smiles.

"You're very welcome."

The pass which they had been given was vetted by a security man before they were ushered into the garden. "Oh, I say this is posh, isn't it, Sarah. Look at some of these women they appear to be rather scantily clad and there's an awful lot of flesh on show," Dotty said in a loud voice.

"Shoosh, Mum, if you are going to say offensive things, please for goodness' sake, speak in a whisper."

"Oh pardon me for breathing," Dotty said scowling at her daughter. "When do you think we might meet up with your new boss then?"

"I'm not sure, Mum, but hopefully we will get introduced to him sometime today. I think that's why we've been invited, well me anyway. Please whatever you do, don't mention you knew his father." Dotty gave Sarah one of her looks, which could turn milk sour. All Sarah could hope for was that her mother behaved herself for a change, as she could be very vocal sometimes! Dotty was right about the house, even from the outside it looked pretty impressive. She couldn't wait to see inside it. The garden was beautiful and a huge marquee had been set up and it had an attractive swimming pool too. It looked inviting, especially on a hot day such as this one and she wondered how many of the revellers would end up in it later on! Waiters and waitresses were mingling amongst the guests, offering everyone drinks and canapés. It wasn't long before Sarah and her mother had a glass of champagne offered to them. "This is the life, Sarah, wouldn't you say!"

"It certainly is, Mum." They were both on their second glass of champagne when Sarah noticed a small group of people coming towards them. She recognised Maxine and the man alongside her was none other than Steve Fountain. Sarah had to admit he was suave-looking in his crisp white shirt and jeans.

Sarah had done some in-depth research on this very successful British Film Director. He'd received a BAFTA for Best Director in one of his films and had been nominated for an Oscar twice and he was well respected in the industry. If you believed all you read in the magazines, he had a different woman on his arm whenever he was out and about, whether it be in LA or London. More recently, he had been dating a young and upcoming Hollywood actress, called Elenour Seymour, but this however, had allegedly been a bit rocky of late.

Sarah gave her mother the nod as to who was coming over. "Oh my," her mother swooned, "isn't he handsome. Better looking than his father and thank God he doesn't have Eddie's nose."

"Mum, please, don't embarrass me." Dotty rolled her eyes at her daughter.

"Hello, Sarah, pleased you could make it," Maxine said, as she greeted them and immediately made the introductions. "Steve, let me introduce you to Sarah, your new Personal Assistant and this must be your mother Dorothy I believe."

"Oh please call me Dotty, everyone does." Steve Fountain smiled broadly at them both and you couldn't fail to notice his piercing blue eyes and, of course, a set of perfect white teeth, no doubt enhanced with the help of a very expensive dentist. She hadn't actually managed to get a really good look at him before when she'd seen him briefly in the lift, after her interview. He shook their hands. "Lovely to meet you," and Dotty began to gush.

"Oh the pleasure is all ours, isn't it, Sarah." Sarah thought her mother rather embarrassingly sounded like a silly school girl. "Perhaps, Sarah, you and I could have a short meeting together before you leave today!"

"Yes that would be absolutely fine. Thank you very much for inviting us to your party!"

"You're very welcome. In fact, Max would you be a good girl and show Sarah and her mum around the house."

"Yes, of course, my pleasure. I will come back in a little while if you don't mind, as I have a few more guests to greet."

"No worries we will see you later Maxine," Sarah answered. A buxom blonde came over and whispered something into Steve's ear and he excused himself.

"I will see you later, Sarah. Enjoy yourselves, ladies."

"Oh we will," Dotty gushed once again.

"Mum, you'll have to ease up on that champagne!"

"Oh Sarah lighten up for goodness' sake. After all it's not every day that we get to go somewhere like this is it?" However, when she saw the look on her daughter's face, she relented somewhat. "Oh all right, I promise to behave myself from now on. Scout's Honour."

"Thanks, Mum, after all Steve Fountain is going to be my new boss."

"Yes love I know that. You have to admit, Sarah, this is exciting though, mixing with all these people, it's given me a real buzz."

"Sure that's not the champers?" Sarah teased her mother.

"I'm sure."

"No you're right, Mum, it's a different world to the one we have come from. Anyhow, I am usually the one behind the scenes organising these kind of events. I do feel a bit like a fish out of water."

"Well you look as good as any of the women that are here Sarah and better than some. Your dress shows off your lovely long legs, as well you know!"

Dotty said giving her daughter a wry look. Sarah laughed, "I couldn't possibly comment mum and anyhow, you don't look half bad yourself."

"Well, I may have to work a bit harder than you, but I didn't want to let you down love."

"You'd never do that, Mum. Sorry I was so snappy with you before but I am just a bit on edge today."

"That's okay," Dotty said. "Anyhow, you're going to have to get used to this kind of thing."

"Yes, but I suspect I will still be working behind the scenes again, if you'll pardon the pun."

"Oh yes I get it," Dotty said laughing.

"Anyway, let's make the most of it today, eh, Mum." A waitress walked by once more and Dotty stopped her and she topped up their glasses for them.

"Cheers, love."

"Cheers, Mum."

"It's weird, but I actually think I am developing a taste for champagne, I've always liked it." Dotty said looking directly at Sarah. "I think I'm going to miss you, love, when you finally move out."

"I know you will, Mum, but I will be coming back you know."

"I tell you what I won't miss though, is your constant nagging about me smoking."

"I cannot help it, Mum."

"Yes I have noticed," Dotty said, knocking back the rest of her champagne. "Oh don't look now, Sarah, but it looks as if his Lordship that is Steve Fountain is coming back again." Sarah didn't have time to say anything before he reached them. She was surprised to see that he was alone and didn't appear to have any of his entourage with him this time.

"Hello, Sarah. I am sorry I had to leave you so abruptly before. How about we have that meeting now?" Sarah looked at her mum. "Dotty, why don't you come up by the pool and sit in the shade. I will introduce you to my mother," Steve said kindly. Dotty had a look of pure panic written right across her face. Both women followed on behind Steve and Sarah just managed to say, "She won't know who you are, Mum. Please for goodness' sake don't mention about your being at the Palladium. Just to be on the safe side, no more champagne until I get back."

"I think I can manage that, love. I will just smile and nod in all the right places."

"Good make sure you do." With the introductions made, Sarah glanced back at her poor mother. Bless her, she really did look like a fish out of water now and Sarah felt sorry for her. She also couldn't fail to notice Steve Fountain's mother had been immaculately dressed and her clothes shouted designer. She was a good-looking woman, but had what her mother would term a hard face. Although she'd smiled at her when they were introduced, Sarah had felt a little self-conscious under her scrutiny. Sarah's head was also feeling a bit light-headed. Maybe she should have taken some of her own advice, and eased up on the champagne!

Sarah followed Steve into the house and was instantly impressed firstly, by just how incredibly spacious the hallway was with an attractive circular staircase and a gorgeous plush purple carpet. Steve opened a door into what was clearly his office, and this once again had been tastefully decorated. It had two black sofas, and several framed black and white pictures adorning its walls.

Many were of Hollywood's most beautiful and iconic women from a bygone era. Marilyn Monroe, Audrey Hepburn and Sophia Lauren were amongst them. Steve noticed Sarah looking at them. "This used to be my father's house years ago. I left the pictures up in his honour. He loved or I should say still loves beautiful women," he said with a wickedly cheeky grin on his face. Sarah thought, *Yes like father, like son.* "Well your father clearly has good taste."

"They're all gorgeous women, but I particularly like the one of Audrey Hepburn. *Breakfast at Tiffany's* is one of our favourite films. Me and Mum that is and she was a very classy lady."

"Yes she really was and the chemistry between her and George Peppard certainly helped in the film's success! Don't you think?"

"Yes definitely." Sarah took in her surroundings. On the whole the room was very stylish and had a contemporary feel. However, a large red leather chair behind the desk, did look somewhat jaded. Perhaps that had also once belonged to the great Eddie Fountain!

"Do take a seat, Sarah. Can I offer you a drink?"

"No thank you, I have already had a little too much champagne I think, for me anyway," she rambled on.

Steve smiled at her. "Right okay," he said as he went over to a small fridge which was in the corner of the room and helped himself to a bottle of water. "Well I have to say, Maxine and James are very impressed with you, Sarah, and it's great to meet you at last." Sarah resisted the temptation of saying that they had shared a lift together when she'd come up to his offices. "I guess they filled you in on everything and by that I mean about me. Clearly it didn't put you off."

"No, of course it didn't."

"Maxine said you used to run a successful business of your own." She'd also told him about Sarah's divorce, which he had no intention of mentioning: "What kind of business?" Sarah had to take an intake of breath, as it was always difficult even now for her to talk about it. Starting up the business together had been Sarah's idea and she'd given her all to both her marriage and the business. It didn't seem fair to her even now, that she'd lost out on everything she'd loved, but as they say it was history. Steve noticed a slightly pained expression cross Sarah's face and felt bad for asking the question.

In a quiet voice Sarah replied, "We ran a Themed Events business, which I started up with my now ex-husband, soon after we got married. I had been to catering college where I qualified as a chef. At the beginning, we catered for weddings. Then as time went on, as well as the food, we offered the whole package, including flowers, discos and wedding singers. It wasn't long before we organised, much larger themed parties for the rich and famous. We also did Corporate events and children's parties. It's surprising the extreme lengths that some parents will go to in the quest to outdo each other when it comes to their children's parties. Fortunately it became very successful and still is to this day." Steve was surprised at how candid she'd been with him, and could tell that it had been a wrench for her to let it go.

"You must be very proud."

Sarah relaxed slightly and answered:

"Yes I am, very proud actually."

"So taking this job on is going to be a huge departure for you then!"

"Yes it will be." Sarah thought he may be having some reservations as to her motive for taking on the job as his Personal Assistant.

"You might be thinking that I am a bit long in the tooth for a job like this, but I can assure you that I am every bit as ambitious and enthusiastic as any 20-year-old! More in fact. I can promise you that I will be the best Personal Assistant you have ever had." He laughed out loud, showing off his perfect white teeth again. "Wow that's a bold statement to make."

"I'm not afraid of hard work Steve and I don't like failing at anything she said in earnest."

Steve smiled at her broadly and he also appeared to be more relaxed than he had been earlier. He looked intently at Sarah as he said. "I don't doubt that for one minute. I should say, Sarah, that whilst I am sure your business background may be an advantage, there is only room for one boss here and that's me. I am used to getting my own way and that's how it is!" Sarah knew he meant it and although he was being very pleasant, he had a steely look in his baby blue eyes. Sarah did, however, respect his honesty. You certainly didn't get to where he was, without being forthright and on occasion, no doubt ruthless with some of the decisions he had to make. She looked directly back at her soon to be boss.

"Well as I told Maxine and James, I am up for a challenge. However, now that I have met you, maybe it's going to be a bit more challenging than I originally thought."

Steve looked surprised and then laughed out loud, before he said, "Well we will have to wait and see won't we!"

"I hope you don't mind me asking, Steve, but what happened to your last Assistant?" Steve smiled, "I think it's fair to say that she lacked commitment and blew hot and cold where work was concerned. It appeared to me that her love life was far more important than the job itself."

"Sarah, the pressure on me is huge, because there is a lot riding on any new film that's made these days and I have to prove to the producers and the backers that I can make it a box office success. I cannot afford to have someone that doesn't give there all to me, or to the job, that's how it is!"

"I do understand Steve, totally."

"Anyway, I am going to be out of the country for a while in LA. You are joining us at a very exciting time actually Sarah. I am about to direct a new film and we will soon be off on location in Tuscany. It's a beautiful place to shoot a film I can tell you. I am pretty sure it will be cinematic gold. Of course, it's going to be a baptism of fire for you though, as you're about to be thrown in at the deep end." Steve looked Sarah straight in the eye.

"It will be long days and some late nights. Your job will be extremely varied. One minute you could find yourself re-typing scripts, or sourcing a speciality cheese which is unique to the particular region we are filming in. Of course, naturally you will have to make sure and I quote 'the stars' have their favourite brand of coffee, or brand of water on hand day and night. An unhappy star doesn't look too good on screen, especially first thing in the morning!"

"Sounds brilliant to me and I couldn't be more excited and I am really looking forward to getting started. I won't let you down, Steve. I guarantee it!"

"Great. I look forward to working with you, Sarah. Maxine will be in touch with you and keep you up to speed with everything that is going on. Any queries just ring her. By the way, did George pick you up okay today?"

"Oh yes and thank you for organising that for us. Mum was in her element."

"No problem. I thought it would make the day a bit more special for you. George is my right hand man and I rely heavily on him. He used to work for my father way back, so he is more of a family friend. He retired a few years ago, to look after his wife, but sadly, she passed away. Poor George was absolutely lost without her. So I asked him, if he would like his old job back He nearly bit my hand off. He only has one daughter and she lives in Washington. He's nearly seventy, but has more energy than anyone I know. Anyhow, he was over the moon and he's great to be around. He has a calming manner about him. If you ever have any problems he's your man."

It would appear that Steve Fountain did have a heart after all. Sarah could hear a buzzing sound coming from Steve's mobile phone and Steve stood up. Sarah realised that their meeting had come to an end. "Excuse me, I'd better check who that is." Steve shook Sarah's hand and said he looked forward to working with her.

"Thank you." Sarah got up to leave the room and just as she opened the door and without any warning, she did the loudest hiccup ever. In an attempt to cover it up, Sarah quickly coughed as loud as she could, well at least that is what she'd hoped she had done. For goodness' sake what was she like and what would her new boss think of her? She would have to give drinking champagne a miss in future, as it certainly appeared to have a rather adverse effect on her. Sarah realised that she could be in for a bumpy ride in the future, but this didn't faze her in the slightest. In fact it made her even more excited. Bring it on Mr Fountain, bring it on. She laughed to herself. He might be a challenge, but she was hardly going into a boxing ring with Tyson Fury.

As Sarah left the room, Steve shook his head but had a smile on his face; he sincerely hoped that he hadn't employed a lush for a Personal Assistant. He certainly wouldn't be able to deal with that. Overall, though, Steve had to agree that Maxine and James had made a good choice.

He hadn't been too keen on taking her on originally, but they had managed to convince him otherwise. In fact, overall, Sarah had made a good impression on him. She was clearly an intelligent woman and an extremely attractive one too, in a non-showy kind of way. She also had a great smile, which reached her rather unusual green eyes and a smattering of cute freckles across her nose. He'd been told she was 38, but if he hadn't known he would have said she looked to be in her early thirties. He did, however, feel that she had been a little guarded with him on occasion, but his gut feeling was that she would be an asset to him and the team. She appeared to be ready to move on with her life and he felt sure that she would be committed to the job and more importantly in his opinion she looked to be a no nonsense kind of woman.

He'd had a few PAs in the past who had tried to use their feminine wiles to charm him, especially when they had screwed up. Somehow he didn't think Sarah would do that. This in itself would be refreshing. He wondered if his mother would approve of her. She could be very vocal and had an opinion on any woman, he either worked or was involved with. She had made it clear to him that she didn't approve at all of Elenour. However, whilst he respected his mother, he was very much his own man and what he did with his life or with whom was his business and no one else's!

He checked his mobile. He had a missed call from his tailor and he decided that he would ring him back later. He had more important matters to address at present, as he had also noticed a few missed calls from Elenour. She was a gorgeous young thing, but rather problematic and she was way too clingy for his liking on occasion. He knew that it would be best to call her back otherwise she would go on calling him and then he would end up switching off his mobile. Steve would have to remain calm for the foreseeable future, and nurture her, as he was relying on her to pull off the performance of her life in his next film. He'd gone out on a limb to help get her the part.

Sarah walked back outside into the bright sunshine once more and was grateful that her meeting with Steve Fountain was now over. She had found the meeting a little intimidating, as it had been just the two of them. She was feeling so much more relaxed now. Steve Fountain had come across as easy going, but he had also been honest, admitting that he was used to getting his own way. She believed she would be able to handle him. She'd managed to deal with Richard, who had needed his ego massaging nearly every single day. She was sure Steve Fountain would be nothing like that.

Sarah noticed Dotty talking avidly to a young man, who appeared to be hanging onto her every word, either that or her mother had hypnotised him, now there was a thought. Her mother was still a striking woman, with her short dark brown hair, which she had coloured regularly. Going grey wasn't an option for Dotty. She looked really lovely in a pink chiffon Charmeuse dress. She had amazing skin and certainly didn't look her age. Typically, she was as brown as a berry even though it was still only early June. One look at the sun and she had an instant tan. Sarah on the other hand was fair with freckles, which she didn't like. She took after her dad, who was of Irish descent and therefore she had to be extremely careful when out in the sun for long periods of time. Sarah really was very proud of her mum, as long as she didn't drink too much! She just prayed that her mother had behaved herself in her absence. Most people were happily tucking into the buffet by now and it looked delicious. There was a huge variety of foods and so colourful too. A real feast. With her meeting now over, she suddenly had an appetite. She was offered a plate which she took and helped herself to some delicious pieces of spicy chicken and some rather tempting, looking prawns, with salad and pasta. The desserts looked simply stunning and there was a chocolate fountain with lots of fresh fruit, tiny meringues and marshmallows, which she knew she would find irresistible later on. A BBQ was on the go as well, but she would give that a miss.

"Dotty called her over. Hello love how did it go."

"Absolutely fine I think, thanks, Mum."

"This is Steve's nephew Scott, lovely lad."

Scott stood up. "Pleased to meet you. Here take my seat," he said as he excused himself. "It's been a pleasure to meet you, Dotty, but I'm going to hit the buffet again." Sarah thought, *poor guy, he probably couldn't wait to get away.* She didn't doubt that Dotty had regaled, some interesting tales to hold his interest, but there is only so much of that anyone can take. She suddenly had a thought and hoped her mother hadn't relayed her anecdote, about her costumes being so tight around the crotch when she was a tiller girl, that she would speak an octave higher for hours after wearing them! Sarah went cold at the thought. *Oh surely not!* "Hope to see you later," Dotty said to Scott as he departed. "Oh what a thoroughly nice young man, so polite. I mentioned I was a tiller girl back in the day. Of course he'd never heard of us. I didn't mention anything about Eddie though."

"That's a relief, Mum, and it looks like you're enjoying yourself."

"I am and fortunately for me, Celia got called away so I didn't have to speak to her that much. I just smiled and nodded as I said I would. In fact, I felt like one of those nodding dogs. Do you remember the one your dad used to have on the back shelf of Betsy years ago."

"Oh yes I do, anyway, well done, Mum, and I think you have passed muster! Lady luck must be shining down on us today," Sarah remarked.

"Oh before I forget," Dotty said, "Maxine apologised as she has had to leave early. One of her children is unwell. She said she will be in touch with you shortly."

"Oh dear, that's a shame, I hope everything will be okay."

"Have kids will worry that's what I say! I still worry about you, Sarah, and of course Tony and the grandkids."

"Yes I know you do, Mum," Sarah said kissing her mother on the cheek!

As dusk began to fall, Sarah noticed that her mother looked tired. It had been a lovely party and Dotty had consumed quite a lot of alcohol. No doubt she would sleep the whole way home. Sarah glanced around her to see if she could see Steve Fountain, but he was nowhere to be seen. However, she did see James and asked if he would let Steve know that she and her mother had both had a wonderful time. It's been the best party ever, Dotty chipped in. He said he would and that he looked forward to her joining them as he gave her a hug and planted a kiss on both of her cheeks. He looked as smart and handsome as the last time she saw him, but his words did sound a bit slurred.

George had given his mobile number to her earlier, so Sarah gave him a quick ring. He said he would bring the car around for them in a jiffy. "Come on, Mum, let's walk round." Dotty slipped her arm through Sarah's. "I think we are leaving at the right time Sarah, as some of the folk have been drinking quite a lot and there's going to be some high jinx later, if I'm not mistaken."

"You could be right, Mum."

"Of course I am right and I could tell you some stories about me back in the day."

"Yes, Mum, but I thought you were going to keep those sort of stories for your memoirs."

"Oh yes so I did!" The two women exchanged a knowing look and laughed. "Oh it's been a fabulous day Sarah and we have been so lucky with the weather."

"It was great to share it with you, Mum. Let's hope they have raised lots of money today for Great Ormond Street Hospital."

"Yes I think they will have, for sure, especially with that auction. Some of the bidding went very high."

"I do envy you, you know. I reckon this new job of yours is going to be exciting, never a dull moment around Steve Fountain. It's just what you need."

"I hope so, Mum. I'm not usually wrong am I love." Sarah gave her mum's arm a gentle squeeze. "No I guess not."

As they reached the gate, George pulled up alongside them and got out to open the door for them. "Hi, ladies, so how did it go?"

"Oh, it was a real eye opener wasn't it, Sarah, mixing with all those people?"

"Mum was a bit star struck, George."

"Yes and that lovely actor James Hunter was there. Ooh, he reminds me of a young Steve McQueen, with his twinkly blue eyes," Dotty said excitedly.

"Yes and Mum rather embarrassingly went up to him and he graciously allowed her to take a selfie of them both. He was very kind to her, but at first he did look somewhat taken aback!"

"Oh he didn't mind," Dotty interjected, "he is so lovely. Also that dreadful weather girl from Breakfast TV was there. Debbie something or other. She loves herself that one and she always shows off far too much cleavage for my liking!"

"Ignore her, George, Mum can be very caustic sometimes."

George laughed. "Well I have actually met James Hunter several times and I know for a fact that, he is a very nice guy."

"Mum also won a special raffle prize which is dinner for two at the Dorchester."

"Oh yes so I did," Dotty said. "I don't know who I will take with me though."

"I'm sure you will think of someone, Mum, as you've got lots of friends."

"That's just it, I don't want to offend any of them!" George ushered them both towards the car door and shut it behind them.

As they drove off, George played soft music in the background and it wasn't long before Dotty fell asleep, resting her head against Sarah's shoulder. Sarah looked down at her and suddenly felt very protective of her mum. They had become even closer over these past months. Living together had been a very special time for them both. Sarah yawned and then rested her head against the comfort of the soft leather seat and stretched her legs out fully. Next week would be a new start and fingers crossed it would all work out for her.

She was struggling to keep her eyes open herself now and was aware that the music had become fainter. Tiredness finally overtook her and she too fell asleep. The next thing she knew, George was calling them both. They had arrived home. It was raining, absolutely tipping it down and George stood at the car door with a large umbrella. "Here you are, ladies, home safe and sound."

"Thank you, George."

"No problem. Well I will see you soon, Sarah."

"Yes I'm looking forward to it." He kissed the back of Dotty's hand and Sarah knew that her mother had been pleased with his gesture. "Might see you again, George," Dotty said rather coyly. Her mother was such a flirt!

"I certainly hope so, Dorothy." Dotty beamed up at him and Sarah was astonished that her mother hadn't even corrected George. She didn't like to be called Dorothy, not by anyone! She appeared not to have noticed, or did she? What was going on here? Sarah had no idea and anyway she was too tired to contemplate any such matters now. She did however feel confident that her mother would be absolutely fine when she moved out.

Chapter 6

Sarah had finally finished packing the last of her bags. She had given a lot of thought as to what she considered necessary to pack and knew that she would have to show some restraint. However, having tried to keep her clothes to the barest minimum, she had still managed to fill two large suitcases. There were other items such as her hair straighteners, hairdryer, laptop and iPad, that she simply couldn't or wouldn't want to live without and those had been neatly placed inside a large plastic storage box. Her hair in particular was always a constant battle. She had even put in her trusty steam iron and a few mementos, including several framed photographs of her family. Hopefully, these would help to make her feel more comfortable and at home.

Maxine had been in touch and had told her, that a car would be provided along with the job. Megan had been having major problems with Horace, her ageing Peugeot 205, which she insisted on driving against Tony's wishes. Naturally she used the family car when the children were with her. Apparently, back in the day she'd been a girl racer and she still liked the freedom, which clearly only Horace could give to her. Sarah had a brand new Mini Cooper and she had the feeling that Sarah would love driving it. Megan very quickly accepted Sarah's kind offer, promising to look after it, just like she did Horace. Her brother and Megan argued constantly about the fact that she should get rid of Horace. Megan knew that at some point, the day would come when there would have to be a parting of the ways. However she was adamant that she couldn't possibly let me him go just yet.

Maxine had also sent through masses of documents for Sarah to sign, in relation to her new role which she'd duly signed and returned. George had rung her out of the blue and said that as the 'boss', which was how he referred to Steve, would be away in LA, it would be his pleasure to come down to Kent and collect her, which she had thought was extremely thoughtful of him. He was due to arrive at mid-day. Unable to sleep, Sarah had been up since 6 a.m. along with the birds who had been chirping away and had become so restless that she'd been unable to lie in any longer. She glanced at her watch and it was still only 10 a.m. Dotty had left a couple of days earlier, after she'd received an invite to go and stay with her sister, Pat, in Devon. Her poor uncle John would have his hands full with the pair of them. Pat was five years older than Dotty, but they were like two peas out of the same pod!

Sarah was thankful really that Dotty wouldn't be around when she left, as she believed it would be a lot easier on the both of them. As it was the two women had been kept busy packing and were fully occupied right up until Dotty had left. Bless her, she'd remained cheery and enthusiastic about Sarah's new venture and had only broken down once, when she'd finally left on the Thursday morning. Sarah had dropped her mother off at the local train station, where they had hugged one another and naturally a few tears had been shed. However, her mother's parting words to her had been. "When I get back, there's one thing I am going to do."

"What's that, Mum?" Sarah enquired.

"Get rid of all those bloody awful plug in air fresheners you keep buying, Sarah!" As usual, her mother liked to have the last word and there really was no need for Sarah to respond, so she'd just smiled back at her mother and blew her a kiss. She could see Dotty's eyes were glistening with tears and Sarah knew she was trying to be stoic. In fact, they both were! Sarah just wished her mother would stop smoking. They had always argued about it and always would, unless Dotty stopped smoking of course! Sarah was pleased that her mother would be spending some time with her sister and her Auntie Pat would look after Dotty and spoil her rotten. Pat was a fantastic cook and a real homemaker. She'd raised four sons and with six grandchildren, she loved nothing more than to fuss over everyone, especially her youngest sister.

With time to spare, Sarah had decided to give Annabel a call. Last time they had spoken, she had been so excited as her firm had won the big ad campaign contract, which they had been working so hard towards. Sarah was pleased for her friend. No one would have worked harder than Annabel, or be more committed. She had always put her work first and it had paid off finally, as she had been promoted to Executive Creative Director. Annabel was extremely passionate about her work and knew how to get the best out of anyone who was lucky enough to work alongside her. Yes she was a hard task master, but at the same time, a most generous person who championed any young person who joined the firm. She most certainly would have played an integral part in securing this huge deal with a major client. This no doubt would have been at a cost to her own personal life, which was still as complicated as ever. Annabel predictably wouldn't talk about her situation with Liam. She did, however, tell Sarah that they were still seeing one another. Sarah doubted that Liam would ever leave his wife. It irritated the hell out of her that Liam had always maintained he and his wife had an open marriage and were only staying together purely for their children's sake. He had two boys, aged 9 and 12, and a daughter who was 14. Sarah wasn't sure if deep down Annabel believed him or not, but how could she know for sure, unless, of course, she spoke with Liam's wife. This was hardly ever likely to happen. Anyhow for now Annabel was buzzing and on a high.

A massive party was planned for everyone at Brighter Visual Creations, as they had all worked so hard on this particular ad campaign for months. For now at least, it also looked like Annabel's relationship with Liam was still very much on.

Sarah went upstairs and just about managed to bring down her cases one at a time and the all-important box with her must-have items in and left them all in the hallway. She went into the kitchen. It was very warm, as was the norm, due to the Aga which was permanently on. She opened the back door to let some fresh air in and put the kettle on and made herself a cup of coffee and sat down at the kitchen table. She loved this kitchen so much, as it brought back so many happy childhood memories of all the times she'd shared with her parents and Tony when they had been children. At Christmas, family and friends would all be crammed around the large oak table. The more the merrier was always her parents motto They would be laughing and joking as they prepared the Christmas dinner, after consuming a few glasses of alcohol. Some mishap would occur, like the time when her dad had accidentally cooked the turkey upside down and discovered that it was even tastier and moist cooked that way.

Sarah glanced at her watch and it was almost 11.45, George would soon be arriving and then she would be on her way to her new venture. For how long she didn't know at this precise moment. *One day at a time,* she thought. On the whole she still felt excitement about what lay ahead, but still had a little knot in her tummy! She wondered what Steve Fountain was up to, but she would find out soon enough.

Sarah had the feeling that she would be able to rely on George as he appeared to be a man of the old school and a true gentleman. A rarity these days. No doubt, like her mother he would have some good stories to tell and she looked forward to hearing all about them. Dotty had seemed a little disappointed that she wouldn't be around when George came down to collect her. Although her mother would never admit it, but it was clear to Sarah that Dotty was quite taken with George. In fact, Sarah realised that this was the first time she had ever shown the slightest interest in any other man, since her dad had passed away, almost three years earlier. There were a few suitors at the Friday lunch club, but her mum had always said no one could ever replace her husband. Dotty, however, was a social butterfly and the most terrible flirt and always had been. Her poor dad had accepted it as part of her charm, which of course it was. However, maybe this went beyond her mother's usual flirtatious nature!

Although, she couldn't really be sure as yet. Sarah heard a car pull up outside, and looked out of the window and it was indeed George. She opened the front door just before he had a chance to ring the bell. Hello George, come through. "Can I offer you a coffee or tea?"

"Coffee would be fine, thank you." George followed Sarah into the kitchen.

"Please sit down, George, and make yourself at home." He pulled a chair out and sat himself down at the old oak table, as Sarah filled the kettle.

"This is a lovely cottage, Sarah, and the kitchen is very homely."

"Yes, it is. Mum likes to call it shabby chic. Both my brother, Tony, and I were born here. Well not in the kitchen, of course, I mean the cottage."

"Well I'm glad you clarified that," George quipped and they both laughed. "My dad grew up not too far from here in Tonbridge Wells. And if you didn't know it, Mum is a real Essex bird, so she had to adapt to a different way of life here. She found it too rural in the beginning, but she soon grew to love it. She has had a wonderful life here and has some wonderful friends too."

"Did you have a good journey down today, George?"

"Yes, it was absolutely fine and I love getting out of London and it makes a nice change to be in the countryside. I used SatNav, which brought me straight here, just as before. Although I always carry a map for emergency situations."

"Were you ever in the Army, George?"

"Why do you ask?"

"Well, you always seem to be so organised and you arrived here exactly on time. Maybe the biggest giveaway is that your shoes are always so shiny!"

"Well actually, your instincts are spot on, Sarah, as I did in fact join up as a young man at just 17. I stayed in the army for 10 years."

"Oh did you. That must have been interesting."

"Oh it was definitely and I got to see a bit of the world. I'm not saying I was a bad boy, before I joined up like, but I was a very impressionable young man and a bit hot headed, like most lads of that age. But the army teaches you discipline and about life and what is expected of you. It certainly made me the man I am today. So where's Dorothy then, has she gone out?"

"No, George, she's gone to stay with her sister down in Devon for a week or so." George looked surprised.

"Oh I see, Devon, yes it's lovely down there," he said, trying to hide his disappointment! Sarah handed George his coffee and a piece of her mother's famous fruitcake.

"Yes it is, George, and we all love Devon so much and we have had some great holidays down there when we were kids. Mum and her sister are so alike I almost feel sorry for my uncle John, as they will certainly drive him potty with all their talking. Still it will also be a good excuse for him to nip out to his local pub. It was probably a good thing that Mum left when she did.

"I think she'd got used to me being around. It was only ever meant to be a temporary arrangement, but things got rather complicated with my divorce and so it turned out to be a bit longer than originally anticipated."

"I don't doubt for one minute that your mother will be fine, Sarah. Dorothy strikes me as a very strong and forthright woman."

"Yes you're right with your observation, spot on, George, she really is."

"It's her way or the highway! So you've been warned, George." George blushed slightly and looked slightly taken aback at Sarah's comment, and scratched his head. "I'm only teasing you, George."

"Anyway, young lady, I guess we'd best think about getting a move on. Molly is going to have a nice roast dinner ready for us later on."

"What does Molly do?"

"Molly is Steve's housekeeper and she is originally from Ireland and she doesn't stand for any nonsense. She runs the house like a sergeant major and she does all of the cooking."

"Oh dear, should I be afraid."

"Maybe, she cannot abide anyone in the kitchen."

"It's her domain and woe betide anyone who enters it."

"Right, I think now I've been well and truly warned."

George laughed, "Oh she's okay really! That's a lovely fruit cake," George said as he ate his last mouthful.

"It is Dotty's signature bake and an old family recipe belonging to my great grandmother, who used to be a cook for some Lord and Lady back in the day, or, Mr & Mrs Snooty as my old Nan used to say! Mum does, however, have a very light touch!"

"Anyhow, don't you worry about Molly, Sarah, as her bark is much worse than her bite. As for me, I am happy to keep out of the kitchen, as I am useless and I cannot even boil an egg! My wife used to do all of the cooking for me and she was a great cook. She was a bit like Molly, as she didn't like anyone meddling in the kitchen either." For a brief moment, Sarah noticed a sad expression cross George's face, before he said, "Right, I really do think we should be getting on our way now, Sarah. I will pop your suitcases into the car."

"No, George, I can do that, don't worry."

George shook his head at her. "Oh no you won't, young lady," he said lifting one of her cases.

"Crikes have you got the kitchen sink inside here?"

"OH NO, I knew I had forgotten something." Sarah laughed, "Anyway, at least one of the cases has some wheels on it. But please, George, don't do yourself a mischief." Sarah followed him out with the last of her gear, which George placed into the back of the Range Rover. Sarah returned to the house and took one more look around it, to make sure that she had left it all safe and secure, then she smiled and said, "Goodbye home," and made her way outside to join George. The Sunday traffic hadn't been anywhere near as bad as a weekday and they had had a good run up to North London. George had mentioned that Steve Fountain was expected back sometime during the week. "Well, we're here, madam, we have arrived at your new home."

"I think it's a bit too grand for me, George, but I will just have to get used to it," Sarah said rolling her eyes.

"Of course you will."

Sarah stepped out of the Range Rover and helped George with some of her bags and followed him up to the front door. Sarah thought about Annabel and silently thanked her friend for her encouragement. If it hadn't been for her, she wouldn't be here! She was feeling so optimistic about her future, for now at least!

As soon as they entered the house, a rather attractive, fresh-faced woman with long wavy auburn hair and a fair amount of freckles on her face greeted them both. At a guess, Sarah would say she was in her mid-forties. A large dog who George called Buster, came bounding over towards them and George made a huge fuss of him. Sarah thought that he may be a Labradoodle. Eventually, George had to tell him to calm down as he was becoming extremely excited. Buster sat down wagging his tail furiously and looked at Sarah, who stroked him for a while, until he laid down. "Well there you are, I thought you were never coming for goodness' sake. You must be Sarah and I'm Molly. Welcome to our humble abode!"

"Thank you, Molly, pleased to meet you," Sarah replied.

"I was just on me way to check on the dinner, but I expect you would like to freshen up Sarah, and see your room?"

"Yes I would, thank you very much, Molly."

"Okay, follow me," Molly said in a soft Irish lilt. "Righty-ho, Sarah, I will bring your cases up for you in a minute."

"Thank you, George." She knew there was no point in arguing with him and she wouldn't have wanted to upset him. She followed Molly up the stairs and once again, as before she was totally bowled over by this house and in particular by its grand staircase and the purple carpet which was so thick and sumptuous, a bit like walking on air. Molly stopped outside a door on the first floor and opened it. "Well, this is your room, Sarah."

Sarah followed Molly into what was to be her room. It was very impressive and in keeping with the rest of the house, with a contemporary feel to it, and decorated in neutral colours. And fortunately for her, it had masses of fitted wardrobes. A massive TV was fixed to the wall and she was pleased to find that it also had an en-suite. "What do you think, Sarah?"

"It's lovely, too posh for me of course, but it will do nicely thank you!" Sarah said rather cheekily. "Yes it's not too shabby, is it? Anyway, you're more than welcome. I will leave you to it now, Sarah, so that you can get yourself sorted out. Dinner will be around 6 o'clock, so there is no need to rush."

"Thanks, Molly." Shortly after Molly left, there was a knock at the door. It was George with her suitcases. "Thanks, George, but you really shouldn't have done that because I'm quite capable."

"So am I he said raising his eyebrows and anyway, it's my pleasure. Right, Sarah, I will see you when you've freshened up and don't forget to make yourself at home."

"Will do and thank you, George, you've been so kind to me and I want you to know that I really appreciate it."

"You're very welcome," he said before leaving her on her own.

Sarah took off her pumps before she laid fully onto the comfortable king-sized bed and took in her surroundings and by the quality of the décor, no expense had been spared in this room either. However, the biggest shock for Sarah so far, had been meeting Molly. She was nothing like what she had imagined her to be. From the little George had told her, she'd expected her to be a woman of more mature years and possibly a bit of an old tartar. Well it looked as if Sarah had been way off with her assumption. Molly so far had been nothing but friendly towards her and she had a wonderful soft Irish lilt in her voice, which Sarah found charming. Providing Sarah didn't interfere in the kitchen, they should get along fine, like a house on fire! From her own experience, there is only ever room for one woman in a kitchen, and Sarah had no intention of stepping on her toes. Each to their own and anyhow, her role in the house would be an entirely different one to Molly's. Sarah had a quick look at the en-suite and once again it was beautifully decorated, just like the rest of the house. With a sunken bath and the best selection of bath products a girl could ever wish for! In addition to the bath, there was a state-of-the-art shower too. The room she'd been given was so fabulous which made her wonder, if she'd actually been given the wrong room!

Sarah began to unpack some of her clothes, and placed the pictures which she'd brought with her onto the dressing table. After she'd freshened up and changed her clothes, she made her way downstairs to find George and Molly. She could hear their laughter before she reached the bottom of the stairs, so she followed it, and also the lovely smell of food, which was emanating around the house. She found herself in a very spacious and modern kitchen. George looked up. "Oh there you are, Sarah, come through. We're taking full advantage of Steve being away and having pre-dinner drinkypoos."

"I think that's what they call it isn't it, Molly?"

"Last I heard it was called alcohol, George," she said with a big smile on her face, "but let's pour Sarah a glass of something."

"Well I'm on the Rose, Sarah, and as you can see George is having a beer. What will you have?"

"Oh a small glass of Rose will be fine thank you." Sarah noticed Buster was now lying fast asleep in his rather sumptuous bed, and only just about managed to lift his head albeit, briefly before opening one eye and then returning to his slumber.

The noise that they were making clearly didn't appear to bother him too much. With their glasses charged, George raised his glass as did Molly and made a toast. "Well, here's to you, Sarah, and we hope you will be very happy in the Fountain household. It's a bit manic and chaotic here sometimes but it's okay."

"Don't listen to George," Molly said. "It's grand, Sarah, is what it is."

"Thank you and I am sure I will be fine, once I know what I am doing and of course, your help would be very much appreciated too!"

Molly was indeed a wonderful cook and the roast beef had melted in the mouth. She'd also made a wonderfully buttery rhubarb crumble and home-made ginger ice cream, which was superb. It was real comfort food. Sarah thought she would have to watch her weight whilst here. She'd worked hard to keep herself trim and toned with regular visits to the gym and of course her Pilates. Although, if she was totally honest, there hadn't been much else going on in her life of late.

Fortunately, from now on, that was all about to change and her life would indeed become a lot busier. After they had cleared away the dishes, Sarah decided to finish off her un-packing, and have an early night. George said he would turn in for the night too. He had mentioned earlier that he had a small self-contained flat over the garages. It was just right for someone on their own he'd said. Sarah could tell that he still missed his wife and felt sorry for him. Molly mentioned there was a film on Sky that she didn't want to miss and disappeared to her room.

Both Molly and George had been nothing but kind to her and had told her to make herself at home. Molly also mentioned to her, that Maxine had been in touch and would like her to go up to the offices, in Kensington the following day, whatever time suited her the best. Suddenly Sarah felt nervous as the reality of it all set in. She picked up her mobile and rang her mother, who was delighted to hear from her. "Oh hello, love, how did it go?"

"Well, I'm here ta da, and, Mum, you should see my room, I'm not sure if they've given me the right one but it is very palatial indeed. I always thought Richard and I had a wonderful home, but this is something else."

"Sounds fabulous love and you jolly well deserve it."

"So what have you been up to, Mum?"

"Well, me and Pat have been to Exeter today and of course we did some retail therapy. I treated us both to a lovely pub lunch at the Crab and Lobster Pot, the seafood is simply amazing in there."

"Oh I'm jealous, but I did have a very nice roast beef dinner, cooked by Molly. She runs the house here and does all of the cooking."

"Crikes you are being spoilt. What about his Lordship."

"Mum, will you stop calling him that."

"Well you know who I mean!" Sarah laughed.

"Of course I do. He's in LA at the moment. Apparently he's expected back some time during the week. Anyway, it sounds like you're having a ball down there, Mum."

"Oh I am and Pat has invited me to stay for another week so I am going to do just that. The weather is glorious too, so I might as well make the most of it. I've already rung Shirley next door to see if she and Ted would carry on watering the plants for another week. She said that was absolutely fine. I will have to make sure I bring them a nice little pressy back from Devon."

"How's Auntie Pat and Uncle John?" Sarah asked.

"Oh they're fine, mind you John spends quite a lot of time down the pub or pottering around in the garden. I think he has been hiding in his shed too."

"He's probably keeping out of the way poor man. You can hardly blame him, can you, Mum."

"Suppose not, love. Oh by the way, did George come and collect you this morning?"

"Yes, he was very punctual as usual and I think he was a bit disappointed that you weren't there."

"Oh don't be so daft, Sarah!"

"It seemed that way to me, Mum," Sarah said teasing her mother.

"Oh really, well say I said hello."

"Of course I will and he really is such a nice man, a real gentleman and there aren't enough of them around these days, are there?"

"Um, yes I suppose you're right, Sarah," her mother said.

"Well, Mum, I think I will turn in now, I'm bushed."

"Okay, love, and do take care and keep in touch."

"Of course I will, that's what I'm doing now, isn't it, silly! Night, Mum, speak to you soon."

"Okay, I love you."

"Love you too, Mum." With that Sarah got undressed and took a hot shower and let the water cascade over her body as she began to relax. She used some of the expensive-looking papaya and coconut shower cream and rubbed it all over her body. It smelt gorgeous. Good enough to eat in fact! After that she blow-dried her hair, jumped straight into bed, before she fell sound asleep.

Chapter 7

Sarah woke up with a jolt, after waking up a couple of times during the night, but each time she had managed to get back to sleep. It was now 6.30 a.m. and although she couldn't hear any movement in the house, she got up. She put a plain white tea shirt on and a pair of black leggings and her pink fluffy slippers. She made her way down to the kitchen and the closer she got to it, a welcoming smell of coffee hit her. Molly was sat at the kitchen table speedily typing onto her laptop. She stopped what she was doing and said. "My, aren't you the early bird."

"You could have had a lay in you know, no one would have thought any the less of you."

"No, Molly, I must start as I mean to go on, I haven't worked in ages, so I need to get into some kind of routine. I have been living with my mother for some time now and she isn't a morning person, so I have got into rather bad habits!"

"Well between you, me and George, we do take a little advantage whilst his Lordship is away." Sarah laughed out loud. "What's so funny, Sarah."

"It's just so funny because that is what my mother insists on calling him."

"Does she, well really it's a term of endearment, Steve's all right, as bosses go and he's been nothing but kind to me."

"Well that sounds promising, Molly. Sure, you've nothing to fear. Would you like some coffee or tea?"

"I'd love a cup of tea please. No sign of George yet?"

"Oh yes, George is always up before the birds every morning. He's taken Buster out for one of his daily constitutionals."

"Oh, of course, I should have noticed that Buster was missing."

"Don't you worry; he will always make his presence known to you, especially when there's food on the go and he loves a big fuss."

"Are we still talking about Buster?" Molly laughed. "Sure we are. Aren't you the funny one. I think we're going to get along just fine."

"Thanks, I'd like to think so. If you want to see a real romance, just wait until you see what Steve's like with Buster when he returns. They're smitten with each, it's true love."

"He does seem to be very good natured."

"Oh he is and Buster's not too bad either." Sarah laughed, "Ha-ha, you got me back."

"Touché, Molly."

"Oh, it will be nice having some female company here, well at least someone I can get along with," Molly said, passing Sarah's tea to her. "If you like, Sarah, I can cook you some breakfast, a full English, eggs, bacon whatever you like."

"That all sounds wonderful, but I think if you don't mind I will stick to porridge and fruit, if you have some."

"Yes, no problem."

"I'm more than happy to do it myself Molly."

"No, you're fine it's my job, Sarah."

"Thank you very much then, but there isn't any hurry."

"No, I will make a start on the porridge, I like to make sure it's done the traditional way, no microwave cooking for me."

"Anyhow, I was getting carried away on that thing," she said referring to her laptop.

"Yes, I know what you mean, I'm always on the internet." Molly set about preparing Sarah's breakfast and it wasn't long before she placed her breakfast in front of her. "I hope that's the way you like it."

"It certainly looks good to me. Thank you, Molly."

"You're welcome."

"Well, I have some things to get on with now with himself back sometime this week, I need to plan out my menus."

"I will see you later on and perhaps if you like, I can give you a grand tour of the house."

"Thanks, Molly, I look forward to it."

"Yes, me too."

Sarah sat down at the table and ate her breakfast and was quite happy to be alone. She looked out through the window at the stunning garden which was awash with colour. It was refreshing to be in a totally new environment. Molly had made the porridge perfectly, just how she liked it, and there was a wonderful selection of fresh fruit which tasted as good as it looked. So far all was going well between her and Molly and although it was early days, she liked her. She was also looking forward to having a good old nose around the house. Sarah was just about to go up to her room when Buster rushed into the kitchen wagging his tail enthusiastically and panting slightly, "Morning Buster, how are you?" Sarah made a fuss of him and he looked at her adoringly with his big brown eyes.

George entered the kitchen. "It's clear he likes you, Sarah, he usually saves those goo-goo eyes for Steve."

"Oh really."

"Morning, George."

"Morning, Sarah."

"Oh he's such a lovely dog, isn't he."

"He certainly is, and he's due for a doggy pamper at the salon this week. Buster is well looked after, aren't you, boy." Buster jumped up at George, who by this time had gone to the cupboard to get his food out. "Here you are Boy."

Sarah had never seen food disappear from a bowl so quick. "Crikes he's got an appetite, hasn't he?"

"Well he's a youngster really, as he's only just turned one."

"Did you sleep well in your new surroundings, Sarah?"

"Not too bad, thank you. I did wake up a few times, but still managed to get myself back to sleep. I woke up really early as I told Molly, I have got myself into bad habits living with Mum. She is so not a morning person and what with not working. Anyway, that is all about to change!"

"You'll soon get into the swing of it, Sarah."

"What will you be doing today?" George asked her.

"Well, I have to go up to see Maxine at the Kensington Offices and I guess I will find out more then. Maxine has already sent me through lots of paperwork for me to read through and I have been up late every night doing my homework. But I cannot wait to get started now."

"Well, I think you will find it interesting, Sarah. It's a crazy world but I think you will be able to handle it."

"I hope so."

"What will you be doing today, George?"

"I shall make sure that all of the cars are cleaned and do my usual odd jobs around the house. The boss will be home again soon."

"Yes so I hear." With her breakfast finished, Sarah said goodbye to George, "I will see you later."

"You most certainly will and don't forget, if there is anything you need Sarah, you only have to ask."

"Thanks, George."

Sarah arrived back at the house mid-afternoon, after a very hectic morning at the Kensington Offices. Maxine had gone through the script with her for the film Steve was directing and highlighted some of the areas which she would definitely be involved in, and just about everything else to do with working on a film set. She'd also told her that confidentiality was of paramount importance. "What happens on set must stay on set," Maxine had said with a smile on her face. Apparently, the actress Elenour Seymour would be returning with him on Thursday and she should liaise with Molly and prepare a room for her, Molly would know which one she should have. Sarah was to order flowers and lots of them, all in pink from the local florist and be placed in the film star's bedroom and also strategically around the house. Molly was to stock up on fresh organic vegetables and juices. All the alcohol was to be locked away. Sarah also had to ring Steve's Saville Row tailor, to check whether his suits would be delivered before he returned. Also she had to make sure that all his white shirts were back from the dry cleaners. Well it had started, she'd got something to do, albeit nothing too taxing at present. The house was quiet and there was no sign of Molly or George. However, Buster was pleased to see her.

She quickly looked at one of the lists she'd been given by Maxine with the necessary telephone numbers she required and then made the calls. The tailor had assured her that Steve's suits would be with them by the following evening and the dry cleaning would be back in the morning. She looked at the time and it was almost 4.30. As the florist was fairly local, Sarah thought it would be a nice idea to walk up to the High Street and sort out the flowers. However, just as she got to the front door, Buster came bounding towards her and began jumping up and down, looking in the direction of where his lead was kept. Sarah decided to take him for a walk too.

Once his lead was on, he became even more excited if that was at all possible. "Come on, Buster, calm down." Bless him, he sat down as good as gold, whilst she scribbled a note for George and Molly to say that she'd taken Buster for a walk. She wouldn't want them worrying about him. It was a pleasant day, just warm enough that you didn't need to wear a jacket and fortunately, Buster was a well-behaved dog on his lead and looked to be enjoying his outing. They arrived at the florist shop, aptly named 'In Bloom', which was certainly one of the smallest florist shops Sarah had ever been in but it did have the most spectacular flowers and their fragrance filled the air. You could barely move for them.

A young woman popped out from behind the counter and greeted her. She was dressed casually in a white T-shirt and a pair of denim shorts, pink wellies and a black and a white bandanna tied around her short curly hair. Sarah asked if she had any objections to her bringing Buster into the shop. "No worries; of course you can." Buster was very obedient as he sat down and for once he didn't wag his tail. It was as if he knew he'd be in trouble if he did! As soon as Sarah mentioned flowers for Steve Fountain, the woman became more animated. "I'm Alice by the way, pleased to meet you."

"Sarah, likewise."

"Can you hold on a sec, I'll just call my husband down and then I will take you through to the back."

Alice disappeared for a short while, but she could still hear her as she called out. "Ben, come here a minute, will you, love."

"What now, Alice?" Sarah could tell by the man's tone that he wasn't too happy.

"Um I just need you to mind the shop for me," she said in an overly loud whisper.

"Okay, but I wish you would make up your bloody mind. I thought you wanted me to go through all these invoices for you."

"Just come down, Ben, please!" Alice came back into the shop looking a little flustered but smiled sweetly at Sarah, who in turn tried to pretend she hadn't heard any of their conversation. Ben duly did as he was asked and came down into the shop, albeit rather huffily Sarah thought and only just about managed a weak smile at her.

She followed Alice out of the shop as they went across a small courtyard and entered a very large shed, which was full of fairy lights, and extremely girlie. A young woman was working on some beautiful flower arrangements in a corner of the shed and Alice confirmed it was for a large wedding the following day. The two women, sat down in a nice seating area, with lots of pretty cushions and Buster laid down beside her. "Would you like a drink, Sarah?"

"No thank you." Alice picked up her note pad. "So when do you need the flowers for, Sarah."

"We need them ready for Thursday morning of this week please." Alice scribbled onto her pad. "Have you any idea on what you would like and the quantity." In her mind, Sarah made a quick calculation that there would clearly have to be one flower arrangement for Elenour Seymour's room and another for the hallway and definitely on the two landings.

"I think six would be fine, and this would give her a couple of extra ones to place somewhere else around the house. All pink flowers too! I guess that you have made flower arrangements for the house before."

"Oh yes lots of times, but never just all pink flowers. That'll be interesting but I will probably mix in a bit of white and green, just to complement the arrangements. So have you any idea of what you have in mind?"

"No I'm happy to leave that completely to you, although I think the one in the main hallway should be a statement piece. Big and bold and the one for the bedroom should be subtle and pretty." Alice raised her eyebrows. "No problem." Sarah felt confident that she could trust Alice to do a good job for the Fountain household. "Would you be able to invoice us for the flowers?"

"Yes, of course, we can."

"Thank you, Alice."

"Thank you and hopefully I will see you again, Sarah."

"Oh I expect you will, bye for now," and with that Sarah left the shop and returned to the house. She let Buster off his lead and hung it up and he made a quick dash for his water bowl. The house appeared to be in silence still, but it was difficult to tell in a house this size. Sarah walked into the office to carry on with some work. A short while later, she heard Molly shout out. "Hello, is there anyone at home?"

"Me Molly I'm in the office."

"Oh hiya," Molly said as she sat down opposite Sarah. "You wouldn't believe the day I have had."

"So tell me all about it then, what's happened?" Sarah asked.

"Well, after I finished my work, I met up with one of my cousins, Shannon from back home and she's a proper chatter-box, believe me. You see we live in a very small village near Cork and everyone and I mean everyone knows each other's business, so she's been filling me in on all the gossip. We've a large family so now I feel absolutely exhausted and I couldn't get a word in edgeways." Sarah smiled and doubted that very much, because Molly was clearly a chatter-box too, just like her cousin Shannon, and she was sure that she'd enjoyed all of the juicy gossip too.

"So what's been happening back in the village then?"

"Well apparently the Priest married a young local couple recently and he was as drunk as a skunk at the Wedding and made a right show of himself."

"You're kidding."

"Oh I wish that I was and it's not that unusual back home."

"Right I am going to put the kettle on, Sarah, do you fancy a cuppa cos I'm gasping for one."

"Yes please, I can finish this off later anyhow," Sarah replied, switching off the laptop. Molly made their tea and the two sat down at the kitchen table. "I take it you've heard from himself about the infamous Elenour Seymour whose arriving back with him on Thursday."

"Yes, I have, Molly, and I've just been to the florist and ordered the flowers. I took Buster with me."

"Oh that was good."

"He needs plenty of exercise that one. I hope he didn't mark too many lamp posts along the way did he," Molly quipped. "Maybe one or two and I'm relieved to say, nothing else!"

"We are all going to be very busy over the next few days now, for sure."

"Have you ever met her, Molly?"

"No, but I've read all about her. A proper little diva by all accounts."

"Yes that's what I have read also and apparently demanding when on set. Still, to be fair you cannot believe all of what's in the press, whether it be good or bad."

"Yeah, I know what you mean but it's the bad stuff that sells newspapers and magazines."

"Yes that's true, Molly."

"Anyhow we're about to get the pleasure of meeting her any day now, aren't we, Sarah."

"Yes and I for one am rather keen to meet her. I think she'll be a challenge and I need some excitement in my life."

"Well as they say, remember what you wish for. I've got Mary and Eva coming in to give the house a good going over. Not that it needs it really. I will give madam the large guest room on the second floor."

"Only the best for Miss Seymour then eh, Molly. Oh and I think it may be a case of us having to be on our best behaviour. Where's George?"

"I don't know; I expect he'll probably be back soon. He could be having a little cat nap up in his flat."

"Well, he does get up early, doesn't he?"

"Yes, and he sometimes falls asleep whilst reading his newspaper. He'd fiercely deny it of course, but I know he does do it occasionally, Molly said laughing. One thing is for sure, our George will be in his element. He's never happier than when Steve has guests staying here and a big Hollywood actress will put a smile on his face."

"He's such a nice man, isn't he, Molly, not judgemental at all."

"Not like me and you, you mean!" Sarah laughed. "Perhaps, Molly, we should give Elenour Seymour a chance."

Molly raised her cup and said, "Let's drink to that," and they clinked their cups together each with a smirk on their face. "Anyhow, Sarah, before all the mayhem starts here, would you like me to give you a grand tour of the house, proper like whilst we have the time."

"Oh that would be great. Lead the way, Macbeth," and Sarah followed Molly up to the first floor. She could hardly wait to be shown around this two-storey home.

The house was amazing and the last room Molly showed Sarah, was the cinema. She was like a child in a sweet shop and Molly had said she had things to do and would leave her to it. Sarah had quickly come to the decision, without a shadow of a doubt, that this, was her most favourite room in the entire house. It was impressive and tastefully decorated from its plush red velvet comfy cinema seats which to her surprise were even tiered, to the red velvet curtains that surrounded a huge screen.

It had a real feel for the 1940's Hollywood Golden era about it as well. The walls were full of pictures and memorabilia. John Wayne and Humphrey Bogart stared back at her and they were just two of the old Hollywood greats. Steve McQueen so handsome, with his twinkling blue eyes, along with Faye Dunaway from the great film *The Thomas Crown Affair*. The attention to detail in the cinema was impressive and none of it had been lost on her. Homage had also been paid to some of the greatest British films ever made, *The Dam Busters, A Bridge too Far*, and even the *Carry On* films, which were a firm family favourite in her house.

It was good to see that Steve Fountain had a sense of fun about him. It didn't matter how many times she'd watched them herself, they always made her laugh. There was even a popcorn machine and a sweetie counter. She looked up at the ceiling where hundreds of tiny lights glistened like stars against a pitch-black sky.

Sarah had also been very impressed with the library too, as it had some really good books in it, mostly about the film industry and its stars, which Sarah thought she may well enjoy reading at some point in the future. It was great to be doing a job that in many ways had always been a passion of hers. When she had been a little girl, she would visit her dad, whilst he had been at work and he would craftily sneak her in to watch the films from the Projection room. She'd been absolutely mesmerised by them and had always felt extra special on those occasions. She knew that her dad would have been extremely impressed that his daughter had found herself working for a British film director.

Sarah dragged herself away from the cinema room and found Molly in the kitchen. "So what do you think of the house then, Sarah, now you've seen it all?"

"It's extremely impressive and I can see that no expense has been spared."

"My favourite room, of course," Sarah continued, "is the cinema."

"No, I'd never have guessed, you're kidding me, Sarah, you were in there bloody ages. However, I do have to agree with you."

"For me it's great having a gym here too and it saves me having to go out into some huge gym. It's so competitive and there is always some sweaty guys who are all trying to outdo one another with the weights."

"Yes I know what you mean."

"I don't generally like gym's but I love doing my Pilates and running."

"Well, feel free to use the gym any time. Callum comes here a couple of times a week when Steve's around. If you asked him, I am sure he would work out a fitness plan for you. He's a bit of a hunk too. That's if you're into muscly men!"

"Oh really," Sarah said raising her eyebrows and winking at Molly. "No don't you give me that look lady. I'm off of men totally," and Sarah could tell that she really meant it too.

"Well that makes two of us then, Molly," Sarah said and gave her a high five.

The next couple of days whizzed by and the house had been extremely lively. George had been busy making sure Steve's cars had a thorough wash, polish and valet and that they were full to the brim with petrol. Molly had ensured that the house had sparkled from top to bottom with the help of Mary and Eva who had worked their magic with the cleaning. When they had left earlier, you could clearly see the relief on their faces!

Elenour's room looked amazing with its soft dove grey walls, and a matching plush grey carpet. Molly had splashed some of Steve's cash and bought a new, soft, pink silk bed cover and matching scatter cushions which set it all off perfectly. Alice had delivered the flowers earlier, as promised, and they were absolutely gorgeous and they smelt wonderful too. She and Molly had been meticulous over every detail in both the bedroom and en-suite.

Elenour's favourite perfumes and soaps had been strategically placed in the rooms. The fridge had been stocked up with fresh organic juices and natural spring water which, Elenour allegedly drank. The two had agreed that they couldn't do any more! They would just have to wait for their guest of honour to arrive. Molly had been right, George had indeed been excited about the prospect of meeting a young Hollywood star. He'd said it was about time it got a bit more lively around the house again, as it had been way too quiet of late.

Sarah had received a list of jobs to complete for Maxine before the end of the week. They would be going on location in less than two weeks' time and she could hardly wait. She had butterflies in her stomach whenever she thought about it. Molly suddenly burst into the room. "Come on quick, herself has arrived. George has just pulled up outside."

"Why, do we have to form a welcome committee?"

"No, but aren't you a little curious?"

"Are you kidding," Sarah said as she laughed and pushed past Molly to get ahead of her.

Buster suddenly made a mad dash out of the kitchen upon hearing his master's voice. He was quicker than a rat up a sewer pipe, but when Steve finally entered the kitchen, he was alone. Buster began jumping up in the air like a crazed puppy until Steve made a huge fuss of him by rubbing his tummy, which he clearly loved. Eventually, on Steve's command, he returned to his bed. "Hello, ladies, I'm back."

"Indeed you are, Steve, how are you?"

"I'm fine thanks."

"Coffee?"

"Yes please Molly, thanks."

"So Sarah, how are you getting on?"

"Fine thank you, everyone has been very welcoming."

"That's good, because now I'm back the fun will really begin!"

"Well I cannot wait and I am looking forward to it, Steve."

"Good."

"So come on, Steve, where's Elenour, we're dying to meet her, are we not, Sarah?" Molly said in a mocking tone Sarah nodded in agreement.

"I've just taken her up to her room."

"Elenour's gone for a lie down."

"I told her not to because really, it's best to try and stay awake and then hopefully the jet lag won't be so bad. However, she knows best." George popped his head through the door.

"Boss, shall I take up Miss Seymour's cases now?"

"No, hang on a minute, thanks, George. I will take them up later. You go and take a break, because you were up very early today."

"No I'm okay boss, really."

"Well, at least sit down and have a coffee."

"Sarah, would you make our George a coffee please and Molly would you mind just checking to see if Elenour needs any help?"

"Yes, of course," Molly said rolling her eyes at Sarah.

"Also you'd better check if she wants her cases up yet."

"Right," Molly said as she left the kitchen.

"Well, Steve said trying to stifle a yawn, I'm going to get myself into the shower now and freshen up a bit." He picked up his coffee and walked towards the door and then stopped. "I'd like to have a meeting with you later, Sarah."

"Yes of course."

"I hope you don't mind, Steve, but I have been working in your office whilst you've been away."

"No, of course not." Steve made another huge fuss of Buster, promising him a walk later before leaving the kitchen.

"Here you are, George, one coffee and two sugars."

"Thank you, Sarah. So come on, George, let me know what is this Elenour Seymour like then?"

"Well, she seems nice enough, bit of a blonde bombshell, but she slept most of the time in the car."

"Gosh the anticipation. I will just have to wait a bit longer before meeting her then, now she's gone up for her so-called nap!"

"How's your mum, Sarah?"

"Oh she's fine thanks, George. Actually I noticed earlier that she'd sent me a text. I had better give her a ring when I have finished work. She has decided to stay an extra week in Devon because she is having such a good time and the weather has been great too."

"Lucky her."

"I'm going to put the car away now, Sarah, and I will take my coffee with me. Mind you, the boss did mention that he would like me to be on standby to take Miss Seymour wherever she wants to go."

"He didn't seem to think that it would be very likely today, but I will be ready and waiting if she does from now on. Actually I'm really looking forward to having a bit more to do now. It's been a bit too quiet round here of late as Steve has been away quite a lot of the time. Tell Molly I have taken the newspaper as I like to see what's going on in the world."

"Right then, I'm off. All right, see you later, George." Sarah was just about to go back into the office when Molly came down. "Oh there you are."

"Hi, Molly, so have you met her?"

"What is she like then?" Sarah asked in a hushed whisper.

"Didn't get to see much, she was already lying in bed with her eye mask on. All I know is that she is definitely blonde."

"I already knew that! Did she say anything at all?"

"Let me see now. Oh yes, hi and could I wake her up at 4 o'clock if she hasn't surfaced by that time."

"A woman of few words then."

"Definitely. Anyway, I'm going to crack on with the preparations for dinner."

"Well, I will see you later," and with that Sarah went into the office and continued with her work. She would have loved to have given her mother a call, but thought better of it. She would ring her later when she had finished her work.

An hour later, Steve came in. He certainly looked fresh eyed and bushy tailed for someone who had just done a long haul flight, taking into account the time difference. His hair was still wet and Sarah thought he looked rather boyish, even with his dark stubble. "Hard at it still, Sarah."

"Naturally."

"That's what I like to see," he said in a mocking tone.

"Right I know, Maxine has already brought you up to speed on most things, but as you probably are aware, it's going to be really tight from now on, what with pre-production well under way and we're leaving for Italy quite soon. I really need to explain to you the real reason why I have brought Elenour over to the UK. The thing is she's really struggling with her British accent.

"I have arranged for a very good friend of mine, Jane Sinclair to tutor her. She is an excellent drama teacher and voice coach from RADA. She's retired now, but she is doing me a massive favour.

"Elenour's got less than two weeks to nail this. It's absolutely essential that she gets the accent just right. It's also crucial that Elenour's character shows extreme vulnerability for this part too and a dodgy British accent is something we don't need!

"Actually maybe I am being somewhat harsh, but there is room for improvement. It has to be completely convincing!"

"There is nothing worse than when you watch a film and someone drops their accent, I don't want that to happen with Elenour. This film is a complete departure from anything she has ever done before.

"To be honest, Sarah, I've totally put my neck on the chopping board in getting Elenour cast for this part. Between you and me, the producers and the financial backers weren't too keen to have her in this film.

"They had someone else in mind and she does have a bit of a reputation.

"She is however, a very good actress and the camera absolutely loves her, which is a gift in itself and trust me, it doesn't happen all the time.

"I know that she can do it."

"She is undoubtedly a gorgeous creature, Steve."

"Yes and she's going to need some cajoling, a bit like a babysitter if you like. I need you to accompany her whenever she goes to Jane's house."

"The last thing I want to happen is that she is recognised, so she is going to have to wear one of those wigs that you bought when you accompany her."

"George will drive you both. Become her friend if you can and just make sure she's happy and hopefully we will get there. She's not the easiest of persons to get along with at times. Of course she likes nothing more than to play the big star, but deep down, she is also very vulnerable, a bit like the character she's about to play. Do you think you can do that?"

"It doesn't sound too taxing, but then I've not met Elenour yet, have I."

"Well then you're in for a treat. Like every major star I've ever worked with she has insecurities and of course she's young. But Elenour is extremely charismatic and good fun. I'm counting on you, Sarah."

"Of course, Steve, you can definitely count on me. I also have a thick skin too, which I think may help."

"Thanks. So you're settling in okay?"

"Oh yes thanks, it's only been a few days, but everyone has been so nice to me and I'm enjoying getting stuck into the work. It's full on but it's totally consuming and I love it. I am genuinely excited about being here and I am ready for any challenges that are thrown at me."

Steve smiled at her and raised his eyebrows. "I'll remind you of that when you're dying to go to sleep and I'm keeping you up all hours with some crisis or other."

"Yes maybe you've got a point there!"

"Have you had a good look around the house yet?"

"Oh yes, it's beautiful and my favourite room by far is the cinema. I absolutely loved it."

"Yes, it's mine too," he said with a big smile on his face. "Whenever I'm struggling for inspiration or have a problem, I just put on some old film and it always gives me the inspiration to get my creative juices going again. It helps to lift my spirits. Some of them take me right back to my childhood."

"I know exactly what you mean, Steve. My dad was a projectionist up in the Odeon, Leicester Square, for many years and when I was a young girl, he used to sneak me in to watch the films."

"I would watch them all from the best seat in the house and I was totally mesmerised. Dad had a real passion for his work and according to him, he was a born natural, especially when things went wrong. He had a gift apparently, as he could always repair any electrical and technical faults when they went wrong."

"I must admit, Sarah, I didn't know that about your dad."

"Well it was on my CV."

"Sorry, Sarah, if I'm honest, I only flicked through it. I trust Max and James' opinion one hundred percent."

"That's okay, Steve. I love the fact that you have the *Carry On* films in your collection, alongside some of the big blockbusters."

"Of course I do, and they are the best of British humour and personally, I can watch them over and over again."

"Me too, it's the double-entendres that get me every time and they were made on a shoestring back then, weren't they?"

"Yes, they were, but somehow none of that matters, because they were all so funny."

"I myself am extremely fortunate to have a massive budget to work with, but with that comes an awful lot of stress to deliver the goods! It's a wonder I haven't gone totally grey!" Sarah thought that he would probably still look as handsome even if he did have grey hair! At that moment, Steve's phone rang and he indicated to Sarah that he would take the call and left the room. Sarah was certainly beginning to discover just how much hard work was involved before a film ever hits the big screen; everything was done meticulously and clearly, no stone was allowed to be left unturned.

Sarah had been engrossed in her work, not realising the time when Molly popped her head around the door. "Hey you, dinner will be ready in about 10 minutes."

"Oh thanks, Molly, I didn't notice the time. Steve gave me an urgent spread sheet to work on, boy it's intense."

"Well you look done in and your eyes have glazed over. You have been staring at that screen for far too long. So it's time to stop for sure."

"Yes you're right."

"Anyway, I'm starving."

"Has Elenour surfaced yet?"

"Well, she hasn't come down so far, but I woke her up at 4 p.m. with her peppermint tea. She didn't have a lot to say except OMG is that the time."

Sarah hurriedly finished up in the office and finally shut down her laptop. She stood up and did some stretches. Molly was right as she had definitely been sitting at the desk for far too long and gently began moving her head from side to side, to relieve some of the tension in her neck.

Sarah walked into the kitchen, where Molly was busy working away. I thought we three could eat in here tonight and let Steve and her Ladyship have dinner on their own. Go and look in the dining room. It looks gorgeous. "I must have lit about 20 candles."

It certainly did look romantic as Sarah checked it out and the table was elegant and pretty. As she made her way back to the kitchen, Steve followed on behind her. He looked a bit sheepish before he said. "Molly, I'm so sorry, but Elenour appears to have found her second wind and now wants to go out for dinner." Sarah looked at Molly, who looked crestfallen, and her face had also gone a deep shade of red. Sarah could almost feel her pain.

"Oh it's okay, Steve, I've only been slaving away here all afternoon."

"I know you have," Steve said, as he walked over to her and placed his hand onto her shoulder. "I've got to keep her happy, you understand, don't you?"

"Yes of course I do, Steve."

"Well, it looks like we're going to be having a feast tonight, Sarah."

"That's music to my ears, Molly, bring it on."

"Well, ladies, I'd better go and get changed. I will see you later."

"Oh, by the way Sarah, Steve said, Elenour's first appointment with Jane is tomorrow at 11.30. Better make sure George is available for about 10, as I don't want her to be late."

"You will keep your eye on her won't you."

"Of course I will, Steve."

"I hope you both have a good evening Steve."

"I will try, but to be honest I am a bit bushed myself and was in fact looking forward to an early night."

"Can you please tell George not to panic, because I won't be needing him tonight."

"I am going to drive us out of town, somewhere nice and quiet and less public and I know just the place. Elenour wanted to go to the Ivy, but I told her no chance, as I want to keep her out of the limelight for now. I certainly don't want the Paparazzi photographing us, not yet anyway!" With that Steve left the kitchen.

"Oh, Molly, I'm so sorry you worked so hard and the dining room looks amazing."

"Shall I go and blow the candles out for you?"

"Certainly not, none of this will go to waste will it, because you, me and George will dine out in style tonight and make the most of it."

"George should be here any minute now, he isn't usually late."

"I thought you handled the whole situation very well Molly. Thanks, Sarah, but my blood is boiling inside. I've done a meal fit for a queen here."

"Still it's their loss. We are going to have a great night, Molly."

"You bet ya."

"Steve has a lot riding on this new film, doesn't he Molly."

"Oh for sure, it's exciting, Sarah, but a lot of bloody hard work and pressure on him and it has been for some time. Now where is George?" Molly asked.

"I'm here, Molly," George answered. "Sorry am I late."

"Oh you're not really George, but I am just about to serve up our meal." Sarah noticed that for once George looked more relaxed, as he was off duty and casually dressed in a T-shirt and a pair of smart jeans. Sarah also observed that for his age, he was still a remarkably handsome man.

"Get a move on then," George said as he looked at Sarah and winked at her, "cos I'm starving, Molly."

"Oh aren't you always, George. Did you know that himself and our big super star, Molly said with more than a hint of sarcasm are going out to eat now."

"Are they?"

"YES."

"Oh dear I'd better get the car out ready as I will be needed then, won't I?"

"No don't worry, George, Steve said he will drive himself and Elenour out of town somewhere which is less public," Sarah informed him.

"Great as that means I can still have my dinner with you two lovely ladies then."

"Indeed you can, and we will be having the dinner that I had prepared for them both in the dining room."

"Right, you two, go take your seats and I will bring it through."

"Are you sure, Molly?" Sarah asked her.

"Yes, of course," she said as she raised her eyebrows! "Away with yous."

Chapter 8

The three of them sat around the table and happily tucked into their starter, which was a creamy goat's cheese tart. Every course was perfect and after a delicious lemon sole, Molly served their dessert, which was a take on a Tiramisu, but Molly had replaced the coffee with black cherries and Kirsch. It was gorgeous, but unfortunately for Sarah a cherry dropped right down onto her white shirt. "Oh for goodness' sake. Blast, look what I have done."

"A regular little 'miss messy' aren't you," Molly said, laughing. "You'd better go and wash it off, Sarah; otherwise, the stain may not come out."

"Yes, you're right. I will be back in two ticks. Hey, whatever you do, keep your hands off my dessert cos I'm coming back for it."

"Will you go, woman," Molly said, laughing at her once again.

Sarah dashed out of the dining room and right into the path of Steve and Elenour Seymour. In fact she'd practically collided with them. She was completely taken by surprise and rather embarrassed. Steve spoke first. "Hello, Sarah, let me introduce you to Elenour."

"Elenour, this is Sarah, who is my new assistant."

"I'm very pleased to meet you, Elenour," Sarah said, smiling at them both.

"Hi," Elenour said, rather dismissively and in a slightly bored tone. Sarah quickly realised that there wouldn't be anything else forthcoming from Miss Seymour.

Feeling even more awkward, if that was possible, Sarah said. "Right I'd best let you two get on your way. I hope you have a lovely evening."

"Thanks very much," Steve replied, "You too. Oh and by the way, Sarah," he said looking her up and then down to her bare feet, "it's really good to see that you are making yourself well and truly at home." Sarah had not missed the wry look upon Steve's face before they had left and she blushed.

She was totally mortified, as she looked down firstly at her bare feet and then at the ugly black cherry juice stain clearly evident on her shirt, not to mention her messy unruly hair. Earlier she'd just scraped it back into a ponytail with an elastic band. What must they have thought! She actually felt like an errant child, who had been caught out! However, she certainly wasn't disappointed in Elenour Seymour, not one bit. She was gorgeous and every bit the movie star that she was.

She was slim and had smooth silky ash blonde hair, which fell half-way down her back. She certainly looked to be taller than Sarah and was on trend in an amazing white trouser suit, which looked designer and from what she could see, little else underneath it. There was definitely no VPL and a fair amount of cleavage on show too.

She'd finished it all off with a pair of red high-heeled patent shoes and a bright red lipstick. Sarah thought she carried the look off extremely well and she certainly came across as one very confident young woman. Her skin appeared flawless and her make-up was perfect, as if a make-up artist had done it for her! Her cool bright blue eyes didn't give an awful lot away, but Sarah had the feeling that this young woman didn't miss much.

Once they had left the house, Sarah nipped into the kitchen and dabbed away at her shirt with a wet tea towel. She felt a complete mess. To be fair, Sarah thought that Steve and Elenour had made a handsome couple. Steve had been dressed immaculately in a navy blue jacket and white shirt, teamed with a pair of expensive jeans. Sarah could barely contain herself any longer, as she stopped trying to get the stain out of her shirt and decided that it would be better to leave it to soak overnight.

She darted back into the dining room like grease lightening. "Guess what, I have actually met her now," Sarah beamed unable to hide her excitement. "I bumped into them quite literally as they were going out."

George and Molly looked at her. "By them, I guess you mean Steve and Elenour," Molly said, "so, what did you think of her then?"

"She's gorgeous and, of course, she knows it!"

"Still I'm not going to blame her for that."

"I didn't feel too great myself, stood there in my bare feet with a black cherry stain all down my white shirt, I felt a complete numpty."

"Oh don't be so silly."

"Anyhow, she probably knows all the tricks of the trade and she's only 26 years old, which helps for God's sake."

"Yes rub it in why don't you, Molly." Sarah laughed, "Yes I know!"

"I have to say, she barely acknowledged me as she slept in the car the whole way home from the airport," George piped in.

"Perhaps she saves all of her dialogue for when she's on set," Molly said with more than a hint of sarcasm. "Right come on finish off your dessert, Sarah. We have cheese and biscuits after this!"

"Right before you do that, Sarah," George said, "let's raise our glasses to Molly for such a wonderful meal."

"Absolutely, thank you so much, Molly." They all clinked their glasses together. "Oh sure it was nothing."

"Oh yes it was and we appreciate it, don't we, Sarah."

"Most certainly we do, and as I said before it was definitely Steve and Miss Seymour's loss. I doubt they will get finer food where they are going tonight."

"Oh will you shut up the pair of yous, me head will be too big for me to get through that door, otherwise!"

Chapter 9

Before going to sleep that night, Sarah had made a quick call to her mother, who was still having a good time in Devon, and the weather had been fabulous, which of course made a difference. She'd been eager to hear Sarah's gossip, especially about Elenour Seymour, but as Sarah had told her mother, there wasn't a lot to divulge as yet, as she'd barely spoken to her.

The following morning, Sarah woke early and as hard as she tried, couldn't get back off to sleep again. For some reason she was really looking forward to the day ahead and saw the young Elenour Seymour as a challenge. She wondered what time she and Steve had got in the night before! Sarah was restless and made her way down into the kitchen to make herself a cup of tea. Before she'd even reached the kitchen, she could smell cigarette smoke and there was a distinct chill in the air, as she entered the kitchen. Someone was definitely outside smoking. Buster got excited and wagged his tail and came over to her and then began jumping up at the cupboard where his food was kept.

Sarah stroked him and rubbed his tummy and because he was still looking up at the cupboard door imploringly, she slipped him a few doggy biscuits, which she knew was naughty. George wouldn't approve, but still what the eye doesn't see, the heart won't grieve over! The patio doors were wide open and Sarah could see Elenour sitting outside on one of the garden chairs. She obviously hadn't heard Sarah and looked surprised to see her. "Okay, it looks as if I'm busted. Please," she said in a whiny little voice, "don't tell Steve, will you," as she continued to puff away once more on her cigarette. "I have had to give up the booze, but I simply cannot give up the cigarettes as well."

"Of course not, I give you my word."

"Your secret is safe with me."

"It's freaking cold out here, but at least it's kinda waking me up a bit."

"Look at my hair, it's like a frizz ball after Steve made me put on that stupid wig last night, before we went into the restaurant! It ruined my hair!"

"He's only looking out for you, Elenour."

"Huh maybe." Sarah felt mean for thinking it, or was she secretly pleased. Because Elenour Seymour certainly didn't look quite as hot as she had the previous night. She looked pale and tired, and had dark circles under her eyes, probably due to a late night or more likely, an early morning. Her glamorous outfit from her night out with Steve had been replaced with a baggy black T-shirt and a pair of grey jogging bottoms. Elenour's skin had looked flawless the night before, but in the cold light of day, and completely make-up free, a few tiny spots were visible on her face. Sarah felt sorry for her, as she looked as if she had the weight of the world on her young shoulders.

"So how come you're up so early, it's Sarah, isn't it." Sarah was impressed that she'd actually remembered her name, having shown no interest in her whatsoever the night before.

"Yes that's me, well I couldn't sleep and then I really fancied a cup of tea."

"Can I get you one, or a coffee?"

"Actually, a cup of peppermint tea would be nice." Sarah went inside to make their drinks and Elenour came in from the kitchen and both women sat down at the kitchen table and sipped their tea.

"Thanks for that."

"I hear that you're coming with me to this voice coach later!"

"That's right," Sarah said.

"Well, I can hardly wait," she said unenthusiastically, as she stretched her arms up into the air and yawned. "I'm sure it won't be that bad."

"Easy for you to say, because you're not the one that has to go through it."

"Yeah you're right, but I will be right by your side and what is it they say, what doesn't kill you makes you stronger!"

"Whatever! I certainly hope you're right!"

"Anyway, Elenour, if you don't mind, I'm going to take my tea up and see if I can catch up on some sleep and I am sure today won't be as bad as you think." There was no reply from Elenour, who seemed rather preoccupied fiddling with her phone and didn't appear to notice Sarah leave the kitchen.

Back up in her room, Sarah sat up in bed and enjoyed her tea, and flicked through a couple of magazines for a while, but once again was feeling restless and had a shower. She then decided that she may as well get on with her work. She went back into the kitchen and this time, there was no sign of Elenour. She quickly grabbed a bowl and made herself some porridge, as she was beginning to feel hungry by now and took it through to the office. A few urgent emails had to be dealt with first and she sorted out the post which had piled up in Steve's absence. She placed it in order of priority as she saw fit, for Steve to deal with. She wasn't sure just how long she would be out with Elenour today.

Sarah glanced at her watch and realised that it was time she got herself ready. She didn't want to keep Elenour waiting! Half an hour later, she was ready after she'd had a good old rummage through her wardrobe and taking out a selection of clothes. She eventually chose to wear a pair of white jeans and a white shirt, with her favourite cornflower blue jacket and matching blue pumps. She'd made a concerted effort with her appearance and an even bigger effort with her hair and make-up today than she normally would. Before she left the room, she sprayed a generous amount of Coco Chanel, which was her favourite perfume and then made her way downstairs to see if Elenour had surfaced again.

It was almost a quarter to ten and George was sat at the kitchen table talking to Molly. Sarah greeted them both. "Where have you been hiding then?" Molly asked.

"Oh I couldn't sleep this morning so I had an early breakfast and cracked on with some work. I would imagine we're going to be out for quite a while today with Elenour."

"Do you have any idea of how long, George?"

"No I don't I'm afraid, I guess, as long as it takes. I have already dropped Steve off at the office this morning."

"Apparently, George said I have to make myself available to Miss Seymour at all times. He will probably get a taxi home, depending on what time he finishes today."

"No sign of her yet then?"

"Oh yes she had her breakfast in bed, about an hour ago now. It was just juice and fresh fruit oh and I nearly forgot Molly laughed a yogurt!"

"So that's the secret to staying slim, is it! It would appear so, Sarah."

Sarah noticed that George was beginning to get extremely fidgety, and although she didn't know George that well yet, she knew that he was a stickler for good time keeping and didn't like to be late. However, Elenour finally appeared at 10.15. "Hi, I'm ready to go." George was all smiles as he greeted her. "Ah there you are, Morning Miss Seymour, the car is out the front."

"After you, Miss Seymour."

"You don't have to be so formal, George, it's just Elenour!"

"Okay, miss, I mean Elenour," George said, pulling a face at Sarah, behind her back!

As they both left the kitchen, Sarah held back a bit. "See you later, Molly, wish me luck."

"Oh you've probably survived worse."

"Yes but she doesn't say an awful lot, does she?"

"That's true."

"Back in Ireland we'd more than likely say she was a bit aloof."

"Anyhow, I have to say I don't envy you today."

"Me neither, do you want to swap?"

"No, now go, woman, don't keep her Ladyship waiting."

Sarah made her exit and joined Elenour in the back seat of the car. George turned round. "Right, ladies, fasten your seat belts we're off." Elenour turned to Sarah looking thoroughly miserable. "To say I'm not looking forward to today is an understatement."

"Steve told me to dress down, so I have followed his orders," she said in a rather sardonic way.

"How do you think I have done?" Elenour asked.

"You look lovely."

"Are you sure?"

"Yes, of course."

"I have a baseball cap to put on later and dark glasses for when I get out of the car."

"I am definitely not putting on one of those silly wigs, whatever Steve says, it's totally crazy!" Sarah thought that even dressed casually as she was, in jeans and a hoodie teamed with designer trainers, she was still a gorgeous creature.

She had really perked up considerably since Sarah had seen her earlier on in the day, smoking in the garden. "Where the hell are we going today anyway, George?"

"It's a place called Dulwich in South London, Miss Seymour, and provided the traffic isn't too heavy, it shouldn't take long and hopefully we will be there in no time." Elenour gave Sarah a resigned look, as it was clear that George would never call her by her first name! "Actually, Miss Seymour, our first-ever British female Prime Minister, Margaret Thatcher, used to live there for a short time. She was a great leader and a powerful and influential woman in Politics, if ever there was one. I had the privilege of being her chauffeur, when she was an MP. Of course that was before she moved into No. 10."

"Oh really," Elenour replied, looking out of the window, completely unimpressed and disinterested. Poor George, he didn't quite get the response he would have expected to and Sarah felt sorry for him. "This sucks totally you know, me having to go to see a voice coach. I don't think I need one."

Sarah had some sympathy for her, but said. "I guess Steve knows best."

"Oh you think so do you and how long have you been working for him?"

"Not long really, but enough to know that I would respect his judgement." Elenour gave Sarah a sullen look and then put on her headphones and listened to her iPhone and was silent for the rest of the journey.

They were now in the leafy suburb of Dulwich, as they turned into a side road which had large attractive Victorian houses with rows of huge trees on either side. George stopped the car and came around and opened the door for them. "Oh God, are we actually here finally," Elenour said as she took the headphones off and placed her iPhone back into her handbag.

"Yes we are, Miss Seymour," George said politely. Sarah had to remind Elenour to put her baseball cap and sunglasses on. Elenour sighed once again, and even Sarah thought that maybe it was a bit over the top. However, Steve didn't want anyone to recognise her and the reason she was there herself was to make sure his orders were carried out. They walked up a number of steps and Sarah rang the bell on a newly painted shiny red front door. It was a while before it was finally opened by a woman of mature years, rather attractive with short spiky pink hair. Sarah thought she could possibly be in her early seventies. She was a vision of colour in a bright orange Kaftan, which rather clashed with her hair, but she did look quite youthful. She had a ton of heavily applied sparkling blue eye shadow on, which was rather difficult to ignore. What is it they say, sometimes less is more.

"Oh there you are," she said in an exuberant manner. "Come this way." Once they were inside, Sarah made the introductions.

"Good morning, Miss Sinclair. May I introduce you to Elenour Seymour."

"Of course, pleased to meet you both, but please it's Jane and you must be Sarah," she said shaking both of their hands enthusiastically. "Righty-ho, are you ready to make a start young lady?"

"As ready as I am ever gonna be," Elenour said flatly.

"Sarah, if you would like to come through to the study, dear, and I will see if I can find that errant husband of mine to make you a coffee, or a tea if you prefer."

"Mind, he does have a habit of disappearing sometimes, but he can usually be found down in his hidey hole, commonly known as the shed!"

"Thank you very much, Jane. I've brought my laptop with me so that I can get on with some work."

"That's fine just make yourself at home, dear. You can use my desk over there in the study if you would like to," she said before turning her attention to Elenour. "Okay, let's see what we can do with you young lady, follow me dear." As they were leaving the room, Elenour looked over her shoulder and pulled a face at Sarah, who thought she looked more like a sulky teenager, than a famous actress! She really was a dramatic little soul. George had gone off to visit some friends, who lived nearby and Sarah was going to call him later when they were ready to leave.

Sarah glanced around at her surroundings, which could best be described as really messy and cluttered. There were many strange objects in the room, including an angry looking stuffed owl with large brown eyes, which glared back at her. Several candles had been lit around the room with a couple of joss sticks burning. Two large book cases had shelves which were all stuffed tightly full of books and the desk that she was expected to use, was littered with paperwork and dirty used mugs. She tidied it up as best she could and got her laptop out ready to use.

Jane Sinclair had certainly been a revelation and a delight and she was clearly a little bit eccentric, which Sarah found endearing. She couldn't help but wonder what Elenour would make of her though.

Three and a half hours later, Elenour reappeared with Jane. She looked tired with a slightly bored expression on her face. Jane smiled and winked at Sarah. She's all yours now dear. "I do hope Jim found you."

"Oh yes thanks, Jane, and he made me a nice cup of coffee."

"Did you get biccies?"

"Yes, I did."

"Oh good."

"Righty-ho, well, we will meet here again on Thursday then and please don't forget to do your homework young lady."

"Yeah, of course, I will, sure."

"Can we go now please, Sarah, I'm exhausted."

"Yes, I will just give George a quick ring," but before she had a chance to ring George's mobile, she received a message to say that he was actually outside. They said their goodbyes. Once in the car, Elenour could barely keep her eyes open and was yawning constantly. "So how did it go?" Sarah enquired.

"God she's one batty old woman and it's like a mausoleum in that house."

"Don't be ridiculous, Elenour, there are no dead bodies in there, just a few stuffed animals."

"I barely had a break today it's been so full on. I hope she knows what she's doing."

"OMG! Some of it was crazy and I felt like a fool."

"I am sure she does, because she was at RADA for many years. So do you think you are speaking the Queen's English yet?"

"You'd best ask the batty old woman that! But, I do feel a bit like Eliza Doolittle," and then Elenour surprised Sarah by saying, "The rain in Spain lies mainly on the plain," in her best posh aristocratic accent and then laughed as she continued. "How did I do, all right gover'nor," she said in a brilliant cockney accent.

"By Jove I think she's got it," Sarah quipped and all three of them laughed. It was nice to see Elenour lighten up a little bit and show that she did in fact have a sense of humour. When they arrived back at the house, Elenour soon disappeared to her room as usual, but not before requesting Molly to bring her up some peppermint tea and a sandwich and explained to Molly, exactly how she wanted the sandwich made in great detail!

"Oh me and her are going to fall out big time, before long, Sarah."

"She's a right little madam, isn't she? I think she's been rather spoilt, Molly."

"Eva said her room was like a tip this morning and she spent ages putting her clothes away."

"Goodness knows what she gets up to! She's hard work for sure!"

"Well don't worry, Molly, I think she'll be tired now and sleep for a while. From what I could tell, she found her session with Jane Sinclair pretty full on. Gosh she was a real surprise and nothing like I had imagined."

"Why was that?"

"Well, she is extremely laid back and a little bit eccentric. I had to share a room with a stuffed owl whilst I was waiting for Elenour and there was clutter everywhere. You most certainly would have hated it. Molly it was extremely and I'll be polite when I say untidy!"

"Still she is a lovely lady, and as long as she does her job that's all that matters."

"Steve knows what he is doing," Molly said. "Oh yes and I'm sure he has every faith in her. Well if I'm honest with you, Sarah, I cannot wait to see the back of our little star. Me thinks her head is so far up her own arse, it's a wonder she can see!"

"Oh, Molly, you're so funny. I don't think she's that bad, more like a petulant child."

"Except she's not a child, Sarah!"

George came into the kitchen at that moment. "Hi, Molly, any chance of a coffee."

"Of course, sit yourself down." Sarah left them to it. She had work to get on with and in particular she still had to go over the timetable for the up-coming shoot once more.

Chapter 10

It had been full on and manic leading up to their departure to Italy and most days had gone through late into the night. Steve was missing most of the time and when he was around, he was very distracted and short tempered. Sarah kept her head down as much as she could, and did as she was told! She used her initiative wherever she was able to. She quickly realised that she couldn't keep interrupting Steve. It hadn't been easy looking after Elenour either. It had been a struggle to get her to turn up at Jane's house as she had become bored with it and still thought Jane was a batty old woman and that the whole process was totally unnecessary. Rather than becoming her friend as Steve had suggested, Sarah felt more like her mother at times, or gofer, but Sarah didn't really mind. She'd also been enlisted by Elenour to do an excessive amount of shopping for her, mainly on line, as she loved British high street fashion.

In many ways she found Elenour rather amusing and even when at her worst, Sarah found it hard not to like her. Anyhow, according to Jane Sinclair she had come on in leaps and bounds and now had a convincing British accent, so mission accomplished. Steve's mood didn't change much as he had been rather grumpy prior to his departure, and he certainly hadn't been easy to work for whatsoever. She knew his work schedule had been horrendous right up to when he'd left for Italy. Elenour had insisted that he took her out practically every night. Sarah did have a certain amount of sympathy for Steve, as he was being pulled in two directions. Firstly, trying to keep up with his workload and then making sure Elenour was happy. In fact Sarah worried that it may become too much for him, but she guessed he must be used to it. She still wasn't any the wiser regarding their relationship either. If anything was going on between these two, they were being extremely discreet. Hopefully once they were on location, Steve would relax a little, even though it would undoubtedly be a tough time, but this had been what Steve had been working towards for months. Months of hard work and stress.

From her own viewpoint, there could be a lot worse places to be other than on location and she could hardly wait, to soak up some of the Tuscan sun. Although perhaps she was being a little too optimistic, because in reality she probably wouldn't get the opportunity to do it that much. This whole experience would be a challenge, and she wondered if she should have been issued with an L Plate. Hopefully her own work ethic, of always working hard and her unfailing enthusiasm would certainly be an advantage.

Elenour had eventually got her own way, and Steve had taken her out to the Ivy one evening, coming home in the early hours of the morning! Probably not ideal, but an awful lot was riding on this young lady's shoulders. Steve clearly thought she deserved a break, however she was one little diva, when she wanted to be, so goodness knows what she was going to be like on set!

Sarah had also managed to fit a night out with Annabel before her departure to Italy. She appeared to be happy, but still not her usual bubbly self. Normally a real firecracker, Sarah had noticed that she was rather subdued and unlike the last time when they had caught up, she clammed right up at the mention of Liam's name. When Sarah had been on the verge of mentioning him to her, Annabel had given Sarah a look that said I'm not saying anything, so don't ask!

Annabel had also looked tired, but she assured Sarah that she was feeling fine and it was because she'd been working long days yet again. She was a workaholic, but you could not tell her to slow down, it just wasn't something she was good at. In the business she was in, you worked hard and played hard and that's how it was. Annabel was still extremely jealous of Sarah's visit to Tuscany, as it was one of her favourite places to visit. She'd also enthused about Florence telling Sarah it was a stunning place with so much history and that she would love it. Sarah had promised Annabel that she would keep in touch and let her know how she was getting along. She would also be the first to hear any juicy gossip too!

Chapter 11

The morning Sarah had left for Italy, had been fairly fraught with George and Molly both to see her off and each had tried their best to calm her down. It wasn't just the nerves, it was also the excitement too, because she was looking forward to throwing herself wholly into her new job. She believed she had something to prove and even if it killed her, which hopefully it wouldn't, she was determined to do her absolute best to deliver on what she'd promised both James and Maxine at her interview. But really deep down, she knew it was Steve that she wanted to impress the most! He had left a couple of days earlier, along with the film's major stars. Sarah would travel with the camera crew, and the production assistants.

The plane had touched down at Pisa Airport almost two hours late, after their plane had been delayed on the runway. Unfortunately, some poor man had been taken ill, just before the plane took off. Paramedics had come on board the plane and he was then taken off to hospital. However, removing the man's luggage from the plane had proved a rather lengthy affair. She hoped that her message had got through and that their fleet of taxis would be waiting to whisk them away to their respective hotels. The film would be shot in and around the stunning location of Florence and other spectacular locations in Tuscany. Sarah had been so excited to find out that she would be staying in the same Hotel as Steve, which was the Il Salviatino. He'd told her that it made sense to have her close by and she certainly wasn't about to argue on that front. She had looked it up on the internet, and it was in a stunning location and its grounds overlooked Florence. Who could ask for more.

Sarah took the last taxi to leave the Airport and joined the others. It had been Sarah's responsibility to make certain that all of the luggage, including some of Elenour's was all present and correct. Several other crucial items, were also her responsibility and she had made sure that it had all arrived safely and that nothing had got lost, or left behind.

Plenty of banter was taking place inside the taxi and everyone appeared happy and it was very loud, with people talking over one another. She was sat with a very experienced and eclectic bunch of people, including a couple of Brits, two Australians and Marie, a pretty and rather petite French camerawoman. Sarah thought she didn't look strong enough to do such a job, but she had assured Sarah, that she was super fit, as you clearly had to be. The anticipation was extremely high and they were all charged and eager to get started on this new and exciting project with everything that lie ahead. It was obvious to Sarah, that each one of them relished the prospect and although this was their chosen profession, more importantly it was their passion too.

The hotel certainly didn't disappoint either even if Sarah's room wasn't as grand as some of the others in this Hotel, but it was a good size, and it had a timeless elegance. She laid down onto the bed which was very comfortable and huge. The bathroom had the most amazing bathtub, and she had already made good use of it. After a long soak in the bath, her hair was now neatly wrapped in one of the hotel's soft white fluffy towels, and she was wearing the hotel's white robe and slippers. Ooh impressive she thought and the view from her bedroom was stunning. Sarah had been horrified to discover that she had not brought her special hair conditioner, which cost an absolute fortune, but it relaxed her hair and made it easier to control! She was extremely cross with herself. How could she have been so stupid!

She would have to get hold of some product and sooner rather than later, or else it would drive her mad without it. She took the towel from her hair and dried her hair off. As she did so, she could already see the odd curl threatening to spring back into action as her hair began to dry. It looked a total mess as she tried to run her brush through it. Her straighteners would help, but would in no way be as effective without her hair product. Sarah had decided to pamper herself, and had put on a refreshing cool cucumber facemask. Her skin was dry, after spending hours on the plane. She'd laughed at her reflection when she saw herself in the mirror, it certainly wasn't a glamorous look, and her wayward hair made her look mad, like the nutty professor. Earlier she'd sent Steve a short text to say that she had arrived, but he hadn't replied so far, and therefore she assumed he wouldn't need her that night, which she was very grateful for.

It had been a long day. Some of the crew she knew would be meeting up later on in the bar for drinks at a hotel close by, but she had already decided to have room service and make some phone calls. They had to be down in reception and ready to leave by 6 a.m. the following morning and the hotel would be serving an early breakfast for everyone. There was a knock at the door and Sarah thought that at last her dinner had arrived and she was more than ready for it. She hadn't ate much whilst on the plane. The food had been held in the warming drawer for far too long, whilst they were held up on the runway and it hadn't been very appetising. Sarah opened the door and was surprised to see Steve standing in front of her. She looked at him and knew there was nowhere for her to hide, what with her damp unruly hair, and in just a dressing gown, her face caked in a mask. "Oh hello, Steve," she said pulling her dressing gown tighter around her. "I thought you would be my dinner arriving."

Steve smiled at her and said, "Oh excuse me, I must have the wrong room number, I'm looking for Sarah Carrington, sorry to have disturbed you," he said, turning away.

Sarah laughed, not an easy thing to do with a mask on. "Oh very funny, Steve. I know I look a sight, something out of a horror movie!"

"You certainly do I thought it was Halloween. To be honest with you, Sarah, if this film we're making doesn't make loads of money at the box office, I could end up making those kind of films. Anyhow, I'm just checking that you're okay."

"Yes, thank you, I'm fine. Really looking forward to tomorrow and getting stuck in."

"That's good to hear."

"Well, see you in the morning and I just wanted to thank you for doing such a good job and he hesitated slightly before saying, with a wry look on his face, thus far that is."

"I know I have been difficult to be around lately and I doubt that it will change, but I do appreciate the efforts you have gone to."

She wanted to say to him that he was a hard taskmaster but thought better of it. So she said instead, "Well, I'm just doing my job, but thank you. Night, Steve." As Steve walked back to his suite, he couldn't help but smile to himself. Sarah had looked a bit of a sight, and even with all that gunk she had on her face, he could see that she'd gone bright red.

Meanwhile, Sarah was in the bathroom, staring at herself in the mirror and removed all of her facemask, feeling like an absolute fool. She knew Steve had found it rather amusing to see her totally embarrassed, but there was nothing she could do about it now. It appeared that it was becoming a bit of a habit!

Chapter 12

A few days later, finally, the day had arrived when they would begin filming, which was on the outskirts of Lucca, a town about 30 miles from Florence. This would be their first full day on location. Breakfast had been a hurried affair, as time had been of the essence and everyone was eager to get going. Finally they had arrived and Sarah stepped out of the mini bus, with yet again a feeling of nervous excitement. Some of the crew had already alighted and very quickly disappeared into their little huddles to prepare for the day, and possibly the night ahead. So far she hadn't seen any sign of Steve or Elenour or Jake Edwards and James Hunter, who also had lead roles in the film. Jake Edwards was an upcoming young British actor from the East End of London, who up until now, had played some gritty roles in several British films. However, this would be a whole new departure for him in this film, just as it would be for Elenour. No wonder Steve was so stressed. He had every right to be. Sarah had read some of the script and in her opinion, it was exceptionally good and very moving. She could hardly wait for it to be played out in front of her very own eyes, in its raw state, before it hit the big screen. She hastily pulled her hair back into a ponytail, and put a baseball cap on to protect her head from the heat. Marie had kindly given her a pair of green combat trousers of which she had several pairs apparently, and had told her they were invaluable, because they were made of cotton. For once she had been sensible and worn a pair of comfortable trainers. She'd also made sure she had applied plenty of Factor 50 onto her face and any other exposed areas. Sarah was feeling pumped with adrenaline and excited about the day ahead. From the little she'd seen of Lucca, it was a beautiful old city.

Having arrived on location, Sarah was soon dashing around everywhere, with her timetable for the shoot firmly in her hand. Part of her job was to ensure that the actors were in the right place at the right time. Most of the morning went by in a massive whirlwind. Sarah had a walkie-talkie permanently glued to her ear and had been running around like a headless chicken, but she was loving every minute of it. She found everything and everyone around her exciting and enthralling. She was particularly impressed by Steve, who was the consummate professional and she was kind of in awe of him.

He certainly knew his craft and was totally focused. So far she hadn't heard him raise his voice to anyone, at least not whilst she'd been around anyhow. He appeared to be very calm and was clearly in the zone. Mind it was after all, only day one, but he clearly knew how to command respect from those around him. The sun was shining with an intense heat, and a perfect bright blue sky above, with not even one little white fluffy cloud around. It was the kind of day you dreamed of back in Blighty on a cold rainy day. As it was so hot, she made sure that she drank lots of water and also ensured that plenty of it was on hand for all of the cast and crew.

She was keeping the runners on their toes too. Before she'd left, she had managed to fit a few sessions in the gym with Callum. He had kindly given her some good tips on how to keep her energy levels up and also some dietary advice, which was proving invaluable. He was a nice guy, but he was just a bit obsessed with himself and she had an idea, that Molly had a little crush on him!

By 1 p.m., everything suddenly came to a halt and they stopped for lunch and she realised just how hungry she was. At breakfast, she had felt so nervous, and all she'd managed to eat was some fresh fruit and a glass of orange juice. Steve was busy talking to Dave, one of the cameramen and she just stood back waiting for an opportunity to speak with him. She wanted to check if he had any jobs for her to do, before going off to get herself some lunch. They appeared to be having an in-depth conversation and she didn't feel as if she should interrupt them. However, Steve eventually looked across at her, and beckoned her over as Dave smiled at her before heading off in the direction of where the canteen had been set up. "Hi, Steve, I wondered if I could do anything for you before I go and grab some lunch." Clearly Steve was unhappy and his tone when he spoke to her was sharp!

"Yes actually, there is," he said. "You need to go and sort Elenour out! She's in her trailer. She's just thrown a hell of a hissy fit and upset Amanda, who you apparently assigned to her today and she's more or less told her not to come back for the rest of the day. You'd better go to her trailer immediately, as I really need Elenour to be calm right now. She's due on set after lunch." Sarah thought that at this precise moment Steve looked as if he had the weight of the world on his shoulders. He obviously hadn't shaved, but his piercing blue eyes stood out even more against his dark stubble, which she hated to admit, rather suited him. This was the first time she'd seen Steve's feathers ruffled and he clearly could do without any kind of upset and certainly not on the first day of the shoot.

Elenour being fractious was something he could well do without, and Sarah didn't hesitate in responding as she said, "Of course I will, Steve."

Sarah also got the distinct feeling that somehow Steve blamed her for this particular drama, as she had chosen Amanda to assist Elenour today. Still how could she have known that something like this was going to happen, if only she'd had a crystal ball.

Amanda was a lovely young girl and willing to do anything for anyone. However, as she knew herself, Elenour could be extremely unpredictable when she wanted to be. "Can I get you some lunch before I go Steve?" Sarah asked.

"No thanks, I doubt I will have time for lunch and will probably grab something from the canteen later. Just you bloody well make sure you get Elenour on set, Sarah."

"Will do," Sarah replied, not feeling nearly as confident as she had sounded, and dashed off in the direction of Elenour's trailer.

Sarah knocked on Elenour's trailer door a few times, but there was no reply. "Elenour, it's Sarah, can I come in please." There was silence. Sarah left it for a short while before knocking again and then she tried the door, which was in fact unlocked and let herself in. Elenour was lying down on the sofa with a pretty pink silk dressing gown covering her head. Sarah noticed an e-cigarette on the table. Poor Elenour was still trying to give up smoking. Sarah knelt down beside her. "Elenour, what's wrong," Sarah asked softly.

"Oh go away, Sarah, you wouldn't understand."

"Well, you could try me. I'm on your side remember."

"I suppose Steve has sent you. Oh God I'm a fucking wreck!"

"Yes, he did actually."

Elenour sat up throwing the silk dressing gown to the floor and Sarah could tell that she'd been crying as her eyes were bright red. But at that point, Sarah was even more shocked to see that Elenour's beautiful long hair had been cut into a short elfin hairstyle. She looked stunning, even though she was extremely pale. "Wow, your hair looks amazing, Elenour, it really suits you. That was a brave thing to do."

"Well, not really because you of all people should know how much I hate wearing wigs. Also, I do know this film means so much to Steve and he thinks I don't know, but I do realise that he went out on a limb for me to get this part. I thought this may show him, albeit it in some small way, integrity on my part and commitment to the role that I'm playing."

"What like Ann Hathaway in *Les Mis*," Sarah remarked.

Elenour looked sad and shook her head. "I hardly think so, Sarah, I am not in the same league as her."

"You never know, Elenour, you're so young and still have plenty of time to win an Oscar."

For the first time Elenour smiled and looked directly at Sarah. "Do you think?"

"Why not! Obviously, I don't really know, but if you want to even get nominated, you know what you've got to do. Steve obviously believes in you. You now have the most wonderful opportunity to go out there today and bring your character, Hope to life. This could be the role of a lifetime that catapults you into super stardom and changes your life forever more."

"I would like to believe that."

"Well, then you should. Come on how about a nice cup of peppermint tea," Sarah said taking a teabag and putting it into a small china teapot.

She took some hot water from a large Thermos flask that Sarah had asked Amanda to put into the trailer earlier. "Yes that would be great, thanks, Sarah."

"So what happened with poor Amanda then?"

"Oh, I was a bit of a cow to her if I am honest. She's young and overly enthusiastic you know, all singing and dancing and she was a bit star-struck around me, that's all. As you can see I am a bit strung out and on edge today and I'm just not in the mood to deal with any of that right now. I guess I will apologise to her later."

"Oh, that's very gracious of you, Elenour," Sarah said with a hint of sarcasm.

"Yeah it is actually," Elenour replied as she began to smile. "Contrary to what some people think around here, it may surprise you to know that I'm not a total bitch."

"Oh well, you could have fooled me Elenour. See, there you go. You should definitely believe in yourself more, because you clearly are a very good actress," Sarah said teasing her.

"Oh you Brits and your sense of humour, that's quite funny, Sarah."

"Well, I try to be."

"Anyway, Elenour, tell me what is the real problem here?"

Elenour looked anxious and paused slightly. "I'm really, really nervous, in fact shitting myself about this first scene I have to do. You know, it's where I am the tour guide in the San Michele Foro Church and for some reason right now, I am really struggling with some of the script, especially the bits in Italian. I was word perfect before, but now it's killing me. I am actually going to be in the Church and I'm so frigging nervous."

"Oh don't be so dramatic, Elenour!" Sarah handed Elenour's tea to her. "Just relax a little and drink your tea and it will calm you down. Getting wound up is not going to help you at all is it? If you like, I could go over the script with you."

Elenour reached over and took Sarah's hand into her own tiny one. "Yeah that would be great, thanks, Sarah."

By the time Sarah left Elenour's trailer, the make-up artist and hairdresser had returned and were working their magic on her once again. Sarah was confident that she was certainly in a much better place now and a lot calmer than she had been before. Hopefully she would have more self-belief in her ability to go out on set and do what she was put on this earth to do. She herself was now behind with her own work schedule, which she still had to get through.

However, firstly she must let Steve know that Elenour was okay and back on track, well at least she hoped so, fingers crossed her pep talk had worked! Sarah firmly believed that Elenour would steal every scene that she was in!

It had been a long and tiring day and by the time she arrived back at the hotel, the sun had well and truly gone down. Sarah had had her sights set on a long hot soak in the bath, but Marie had persuaded her to meet up later in the bar to have supper together. So she'd have to make do with a quick one now. In the end, she'd only managed to eat a sandwich earlier, as there hadn't been enough time to get a proper meal from the canteen. She was certainly ready for something more substantial now. Today had been so much more than she could ever have imagined, and she had been in awe of everyone, and even though she was beyond tired, she could hardly wait to see what would unfold the following day.

Chapter 13

So far Sarah had thoroughly enjoyed the bonkers world of film making, even if it was somewhat exhausting. After her bath, she immediately began to feel refreshed and somewhat calmer. She had sweated a good deal during her long day, what with the heat, or rather perspired isn't that what they say women did. The Hotel had been very accommodating towards them, and they were bending over backwards to keep the cast and crew happy during their stay, which would be a lengthy one! Nothing was too much trouble and naturally, they were making a lot of money out of the film crew and some of its big stars. Before Sarah left her room, she checked herself out in the full-length mirror and thought she'd do, as her mother would say and more importantly her purple jump suit was so comfortable to wear. She'd brought several with her, as they were not only easy to pack, but they never creased. Earlier when she'd taken her bath, she couldn't believe just how grimy she'd been. It had been an extremely hot day and clearly there were more to come!

She made her way downstairs and found Marie who was sitting at the bar waiting for her. Sarah could not believe her eyes, as she looked so cute in a crisp white shirt and a pair of black leather shorts and a fabulous pair of shoes. Sarah had proper shoe envy as she quickly realised the black patent shoes she was wearing with the killer heels were none other than Christian Louboutin, with their distinctive red sole. She looked very glamorous out of her usual mode of clothing, namely a dark green sweatshirt and a pair of combat pants and heavy-duty boots.

Marie came across as the kind of woman who took no crap from anyone and preferred to be one of the boys whilst at work at least. However, this girl certainly scrubbed up good.

She had a great figure, and you could clearly see that she worked out regularly, as her legs were well toned and muscular. "Hi, Marie, I hope I haven't kept you waiting long," Sarah said kissing her on both cheeks!

"No, I have only just arrived myself, Cherie. What will you have to drink?"

"Oh something long and cool please, and non-alcoholic, as I need to keep a completely clear head for tomorrow's shoot. Fresh orange juice and lemonade would be refreshing with lots of ice please." Marie ordered herself a large red wine and once they had their drinks, they were shown to their table, which had been reserved for them in the dining room earlier.

Both women studied the menu and Marie beckoned the waiter to come over. They were hungry and quickly made a decision on what to eat and ordered a massive pizza with salad and chips to share! Marie took a long sip of her wine. "Ah that's better, I feel normal now. It's been a hell of a first day she said placing her glass back down onto the table and the first of many more to come, Sarah. How are you finding things so far?"

"Mad but wonderful, I'm loving it at the moment."

"Well, that's a good start, but I will ask you the same question in a week's time."

"Yes you do that, Marie, and I have a feeling that I will be saying pretty much the same thing, well I hope so anyway."

"What I love the most is that there is no time to think about anything else, but getting on with the next job and trying to stay one step ahead of Steve, which is hard."

"I think you are doing an okay job, and if you're not, Steve will soon let you know."

"I have worked on a couple of his film in the past, and he is one of the best directors that I have ever had the pleasure of working with. He knows his craft and everybody else's inside out! The nicest part is he wouldn't ask anyone to do something that he wasn't prepared to do himself."

"So was this a typical first day for you, Marie?"

"I'd say pretty much and luckily there were no major problems, but it was still extremely hectic and demanding as usual, but I am of course used to it and it's what I expect."

"If it wasn't like that, then there would be something very wrong!"

"I hear Elenour had a major strop today!"

"Oh, that's a bit unfair, Marie, she just had a severe case of nerves and I merely calmed her down."

"Oh, Cherie, you see the best in everyone."

"No I don't. Poor girl, I always end up defending her and anyway for what it's worth I like her." By now they had both finished their meal and it had been amazingly good and they had finished it off with some fresh fruit, and delicious Italian gelato. It was the best ice cream Sarah had ever tasted. Bellissimo!

Marie said she was going outside for a cigarette and Sarah decided to join her, despite her dislike of smoking. Somehow it didn't seem to matter to her quite as much right now. They took their drinks out into the garden and Sarah found the slightly cooler air refreshing after the heat and humidity earlier in the day. She looked up at the twinkling stars above and breathed in some of the fresher night air, even though Marie was about to pollute it somewhat!

It was a glorious garden and by day it looked beautiful, bursting with colourful flowers native to the Mediterranean. Sarah noticed Marie's glass was empty. "Right are you ready for another drink, Marie."

"You bet, but I guess I'd best make this my last one for tonight she said lighting her cigarette."

"Okay, I won't be long."

It was a lot quieter in the bar now and Sarah was served quickly. As she returned a short while later with their drinks, she noticed Jake Edwards making his way over to their table. He was a really nice young man and appeared to be friendly with everybody and he also had a great smile. Whenever he'd spoken to her, Sarah had found him extremely charming and he always appeared to be in an upbeat mood, and looked as if he was enjoying life. He was very popular with the ladies, as he was also very good looking, but he certainly wasn't full of himself, like a few she'd met on set recently.

"Hi, ladies, may I join you?" he said with a cheeky grin on his face, and then sat down next to Sarah. "What a brilliant place to shoot a film, don't you think? I feel like I have won the lotto. I have never been to Italy before, but this place is just amazing isn't it?"

"Yes it is, Jake, and this hotel is in such a lovely location and Florence has more than lived up to all of my expectations," Sarah replied. "The Churches here are amazing and I love the rustic feel of the place and then there is the magnificent architecture."

"What about all those saucy statues," Marie said raising her eyebrows.

"You don't have to look, Marie," Jake said.

"Now why would I do that, it wouldn't be any fun at all then would it," she said with a huge smile on her face. Sarah could tell that Jake had been drinking,

110

but she also felt sure that he would know his limit. He confirmed this by saying that he had been out with some of the crew in a nice lively bar and restaurant where the food was superb, which he had spotted earlier, whilst filming in Lucca.

Jake was a good conversationalist and easy to be around and had mentioned that he was from the East End of London and spoke non-stop about his beloved football team, West Ham. He had kept both women entertained with his wicked sense of humour, but as it was almost midnight they all agreed that it was time to call it a night.

However, Marie decided that she was going to have one last cigarette, before turning in for the night and whispered to Sarah, "I think Jake likes you, Cherie. J'Taime mon amie! (*I love you my friend*)."

Sarah shook her head, "Oh don't be so ridiculous, Marie."

Jake and Sarah took a slow walk back towards the Hotel where a number of steps had to be negotiated up from the garden and Sarah tripped on one of them and nearly fell onto her knees. Jake immediately swept her off of her feet and carried her up the rest of the stairs. "Put me down, Jake, please I'm fine," Sarah said laughing as they entered the reception. Jake still wouldn't put her down, but eventually after she protested again, he did as she asked, but he took hold of her hand.

"I'm going to make sure that you get back to your room safely, you're not to be trusted, Sarah!"

"How much have you had to drink?"

"I've only had an orange juice and I am fine honestly." They walked the short distance to the stairs. "So how did you find your first day, Sarah?"

"As I said to Marie earlier, it has been very full on, but I absolutely loved it."

"Yeah it's not a bad life at all is it?"

"Look at us lording it up out here in Italy and getting paid for it," Jake said with another one of his cheeky grins.

Sarah smiled, "Yes I guess there are worse ways to earn a living for sure."

"Do you know you have a lovely smile, Sarah."

"Thanks, Jake." Sarah blushed slightly under his gaze and had been tempted to say "so do you", however, that might have sounded a bit too cheesy. At this point Jake nudged Sarah.

"Eyes right look who's coming." Sarah looked across towards the main entrance to see Steve and Elenour, who were walking through the rather palatial reception, and deep in conversation with one another. They looked happy and relaxed together, and obviously he had forgiven Elenour for her earlier wobble. Steve acknowledged them both before getting into the lift.

Sarah and Jake made their way up the stairs to the third floor. "I'm not sure what to make of my co-star," Jake confided in Sarah. "She's a gorgeous creature, but she blows hot and cold around me. To be honest, I am a bit concerned as some of the scenes we will be doing later on, will see us, getting up close and personal, if you get my drift. It would certainly help if we at least both liked one another."

"Oh I'm sure you can charm her, Jake; however, the Americans do not always get our sense of humour, you know. Maybe you should tone it down a little and be more patient. Just show her you are a real gent and you'll probably win her over. I have spent quite a lot of time with her recently, before we came out here and I know she can be a bit temperamental, but maybe it's because, believe it or not, she lacks confidence. Anyway, that's what I think, for what it's worth!"

"From what I have seen, Sarah, she knows exactly how to wrap Steve around her little finger all right," Jake said somewhat harshly.

"I don't know about that, Jake, but I have to admit that I've actually become quite fond of her."

"Well, I will take on board what you've said and try to be on my best behaviour from now on, if you think it will do the trick."

"Oh I'm sure if anyone can do it, you're definitely the man, Jake."

"Oh I love your confidence."

"Well this is my floor, night, Jake."

"Night, Sarah," he said and kissed her on the cheek. "Thanks for the advice."

"You're welcome, my pleasure."

Once Sarah was back in her room, she couldn't help but be flattered by Jake's attention. However, she got the feeling that it was all just part of his charm. She found herself thinking about Steve again and in particular, whether he was in a relationship with Elenour. She was still none the wiser. It didn't matter to her, did it? After all, it really was none of her business. Once in bed, Sarah soon drifted off to sleep, but her mobile phone woke her up out of her slumber violently. She sat up sharply and pushed her eye mask onto her forehead. She was worried that it may be her mother and that something could be wrong. Her heart was pounding as she took the call, but it was in fact Steve. "Oh sorry I hope I didn't wake you up, Sarah?" He didn't even wait for her to reply. "I'm going to need you to type up some last-minute alterations to the script ready for tomorrow.

I will pop them down to you, if that's all right." Once again, he didn't wait for her to reply. She quickly put the hotel's towelling dressing gown on and waited for Steve. A few minutes later, he was knocking at her door and she let him in.

"Not interrupting anything, am I," he asked.

"The only thing you've interrupted, Steve, is my sleep."

"Oh, sorry but this is extremely urgent."

"Well I cannot say that I wasn't warned, can I."

Steve went over in detail with Sarah, the changes that needed to be made to the script and then suddenly said, "So did you have a good evening with Jake tonight?"

"Oh fabulous thank you, Steve, and Jake is so charming and he knows how to treat a lady." Sarah was being wickedly naughty by not being entirely honest with Steve, but he had just woken her up at silly o'clock for goodness' sake! "Anyhow, I'd better make a start on this," she said looking down at the paperwork which had been put down next to her laptop.

Steve smiled. "Yes you're right, I'd best leave you to get on with it."

"Just a word of warning, though, Jake is a bit of ladies' man, Sarah."

"Thanks for the warning, Steve, but really I think I'm old enough not to be sucked in completely by him. Anyhow, I happen to like him and he's very good company." Sarah was somewhat miffed at Steve's comment, but had tried hard not to show him, but knew she'd failed miserably.

"Fair enough. Night, Sarah," see you in the morning.

"Night, Steve."

Steve walked back to his room and hoped he hadn't over-stepped the mark with Sarah, as it was absolutely nothing to do with him, who she spent time with. Of course, deep down he knew she was more than capable of making up her own mind. He did in fact really like Jake, but on the other hand, he wouldn't want to see Sarah get hurt. God he was behaving like an overbearing father and he really shouldn't interfere in other people's lives.

For a start off, he had more than enough on his own plate at the moment. Elenour as he'd predicted was hard work, but so far the time he had given to her, was paying dividends. She had stepped up to the mark today after her hiccup and was performing really well, at least for now!

Elenour would always be high maintenance and have tantrums and he would prefer it if she and Jake got on better, but he'd given them both a good talking to earlier. He had zero tolerance now as an awful lot was at stake with this film and there was a long way to go. Nothing must get in the way of its progression and completion.

Meanwhile, Sarah felt slightly annoyed at Steve's comments earlier regarding Jake. How dare he! She wasn't a child for goodness' sake and she had no intention of being treated like one either. She would make up her own mind about who she spent time with and Steve should quite simply mind his own bees' wax!

Sarah yawned once more and sat down at the desk to make a start on the alterations to the script, and by the time she had typed up all of the changes it was almost 3 a.m. She just hoped she could get back to sleep as easily as she'd done earlier.

Chapter 14

The weeks were whizzing by and every day was fascinating and Sarah was still enjoying everything about her new job, even running around and taking care of Elenour! Watching Steve do his job was enlightening. He knew exactly how to get the best out of all of his actors and crew alike and it was obvious that they not only respected him, but admired him too. With yet another exhausting day on set over, Sarah returned to her room and just laid on her bed and stretched out fully.

Yet again she'd opted to have a quiet night in, with room service. It was late anyway and simpler to have a meal in her room and she also had a couple of phone calls to make. Her mother had been sending her a few sarcastic texts of late, asking her if she was still alive. Dotty was overly dramatic as always. The following day was Friday and the cast and the crew had a free day and Steve had organised a day out for them all. He'd hired out a private part of the beach at Forte dei Marmi. He'd promised them all a day of fun and relaxation to thank them for all their hard work so far. It was going to be the first complete day off for the majority of them in weeks.

Of course there had been a few dramas here and there along the way. One day was practically lost when a major problem with the lighting had occurred. On another occasion, a freak storm had set them back, but so far they were still ever so slightly ahead of schedule. Elenour and Jake had had a few ups and downs, but both had resolved to be on their best behaviour from now on. It was understood that it would not be tolerated by Steve and ultimately it could potentially be detrimental to the film if they didn't.

Every day had been full on and demanding but Sarah thrived on it. She and Marie had become really good friends and they generally hung out together, if they had enough energy to, after a long stint on set. She had also become like a Mother hen to Elenour, who still needed the odd bit of cajoling and support. Sarah had come to the realisation that she was far happier than she had been in a long, long time. Not only did she feel more like her old self, perhaps if she was really honest, even better than before. There was no more pussy footing around Richard and walking on eggshells for fear of an argument. She was free and she only had herself to answer to thankfully.

After she'd eaten, she decided to give her mother a call and as Sarah had expected, she was as caustic as ever exclaiming, "Oh, you've finally remembered that you still have a mother then! Anything could have happened to me and my only daughter hadn't even bothered to call."

"Oh don't be so silly, Mum. I just don't get that much free time at the moment." Fortunately, after a while, Dotty piped down saying that it was lovely to hear from her.

"So how is it going out there in Italy, as hectic as ever?"

"It is but I love it. So what are you up to, Mum?"

"Oh this and that keeping myself busy, you know me, I never let the grass grow under me feet. I went into The Bake Stop the other day and Iris asked how you were getting on."

"She also said that the girls are all missing your classes."

"Well I miss all of them, not that I have a lot of time to think about my old life. Oh blimey, you've not been away that long yet, love."

"If I'm honest, Mum, it does feel like I have been away for ages. It's just what I needed and I am so very grateful for this job."

"Well then, I am pleased for you, I really am Sarah. When you're back love, I would like to talk to you about something."

"Is anything wrong, Mum?"

"Oh no, absolutely nothing for you to worry about, but I'd rather speak to you face to face."

"Oh now you've set me thinking."

"Don't be so daft, put it out of your mind. There isn't anything for you to get your knickers in a twist over," Dotty said laughing.

"Okay, Mum, I trust you, night, love you."

"Nighty night, love you too." Sarah was curious to know what her Mum wished to discuss with her, but she would just have to wait and see!

The following day, everyone had grouped together outside the hotel promptly at 10 a.m. and taken by convoy in mini buses to Forte dei Marmi, which at first glance looked to be a fantastic resort. It had a beautiful sandy beach, which stretched for miles and a whole section of it was exclusively for their use only.

The best-looking chalets Sarah had ever seen were at their disposal to get changed in and luxury loungers had been neatly lined up, with Bedouin tents, for those who wanted to keep out of the sun totally.

It was clear that everyone was happy and in a playful mood and it was on the cards that there would be some heavy partying at some point later on. Sarah and Marie both found themselves sun loungers and were soon stretched out on them in their swimwear. Marie had a natural deep tan and Sarah felt pale in comparison, although naturally since she'd been in Italy she now had a light golden tan. She'd brought plenty of factor 50 with her, as she certainly didn't want to burn and a straw hat, to protect her head from the heat. "Oh, babe, this place is amazing," Marie enthused. "I have been looking forward to this day so much."

"Me too, Marie, and this is a wonderful beach and I cannot wait to go in for a swim. The Italians really know how to do luxury, don't they?"

"They do and it was so nice of Steve to treat us to this day out."

"I think we deserve it, Marie, don't you."

"Yes but not all directors would do something like this, trust me on that one." Sarah started to put sunscreen onto her legs when Jake suddenly appeared and offered to help.

Sarah was slightly embarrassed and quickly replied, "No, I'm fine thank you, Jake." Behind Jake, Marie was blowing kisses and pulling all kinds of silly faces at her, which she tried her hardest to ignore.

"Come on let me help you," he said as he sat down next to her on her lounger. "I can get to all of those hard-to-reach places for you."

"Oh all right, I give in, you can do my back for me if you like." Sarah turned onto her tummy and Jake began to rub sun cream gently onto her back and she had to admit that Jake had a fantastic light, but effective touch and it was more like having a massage. He was doing a really good job and she began to relax instantly. It felt heavenly and so sensuous!

"There it's done, how did I do?" Sarah would have liked to say she would give him an 'A Star', but played it down somewhat!

"Yeah not bad," Sarah said and noticed that Jake looked somewhat offended. "No don't worry, I'm only kidding, it was amazing and you did a great job, thank you very much."

"You're more than welcome."

"Right, girls, later on, we're going to play a game of volley ball and I hope you two are going to play? How come Steve agreed to that?" Sarah asked. "Oh a long as I don't drink alcohol, he said it would be okay! Anyway, I am mostly organising it really!"

Sarah pulled a face, "I'm not sure it's my thing."

"Oh come on, Sarah, say you will," Jake said trying to encourage her.

"I will have to think about it."

"You can count on me," Marie said. "I am definitely up for it."

"That's good I will put your name down." Jake's parting words were: "I am going to put your name down too Sarah."

"He can be very persuasive, don't you think, Sarah?"

"Maybe, you will just have to wait and see." In fact, Sarah was actually thinking more about when Jake had rubbed sun cream onto her back and how sensual it had been. Her head felt light with all kinds of naughty thoughts. He was not only good looking, but had an impressive bod, which was honed and toned, and after weeks in the Tuscan sun, he now had a deep tan. He also looked cute in his red Bermuda shorts! However, he was way too young for her and she didn't want to become a cougar! Still after all, it was really only a bit of harmless flirtation and there was nothing wrong in that, was there?

"He is as you Brits say, well fit no," Marie remarked.

"I couldn't possibly comment!"

"No need to, babe," Marie smirked "as the sparkle in your eyes says it all!"

"Please say you will play volley ball this afternoon we could always do girls versus the boys and whip their pretty asses."

Sarah laughed. "I have never ever played volleyball in my life and I would probably be a hindrance."

"Oh me thinks Jakey will be so disappointed if you don't come out to play," Marie said mockingly.

"Don't be so immature, Marie!"

"It's okay, Cherie, I am only jealous, you are the jammy cow." In many ways Marie reminded her so much of Annabel. Both were strong and independent women and as feisty as they come.

Marie was definitely a ballsy kind of woman, who had told Sarah that it was far from the norm to have females in the camera crew within the film industry. She had Steve to thank for this opportunity which had been afforded to her. She would also have to work harder than most of the others to prove she was more than capable! On the whole it was a male dominated industry and she had told Sarah that she had every intention of training to become a cinemaphotographer in the future. Sarah had no doubt that she would achieve this eventually, because she was one determined woman for sure. She had found a good friend in Marie and they had clicked from day one.

"I'm going in for a swim now Sarah, are you coming in?"

"Not yet, I fancy a nice relaxing morning and I'd rather like to get back into my book. I've lost count of how many times I've picked it up before I go to bed and then fall fast asleep, barely having read a single page!"

"See you in a while crocodile!"

"Be careful, Marie."

"Of course, don't worry about me." Sarah made herself comfortable once again, happy to be settling down with her book at last. She like Marie was going to make the most of today.

Lunch had been a fabulous affair and everyone was in good spirits as plenty of wine had been flowing. However, Sarah was still sticking to non-alcoholic drinks, as she preferred not to indulge today. Alcohol and sun were definitely not a good combination in her opinion. She'd observed that Elenour was in a good mood and apparently was even going to play volleyball later. It looked like she was making an effort to mix with everyone, which was nice to see.

Steve, she'd noticed had been constantly on his mobile phone and had gone outside several times during their meal. Hopefully there wouldn't be any problems for him to deal with. Surely, even he was entitled to one day off! With lunch over, Marie and Sarah went back to their loungers. "So," Marie said rather bluntly, "what do you think Steve's relationship is with Elenour?"

"Now that is the million-dollar question. I don't know and even if I did, I wouldn't comment. I am paid to work for Steve as his personal assistant and his love life is his own business and must remain private!"

"I know, Cherie, but you must have some thoughts on it."

"Not really, she's the major star alongside Jake and James in this film and he needs her to give the best performance ever. So who knows!"

"You're being very diplomatic. You should have been a politician."

"Maybe, but they're clearly good friends and I will say that he does appear to be very protective of her. An awful lot is riding on this film for Steve."

"Yes you're right, Cherie, but she's a lot younger than him."

"Yes she is, but I don't think that's ever a problem for Steve from what I have read about him."

"True, and it probably does his ego good, like all men," Marie said sarcastically!

"Yes, I know, don't worry I have done my research on Steve Fountain and read some of the gossip magazine articles."

Marie looked at her watch. "Hey look at the time, come on it will soon be time for volleyball."

"Oh no, not me Marie. I am not playing, it's too hot, so you can go and whip their asses on your own."

"What with Elenour playing, you're joking me, no. She'll be useless and too scared that she will break a nail! Come on please, Sarah, come and play."

"No, anyway, you'll have Sam and Amanda and Jessie on your team!"

"Oh you are such a lazy woman," Marie said as she placed her baseball cap firmly onto her head.

"See you later then." Sarah laid back down and closed her eyes. *Oh this is heaven*, she thought and realised that she might even have a little snooze, it was so peaceful with everyone either going to play or to watch the volleyball.

Even though it was hot, she was happy that the umbrella protected her from the direct sunlight. Suddenly, Jake caught her off guard. "Oh don't think you're going to get away without playing, Sarah," he said sweeping her up from off her sun lounger and placing her over his shoulder in a fireman's lift. He then ran back down the beach with her protesting loudly for him to put her down.

Everyone was laughing and clapping their hands, as he placed her down behind the net with all the other girls on the team. She tried her hardest to give Jake the fiercest of looks but wasn't sure if she had succeeded as she too began to laugh. "You wait, Jake, I'm going to get you for this she shouted across at him!"

He just smiled and said, "Let the games begin."

After around 15 minutes or so of playing, Sarah had become so hot and bothered that she thought she would explode. A ball had nearly hit her full on in the face, which she had only just managed to dodge. She wasn't enjoying it, one little bit. The competition was on and the girls were a highly competitive bunch, and hell bent on beating the boys. Marie was very good at volleyball and clearly athletic and enjoying it far more than she was. There were some things Sarah just wasn't any good at and clearly volleyball was one of them. The ball came in her direction once again and she made a real play for the ball this time, as she jumped up as high as she could in an attempt to hit the ball back over the net. She failed spectacularly falling to the ground. Sarah thought this could be her best chance of getting out of playing and taking her leave. She sat up and began rubbing her right ankle and Jake immediately came over to her and placed his hand on her ankle. "Ouch, don't touch it, Jake, it's soo very sore," she said in a whimpering voice.

"Are you okay Princess?" he said looking concerned.

"I think I must have sprained it, Jake."

"What is up, Cherie?" Marie asked with a wistful look on her face.

"I'm not sure, but I think I am out of the game, sadly," she replied, trying her best to sound disappointed. "So sorry guys, you're going to have to manage without me!" Jake and Marie helped her up.

"Come on," Jake said as he kindly lifted her off of her feet for the second time in one day, but more gently this time and took her up to her sun lounger and placed her onto it and said, "I'm so sorry, Sarah, I feel a bit responsible for what happened to you, as I forced you into playing."

"Oh don't be silly, don't give it another thought!"

"Will you be all right?"

"Oh yes, I think so and if I am honest, I am a bit of a drama queen, so I'm sure I'll be fine. Anyway go. Your team needs you."

"Yeah you're right. Okay, see you later."

Sarah watched Jake run back down the beach in his red shorts once more, to join the others and couldn't help but admire his body with his six pack and those muscular thighs.

In fact he reminded her of a young David Hasselhoff back in the day, running down a Californian beach, but without the slow motion imagery. As Marie had said, he was some hunk. Sarah took a bottle of ice-cold water from the ice bucket and took a long sip to cool herself down after her eventful volleyball game. She was feeling so hot that she poured the rest over the back of her neck to cool herself down. She grabbed a mirror from her bag and smiled when she saw her face, and thought she looked like a cooked lobster!

She so longed to go for a dip into the sea now, but she was feeling extremely guilty for feigning the injury to her ankle. Maybe she'd gone too far! Her performance was worthy of an Oscar in her opinion. Oh dear, well at least she'd got out of playing volleyball and that had been her aim. She would no doubt have some explaining to do later on, or perhaps she may even continue with the lie. Sarah could hardly believe Elenour, as she was really throwing herself into the game and looked at last to be having some real fun for a change, which surprised her. Sarah tried to relax but was becoming restless, still itching to get into the beautiful glittering sea. Hopefully no one would notice her leave, as they were all so busy with the volley ball game. She wrapped her sarong around her and quickly stuffed her towel and sun cream inside her beach bag.

She walked down towards the sea and along the water's edge, as the waves gently came lapping over her feet, forming a white frothy foam which reminded her of fizzing champagne. She splashed through the water, which was so temptingly warm and immediately a feeling of calm came over her. She was enjoying being alone, soaking up the atmosphere and collected some pebbles and shells along the way. She'd been doing it ever since she was a child and would take the best ones home with her. She had a collection from various places all around the world.

This was a stunning beach, surrounded by beautiful mountains and it was certainly the cleanest and tidiest beach she'd ever been on. However in her opinion, it was almost too perfect and she would rather have a completely natural and rustic beach. She found herself a nice little spot which was fairly close to the water's edge and laid down her towel. She wondered what everyone would be doing back home and realised that it was Dotty's day for her lunch club, so no doubt she would be holding court and would be in her element. She was never happier than when she had a crowd to entertain. Sarah began to do one of her favourite pastimes, which was people watching. Human beings were such fascinating creatures. She was surrounded by several young couples, some with their young families.

Many of the children were building sand castles, either with the help of their enthusiastic dads or grandfathers. Sarah smiled as one small toddler sat on her older brother's sand castle and he rather naughtily pushed her over onto the sand and she went screaming back to her Mother. "Hello," a voice said interrupting her thoughts, and Sarah looked up and shielded her eyes from the bright sun to see Steve standing over her.

"I saw you disappearing when you thought no one else would notice," Steve said with a smirk on his face. "How's the foot by the way? You appear to have made a miraculous recovery by the looks of it! I thought it was the right ankle you injured. You appeared to be hobbling with the left!"

"Oh great, I guess I've been busted haven't I," Sarah said wryly pulling a face. "I had hoped to keep it up for a bit longer."

"Did you now! I saw your knight in shining armour, Jakey boy came to your rescue," Steve said with just a hint of sarcasm in his voice as he sat down beside her.

"Well, I think he just felt guilty really because he'd practically forced me into playing volleyball."

"I see, well don't worry I won't spill the beans, Sarah!"

"Steve, I simply couldn't stand all that exercise in this heat and to be honest, I was beginning to overheat like a car's radiator! What have you been up to anyway? I saw you rush off earlier before the game started, so I guess you weren't overly keen on playing volleyball either?"

"I had other things to do."

"Is everything all right, Steve?"

"Yes, of course, I just went to meet up with a really good friend of mine, Sam at a local bar he frequents. We had a great catch up as I haven't seen him in ages. He's a film producer, who I've known for years and he now lives here with his Italian wife Isabella."

"Oh that's okay then, as I was a bit concerned that perhaps you were not having such a free day as everyone else is! You seem to have been on your mobile most of the time."

"Just making good use of my free time. I had to make a call to my mother he said, pushing his sunglasses to the top of his head. She worries if she doesn't hear from me now and again," he said with a rueful look. Then he smiled at her with his piercing blue eyes looking directly into her own. "But thank you for your concern Sarah. Suddenly she felt somewhat disconcerted under his gaze and her face flushed slightly!"

"No really, I should be thanking you, Steve," she said not wishing to sound flustered, "and I am really having a great day."

"Yes, it looks as if everyone is having fun and by the way, it's my pleasure."

"Is this a hobby of yours?" Steve said picking up a few of her pebbles.

She nodded, "Yes but it's more like an obsession really, as I've done it since I was a kid. In fact," she said looking around her, "that's just how I feel when I am on a lovely beach like this one."

"Young and carefree."

Steve didn't say it, but that's exactly how she looked with her hair scraped back into a ponytail and her cute freckles which stood out right across her nose. "I have large glass jars full of them back at home, all the white ones are in one jar and the black ones in another and so on. Cornwall and Devon are the best places to find them for me. We had loads of brilliant holidays down that way when we were young, as my aunt and uncle live in Devon." Sarah knew she was talking way too much but she always found Steve so easy to talk to, at least when he was away from his work.

"You're a real quirky little character aren't you."

Sarah smiled, "Well, I've never been called that before."

"Perhaps you should get out more," Steve said teasing her.

"Maybe, you could be right."

"Are you still enjoying all this madness that we call the film industry?"

"I absolutely love it, Steve."

"So what is it that stands out for you?"

"I'd say the intensity of it all, the commitment and enthusiasm that everyone has. Each person works so well together and of course I've made some very good friends."

"I see I didn't even get a mention there did I," Steve remarked, pretending to be put out.

"Oh that goes without saying, I am very thankful to be working with the infamous film director that is Steve Fountain and I'd like to thank you for taking a chance on me."

"Well you have James and Maxine to thank for that really, and anyway you have more than repaid us all. I know I can be difficult to work for at times, especially when I'm under pressure."

"Well, I was warned about that, wasn't I?"

"Yes, but I want you to know that I do appreciate the commitment you have shown to me and you too have had to make some big adjustments. Not only do you keep up with me, sometimes you're ahead of me, which is great. And you're mother is right; you definitely did invent the word organised."

"Oh please I'm blushing now," she said and she really was, but she also had a warm feeling inside. In fact she was more used to his bellowing orders at her, rather than receiving a compliment, which she found a little embarrassing. Somehow she would have found that easier to deal with.

He could be so charming when he wanted to be, which could throw you completely off kilter on occasion. "Well, I'm going in for a swim, Steve, as I really need to cool down."

"Great idea, I will join you." They walked to the water's edge together where the sea was warm and inviting. Steve ran off into the water speedily and took the plunge and soon swam out into the distance, whereas she continued to tentatively walk into the sea, and it got decidedly colder and she stopped just as the water reached her waist. Steve swam over and began splashing her. She begged him to stop. However, he carried on and threatened to splash her even more if she didn't get into the water.

"Come on, you wimp," he chastised her, "get in." Sarah thought *what the heck* and also took the plunge and swam off doing her usual breaststroke, but as always she kept her head out of the water and swam as fast as she could, to warm herself up. It wasn't long before her body became accustomed to the temperature of the sea and it didn't feel so bad. Steve had swam out further now, whilst she continued to swim closer to the beach, which she found safer. She wasn't the strongest of swimmers. After what she perceived to be a decent amount of time, she decided to get out of the sea and quickly dried herself off with her towel. She looked for Steve, but she couldn't see him anywhere. He was obviously a competent and strong swimmer. A young Italian couple who were sat quite close by caught her attention, as they were all over one another like a rash and she thought they should get themselves a room. The Italians were so much more tactile than the British ever were and she'd also observed that they talked incessantly on their mobile phones in overly loud voices! This reminded her that she hadn't looked at hers at all since leaving the hotel and checked to see if she'd received any new messages. She noticed a couple of missed texts from Annabel and quickly sent her a text to say she would ring her later that day. Dotty had also sent her one, which simply said, *Are you still alive? Kisses Mum.* Her mother was always so sarcastic!

Steve had noticed Sarah getting out of the water and thought she was clearly a real lightweight when it came to sports. He also observed too that she had a fantastic figure and looked great in her peach poker dot bikini and her legs were sensational, they went on forever. She had a natural beauty which was in total contrast to most of the women he met in his everyday life and her breasts were all her own, he was sure of that. Hollywood in particular was full of women, who'd either had a nip and tuc done or fillers and Botox. It wasn't any different in the UK these days, especially in the world that he was heavily involved in. He personally found it extremely refreshing to know that there were still some real women around like Sarah.

He wasn't in a hurry to get out of the water just yet as he had every intention of making the most of his time in the sea. He had always found swimming relaxing and this would probably be the one and only chance he would have to swim in the sea, whilst here. Most mornings he managed to swim in the pool at the hotel, at some unholy hour, but it wasn't as enjoyable as this. Tomorrow it would be back to their tight Schedule, but he believed that today would prove to be a productive one, as everyone would be refreshed for the days ahead. Well, that is what he was hoping for at any rate.

Sarah sneaked a quick look at Steve as he ran back up the beach towards her, and although he wasn't quite as muscular as Jake, you could see that he worked out and looked extremely fit. Before he reached her, she laid back down and pretended to be asleep. Suddenly the shock of cold water on her warm body, made Sarah jolt and sit right back up again, as Steve shook the salty seawater from off his body all over her. "You bugger, that was so uncalled for," she shouted at him and grabbed her beach bag and tried whacking him around his legs with it. He laughed, but managed to successfully get out of the way before drying himself off with his towel. Sarah thought he looked handsome and rather boyish as he smoothed his dark hair back and his gorgeous blue eyes made her heart skip a beat. What was she like. Anyway, she wasn't really annoyed with him, but she pretended to be cross, and tried her hardest not to laugh. "You can pack that in, thank you very much."

"Well, you looked as if you needed to cool down to me. Too much heat isn't good for you, you know."

"Oh really so what you're actually saying is that I should be thanking you."

Steve laughed once more as he said, "Do you think we should make our way back to the others now?"

Reluctantly, Sarah agreed, "Yes I guess so, but in actual fact I could stay here for ever."

"Yes it's beautiful, but you can't so come on," he said as he pulled her up onto her feet. Sarah gathered her bits together and they walked back to join the others and she spent a wonderful restful afternoon, chatting with the others and chilling out and even managed to read her book. The boys had apparently thrashed the women at volleyball, but fortunately, there didn't appear to be any animosity now, as most of them were sitting together in their little groups, laughing and joking.

It was great to see everyone enjoy themselves after all the mayhem of work. Marie had quizzed her about her ankle, saying she'd made a very remarkable recovery. Sarah realised it was probably time to come clean with her friend, but before she had a chance to say anything, Marie put her arm around her. "I don't blame you, Cherie, it was a very tough and competitive game and you were definitely shit at it. However, as good a performance as you gave, you didn't fool me."

"What about Jake?"

"Oh no, he is still concerned about you. I do think you owe him an explanation!" When Sarah had enquired where he was, Marie had told her that he'd gone off shopping into the town of Forte Dei Marmi. It was only a small place, but it was full of very exclusive designer shops apparently. She'd been told that many wealthy Italians holidayed there. She already knew that Jake was very taken with both the Italian designer clothes and shoes, so no doubt he would be like a kid in a toyshop. Marie had made Sarah promise to come clean with Jake over her feigned injury and Sarah had said with a glint in her eye, that she would eventually.

Sarah arrived back at the hotel at 7.30 along with Marie and Elenour, and a few others ahead of the rest of them, who looked as if they were intent on staying for the long haul! Elenour had been moaning that Steve had stopped her from playing volleyball earlier. He didn't want her to injure herself he'd said, as it could jeopardise the whole film and set it back and she had reluctantly seen sense.

Those who had returned to the hotel, appeared to be tired from their day out, including herself. Sarah went up to her room and was really looking forward to speaking to Annabel. They'd not had a proper catch up in ages. She was feeling a little guilty that she hadn't rung her back earlier, but she was more than ready now for a full-on girlie chat with her best friend. Anyway, calling her from a lively Italian beach just hadn't been an option.

Chapter 15

After Sarah had taken a bath, she got herself dressed and wrapped her hair in a towel and rang Annabel's number. The phone rang for quite some time, before Annabel finally answered it. "Oh hi," she said sounding a bit down. "I'd almost given up on you, Sarah!"

"Yes I am so sorry I didn't ring you earlier, but I've been sunning myself on a beautiful beach in Forte dei Marmi."

"How are you hun?" There was silence from the other end of the phone when suddenly, Annabel burst into tears and said, "I'm bloody well pregnant!"

"Oh my God, Annabel, how did that happen?" Dumb question to ask, she knew immediately after she'd said it.

"How do you think, you silly mare."

"Oh sorry, Annabel, I'm shocked that's all."

"You're not the only one, how do you think I feel?"

"It must have been when I was sick some weeks back with an upset tum."

"I guess the pill must have left my system and then bang I'm pregnant." Sarah hesitated before asking, "Are you pleased?"

"No of course I am not," Annabel said emphatically.

"What about Liam, what did he say?"

"I haven't actually told him yet, but I know for a fact that he will run a mile."

"You cannot be sure of that and he has a right to know, doesn't he?"

"Maybe. Anyway, I have made up my mind and I'm not going to have it. I don't want to be a single mum."

"It is something that would absolutely terrify me."

"And you know that I have never ever hankered after having children. It's not for me, Sarah and I feel guilty because I know, if you'd only had the chance, you would have made the most wonderful mother."

"Annabel, this is your life we're talking about and I just don't want you to do anything hasty. You need time to think about this thoroughly, before making such an important decision!"

"Oh damn it, I wish I wasn't so far away from you, as I can't do much from here can I?" Sarah began to feel emotional.

"How far gone do you think you are, she said grabbing a tissue from a box on the dressing table to wipe away a tear that was rolling down her cheek?"

"About six weeks."

"I haven't been to the doctors yet, but I have done umpteen pregnancy tests and all of them are positive." Annabel sobbed again. "I feel like shit and I am so nauseous all the time. It's getting harder for me to hide it at work, because of how I feel."

"Oh you poor baby, that must be awful."

"I miss you so much, Sarah, and I just wish you were here with me."

"Oh, hun, I wish I could be with you and I am so sorry, Annabel."

"Oh it's not your fault, ignore me. As usual I'm being a selfish cow. You have had such a rough ride yourself and finally you are enjoying life again and so you should be."

"Yes, Annabel, but you were always there for me, right by my side and I want to be there for you."

"I feel awful, because unfortunately, I'm not going to be back for quite some time."

Sarah knew this was a sensitive matter but she had to ask the question. "Have you spoken to your mum about it?"

"No of course not, Sarah, why would I do that, and anyway I don't want to. I haven't spoken to her in ages."

"Yes I know, but you should give her a chance, Annabel."

"She isn't interested in me, Sarah. She never has been." Sarah knew that wasn't entirely true, but there was no point in arguing with Annabel, especially the mood she was in right now. Annabel continued with her rant. "All she's ever cared about are my baby brother and sister."

"Annabel, you cannot go through something as emotional and difficult as this by yourself. You need to wait and give yourself some time, please say you will think about it. You could be making a huge mistake."

"Oh I've done that all right."

"No seriously just promise me that you will get in touch with your mum. As friends we have been through so much together. Don't you think that this may be a good opportunity for her to make amends and for you to get close again. I don't expect you will agree, but I think you owe her that much at least. Do it for me please, Annabel." There was a loud sigh from the other end of the phone.

Annabel answered her in a very quiet voice. "I'm not sure if I can, Sarah, I feel so hurt and you know what me and Mum are like, we never sing from the same hymn sheet and will end up arguing."

"Perhaps this is the time for you, to forgive and forget and to move on before it's too late, please, Annabel!"

"Okay, I will think about it, I promise."

"Good girl, I won't sleep tonight for worrying about you, but just know one thing that I love you, Annabel. Also for the record, I think I would make a really good auntie," Sarah said cheekily.

"I know you would, you big softie, but as you said, Sarah, this is my life and, of course, I love you too and you have always been like a sister to me." The two said their emotional goodbyes and Sarah had tears in her eyes once more as she ended the call. How she wished she could be back home, comforting her best friend and to be able to give her a hug, in her hour of need.

Chapter 16

The next couple of weeks were extremely full on with long days, which went on well into the night and by the time Sarah eventually got into bed at night, she had fallen asleep as soon as her head hit the pillow. However, they'd finished at a decent time today for a change and Jake had suggested that tonight would be an ideal opportunity to take Sarah to dinner. He'd previously invited her out after the infamous game of volleyball, by way of an apology he'd said, because he felt responsible for what had happened when she'd hurt her ankle. At that point, Sarah knew that it was time to confess all and she told him about how she'd feigned the injury. "Can you forgive me, Jake?" she had asked, putting on her sad face and fluttering her eyes at him. "I'm just not that sporty you see!"

Jake had laughed. "I guess so," and then said he'd suspected as much, because of her remarkably quick recovery. However, he was a real gentleman and had insisted on their dinner date, because at the very least he said he had forced her into playing, when she clearly hadn't wanted to. She had accepted his invitation and was really looking forward to going out for a change. Marie had been teasing her mercilessly all day, saying that Jake had the hots for her. Sarah didn't believe that for one minute, but she was feeling good about herself. She had taken a leisurely and luxurious bath. Her hair looked sleek and smooth after she'd spent ages on it, but the outcome had been worth it.

She had made up her mind earlier, that she was going to wear her soft pink lace dress, with a sweetheart neckline, which she'd found in a little boutique back home. It was an expensive designer dress, but she had loved it the minute she'd seen it. It showed off just a small amount of cleavage. As her grandmother used to say, "Don't put all your goods on show love, a hint of the mint was just enough!" A very wise woman, her grandmother, she thought. Anyhow, she believed tonight would be a worthy enough occasion to wear it. Jake hadn't revealed where they were going for their meal, but had said that it was one of the best places to eat in Florence. Sarah was going to meet him downstairs in the bar for a drink, before their reservation at the restaurant which was 8 p.m. With her make-up complete, she put on her gold wedges.

Sarah was in such good shape now, since she'd been going regularly to the hotel's gym most mornings at an ungodly hour, with Marie, who was a total gym bunny. She had little butterflies in her stomach, which was ridiculous, it wasn't as if she was going on a date or anything, just out for a meal. The door knocked and it was Marie and as soon as she saw her, she gave Sarah an extremely loud wolf whistle! "OMG, you are looking so hot tonight, Sarah."

"Well, thank you, Marie. I just wanted to come and wish you good luck Cherie."

"Also please promise me that tonight you will let go of any inhibitions you might have. You need to get any ideas out of your head that Jake is too young for you, because he is so NOT! Just loosen up, and let your hair down and have some fun!"

"Crikes, Marie, you sound just like my best friend Annabel."

"Oh, do I, well we can't both be wrong, can we?" *The jury is still out on that one,* Sarah thought. "Anyway, I am off as I am meeting up with some of the lads tonight, but I have made a pact with myself not to drink too much! See you tomorrow and by the way, I will want to know everything okay, everything!"

"All right, but I doubt there will be much to tell. Au revoir, Marie, see you in the morning."

It was uncanny how alike Marie and Annabel were and now she had another good friend in Marie. She still felt bad about being unable to be with Annabel, at a time when she really needed her love and support. However, they had kept in regular contact with each other and Annabel had now spoken with her mother and arranged to meet up, which Sarah had been both happy and relieved to hear. She hoped that for once these two women would finally get their act together. Annabel certainly hadn't had the best of childhoods and her relationship with her mum, Julie, had been fraught to say the least.

Julie had become pregnant at the age of 16 and gave birth to Annabel shortly before turning 17. Julie's parents were going through a messy divorce at that time and were not overly supportive towards their daughter as she'd struggled to cope as a single mum at such a young age. She had tried to manage, but after a while, she was eventually persuaded to put Annabel into temporary foster care. Although she always had regular contact with her daughter. However, it wasn't until Julie met and married John when she was 19, and Annabel was two years old that she went back to live with her mum and new stepfather permanently.

Sarah understood that for a while Annabel had settled down happily, pleased to be back living with her mum and John, who had always treated her like his own daughter. All was well for a time, until Julie and John had twins together, Jamie and Samantha, when she was 8 years old. Somehow, Annabel felt pushed out once again, as if she didn't fit in any more. By the time Annabel became a teenager, she was as feisty as they come and just as hot-headed. Sarah had found her difficult to be around at times when they were growing up, as she could be very unpredictable and moody at times. But she had stuck by her friend, who constantly clashed with Julie. When the two fell out, Annabel would often come and stay round at Sarah's house and her parents became very fond of her and Dotty still was.

Annabel had eventually moved out of the family home at 18 and shared a flat with a couple of workmates. Even back then, she had been a strong and independent woman! Annabel had confided in her some years back that she had always believed that her mother had never loved her as much as she loved her younger brother and sister. Sarah however, didn't believe that was true for one minute, but Annabel would not be convinced otherwise.

Sarah had tried to encourage her many times over the years, to confront her mother about their past, not an easy thing to do she knew, but to no avail. Of one thing Sarah was sure of, these two women loved each other, but so much had happened in their lives. Please God there would still be time for them to move forward and put what had gone on before, truly behind them. Maybe if Julie could persuade Annabel to keep this baby, that would surely be a good place to start from. She would just have to wait and see.

Chapter 17

Jake was waiting for her in the hotel's bar and he looked very cool in an electric blue suit, designer no doubt, and he was wearing a crisp white shirt and a few buttons had been left undone, revealing a tiny amount of chest hair. He immediately came over to greet her and Sarah was once again struck by how extremely handsome he was. Jake looked her up and down with his deep chocolate brown eyes staring into hers. "Hey, you look gorgeous, Sarah," he said and kissed her on both cheeks, before helping her up onto one of the bar stools. Sarah got a waft of his aftershave and he smelt as good as he looked. "So what do you think of the whistle and flute then? I think I scrub up all right for an East End boy?"

"You certainly do, Jake."

"I bought the whistle and flute the other day in Forte Dei Marmi. Boy, the shops are fantastic there."

"So I hear and expensive!" Jake smiled and brushed her comment aside. "Right what can I get you to drink?"

"Just some iced still water for now, please."

"Oh come on that's hardly pushing the boat out is it? Why don't you try a cocktail," he said trying to coax her.

"All right but not too strong I like mine fruity." Jake shook his head and looked at her as if she was mad and ordered her cocktail. Sarah sipped it slowly and she found it surprisingly refreshing, with a strong taste of raspberries, which clearly masked some of the alcohol. "What do you think?"

"It's lovely thanks, Jake. So where are you taking me to tonight, I'm dying to know?"

"It's top secret and I am not telling you, it's a surprise, but I think you're gonna love it."

As soon as they had finished their drinks, they were taken by taxi into Florence, where it stopped right outside the most iconic restaurant in Florence, the Il Limone Albero Ristorante, (*The Lemon Tree Restaurant)*, which she knew had just received its second Michelin Star. She was thrilled. They were immediately greeted at the door and swiftly ushered into the restaurant, where they were seated at their table within minutes. It was an amazing place and somehow gave you the impression that you were in a rather grand villa. The décor was extremely impressive and stunning pieces of artwork were hung upon the walls.

Each course they had eaten had been a surprise and absolutely delicious. Everyone was so attentive towards them and the service they had received was first class. The Sommelier had found a wonderful bottle of champagne especially to suit her taste. She wouldn't even want to hazard a guess at how much it had cost! It tasted amazing to Sarah, perfect and she appeared to be acquiring quite a taste for it! She had told Jake not to worry, as she probably wouldn't drink that much of it. He had however insisted that she have it and ordered himself a fine bottle of Chianti red wine, which was produced locally. Jake had said it was the best he'd ever tasted. The restaurant was beautiful and the ambience was not only charming but also warm and inviting. The Maitre'd came round to each table to personally check that everything was as it should be and they were happy to report back that it truly was.

Once their meal was over, they sat chatting to one another with such an ease between them. It may have been the champagne, but Sarah's heart was all of a flutter. Jake was so handsome and so attentive towards her. This restaurant was magical and it had been the most amazing experience. They left the restaurant and both decided that as it was such a beautiful night they would walk back to the hotel.

Lots of people were still wandering around the streets, making the most of the warm night. Jake spotted an elderly gypsy woman holding a large wicker basket, full of red roses and insisted that he buy one for her. Jake gave the woman a handful of Euros and she looked highly delighted, as she gave him a beaming, but toothless smile. "Here you are Signorina, a beautiful red rose for a Bella Donna *(beautiful woman)*."

"Oh, Jake, thank you, but you paid well over the odds for it."

"Yeah, but it was worth it to put that smile on her face."

"Yes I agree, that was a lovely thing to do, Jake."

"Come on you," Jake said as he took Sarah's hand. "Are you sure you're going to be able to walk in those wedges?" and she assured him that she would be fine. They walked a short distance before stopping to soak up the atmosphere in one of the many beautiful squares in the heart of Florence. People were still sat outside the bars and restaurants, chatting away and laughing. "This really is an amazing place isn't it, Sarah, and so romantic, even though there are a few dodgy statues here and there!" It was true to say that there were a lot of naked statues in Florence, but they were eye catching to say the least!

"Not feeling threatened are you, Jake," and Sarah laughed.

"No, not at all cheeky." Sarah had fallen in love with Florence, what with its beautiful architecture and art, which were sublime. It had certainly given her an appetite to see more of Italy and she now had a desire to visit Rome one day too. Jake looked at her intently as he said in a seductive Italian accent. "So, Bella tell me, did you enjoy your evening he asked her."

"I did thank you very much."

"What about you, did you enjoy it?"

"Of course I did, the company speaks for itself and that restaurant was fabulous. However, I would have been just as happy myself with some good old fish and chips back home," he said in a mocking tone, but with a huge smile on his face.

"I've come along way though. What can I say, the boy's done good, well so far anyway. What do you think, Sarah?" Jake clearly sought reassurance from her, which she found somewhat endearing about him.

"You certainly have, Jake, and I agree with you, as I also love fish and chips. But this was surely more about the whole experience and it was way above all my expectations, it was fabulous. You certainly don't go to somewhere as lovely as that every day."

"Anyhow, don't be so modest, Jake, you're going places, absolutely no doubt about that."

"I hope so, Sarah, but I will never forget where I have come from."

"I don't think you will either. You really are a down to earth geezer and that's what is so charming about you," Sarah said and she meant it.

"My mum would adore you. She's from Essex and extremely proud to be. She's also a handful, just like you in fact."

"She sounds like my kind of woman and maybe I will get to meet her one day."

"You never know, she'd certainly be up for it Jake, I can tell you that much! She's a bit of gal, is my mother!"

"Anyway," Jake said, squeezing her hand gently, "thanks for the vote of confidence, Sarah," and then he promptly kissed her softly on the lips, which left her wanting more!

They took a rather leisurely walk back, which was mostly due to her wedges and Jake had had to pull her up any inclines, but finally they arrived back at the hotel. As they strolled through the hotel's gardens, they both stopped to look up at the clear night sky. A giant-sized moon shone brightly down at them and what looked like a million stars, sparkling like diamonds in the sky.

It was indeed the most perfect night and a gentle breeze was blowing and the sweet fragrance from the flowers was in the air, mixed together with the heady smell of the fresh herbs, which were also grown in the hotel's gardens. It was a magical night for Sarah. Sarah felt totally at ease in Jake's company and realised that she had drunk far more of the champagne than she'd intended to do and now her head was a bit woozy. Jake took her into his arms. "Do you even realise just how lovely you are, Sarah?"

"Oh thank you, Jake, but I don't think I am anything special."

"Oh really, so now who is being modest," he said teasing her.

"Anyway, I bet you say that to all the girls, don't you, Jake!"

"No I don't actually," came his quick response. Sarah laughed and their eyes met and he pulled her closer towards him.

"Well I happen to think you are," he said and kissed her softly on the lips. Her heart quickened and she knew she was being drawn to Jake, like a bee is to the pollen in a flower. They continued walking through the gardens and back up towards the hotel, holding hands in total silence and then made their way up to Sarah's room. Once inside, Jake took her into his arms again and kissed her with a real sense of urgency and passion. A fire had been lit inside of Sarah, which Jake had ignited, as Sarah returned his kisses in equal measure. It had been a long time since she had been that physical, with any man, not since Richard and Jake really was some man. There was nothing she didn't like about him. He was handsome, funny and easy to be around. Her head was all over the place and her heart was racing with excitement.

Her sex life with Richard had always been healthy, and she hadn't been aware of just how much she'd missed it. However, out of the blue she suddenly panicked and pulled away from Jake, slightly breathless. She had put the brakes firmly on and she didn't really understand why. "I'm sorry, Jake," she said in a hushed, breathless whisper, "but I cannot do this at the moment. It's getting late and we both have to be up early in the morning, don't we!" What was wrong with her? No doubt Annabel and Marie would chastise her and think her totally off her head! Maybe the timing wasn't right, or was it possible that Jake wasn't the one for her? Could it be the age difference? Jake was 29! She was confused and her head was really thudding by now. Sarah looked into Jake's eyes, but she couldn't really tell how he was feeling, as she said, "I'm so sorry, Jake, I hope you can forgive me?"

"Don't look so sad, Princess, you haven't done anything wrong. Night, see you in the morning," and then he kissed her on the forehead.

"Night, Jake." She closed the door behind him and lent back against it for a while and closed her eyes.

She felt a complete fool, but also if she was completely honest, slightly relieved. She told herself she just wasn't ready for any kind of relationship, physical or otherwise, not yet anyway. She was still holding the red rose which Jake had given to her and she filled a glass with cold water and placed it onto the dressing table.

A tear rolled down her cheek and she knew with some certainty that when she went to bed, she would more than likely lie awake, unable to sleep because she would be over analysing what had just taken place. She must need her head examined. There was an undeniable chemistry between the two of them. Jake was such a lovely guy and earlier in the evening she had warmed to him even more, especially when he had told her how he had got into acting. It had been purely by chance when he had been spotted by a talent scout. He had joined a local drama workshop in Hackney when he was 16 years old. He had played the part of the Artful Dodger in *Oliver*, a role that must have surely been made for him. He had also admitted to her that after his dad had died, he'd begun to hang around with the wrong crowd. Some of his former friends had since done time at Her Majesty's pleasure! The worst thing for him had been how it had impacted on his mum, as he'd put her through hell apparently, at a time when she was still grieving over his dad. Sarah had pointed out to him, that he had been grieving too. Losing your dad at such a young age would have been extremely hard to deal with. With the money he had earned from making some very successful British films and TV work, he'd also been able to buy his mother an apartment in Hove, Sussex. This was close to where Jake's eldest sister lived with her family. He'd said that his old Ma, as he referred to her, adored her three grandchildren. From what he had told her, the drama workshop had kept him off the streets and

138

out of trouble. Life had been good to him and he said he'd been very fortunate indeed, as he could so easily have gone down a different path.

Sarah hadn't gone into too much detail about her own life, but she had felt comfortable enough to mention her divorce and more importantly, how she had now drawn closure on it all and was in a much happier place. He had been particularly surprised to discover that she had also trained as a chef. He'd said that he would love it if she would cook for him one day. Sarah really hoped that things wouldn't become too uncomfortable between them from now on, as she really liked him rather a lot in fact!

Chapter 18

The following morning as soon as Sarah woke up, after very little sleep, she lifted her head from off the pillow and was reminded that she was paying the price for drinking way too much champagne the night before! She was fast becoming a bit of a lush! Hopefully it would go away. She had as she'd predicted spent most of the night lying awake and when the alarm had finally gone off, she felt like she hadn't had a wink of sleep. She thought about Jake once more and immediately became embarrassed with herself, all over again. Still she didn't have time to dwell on him right now, as it was almost 5 o'clock and today was going to be a busy one. She'd best get her skates on, otherwise she would be late and no doubt she would feel Steve's wrath!

After a quick shower, she got dressed and went to call for Elenour. This had become part of her daily routine now, as Steve had asked her to make sure that Elenour was supported in every possible way. Elenour still had the occasional melt down, especially before any big scene, which she was involved in and Sarah had grown closer to her over the past few weeks. She often behaved just like a petulant child, but Sarah was usually able to talk her around. Her job was to smooth things over for her as much as possible and to make sure she didn't become too stressed, not an easy task, but she loved a challenge.

Sarah knocked on the door to Elenour's suite and called out to her, but received no reply. Maybe Elenour wasn't up yet, which was often the case. She knocked once more and then as she had done on many occasions, she let herself in. However this time, there was no sign of Elenour and it didn't look as if she'd slept in her bed, which was a first. Sarah realised she had better inform Steve of the situation and then a thought came into her head, what if they'd spent the night together in his suite? Now that could be awkward. However, she'd be in even bigger trouble if she didn't let Steve know, because today Elenour had a major scene to do. Sarah made her way to Steve's suite and drew an intake of breath before she knocked on the door.

He eventually opened the door with an electric shaver in his hand. He looked surprised to see Sarah. "Morning, Steve, I just thought I should let you know that I went to call for Elenour just now and she's nowhere to be seen."

"Her bed hasn't been slept in either." Sarah was waiting to see what Steve's reaction would be and she didn't have to wait long.

"Bloody hell, where the fuck is she?" Steve made no apology for his language.

"I'm sorry, Steve, I really don't know."

"Did you see her last night?"

"No, I didn't. I went out for the evening."

"Well, you should have kept a closer eye on her, Sarah, he said angrily."

"Well, she told me she was going to have an early night."

"Clearly, she's not to be trusted. Fuck." Sarah realised that it would be best to say nothing, but she too was angry, after all she was actually entitled to have some free time herself. "Damn it, I bet she's with that time waster Angiolo. I tried to warn her to keep away from him, but as usual she takes no notice of me." Steve looked furious. "This would have to happen today of all days. Right, meet me downstairs in 10 minutes."

"Where are we going, Steve, do we need a taxi?"

"No, I will call my driver, Alfonso. I can trust him to be discreet."

"See if you can find out where Angiolo is staying?"

As she made her way down to the foyer, Sarah took out her iPad from her bag and checked her contact list and hoped and prayed that she had the correct address for Angiolo, otherwise Steve would probably fire her from out of a cannon. Angiolo she had been told was a well-known ex-footballer who had once played for A.C. Milan, and was now trying his hand at acting. He'd been given a very minor role in the film. There was some gossip about him having a bad boy reputation. She knew that Elenour was friends with him, but didn't think there was anything more to it. Sarah had the feeling that she would definitely get the blame for it if they were not able to find Elenour and soon! Elenour didn't really confide in Sarah that much. Most of the time she would just moan about something or other that she wasn't happy about and expect Sarah to sort it out for her. However, she still appeared to be perfectly happy to have Sarah around, in her now all too familiar role, as mother hen. She did also have a kind heart and, on occasion, was extremely generous and had given Sarah some of her cast off clothing, all designer and freebies which had been given to her. .

Steve clearly didn't think highly of Angiolo that was for sure. Maybe there was a good reason for his concerns! Thankfully, she had found both Angiolo's address and mobile number along with his Agent's address and telephone number. Sarah would now have to wait and see what Steve wanted to do when he came downstairs. It could be that Steve was jumping to the wrong conclusion, but she could tell that he didn't believe so! It did look as if she herself may have taken her eye off the ball, where Elenour was concerned. She just hoped they found her soon because, Sarah was genuinely concerned about her now.

When Steve finally came into the lobby, he didn't look any happier than he had before. "I've just checked and she's still not in her room."

"Right, well I have Angiolo's address and mobile number and his Agent's mobile number."

"What do you want to do, Steve, do you want to ring him first?"

"No," he said emphatically, "let's just go."

"If my hunch is correct, she will be with him, I'm certain of it." Alfonso, Steve's driver had brought the car around to the front of the hotel.

It was quiet outside, as it was still early, with just the odd delivery being made to the hotel. Sarah gave Alfonso the address of Angiolo's apartment and he nodded and said he knew where to go, and they were soon on their way. Steve was still ranting. "I cannot believe it, why did she have to choose today of all days to go AWOL." Sarah kept quiet, for fear of getting her head chewed off, as she'd never seen Steve this angry before. They had been driving for about half an hour when Alfonso pulled up outside a smart block of apartments.

Steve asked Alfonso to wait for them until they came back. They took the stairs, which Steve was taking two at a time and Sarah tried her best to keep up with him. Steve rung the bell of No. 24A and left his hand pressing on it continuously. Eventually, an extremely tired and hung over Angiolo came to the door. "Steve, what's going on?"

"Just tell me, Angiolo, is Elenour here?" Angiolo looked stunned and somewhat agitated. "Come on, is she here or not, for God's sake," Steve persisted.

"Yes she is, you'd better come in."

"Right, where is she?"

"Shoosh, calm down, Steve."

"She's asleep, we had a pretty heavy night."

"Oh did you now! And did you know that she's not meant to be drinking. She should have been ready ages ago to be on set this morning."

"No, I did not know that, Steve, she didn't tell me honestly."

"Did you get her drunk?"

"No, of course not. I care about her, Steve, we're friends that's all."

"Do you expect me to believe that?"

"Yes I do." Angiolo looked slightly embarrassed as he said. "Look I'm gay all right, but I don't want the whole fucking world to know. She was out of control last night and I promise you, I was looking out for her and tried to stop her drinking, but she wouldn't listen to me. She was hitting the vodka pretty hard. I brought her back here because she was in such a state."

"Okay, enough with your excuses, Angiolo," Steve hurled at him. "Where is she?" Angiolo pointed to a door and Steve stormed towards it, hotly followed by Sarah and Angiolo. Sarah wanted to make sure that Steve didn't completely lose his temper with poor Elenour, who was still sleeping and looked deathly pale.

There was a bucket beside the bed, which she had actually been sick in. Steve turned to Angiolo and shouted angrily. "Get rid of this now!" Steve then gently shook Elenour. "Come on, Elenour, wake up." It took several minutes before she finally began to stir and slowly opened her eyes.

"What, oh please stop, I just need to sleep," she begged him.

"Oh no you're not going back to sleep, young lady."

"Steve, leave her," Sarah interjected, "please let me deal with her. Get Angiolo to make you a coffee."

"I'm not leaving here without her, Sarah."

"I know that, Steve, but look at the state of her. Can you honestly see her recovering enough to go on set today?"

Steve shook his head. "Just get her cleaned up, Sarah, and be as quick as you can!"

An hour later, they left Angiolo's apartment and Steve's parting words to Angiolo had been. "Don't ever be late on set, young man, and keep away from Elenour, or you'll be cut out of this movie," he said rather menacingly. Sarah had managed with some difficulty to get Elenour into the shower and dressed, but even now she still looked as white as a sheet. The two women sat in the back of the car together and Sarah held Elenour's hand, as she was still shaking slightly. Steve sat next to Alfonso with a stern and worried look on his face. Elenour was full of remorse and had apologised to Steve several times. Sarah wasn't sure if Steve was in a forgiving mood as yet. Once again, Sarah's heart went out to her. She was young and she'd made a mistake. Everyone is allowed to make them occasionally, but unfortunately Elenour couldn't have chosen a worse day to make hers. Steve was silent as he sat next to Alfonso. They made their way back to the hotel, via the back entrance this time, to avoid the Paparazzi, who by now had got wind of where they were staying. They were always eager to get snaps of the stars, but fortunately it was still relatively early.

Back in Elenour's suite, Sarah helped her to get undressed and into bed and pulled the curtains shut tight and then kissed her on the forehead. "You need to sleep, Elenour, and I'm sure you'll feel better when you wake up, I promise." Elenour took hold of her hand and looked at Sarah with her bloodshot eyes.

"Thanks, Sarah, you're always so kind to me and I don't deserve it."

"Just get some shut eye, sweet dreams. I will be around if you need me." Steve had already asked her to stay with Elenour for the rest of the day to make sure she got herself back to normal if that was possible, for the following day. He said he would have to re-work the entire schedule for the day and understandably so, was still in a foul mood when he'd left. He'd also suggested that it might be a good idea to take Elenour out, to get some fresh air later, if she was up to it. Alfonso would be on standby if they needed him.

Steve's parting words to her had been that he was relying on her, so no pressure there whatsoever.

Sarah left Elenour to hopefully sleep off the hangover and went back to her own room briefly to collect her laptop, so that she could at least do some work whilst babysitting Elenour. Steve had already sent some urgent last-minute changes to the script. She made her way back to Elenour's suite, and opened her bedroom door as quietly as she possibly could and crept into see if she was all right. She was in fact sleeping peacefully.

By 1.30, Sarah decided to order room service as she was starving and checked on Elenour, who appeared to be still fast asleep. Sarah was just about to close the door behind her, when Elenour called out to her. "I'm awake now, Sarah." Sarah sat down on the edge of Elenour's bed.

"Hi, so how is the wounded soldier feeling now?"

"To be honest, better than I deserve to. I actually feel hungry."

"Well, that's a good sign and I was just about to order something from room service. I missed breakfast and have been trying to stave off my hunger pangs by drinking loads of coffee and eating biscuits."

"If you're going to have something to eat, I suggest that you stick to toast don't you!"

"Yeah I guess so and some peppermint tea please." Sarah rang down for room service and they didn't have long to wait before their food was delivered to Elenour's suite. Sarah munched her chicken salad sandwich which was enormous, whilst Elenour sat up in bed to eat her toast. She was beginning to get a bit of her colour back, but was still rather pale. "Tell me, Sarah, how do I look?"

"What honestly!"

"Yes of course."

"Like shit!" They both laughed. "Oh, Sarah, I love you, as I can always count on you to tell me the truth and not what people think I want to hear. I have a lot of making up to do don't I?" She paused briefly before saying. "I have screwed up big time haven't I?"

Before Sarah had a chance to respond, Elenour came out with, "What the hell are people going to think of me, Jake for instance, he's going to be so mad!"

"Stop it, Elenour, calm down as it won't do you any good. I, like Steve still have every faith in you." Suddenly, Elenour flung her arms around Sarah in a childlike manner, which was so typical of her when she was feeling vulnerable. "Oh thanks Sarah, I could not have gotten through all of this without you."

"Of course you would have silly."

"How about we get ourselves cleaned up and go out somewhere."

"I could ask Alfonso to take us out for a spin if you're up to it."

"A spin," Elenour said, looking nonplussed. "That's just a drive to you," and Elenour laughed. "Oh I see."

"What do you say!"

"I say yes, it sounds good to me."

"Okay," Sarah said in her usual bossy manner. "You go get yourself into the shower young lady, again and I will nip back to my room and get changed and I will be back in a jiffy."

"Okay, miss bossy boots, get out of here," Elenour ordered, as she threw a wet flannel at Sarah. "I get the message, Sarah!"

Sarah and Elenour were ready within the hour and met Alfonso at the back of the hotel, to minimise the chances of Elenour being snapped by the paparazzi.

She had put on the largest pair of sunglasses they could find and Sarah gave her the big floppy straw hat which she wore to the beach. It was the best they could do, but in reality, she probably looked as conspicuous as hell. Fortunately no one snapped them as Alfonso sped off. The two of them spent a fun afternoon together in Forte dei Marmi and hit the shops and both of them bought expensive jeans and some fabulous shoes, whilst Elenour also splashed out on a gorgeous and expensive soft pink Italian leather jacket. They finished their trip off with a delicious pizza and sat outside a traditional Italian Restaurant in the beautiful Tuscan sunshine and people watched. The Italians certainly knew how to dress which was always stylish and extremely sophisticated. Sarah had never seen so many flash cars like the ones driving around Forte dei Marmi that day, everyone seemed to be either driving a Porsche or a Lamborghini.

Money was clearly no object for the people who holidayed there and it was a real eye opener for Sarah. She had rung Steve earlier to tell him of their intention to go out for the afternoon. She was pleased to find that he had calmed down considerably from earlier on. Sarah was also able to reassure him that in her opinion, Elenour was well and truly on the mend. Apparently, Steve had managed to successfully re-schedule most of the shoot for the following day and he was happy as they had also managed to shoot a few scenes and back shot views in Elenour's absence.

He'd also mentioned that many of the actors and crew were extremely put out about the delay, especially Jake. Steve had also told her, that he'd more or less put everyone in the picture, as to what had taken place. He didn't see the point in trying to sugar coat it, because the truth would have eventually got out, it always did. Jake had initially exploded, but Steve had managed to calm him down again. He asked that Sarah didn't mention this at all to Elenour, which of course she wouldn't have, but gave him her word anyway. He finished up by saying that he'd spoken to everyone and there was to be no backlash towards Elenour whatsoever or they would have him to answer to!

Tomorrow would be a new day and they would all start afresh. Sarah had assured him that she would not let Elenour out of her sight for a single moment! Steve finished by saying, "No you better hadn't." It wasn't just Elenour who had some major making up to do, she had also let Steve down. Well at least in his eyes.

Sarah and Elenour arrived back at the hotel at a respectable time and spent the rest of the evening going over Elenour's script. Sarah had been impressed as always by how well she knew her lines and had barely faltered over any of them. The next day though was going to be an extremely challenging one and not just for Elenour, but for all of the actors and crew.

Several action scenes were taking place and it would be a long day. Sarah had asked Elenour what had happened the night before. She'd hesitated briefly before answering that it was just her nerves getting the better of her and the fact that she also constantly doubted her acting ability. It was clear to Sarah that most of the pressure came from herself. It was that which had led her to hit the bottle and it really had nothing to do with Angiolo. She had told Sarah that she felt really bad about him now, because Steve had been so awful to him earlier.

It soon became obvious that both of them were exhausted. The tension of the day had caught up with them both and they agreed that it was time to get themselves to bed. "Right, Elenour, I'm off now, so I will see you bright and early tomorrow morning." Sarah instinctively kissed Elenour on the forehead as she often did, and before she had a chance to leave the room, Elenour called out to her. "Would you think me pathetic, if I asked you to stay here with me tonight?"

"Please. I know it sounds silly, but I don't want to be on my own tonight."

"Of course I will and I can sleep on the sofa!"

"No, you won't, you can share my bed. It's big enough to sleep three people in, let alone two."

"Okay then I'll just nip back to my room and get my nightie, it's way too hot to wear PJs."

Sarah gathered up her night things, cleaned her teeth and brushed her hair until it shone and returned to Elenour's rather grand suite, which was exactly what you would expect to find in a high-class Italian hotel, with its pure timeless elegance! She could certainly get used to this she thought.

Elenour was already in bed and she quickly slipped into her nightie and got into the bed beside her. "What do you think the Paparazzi would make of this if they saw us together now?"

"They would probably have a field day, wouldn't they," Elenour replied and both women giggled.

"Anyhow on that note, no spooning with me please and respect my space!" Sarah quipped!

"I promise, definitely no spooning." Sarah pulled the covers over them. "Lights out now."

"Yes night, Sarah."

"Nighty night, Elenour. Sweet dreams."

They were both quiet and still for a while and then out of the blue, Elenour suddenly broke the silence as they lay in the dark, "You do know that I'm fucked up in some ways, don't you?" Sarah was shocked by what she'd just heard.

"I don't believe that for one single minute, Elenour." Sarah quickly sat up and put her side light back on. "I think you're just a bit confused and this lifestyle which you lead, is full on pressure. It's an awful lot to deal with and you're still young."

"Yes, but I am the lucky one because I have been given so many opportunities. Some of my friends haven't been so lucky and are working either as a waitress, or temping in offices, or worse still working in a fast food place!"

"That is just the way it is, Elenour, when you get a lucky break, you have to run with it. It is a very tough industry and it's not for the faint-hearted."

"Why then, do I have to go and screw things up for myself all of the time," Elenour said, clearly angry with herself. "If you're referring to what happened last night, then you have to learn from your mistakes, we all do."

"Here's the thing, Sarah, I hadn't actually had a drink in over a year and then wham!"

"You'll get over it, you have to." Sarah was surprised when she went on to say.

"But I mess up everything, Sarah, I really do. I have never even had a proper long-term relationship with anyone. I think sometimes when things are going really, really well, I seem to panic and deliberately screw it all up. I'm a frigging freak."

"Stop it, why would you even think such a thing?"

There was a long silence before Elenour began to cry from a place deep within and blurted out, "Because my step-father abused me when I was younger and I still feel so ashamed," she sobbed. "I felt like it was all my fault."

Sarah grabbed some tissues from the side table and quickly gave them to Elenour. "Come on dry your eyes and blow your nose, missy!" Sarah placed her arm around her and looked directly into Elenour's sad and tearful eyes and said, "Listen, here young lady, you are definitely not the one who should feel ashamed and it certainly wasn't your fault." Sarah could see the pain in Elenour's eyes as she continued.

"It only happened the once, but when I told my mother, she didn't believe me."

"That actually was the worst thing of all and it became so unbearable that I had to leave home and I went to live with my auntie."

"Elenour, I am so, so sorry, it must have been terrible for you."

"I was only thirteen at the time, Sarah."

"I cannot even imagine what you've been through, but you will learn to trust men again one day, I'm sure of it Elenour."

"Steve has been so very kind to me and look how I repay him."

"Oh I am sure he has forgiven you by now."

"Yes but he's never ever been so angry with me before."

"He'll be okay don't worry."

"Elenour, I hope you won't mind me asking you, but what exactly is your relationship with Steve?" Sarah hoped she wasn't being too intrusive. "No of course not, you're my friend."

"We had a little fling a while back, nothing too serious you know, the usual thing, and now we're just really good friends."

"You see, it doesn't do either of us any harm to be seen out together. It also keeps the Paparazzi on their toes too."

"Steve loves women and as you probably know he has had a string of them in the past, but he isn't the kind of man who wants to settle down any time soon."

"No woman has managed to pin him down, well not yet anyway."

"I am not sure if one even exists!"

"He can be a hard nut to crack sometimes, but trust me he has a kind heart."

"He looks after me."

"I know he does, Elenour, and when this film comes out and hopefully it will be a box office success, you will have repaid him."

"From what I have managed to glean from the rushes so far, Elenour, you're giving a powerful performance and the camera simply adores you and I don't want to miss seeing you give the performance of a lifetime tomorrow."

"And for what it's worth, I know you can definitely do it."

"You're going to blow everyone's socks off!" Elenour turned to Sarah with a smile on her face and kissed her on the cheek.

"Thanks, that means such a lot to me!"

"You're welcome; now I'm turning the light off, Elenour, so nighty night."

"Sarah!"

"Yes, what is it now, Elenour?" Sarah said, yawning as she felt a little exasperated, due to her lack of sleep.

"Have you ever thought about becoming a psychotherapist, cos I think you'd be great at it!"

"No I haven't, now shut up and get some shut eye!" It had been a long day and they both soon drifted off to sleep.

Chapter 19

Sarah and Elenour were both up early the next morning and had room service again. As soon as they had showered and dressed, the two women went downstairs into the foyer and were surprised to discover that they were the first to arrive. Elenour was a little uptight Sarah noticed, but on the whole she looked great and certainly, a million times better than she had the previous day. Steve walked out of the lift and glanced in their direction with the same stern look he'd had on his face the previous day. He came over to them and said, "Morning ladies, and how are we?"

Elenour cast her eyes down. "I'm so very sorry about yesterday, Steve."

"Let's just concentrate on today, Elenour! We have a job to do and I just want to know, are you ready for it?"

Elenour nodded and looked up at Steve with a weak smile and said emphatically, "You bet."

Steve looked happier than he had the day before as he said, "Good now, let's go, as Alfonso is waiting for us." As they walked outside, Steve took hold of Sarah's arm, "Thanks you did a great job."

"You're very welcome, Steve." High praise indeed Sarah thought and wondered how long that would last!

Sarah left Elenour with the wardrobe team and after studying her brief again, she realised that her schedule was going to be extremely demanding. Soon she was rushing around like a headless chicken, even more than usual, as she was planning to see as much of the action on set, as she possibly could today! She had already delegated some of her work to Amanda and a very enthusiastic young man called Alex, who was extremely camp and everyone loved him, as he made them all laugh constantly which broke up some of the tension during the shoot.

It was going to be a hard and challenging day of filming for everybody. She had briefly seen Marie earlier, but neither of them had had time for idle chitchat and no doubt she would catch up with her later, much later Sarah thought, if at all. Sarah made time to pop in and see Elenour once more, whilst she was in hair and make-up and she looked stunning. Sue, the head make-up artist had just finished doing her make-up. She looked radiant and back on form in a beautiful, if not rather flimsy looking pure lace white dress.

Sarah knew that several identical ones had been made and no doubt would be used throughout the day. "I just wanted to come in and wish you lots of luck."

"Thank you so much, Sarah."

"Oh and I nearly forgot, here take this." Elenour looked at what Sarah had just put into her hand. "What the hell is that," she said with a look of disgust. "It's a white rabbit's foot, well actually it's a fifty shades of grey rabbit's foot," Sarah said with a cheeky grin. "It's for luck. My mum gave it to me and it works, trust me. Just hold onto it. You could put it down your knickers," she joked, "but please look after it as I will need it back!"

"Give it a good squeeze before going on set!"

"Right I have to dash now, otherwise, Steve will have my guts for garters!" As she left, Elenour turned to Sue and said, "Did you even understand any of what she just said."

Sue replied, "No, not a bloody word, so don't ask me," and they both laughed.

It was the most manic and craziest days ever on set by far and it was only 9 a.m. The pace was always full on, but this was something else, and on a completely different level. Everyone was so busy and knew that time was of the essence. The sun was shining and it looked set to be another scorcher in the most idyllic Tuscan countryside. It was breathtakingly beautiful and as Steve had told her, cinematic gold would definitely happen here. They were filming in Chianti about 30 km from Florence. As far as the eye could see, there was a myriad of lush green colours, as rich olive groves and vineyards surrounded them. Right now, as she stood looking around her, she couldn't imagine a better place to be making a film and as she the thought about leaving it all behind, a feeling of sadness came over her. However, now wasn't the time to ponder such thoughts.

Sarah had made sure earlier, that there would be more than enough ice-cold water and fresh fruit readily available at all times. They couldn't afford to run out of anything. Paramedics as always were on standby, but hopefully they wouldn't need them. It would also be full on for the catering team as there were even more people on set today. It would definitely be the toughest day by far and Sarah could hardly wait for it all to get going now and she was really looking forward to being part of it albeit in a small way.

Over recent weeks, Steve had become slightly more relaxed and had been very kind and generous towards her. On several occasions he had actually invited her to give him some of her own input. She'd been extremely pleased when Steve had said, that in particular, she had good vision, which was a central part when directing any film.

Today, the majority of the filming would be set in and around the beautiful Villa Paradiso, where Elenour's character Hope has been brought to, by James Hunter's character Dominic, a successful art dealer and chronic gambler. She had been pleasantly surprised to discover that James was a real gentleman and highly intelligent, but it was clear that he liked his own space. She'd even managed to apologise on behalf of her mother, in relation to the selfie which she'd inflicted upon him. He had kindly said that he hadn't minded at all.

This was the climax of the film and where Elenour would have to put in her most powerful performance yet. Her character Hope, is a young struggling artist, who up until recently had led a fairly sheltered life. Dominic has duped her into believing that she has immense talent and Hope is totally sucked in by him. Jake's character, Ben is suspicious of Dominic and is convinced that he is not all he is purporting to be. He tries to tell Hope that she should be wary of Dominic, and steer clear of him but she believes mistakenly, that Ben is just jealous.

This is all about to change, however, as she finally begins to realise that not everything is as she thought it was after all, when she inadvertently overhears a telephone conversation. She very quickly realises that her life is in danger and she needs to make her exit from the villa quickly, but how?

Chapter 20

The shoot had gone relatively well, without too many glitches and it had been the best day of filming by far for Sarah. It was action packed and extremely physical for its three lead actors, who had each given their all and none of them had faltered or disappointed. The creative energy was electric. Elenour had truly excelled herself and Sarah was so pleased for her. Despite the obstacles that had presented themselves for her the day before, she'd pulled it off. At one point, her character Hope had been required to run through vineyards and olive groves in order to get away from Dominic's clutches and she had worked tirelessly, even though it had taken numerous takes.

Her energy was boundless and boy could she run, but throughout the shoot, she had managed to do it all with the grace and agility of a gazelle. She had legs that went on forever, and even covered in fake blood, cuts and bruises she had still managed to look gorgeous. How the hell had she achieved that Sarah didn't know. Elenour had received a huge round of applause from everyone on set and her face had been a picture.

Steve knew exactly what he was doing with Elenour, because the camera simply loved her and something even more surprising was the chemistry between her and Jake, after their somewhat shaky start. She looked amazing and not for the first time, Sarah thought she had an ethereal look about her. However, as soon as the cameras stopped rolling, she'd slumped into a heap and looked completely wrecked. Elenour finally finished up wearing several of the lace dresses and each one was ripped to shreds!

Sarah watched Steve, who looked pleased with himself and was high-fiving everyone and looked like the cat who had definitely got the cream! All the actors and crew were clapping and congratulating one another. It appeared that he was never happier than when directing a film and as he looked across at her, gave her one of his cheeky winks.

Chapter 21

The weeks leading up to their return to Blighty had been extremely busy and soon they would be packing up and returning home. Sarah had heard from Annabel and she was over the moon and relieved to hear that she had been back in touch with her mother. More importantly, she had had a change of heart and had decided that she was going to keep her baby. Liam had told Annabel that he would give financial support for herself and the baby. Fortunately, her morning sickness had now passed and she was feeling so much better. Apparently, she was still wearing her normal clothes as she only had a small baby bump, but no doubt when she did eventually show, tongues would be wagging at work behind her back.

Annabel had also said that she didn't care a lot about what anyone had to say. She knew she was a thorn in Liam's side at work, but she certainly wasn't about to walk away from a highly paid and successful job that she'd worked her butt off for either. There was far too much at stake for her to lose. Anyway, there wasn't a thing that he could do about it.

She fully intended to take a year off on maternity leave. Sarah was proud of Annabel, it was as if she was giving Liam the middle finger and if anyone was more deserving of it, it was certainly him.

Life was really going to change for her friend, but for the better she was certain of it. Annabel had asked her to be present at the birth of her baby, which was due at the end of February. Sarah had been both touched and excited and of course she had said yes. She sincerely hoped her work wouldn't interfere and that she would be able to be with Annabel, she owed her that much at least! She was thrilled for her best friend and she was going to be the best Auntie ever!

It was the end of shoot Wrap Party, which Sarah had organised at the Ristorante Gigilio in Lucca for them exclusively. She'd enjoyed sourcing the decorations for the restaurant, who had been extremely accommodating. It would be full on Hollywood Glitz and Glamour and of course a few surprises! Several of the cast and crew had been to the restaurant on numerous occasions and had all raved about it. The staff were so attentive and were clearly enjoying having such esteemed patrons in their restaurant. Everyone had arrived with the full intention of well and truly letting their hair down and who could blame them. Soon they would be leaving Tuscany and lots of them were already beginning to feel sad and nostalgic for the good times they'd had.

It was a great atmosphere and they were all in high spirits, and naturally there was a fair amount of alcohol being consumed, which also helped. A DJ played loud music and many were already up dancing, including Jake who was dancing with Amanda and they looked like they were having fun.

Fortunately, she had got back on track with Jake and as far as she could tell, he didn't appear to treat her any differently after their night out together, when she had most definitely got cold feet. She had confided in Marie about what had happened who, had thought she was mad! So far he hadn't asked her out again and really she could hardly blame him. Anyway, it had also been so busy and full on of late, that there had hardly been any time for anyone to do much socialising. It was work sleep and then work again, everyone was tired. However, tonight Jake so far had been attentive towards her and once more she was extremely flattered. Jake was so easy to be around and more importantly he made her laugh. She herself had had a few glasses of champagne and knew really that she shouldn't, but then again she thought to herself, what the heck, she'd soon be back home in good old Blighty. She fully intended to have a ball, why not?!

It was still going to be busy when they returned to the UK at Pinewood Studios, but they had all agreed that Tuscany had been such a special time. Sarah was however looking forward to the post-production period, which would be new to her. Tuscany would soon be a distant memory, which made her feel sad too! It had certainly been the most magical of times for her in Italy. She almost felt as if she was a different person, who had blossomed and grown in so many different ways, and one she barely recognised sometimes. She was so much more relaxed and carefree, even though most of the time her job had been full-on madness, but she had loved every minute of it.

Sarah glanced around her and everyone was having a great time. Many were just chatting, or still eating, to the revellers on the dance floor. There was plenty of laughter too. Even Steve appeared to be enjoying himself. She had grown close to quite a few of the cast and crew members and they had all become like one big happy family, albeit a large one! The best was still to come later, as she had organised fireworks and flame-throwers who would entertain them all. Marie was chatting away to Dave, one of the cameramen whom she knew Marie had the hots for. She was flirting with him outrageously. He was a really nice guy and single, so maybe Marie would get lucky, she hoped so anyway! Elenour was dancing with James Hunter and even Angiolo was there too, after getting back into Steve's good books. Elenour had now fully explained to Steve what had actually happened the night she'd got herself so awfully drunk and he had apologised to Angiolo! Steve had also acknowledged that he had been impressed by just how good, he'd come across on screen and he had even proved himself to be a half-decent actor.

Sarah noticed Amanda come off the dance floor and Jake came walking towards her. "Come on, Sarah, it's your turn now," he said as he took hold of her hand and pulled her up from her chair. She didn't even try and stop him. Jake was a good dancer and they did a jive together and she really enjoyed herself. Even though every time he spun her round, she was left feeling dizzy and the high-heeled sandals she had on were certainly not helping. She quickly stopped and took them off and threw them aside and carried on dancing.

As the dance came to an end, Jake swept her off her feet, which was a habit of his and carried her off the dance floor. They were both laughing and out of breath. "You're a natural, Sarah."

"So are you, Jake, where did you learn to jive?"

"What can I say?" he said with a big smile on his face. "I was born to dance," and he took a very long sip of his beer.

"Is there nothing you can't do, Jake?"

"Apparently not," he said putting his bottle of beer back down onto the table.

"Do you fancy getting some fresh air, it's a bit hot in here isn't it," Jake said wiping his brow with a serviette.

"Yes let's go outside, I think I'm actually melting myself." Several others were already sitting outside the restaurant. It was a lovely warm night and not much of a breeze either and she noticed Steve was sat in deep conversation with a man and woman, whom she didn't recognise. Marie beckoned them over and they sat down with her and Dave and a few of the other crew members. Marie's eyes were sparkling and she looked so happy. She had been working extremely hard and Sarah really admired her commitment to her job and was confident that Marie would achieve her dream of becoming a cinema photographer one day! She had had to prove herself more than any of the other camera crew these past months and she had come through it all with flying colours. She knew that Steve had also been very impressed with her. Sarah thought that Marie and Dave made a very cute couple too.

Steve had been quietly observing all that was going on around him since his friends, had now left. It was clear that everyone was having a great time. Some however, were certainly looking the worse for wear by now though. It hadn't escaped his notice that Jake was all over Sarah like a rash and for her part, she certainly appeared to be enjoying his company and attention.

He had to admit to himself, she did look particularly beautiful tonight, or was the word he was looking for, sexy in her 1940s inspired white halter neck jump suit. Her hair was in a chignon and she looked sophisticated, and her skin now had a healthy glow, which suited her. She'd also developed a few more freckles across her nose more recently, due to the Tuscan sun. In his mind, tonight she equalled, if not rivalled Elenour!

Sarah being the more mature of the two women had a certain sophistication about her, which Elenour had not yet acquired. She could easily have been taken for one of the film's major stars and the most endearing part about that was, she didn't have a clue herself.

He knew he shouldn't judge her, but in his opinion she was drinking way too much champagne, but really it was none of his business. He couldn't quite understand why it should bother him so much. He had chosen to give drinking a miss tonight, as he knew he needed to keep a clear head for the following day, but he certainly didn't begrudge the others letting their hair down for one night.

They'd been a fantastic bunch of people to work with and each one of them had worked extremely hard. He didn't have a problem with Jake either, he was a great guy and a brilliant young actor too. However, he was a bit of a player and he didn't want to see Sarah get hurt by him. Elenour wandered over towards him. "Come on, Steve, have a dance with me, please!"

"No you should know by now, Elenour, that I don't dance."

"Suit yourself," she said and walked off in a huff, saying he was a party pooper and then dragged poor James up once more onto his feet and they went back inside the restaurant. Phew, he was pleased that he had managed to dodge that bullet. He was no dancer!

Sarah glanced over at Steve, who was sitting by himself now and decided to go over to him. "Hey what's up, Steve?" she said giving him one of her broad smiles. "You don't appear to be having much fun, compared to the rest of us! Why don't you come over and join us for goodness' sake."

"No, actually I am going to have to leave I'm afraid."

"What can be so important that it cannot wait?"

"Well, it can't wait he said somewhat abruptly, it's a little emergency that's cropped up."

"Actually, I was rather hoping you'd come with me, as I really could do with your help."

"What right now you mean?"

"Yes right now."

"Are you kidding me because I'm having an amazing time and if you haven't noticed, I've been drinking, just a teeny weeny bit though," she said giggling, "so I doubt that I will be of much use to you."

Steve had a disapproving look upon his face. "Yes I had noticed, but I'm prepared to take the risk! Now be a good girl, go and grab your shoes and bag and let's get going."

"All right, Mr Bossy Pants, give me a minute," she said laughing, but actually she was really seething inside. She joined the others and as there was no sign of Jake, she asked Marie to explain to him why she'd had to leave so suddenly and she had promised Sarah that she would. She continued to say her goodbyes to just about anyone and everyone and kissed and hugged them all.

This time it was she who teased Marie, before she left whispering to her, "Don't do anything that I wouldn't do, Marie!" as she looked across at Dave and winked.

"Ha-ha, I will let you know, Cherie, now go, before Steve blows his gasket."

"He doesn't look too happy to me!"

"Tough," Sarah replied.

Steve was indeed becoming impatient whilst he waited for Sarah, as she appeared hell bent on kissing and hugging anyone she could lay her hands on. Eventually, she walked over towards him, without any sense of urgency, swinging her sandals to-and-fro.

"Okay, I'm ready to go now!"

"Finally, well you certainly took your time," he said rather tersely looking down at her bare feet. "Don't you think you should put your shoes back on?"

"Nope that's not going to happen, because my feet are absolutely killing me!"

"Well that's your fault for wearing such high heels."

"I know that, Steve, but I love them and it's a woman thing don't you know. When it comes to shoes, sense and sensibility don't come into the equation."

"If you say so, Sarah."

"Well I do."

"How are we getting back? Is Alfonso driving us?" Sarah enquired.

"No, but someone from the restaurant has gone to collect my car from the car park."

"What you drove here?"

"Yes don't sound so surprised and before you ask, I haven't been drinking." He could have said unlike some people I could mention, but thought better of it. "Well, I know you wouldn't be that stupid, Steve."

One of the young waiters from the restaurant roared up behind them and came to a screeching halt in Steve's shiny red Ferrari convertible, which he'd been given to use during his time in Italy. Steve could tell that the young man was impressed with the car, as he had a huge grin on his face when he jumped out of it. "Oh Senyore, Magnifico, magnifico," he repeated again enthusiastically to Steve as he went around to the passenger side and beamed at Sarah as he helped her to get into the car. Steve noticed that the young waiter was also equally as impressed with Sarah by the look he was giving her. Italian men really appreciated their women, especially a good-looking woman and certainly knew how to show it too.

Sarah hadn't got into the car as graciously as she would have liked, because the seat had been lower down than she'd anticipated and she fell onto it rather clumsily. Steve took a large amount of Euros out from his wallet and tipped the waiter, who in turn thanked Steve profusely, before he went back into the restaurant. Steve got into the car beside Sarah and told her to put on her seat belt. "I know what to do, Steve, give me a chance." Once she had her belt secured, Steve pulled away rather sharply and the wheels span slightly on the dirt track as he did so, but the engine purred seductively. As they sped along the open road, Steve put his foot down harder on the accelerator and with the rooftop down, it wasn't long before Sarah's once, neatly coiffured hair began to completely unravel. But she didn't care because she was enjoying the ride.

She found the whole experience exhilarating. Steve was a very skilled driver and the car was out of this world! Like something out of a Bond film. Was there anything that this man didn't do well she pondered! Her feet were still throbbing from wearing her overly expensive gold sandals, which she now regretted buying on impulse, from one of the fancy boutique shops in Florence. On a whim she just decided to lob them out of the car and then shouted out at the top of her voice, "FREEDOM!" Steve smiled and couldn't quite believe what she'd just done.

"Are you mad, woman, I thought you loved those sandals! Do you want me to turn around and go back for them?"

"No, I bloody well don't, thank you and I am never going to wear another pair of 5-inch heels ever again."

"Oh yes, sorry don't believe you!"

"I swear on my life, it's brogue shoes for me from now on," she said and let out a loud hiccup. "PARDON."

"Should think so too," Steve said with a look of disapproval!

"My feet simply cannot take it no more! Anyway, they have given me the pleasure, but boy the pain is unbearable!"

"You're crazy totally nuts!"

"No, I am not, just slightly wild and you've made me like this, Steve."

"Me, why would you say that?"

"Well not just you solely, it's being part of this mad world of filmmaking, I've completely lost my mind," she said laughing. Steve couldn't believe his eyes, when minutes later, Sarah had fallen fast asleep with her head firmly back against the headrest. He wasn't sure what he would tell her once they got back to the hotel and he began to feel somewhat uncomfortable about what he had done. How would he explain himself to her, about why he had brought her away from the party, on some pretext of an urgent matter, which had suddenly cropped up! If he was honest with himself he had to admit that he didn't fully understand why he'd done it.

He glanced across at Sarah again, and her head had now flopped forward, so he gently pushed her head back against the headrest and eased his foot off the accelerator and drove along at a more decent speed. He pushed a button to recline her seat, to make it more comfortable for her. He smiled to himself, as she didn't resemble the once highly coiffured and sophisticated woman, whom he'd been admiring all evening. The wind had blown her hair into complete disarray and although it was a bit too late, he pressed another button and the rooftop slowly began to rise and close effortlessly above them.

You only had to look at Sarah to see that her time in Tuscany had done her the world of good, and once more he thought that she looked as sexy as hell, but quickly dismissed such thoughts.

It was especially good to see how much Sarah had blossomed whilst in Italy he thought that she appeared to be in a much better place right now and a lot happier. She'd told him herself, on several occasions that she loved her job and being around so many mad, but committed people. However, to him she was still rather vulnerable and for some inexplicable reason he had an overwhelming desire to protect her, but from what? This was something he couldn't fathom out for the life of him. Was he really trying to save her from the clutches of Jake, he couldn't really be sure. He knew Jake was a player and currently stringing along an Italian actress called Sofia, who had a minor part in the film. Sarah was however, perfectly capable of making her own decisions.

In the past he had taken it upon himself to look out for Elenour, because she had got mixed up with the wrong crowd occasionally. She was fragile and extremely vulnerable and some people wouldn't believe it but, he knew she was quite an innocent at times. She'd also had some major issues with alcohol and this led to her making some very bad choices with the men in her life. Most of whom were only interested in her for the fame. But she did actually need his help, or should he say intervention, but Sarah was a different kettle of fish.

His own past had not been entirely straightforward. His father had walked out on them all when he had been just 15. After his father had had several affairs, his mother had been left heartbroken and humiliated. He himself had had to grow up fast back then and very quickly stepped up to become the man of the household, taking care of his mother Celia, and his younger sisters, Becky and Lisa. Celia, had relied heavily on him and for a time he'd hated his father for what he had done to her and for abandoning them all. He had always looked up to his him growing up, and was so very proud of his achievements. Naturally he had missed him dreadfully after he'd left.

He had become one angry young man for a while. However, over the years he had begun to develop a good relationship with his father and once again, there was, a special bond between them. He'd also realised that his mother was not the easiest of women to live with, not that he was excusing the way his father had treated her.

His parents had married young, when Celia had just turned nineteen and his father only twenty and from what he had been told, he knew they'd been happy, for a while at least. At that time his father had been a struggling actor whose dream, was to become a famous actor! He certainly had the looks, but when this didn't happen, he decided to work his way up in the industry. He learnt his craft and became a very successful director and then a producer. From a young age, Steve had always known that he wanted to follow in his father's footsteps. Celia's parents were very wealthy and his mother never missed an opportunity to remind him that if it hadn't been for their help, his father would never have made it.

To be fair though his mother had forgiven him for a couple of his father's affairs, before he finally left her for a young French actress called Amiele. His parents divorced and his father eventually married Amiele and he had a half-sister, Francine and they lived in Nice in the South of France. He didn't believe he was like his father, whatsoever. It was true to say however that just like his father he too had a great appreciation for a beautiful woman, but the whole marriage thing wasn't for him he'd always known that.

They arrived back at the hotel and Steve wondered what the heck he would tell Sarah, as to why he'd brought her away from the party. His actions he knew had been irrational and would be difficult to explain. He gently woke Sarah up. When she eventually stirred, she looked slightly dazed and yawned, whilst she tried to wake up fully. "Oh my goodness, how long have I been asleep."

"Ages and you were snoring." Sarah pulled a face and shook her head, she wasn't normally someone who snored! Steve went round to open the car door for her. "Right, out you get." he said rather sharply.

"Okay, give me a minute. Well, at least give me your hand Steve."

"No, you look to be doing an okay job to me!" This wasn't true, but Sarah decided she'd come out backwards and nearly fell over on to the floor! She looked at Steve and spat out, "Thanks for nothing!"

"I will just go and park the car and then meet you upstairs," Steve said passing her handbag over to her, and Sarah made her way into the Hotel and up to her room, barefoot. She nipped into the bathroom and went into the loo, and checked herself out in the mirror. Her hair was a complete mess after the ride in the Ferrari and resembled a bird's nest. Still what did it matter now, as it was almost mi-night and the party was well and truly over, for her at least. She took out the pins from her hair, which didn't come out easily and it was rather painful and she gave it a thorough brush through, before tying it back into a ponytail with an elastic band. She knew she'd overdone it with the champagne tonight, but somehow after her little sleep on the way back to the Hotel, her head did in fact feel a little clearer! However with a clearer head, she also began to feel really cross with Steve for dragging her away from the party.

Everyone else would be partying right into the early hours. She was also going to miss the fireworks and the flame-throwers, which she'd organised. Why did Steve have to go and spoil her night! She wouldn't mind but over the past few weeks, she had occasionally worked some extremely long days, which she thought went above and beyond the call of duty.

Reluctantly, she picked up her laptop and work folder and made her way up to Steve's suite and knocked on the door. After a couple of good hard knocks, Steve finally opened the door and because, Sarah was still feeling a bit irksome, she pushed past Steve and asked. "So what is this big emergency about then, that you need to drag me away from the best wrap party ever."

"Um so how many have you actually been to before?" Steve asked.

"Well, none, but everyone told me it was the best one they'd ever been to!"

"Anyhow, I thought we had done just about everything and ticked all of the boxes until we get back home, more or less!"

Steve knew there was absolutely no point in trying to make some feeble excuse up now, as Sarah would see right through it. He decided to come clean. He hesitated for a while still unsure of what he would say. "Actually there isn't one."

"Pardon, what do you mean there isn't one?"

"Just what I said, Sarah."

"Are you for real, you actually brought me away from the party for nothing and under false pretences!"

"Oh don't be so melodramatic!" Sarah sighed loudly and could feel her blood boil as she hurled at him. "Well, you're jolly well going to have to find one," she said as she sat herself down onto one of the comfy sofas in Steve's suite, "because I'm not budging from here until you fully explain yourself to me!"

Steve looked slightly awkward and she knew she'd put him right on the spot. "Well, what can I say?"

"The truth would be a good place to start, Steve, don't you think?"

"Yes, I guess you're right," he said, smoothing his dark hair back, "and I do at least owe you that much." He took his time before saying. "Well the truth is Sarah, I just worry about you, simple as."

"Worry about me, are you joking? Why would you do that?"

"I don't know I'm struggling with that one myself Sarah right now. Maybe it's because I think that Jake wouldn't be good enough for you and I don't want to see you get hurt." Sarah could feel herself getting even more angry with Steve if that was at all possible, as she got up from the sofa. Who the hell did Steve think he was. He had no right to try and meddle in her personal life.

"How dare you, Steve, that doesn't make any sense to me and my life should be of no concern to you whatsoever. I am after all a grown woman and perfectly able to make my own decisions on whomever I want to spend time with. I work for you, Steve, you don't own me, nobody does! Anyhow, I don't care what you think about Jake, as I happen to think that he is a lovely guy and I love it that he appears to like me too! So what if he's younger than me. Is that it, you probably think that I am some poor desperate divorcee grateful for some male attention?" She didn't give Steve the opportunity to reply before she said, "Well, do you?" she shouted back at him. She knew that she was ranting on somewhat, but she couldn't stop herself now. Her anger had truly come to the fore! However, there was a little part of her that was flattered that Steve appeared to care about her.

This time it was Steve who became angry and his face drained of any colour, as he came closer to her. "Of course that is not the reason, Sarah, I just don't want you to do anything you may regret, that's all."

"What like have a bloody good time for instance!"

"No, I knew you'd been drinking tonight and as I said to you before, Jake has a reputation."

"What and you don't? I have read up on you, Steve, so that's rich coming from you quite frankly!"

"Okay, maybe I will take that one on the chin, but I never ever mislead anyone. I'm always honest and upfront."

"And for the record, I've been too busy for any women of late."

"Oh really, poor you."

"So what are you now, some kind of bloody Saint?"

"Now you're just being ridiculous Sarah!"

"Well, you should at least come down from off that pedestal which you've so clearly put yourself on Steve!"

It had quickly become heated and tense between the two of them, as they squared up to one another. Sarah was secretly pleased to see Steve squirm, whilst defending his actions! The two of them stood opposite one another and it was like a proper stand-off, as they glared back into each other's eyes and Sarah now had the urge to laugh, but managed to control herself. Suddenly Steve took her by surprise as he leaned forward and pulled her towards him, wrapping his arms tightly around her. Their lips locked together in a passionate lingering kiss, which seemed to go on forever. Once again there was a fire burning inside of Sarah, as it had done when she'd been with Jake, but this time the flames were burning right up through to the rooftops. She responded to Steve's kisses with fervour and her heart was beating loudly, but then he pulled away from her, rather abruptly and shook his head and looked troubled. "No, no, we need to stop, Sarah, this is a bad idea!" Sarah was breathless from their kiss and her heart was still beating fast.

She touched his face gently and said, "No, I don't want you to stop," and in a hushed whisper said, "please, Steve." Her green eyes had a fire in them, which were dazzling and full of mischief and ultimately rendered him powerless to resist her. He kissed her once again, but with even more passion this time, and it wasn't long before they found themselves in Steve's bedroom.

"Do you know what you're doing Sarah?"

"Oh yes I most certainly do," she said full of anticipation.

"You know that I don't do the whole commitment thing, but I do, however, happen to think that you are one of the most gorgeous human beings I've ever known."

"Oh why don't you shut up Steve, or should I say, Mr I Don't Do Commitment!"

"Steve, really there's no need for you to panic, because in the long term I don't want or need anything from you, but right now, I do need you and want you." Steve pulled Sarah towards him, and let her hair fall down past her shoulders, as he ran his hands gently through her thick mane. He kissed the nape of her neck and slowly began to undo the zip of her white jumpsuit, which instantly fell to the floor, revealing that she was wearing a scanty little pair of undies and as he'd suspected nothing else. Sarah quickly slipped out of it. He looked at her full rounded breasts, as he drunk in her naked body, and he was extremely aroused by now, as Sarah rapidly undid the buttons on his shirt and he did the rest himself and soon discarded all of his clothes.

He kissed Sarah's breasts and teased them gently with his tongue and took her into his arms and they both fell back onto the bed together. Sarah sat back up almost immediately with panic in her voice, as she said, "Sorry, Steve, but do you have a thingy?"

"What do you mean a thingy?"

"You know, some protection, because if you don't, I have some in my room."

Steve raised his eyebrows and said in a mocking tone, "Oh yes, tell me more!"

Sarah laughed as she said, "Oh, I didn't actually buy them myself, Steve, I swear. My best friend, Annabel, gave them to me and insisted that I bring them with me, well you know, just in case! She said I should always practice safe sex."

"What a sensible friend you have," Steve said as he opened the drawer of his bedside cabinet and took out a small bright pink packet, which he waved into the air. Sarah didn't see any point in revealing to Steve that Annabel was now actually pregnant, by her married boss!

Steve began to kiss Sarah and then cupped her breasts within his hands, and kissed and teased her nipples until they became firm and erect. They explored each other's bodies with an intensity that overwhelmed them both, as they moved around the bed. Steve finally entered her and they made love. There was nothing rushed about their lovemaking, as Sarah squealed with pleasure as they climaxed together. Such was their passion they instantly made love once more and then fell asleep for a short time, only to awake and make love all over again.

Neither of them appeared tired as they chatted idly about some of the funniest moments which had happened on set and, of course, some of the dramas behind the scenes too! There was a definite ease between them and she'd found herself telling Steve about how her marriage to Richard had ended and how they had unfortunately been unable to have children. Steve's only comment was that Richard sounded like a complete arse hole.

Sarah hadn't been this happy in a long time and it was as if they were the only two people that existed, or even mattered in the world. Still this was Steve and she knew that the bubble which she currently found herself in, would probably burst at any moment! Steve was a very good lover and long after they'd made love, Sarah's body was tingling from their lovemaking, before she had finally drifted off to sleep, safe and secure in Steve's arms.

However, sleep eluded Steve because he felt as guilty as hell. What had he done? Sarah was a beautiful and decent woman and the sex he'd just had with her, had been absolutely amazing. She did, however, deserve better than he could ever offer her now, or in the future. He made up his mind there and then, that it shouldn't ever happen again. It would have to be a one-off. He truly hoped that she wouldn't regret what they had just shared and more importantly, that working together wasn't about to become awkward. He couldn't imagine not working with her, as she had certainly impressed him with her commitment and enthusiasm, which were invaluable. But more than that, she was a kind and compassionate woman to everyone on set. In particular, she knew how to handle

Elenour and she had become more like an older sister to her. In fact, just as she had told him back in the beginning, she really had turned out to be the best damn PA he'd ever had by far. As the Americans would say, he wouldn't want to screw things up between them, but maybe he already had.

Chapter 22

Having arrived home some weeks ago, time was flying by and soon it would be Christmas. It had all been extremely busy since their return from Italy and most of that time had been spent at the Studios, and fortunately everything was looking good in post-production. Sarah was loving this part of the film making process as much as she had done whilst on location. She was learning fast on her feet and it was such a joy for her to be in this position. She did however, miss the sunshine which she'd got used to whilst they had been in Tuscany. It was a complete learning curve for her and she was totally absorbed by everything around her. She liked to think that if her dad was looking down on her, that he would be proud of her. It was a path which she knew her dad would have loved to have gone down, for sure.

After their night together, the atmosphere between Sarah and Steve had been a little strained at first, but now their workload was so heavy that there was little or no time whatsoever for her to think about what had happened back in Tuscany.

For her, though it would always remain a moment of madness, but one which she would never forget and certainly had no regrets about. She wasn't under any illusion where Steve was concerned and it was absolutely fine with her. She didn't need to be in a relationship with Steve, or anyone else for that matter. Maybe in the future, if she met the right person, but not at the moment.

Fortunately, they had more or less eased back into their working relationship and as always, she worked and conducted herself in a totally professional manner. Steve still occasionally barked his orders at her when he was stressed and she always did as she was asked, wherever feasible. She would also crack the occasional joke to ease the tension and it seemed to be working so far. Before leaving Italy, they had had a brief and rather awkward conversation and both agreed that what had happened between them, should remain strictly a 'one off'! Neither of them wanted anything to come between their working relationship.

Sarah had also managed to catch up with Annabel who was positively glowing, and now had a rather large baby bump, which was quite noticeable, probably due to the fact that she was so petite. Whilst she'd been away, they had kept in regular contact and used to Skype whenever they could. Sarah had been lucky enough to see pictures of all of the baby scans, which Annabel had sent to her, but so far Annabel had resisted the temptation of finding out the sex of her baby. Sarah had spent a fortune whilst in Italy buying baby outfits and a cuddly bear for baby Armstrong, all in neutral colours and Annabel had been delighted when she had given them to her.

Annabel also mentioned that it had become extremely awkward at work recently and the atmosphere between her and Liam continued to be fairly strained. Everyone either knew or suspected that Liam was the father of Annabel's baby, but most pretended otherwise, with the exception of Tara, Annabel's Personal Assistant, who was more of a friend to her. Annabel could hardly wait now to go on her maternity leave as she was finding the whole situation between her and Liam, stressful. Apparently, her mother had been on the scene a lot more recently and Sarah had been pleased as it was clear that they were now finally becoming so much closer. This was exactly what Sarah had always hoped for and she was delighted for them both.

Sarah wasn't overly surprised with Dotty's news, which had been that she and George were seeing one another. It was clear from the start that there had been a chemistry between the pair and anyway, they both deserved some happiness in their later years. Dotty as always had been overly dramatic by saying that she had a bit of a bombshell to drop on her, which was so typical of her.

She'd, always been a terrible flirt too, which was part of her make-up, but this time it must be different. Tony apparently was less than pleased and had been rather off-hand about it with Dotty. Subsequently, he'd said that he, Megan and the children wouldn't be spending Christmas day with them this year, purely because Dotty had invited George. Sarah knew that like Margaret Thatcher, this wouldn't deter her mother whatsoever, as 'this lady wasn't for turning!'.

Dotty would not change her mind and why should she? Sarah was of the opinion that her mother was entitled to see and do whatever she wanted with her life and Sarah, would never stand in her way. Dotty deserved to find some happiness and George was a fine man. Tony would hopefully have a change of heart soon. He was very much like their dad and he was prone to being a bit intolerant at times. Maybe he felt that it would be disloyal to his father's memory. Sarah had already had a word with him so she hoped that he would see sense and realise that he wasn't being fair to his mother!

Chapter 23

Sarah woke up early on Christmas Eve to a quiet, still morning and as she got out of the bed and looked out of her bedroom window, to her surprise, snow was gently falling and there was a light covering right across the whole garden. *Oh heck*, she thought, she'd have to get her act together now as she still had lots of last-minute shopping to do for herself and Steve. He was flying out to LA to spend Christmas with his mother and sisters that night. She quickly showered and got dressed and went downstairs to prepare breakfast for Steve and George. Poor Molly had had to rush back to Cork to be with her mother, as she had been taken ill suddenly and was in hospital. She'd been so distraught before she'd left and Steve had told her to take as long as she needed and they could manage. Sarah had been happy to take on some of her duties and naturally, cooking was never a problem for her. George was already in the kitchen, trying to towel dry Buster, who had clearly already been outside in the snow and was still trying to shake it off his fur. He did however manage to escape George's clutches and greet her in his usual way by jumping up and trying to lick her face.

She gave him a hug and made a fuss of him and rather naughtily gave him a little treat from the cupboard, and George's disapproving look didn't escape her notice either. "Morning, George, if this carries on, we could go outside later and build a snowman!"

"Morning, Sarah, I'm hoping it is going to stop as I have to run the boss up to Heathrow tonight, but I don't think it will be too bad do you?"

"Probably not up here, but I'm a bit concerned about driving down to Biddenford."

"I think I'd better try and get away earlier."

"Yes, it may be best."

"I've put the coffee on for you."

"Oh thank you, George. I think Steve requires scrambled eggs and grilled tomatoes today, nothing too taxing. What about you, would you like something George?"

"I'll have the same as the boss if that's okay?"

"Of course it is. So are you looking forward to tomorrow and spending Christmas Day with us?"

"You do know Mum's invited her two Pals, Pat and Annie too."

"They're hilarious and very full on, like mum."

"Yes I do, and I'm looking forward to meeting them, as I haven't had the pleasure yet."

"You might not say that after you've met them though."

"I think it best if you have some, paracetamol's handy, just in case." George smiled and said, "So I hear." He was quiet for a while before saying. "Actually, Sarah I was thinking about not going, you know because I don't want to make things difficult for your mother. It wouldn't be right. It's Christmas and families should spend it together, whenever they can."

"Oh don't be so silly, George. Mum will be very upset if you don't come."

"My mother is a very strong and independent woman and she knows her son very well and I am sure he will get used to the idea of you and Mum being together."

"Maybe not just yet, but in time."

"Mum wouldn't ever try to rule Tony's life and she's always been so supportive of everything he has done, and he certainly has no right to do that to Mum," she said emphatically. Sarah put her arm around George's shoulder, "Say that you will come, George."

"I'm not so sure, Sarah."

"Well, you're coming and that's that!"

"Thanks, Sarah, I was a bit concerned about how you'd react, but deep down, I knew you'd be okay about it."

"Why wouldn't I be, and as Molly would say I'm happy for yous both!"

"I could see immediately that there was a little spark between you and Mum and you most certainly have my blessing George. I think the pair of you were made for each other and it may sound silly, but I think Dad would have liked you too."

"Anyhow he wouldn't want Mum to be lonely and even though she leads a full life and certainly doesn't let the grass grow under her feet, I think occasionally she has been!"

"Tony is just being selfish!"

After a busy day up in London and a fairly traumatic journey down to Kent, Sarah finally pulled up outside her mother's cottage. Dotty came outside immediately to greet her wearing her warm winter's coat and a pair of wellies. "Oh my lord, Sarah I have been so worried about you."

"Thank god you're here safe and sound." Sarah got out of the car and hugged her mother.

"I'm glad to be here too, driving on the motorway wasn't too bad, but some of the roads around here are a bit treacherous."

"Come inside love and I'll make you a nice cuppa." Sarah slumped down onto Dotty's comfy sofa and her mother quickly brought through her cup of tea. "Here you are, love," Dotty said, as she sat down next to her daughter. "I thought you would like a piece of my fruitcake as well. It's only a small bit."

"Oh, Mum, thank you I'm ready for this I can tell you. The tree looks lovely and festive as usual."

"Well, I do try, and it took me the best part of three days to decorate it mind. I've told George not to bother to come down tonight, if this weather continues, because I will be worrying about him otherwise. My nerves have been stretched enough worrying about you coming down in this snow!"

"Well I am sure he will be sensible, Mum, he is, after all, a very wise man."

"Oh yes I have noticed, Sarah."

"You have? So should I be looking at buying myself a hat, Mum?"

"Oh don't be so ridiculous, Sarah, of course not. We're just very good friends and he is, as you know, a real gentleman."

"I know he is, Mum. He should be leaving shortly to drop Steve off at Heathrow Airport for his flight to LA."

"Yes, George did mention it to me. What's the weather like up in London then?"

"Not as bad as here, fortunately."

"I shouldn't think it will interfere with Steve's flight."

"George thinks the world of his Lordship, doesn't he?"

"I think, Mum, that Steve has been very good to him over the years."

"Anyway, will you stop calling him his Lordship, he's not like that at all."

"Oh I see, defending him now, are you?"

"Is there something that you should be telling me?"

"Like what, Mum? Don't be daft," Sarah said hurriedly, putting on her best poker face. "I think I am a bit too old for Steve Fountain. He likes his ladies young, as well you know," and to throw her mother completely off the scent said, "Anyway, Jake Edwards has paid me quite a lot of attention whilst I have been in Tuscany."

"You lucky girl. Isn't he a bit young for you though?"

"Not from where I've been standing, Mum," Sarah said giving her mother a smug look and Dotty laughed.

Hopefully she'd successfully steered her mother away from discussing Steve any further. "So tell me," Dotty asked, "how is that handsome James Hunter?"

"He is actually quite shy, Mum, and keeps himself to himself a lot of the time. He's playing the baddie in this film, and I think he is a method actor, so we didn't get to spend too much time with him off set."

"Okay, Mum, I'm going to take my stuff up to my room so I will see you in a moment."

"All right love. I've made us a nice vegetarian lasagne for tonight."

"Yummy, see you in a little while," Sarah said as she walked up to her old, but familiar bedroom with its flowery pink wallpaper and her faithful teddy bear, Mr Ted sitting on her bed with his one eye!

Sarah unpacked her bags, changed her clothes and went downstairs to find her mother who was on the phone. "Okay George, well I will see you when I see you then."

"What's up, Mum, isn't George coming down now?"

"No, apparently that boss of yours has come down with some kind of flu bug and he wasn't well enough to get on the plane to fly out to LA. According to George he almost passed out at the airport and was sick."

"Oh dear, I knew he wasn't feeling too good earlier on, but I thought he just had a heavy cold."

"Well you know what men can be like, he's probably just got man-flu."

"No, Mum, you don't know Steve, he's tough."

"Oh he'll be all right because George is going to stay and keep an eye on him."

"Sorry, Mum, that's rather disappointing for you though isn't it?"

"Well it is, but it's just one of those things isn't it!"

"Poor Steve, he must be feeling rough, if he hasn't flown out to be with his mother for Christmas. She rings him constantly now we're back home."

"Have you seen much of her Sarah?"

"No, because she spends a lot of time in LA."

"But I have spoken to her several times on the phone and although she's always polite she isn't overly friendly!"

"She's quite demanding where Steve's concerned, so I guess she won't be happy that he's not going to be with the family on Christmas Day."

"Well he can hardly help that, can he?"

"No of course not."

"Still he will be going out there in the New Year as he is in negotiations to direct his next film."

"Oh my aren't we moving in fancy circles."

"I love it, Mum, I really do."

"I can see that Sarah and it's so nice for you and it's clear to see that you're much happier than you have been in a long time."

"Yes I am and so are you. I don't feel I have to worry about you as much now you've got George in your life."

"I wouldn't go that far Sarah, but he's very good company," Dotty said rather coyly!

Chapter 24

It was Christmas day, and Sarah woke up feeling sleepy, as she glanced at her watch and was horrified to see that it was nearly 12 o'clock. Oh my goodness, what was wrong with her. She threw back her duvet and got up and threw on her dressing gown and made her way downstairs into the kitchen. She could already smell the turkey, which was cooking in the Aga and Dotty stood at the kitchen sink peeling the Brussel sprouts and had on her red Mrs Christmas Hat that she wore every year. "Oh there you are love, Merry Christmas," Dotty said as she kissed and hugged her daughter.

"Merry Christmas to you, Mum. Have you been drinking already, Mum?"

"Might have just had a small sherry with a mince pie."

"You've started early!"

"Well it's Christmas Day after all," Dotty said. "So did you enjoy your lie in?"

"Yes thanks, Mum, but you should have woke me up earlier!"

"I thought you must need the sleep, which clearly you did."

"Yes, maybe you're right. I cannot even remember the last time I laid in."

"Well there you are then. Here we go, the kettle has just boiled, do you want a cuppa?"

"Yes please."

The two women sat around the kitchen table and sipped their tea. "I feel so guilty, Mum, I haven't done anything."

"Don't you worry about that. You know I love everything about Christmas, even peeling the Brussel sprouts!"

"Would you like your pressie now, Mum, or later?"

"No let's open them up later and it will give us something to look forward to won't it?"

"Okay."

"Come and have a look at the table," Dotty said and Sarah followed her into the dining room, where they always ate their Christmas dinner these days.

"Oh, Mum, the table looks amazing."

Dotty had really gone to town as usual, with lots of candles which had been lit and placed all around the dining room and pretty fairy lights too. Christmas ornaments and regalia were everywhere in red and gold. Maybe just a little over the top, but that summed Dotty up, as she was a way over the top character. She absolutely loved Christmas. Her mother was a traditionalist who took pride in all that she did. Right from the time, when Sarah and Tony were children, she'd always made it fun. Goodness knows how many crackers were on the table and Sarah knew that Dotty would insist on every joke being read. Dotty looked particularly pleased with herself. "Oh I do love Christmas, Sarah."

"I know you do, Mum, and it shows."

"Well I do my best, love."

The doorbell interrupted them. "Oh that must be Pat and Annie."

"Why don't you pop up and get yourself ready. No need for you to worry, because there's plenty of time and me and the girls can have some pre-lunch drinky poos. I'm ready for my G and T now!"

"Thanks, Mum." Sarah stopped half-way up the stairs and called out to her mother. "Hey, not too much drink, Mum eh, don't want you passing out before you've cooked our dinner!"

"Cheeky girl, don't panic, I will pace myself," was her mother's response!!

Considering only four females were sitting around the table, it had been a rather raucous affair and they had all eaten and drunk far too much. Each one of them sat, festooned and bejewelled in their cheap jewellery from the crackers and Dotty had told them that they must all wear their party hats!

"That was a lovely meal, Mum," and they all heaped praise on Dotty for her home-made Christmas pudding.

"It was delicious Mum, as always," Sarah told her and Pat and Annie also agreed and said they were stuffed to the Gunnels.

"You know it's been my pleasure. My Jeffery always loved my Christmas pud, didn't he Sarah?" she said with her eyes misting over.

"Yes he did, Mum, in fact he enjoyed all of your cooking," Sarah replied. After the meal was over, they sat down and played an hilarious and lengthy game of charades and Dotty became completely hysterical when none of them could guess her one, which had been, 'Bend It Like Beckham', exclaiming to them all

177

that she was about to wet herself. Just before 10 p.m., everyone was getting tired and Pat and Annie took their leave. Sarah had insisted both women had a strong coffee before they'd left to sober them up a bit. She'd also offered to walk them both home, but they had insisted that they would be absolutely fine. Sarah, however, was a little concerned for them, because of the snow, but at least it had stopped.

"Right, Mum, you go and sit down and I will clear away and load up the dishwasher."

"I can do that love, no need to worry."

"No you won't, you've done enough today."

"Have you had a nice day, Mum?" Dotty became emotional as she took Sarah's hand into her own.

"It's been lovely to have you back Sarah, just like old times. Of course, I've missed the kids not being here and no George either."

"Well, George will be down with you tomorrow." Sarah had taken the decision to go back up to London, to take care of Steve in his hour of need and let George enjoy some of his Christmas.

"Yes, that will be lovely, but I wish you weren't going back so soon, Sarah. I don't half miss you, you know, love, I think I got used to you being here."

"I miss you too, Mum."

"Still George and me becoming," Dotty paused slightly before saying, "friends has given me a new lease of life. He takes me out most Sundays and we have a lovely roast in a nice pub somewhere. He really spoils me. I've proper got me mojo, and me je ne sais quoi back too."

"I don't think you ever lost it, Mum!"

"Come on why don't we open our pressies up?"

"Ooh yes, how could I have forgotten!" Sarah collected their presents from under the tree, which as usual had the Christmas pudding she'd made out of felt as a child and Tony's wooden star hung upon it. She put their presents into two neat piles and they opened up each of their gifts. "Right, here's mine for you, Mum," Sarah said handing her the pretty little purple and gold box, which she had so lovingly wrapped for her mother.

"Oh I'm so excited," Dotty said as she tore the paper off and opened the present with anticipation. As soon as she opened the box, Dotty went very quiet and then became emotional. "Oh love they're beautiful. You shouldn't have." Sarah's gift to her mother was a pair of sapphire and diamond earrings.

"You're such a naughty girl and I don't deserve these!" Sarah looked directly into her mother's eyes. "Yes you most certainly do, Mum, you're the best mum ever."

"They look expensive, love."

"No, they're not I got them out of one of last year's crackers."

"Oh yes," Dotty said laughing, "I don't think so!"

"Actually I bought them whilst in Florence, I couldn't resist them and I knew they'd be perfect for you. Blue is your colour, Mum, and they match your eyes! And what girl doesn't like diamonds!"

"ME, I love them," she cried. "Would you like yours now, Sarah?"

"Yes please, Mum." Dotty also took a small box from behind the tree which she'd hidden earlier and passed it to her daughter. "I hope you like it, love."

"I'm sure I will, Mum. Now I am the one who is excited," Sarah exclaimed as she unwrapped her present. Sarah looked inside the box and was speechless for a moment, as she just stared at the beautiful gold heart and could hardly believe her eyes. Dotty was beaming at her. "I had it made especially for you, love. You know that lovely picture of you and Dad on your 16th birthday? Well, Tony had it enlarged for me and I took it into Jaggards, the jeweller's shop and they copied it from that."

Sarah began to cry. "Oh, Mum, thank you."

"I have always felt so guilty for losing that locket."

"I know you did. But Dad never knew love, men don't notice things like that and I didn't tell him either."

"Anyway, you've got it back now, well as good as anyway."

"Best present ever, Mum, you're such a clever woman."

"Yes I believe I am love." The two women were both in tears and emotional once again.

"I miss him so much, Mum,"

"So do I, so do I." Sarah grabbed some tissues and they both wiped their eyes and blew their noses.

"Sarah," Dotty hesitated, "I wish you would change your mind about rushing back up to London so soon. Do you really have to go back, love?"

"Yes I do, but it's difficult for me to explain it to you, Mum."

"Are you sure Sarah, there's nothing more to all of this?"

"Like what, Mum?"

"Steve Fountain, for instance!"

"You're like a clucking hen mothering everyone. What with looking after him and that flighty young madam, Elenour Seymour."

"Oh I don't mind Elenour and she's not that bad really, once you get to know her."

"Anyhow, I prefer to think of myself as her elder sister."

"Well, it seems to me that Steve Fountain has you wrapped around his little finger."

"No, Mum, it's not like that at all, he's been really good to me honestly. Yes he barks his orders at me sometimes and naturally I am no more than his gofer. But, there are other times when he has taken the time to share so much of his knowledge of film making with me. He's taught me a lot about lighting and sound and he told me I have a very good artistic eye."

"Oh, did he indeed," Dotty said, shaking her head from side to side.

"Doing this job, Mum, really has helped me to move on and turn a corner."

"Yes, I realise that Sarah," Dotty said, "but just you remember I also know you better than you think and I don't want to see you get hurt again that's all." Sarah had forgotten just how intuitive her mother could be.

"No Mum, there is nothing for you to worry about, it's purely a working relationship," she said. Was she trying to convince her mother, or herself? Sarah was after all telling the truth, yes they'd had sex, but that was all, not a real relationship, not in the way her mother thought anyhow! Would she like it to be, she didn't want to go there and pushed such thoughts out of her mind.

"Yes, and I am telling you, that I'm not sure I believe you Sarah! Anyway, I guess I am going to have to take your word for it, aren't I?"

"I think you are, Mum."

"Also I've promised Molly that I would keep her kitchen pristine whilst she's away. Goodness knows what it will be like now, because although George does have many attributes, keeping a kitchen tidy isn't one of them. He's extremely messy and he leaves the tops off the milk and the marmalade and he cannot cook either. More importantly though Mum, I really want George to come and celebrate part of Christmas with you, it's only fair. He doesn't have any family here what with his daughter living in Washington."

"I guess you're right." Sarah could tell that something else was troubling her mother.

"What's wrong, Mum?"

"I'm not going to lie to you, Sarah, I have really missed not seeing Tony and the family today. Although, it was really nice of Megan to pop round yesterday with the girls and at least, I was able to give them their presents."

"Don't worry, Mum, Tony will come around."

"Yes I know, that's what Megan said."

"He definitely takes after your dad, don't you think?"

"Yes, he is more like him than me."

"What do you mean, stubborn-like?"

"Yes, that's exactly what I mean."

"Yes, he is, I'm afraid," Dotty said and sighed!

Sarah hugged her mother, "He'll get used to the idea Mum, and you're entitled to have some fun and friendship in your life."

"Yes, you're right."

"After all the alcohol, Mum, do you fancy a coffee?"

"I didn't have that much actually," Dotty replied sounding slightly miffed. Sarah rolled her eyes at her mother who said, "Oh shut up and put the kettle on, will ya?"

Chapter 25

The next morning, after an emotional farewell with Dotty, Sarah made good time up to London and thankfully the roads were better than they had been on Christmas Eve. She arrived back at Steve's house just before 11.30 a.m. The roads had also been exceptionally quiet. Dotty had still been a bit upset at her decision to go and look after Steve, or 'his Lordship', as she continued to insist upon calling him. She also wouldn't let Sarah leave without preparing her a huge breakfast and she doubted that she would need to eat for the rest of the day. She would actually be seeing her mother sooner than Dotty realised, as she had a nice little surprise lined up for her early in the New Year, which Steve was helping her out with. She knew Dotty would love it.

Sarah entered the house and went straight into the kitchen, and she wasn't overly surprised to see a sink full of dirty dishes. It was just as well Molly wasn't there, as she would probably have had a fit. She would put them into the dishwasher later. George looked surprised to see her, when he came in moments later, from the utility room, holding the laundry basket. Buster wasn't too far behind him and he ran over immediately and she bent down to make a fuss of him as he tried to lick her face. George had clearly not heard her come in. "Hello George, sorry if I made you jump."

"No I'm all right, as you know, I was trained to expect the unexpected."

"Yes of course, your army training."

"Yes it never leaves you."

"I see you've been busy by the look of it. Yes, and I have just put a load in the washing machine. I didn't want to leave any dirty washing for you Sarah! The girls still have a few more days off, before they come back to resume their duties."

"Thanks George, that's very kind of you," Sarah said glancing towards the sink. "But what about the washing up?"

"You know me, I don't do dishes and I refuse to use that blasted dishwasher. I don't like wasting all that water! Give me a hoover and a dustpan and brush and I'm your man."

"Okay, I will let you off!"

"I was going to do it later, I promise!"

"I'm only teasing you, George. So how is the patient then?"

"He's steadily improving and his temperature has come right down now. He hasn't got much of an appetite at the moment and he still has a bad head according to him."

"Wow, he must be bad if he's in bed, but hopefully with some TLC he'll soon be on the mend, right George! Anyway, now I'm here you can get yourself off to Kent, George, and Mum is really looking forward to seeing you."

"I'm really looking forward to seeing her too," he said with a glint in his eyes.

"I know you are, George. Anyway, I had a wonderful day with her yesterday and her friends and now it's your turn. If you're lucky, there will be some of Mum's excellent Christmas pudding left over for you today!"

"Sounds lovely George said with a smile on his face. I guess I had better get myself off. I have my overnight bag packed so I am ready to go."

"Yes, you do that George and don't worry about that washing, I can pop it into the tumble drier later."

"Okay, thanks, Sarah. Oh and by the way Sarah, that silk tie you bought me was spot on. Thank you so much. It was an excellent choice."

"You're very welcome, George." Sarah had bought George a silk tie from Harrods, as she knew he had a penchant for an expensive tie, which he would no doubt team up with one of the many smart blazers that he nearly always wore.

Sarah waved George off and after putting her bag upstairs into her room, she knocked on Steve's bedroom door and when there wasn't a reply, she opened the door cautiously. She could see that Steve was completely distracted reading through some scripts, which were spread all over his bed, along with some used tissues, which she looked at rather disdainfully.

Without even looking up from what he was reading, it was clear he hadn't noticed her enter the room, as he said, "Hi, George."

"Hello Steve, sorry to disappoint you, but it's me." Steve looked up from what he was reading and said.

"Oh hello, Sarah. You really didn't have to come back for me you know. I think I am hopefully over the worst now, but I still appear to have got quite a lot of mucus though."

"Yes you do look poorly, but that is way too much information for me, thank you very much. Anyhow don't flatter yourself, because I actually came back to relieve George from his duties, so that he can spend some time with my mother."

"Oh, I see."

"Dotty, as you can imagine, was rather disappointed when he wasn't able to come down on Christmas Eve."

"Well, I did try to persuade him to go down, but he insisted on staying here with me."

"Of course, George wouldn't leave you Steve."

"Boy was I ill. I nearly passed out at the airport and that's when George said he didn't think I should make the journey. Reluctantly I had to agree with him."

"You've definitely been pushing yourself way too hard, Steve. I expect your mother was upset that you didn't make it!"

"She was initially, but she knew that I must be feeling real bad, otherwise nothing would have stopped me. I haven't got together with all of my family in a long time."

"Hopefully, you will see them in the New Year."

"Yes, I'm sure I will."

"Right, is there anything that can I get you?"

"I wouldn't mind a nice healthy honey and lemon drink, I'm so thirsty and my throat is still very sore. Also I'm nearly running out of these blackcurrant lozenges, could you get me some more please?"

"Yes of course, sir," Sarah said with a hint of sarcasm, which was totally lost on Steve. "Mum has given me some leftover turkey, so I could make you some nice soup with it if you like and I will add some fresh vegetables, so that it will be healthy for you!"

"That will do nicely, thank you. George gave me chicken soup yesterday, but it was out of a can!"

"Oh, how you've suffered, you poor man," Sarah said in a mocking tone! She was just about to take her leave, when Steve stopped her in her tracks.

"Here, if you get the time," he said gathering up some of the papers from his bed, "perhaps, you would like to read this script. I've cherry picked it from all the others, which have been sent to me and I would very much value your opinion."

"Really?"

"Yes, really."

"Okay, I will cast my mince pies over the script and give you my honest feedback."

"I think you've been spending too much time with Jake," Steve sent disapprovingly!

"No, not Jake, my mother actually!"

"So how is the lovely Dotty?" Steve asked.

"She is very well thank you and she sends you her best regards. She cooked a supreme Christmas dinner yesterday and then today, insisted on filling me up even more by cooking me a mega breakfast, before I left."

Steve laughed, "Perhaps, she thinks you're too skinny now?"

"No, I'm not, am I?"

"No, of course you aren't!" Steve said. In fact he thought she had the most perfect figure, and he found himself thinking about the time they had made love in Tuscany. He suddenly came over all hot, which wasn't necessarily down to the flu either. He forced all such thoughts from his mind as he said. "Oh by the way, I have spoken to James my friend at the Palladium and he is going to arrange it so that Dotty can see Cats. Also, she will get a guided tour around the theatre and back stage too. We just need to sort out a date."

"Oh that's brilliant news! Thank you so much, and it will be such a lovely surprise for her and she will be over the moon. I will arrange a date with Mum as soon as I can if that's okay. I will just say I am taking her out for the day shopping up in London."

"Sure, let me know, but don't leave it too long as it will take a bit of organising." Sarah looked directly at Steve. "I really do appreciate this Steve, thanks again."

"I know you do, my pleasure."

"I will be up shortly with your drink and I will see if we have any of those lozenges you need. I think I am going to be quite busy she said, looking at the script she was holding."

"There's no hurry for that Sarah, take your time."

After sorting out her travel bag, Sarah went down into the kitchen and made Steve his honey and lemon drink and luckily she'd found some more of the lozenges, which he'd asked for in one of the drawers. She took them up to him and went back into the kitchen and made a start on the home-made turkey and vegetable soup.

She also made some bread rolls to accompany it and with her Chef's hat off, she decided to take Buster for a walk to the local park. It was still quite cold outside and she was glad she'd dressed appropriately, but the temperature had clearly begun to warm up slightly, as the snow was beginning to slowly melt now. A snowman in a neighbour's front garden caught her attention, but sadly it was a rather forlorn sight, because it too appeared to be melting, as the carrot, which had clearly been used for its nose was now laying on the ground. With the snow about to disappear, she suddenly felt sorry for the children. What child and even some adults, didn't love to play outside in the snow, until they were horribly freezing cold and wet. Still at least they'd had a white Christmas and after all, that didn't always happen. Several young children were riding their brand new shiny bikes in the park, with their bells ringing loudly and a few joggers, who were probably trying to jog off some of what they had eaten the day before.

Buster tugged at his leash and she quickly let him off his lead and he ran off frantically as usual, but eventually he returned with a tatty old tennis ball which he'd found for her to throw for him. As he came back with the ball for the umpteenth time, she thought it would be a good opportunity to take advantage and slip his lead back on. That's it Buster, we're off home now, come on boy!

Back at the house, she fed Buster, who seemed to woof his food up in record time and retreated to his comfy bed, whilst she went upstairs again to check on Steve. She knocked gently on his bedroom door and popped her head around it, but this time Steve was sound asleep and he was making a loud snuffling noise! A script had been left open in front of him and his large black framed glasses, which he always wore for reading, were perched on the top of his head. She decided to leave him to sleep for a little while longer. He was a bit of a night owl at the best of times, so the more sleep he had, especially at the moment, the better.

Sarah thought it was strange to be in this huge house, practically alone, except for Steve upstairs asleep and Buster for company. She was more used to having lots of people around her as most days, it was quite a lively house. She also really missed Molly, who was such a full on and happy character to be around. She did, however, speak to her on Christmas Eve and she had been hopeful that she would be returning soon. Her mother was fortunately making a good recovery from her stroke. The place definitely wasn't the same without her presence. Still she took advantage of the situation and spread herself out onto one of the large sofas in the main lounge and began reading through the script, which Steve had asked her to read and she had quickly became engrossed in it. Buster was spread eagled at her feet on the sumptuous carpet, fast asleep, *this dog knew no shame*!

The premise of the script was about a young man who wins a huge amount of money on the lottery. Having come from a poor background in Ireland, he sets about changing his life completely, due to the money he now has but loses sight of who he is. He soon discovers that there is a downside to having a large sum of money and that there can be harsh consequences to his actions, before realising he has gone too far.

The time had slipped by and when Sarah eventually checked her watch it was almost 6:30 p.m. and she thought it was time she got Steve's supper ready for him. She popped the soup back onto the hob to heat it up and warmed through the bread rolls, which she'd made earlier in the oven. The kitchen smelt amazing and she now felt hungry herself. The walk in the park with Buster had definitely done her good.

She prepared a tray for Steve and took it up to him. This time he was wide-awake and hungry. At last he said, "I thought you'd forgotten me."

"As if. I'm surprised you haven't got yourself a bell? Or perhaps, given the size of this place, an intercom!"

"Now that's a good idea," Steve said laughing. He certainly looked a lot better, as he had a bit of colour back in his face now. After a second helping of the soup he declared it was delicious.

"Thanks, Steve."

"Well if that's all, I am off for an early night myself. See you in the morning."

"Night Sarah, and thank you."

"You're welcome."

However, after she'd had her supper, she picked up the script once again before jumping into bed. It was really enthralling and she read it right up until she could barely keep her eyes open any longer.

Chapter 26

Within a couple of days, Steve appeared to be making a full recovery and his appetite was certainly increasing. Sarah had now got herself into a routine and was managing to go to the gym early in the morning and what with taking Buster out, she felt a lot fitter. Steve was as demanding as ever, which was a clear indication that his health was indeed improving. He was back to barking his orders at her. She also now knew the true meaning of head cook and bottle washer. Still, Molly would be home by the end of the week, thankfully. She didn't really mind doing the extra work, but Steve, clearly didn't make any allowances for it whatsoever. At the moment, though, he was milking it for all it was worth, and he was still having breakfast in bed and his bedroom looked more like an office with every passing day.

Sarah took Steve's breakfast tray up to him and knocked on the door. "Enter. Oh, thank you M'lord, you're too kind. Here you are, as requested two poached eggs on toast and two rashers of crispy bacon. There is black coffee and freshly squeezed orange juice! If that will be all M'lord, may one please be excused?"

"No need to exaggerate Sarah, I'm not that bad am I surely?"

"I think you are extremely high maintenance actually," Sarah quipped as she raised her eyebrows at him! Steve just shrugged his shoulders.

"This looks good," he said as he began to eat his breakfast. She was just about to leave the room when he stopped her. "Oh by the way, could you change the sheets on my bed for me today. Also can you give Callum a call and cancel my session with him. I am not up to a full on session in the gym just yet."

"Of course, Steve." *Oh the joys of this job*, she thought *were endless*. She had almost made it out of the door, when he called out to her again.

"Oh Sarah."

"Yes Steve, what is it now," she said sounding slightly exasperated.

"I just wanted to say thanks for all you've done for me."

"My pleasure and by the way you've just totally redeemed yourself." Steve smiled and winked at her. The cheek of the man!

Sarah soon knuckled down and began by making some of the urgent phone calls which Steve had asked her to do, and answered a few emails. Callum was perfectly okay about Steve cancelling his session with him that day, because he knew he would still get paid, as Steve was generous to a fault. She realised she should put some washing on, which reminded her that Steve's sheets needed to be changed. Sarah walked back upstairs to the linen cupboard and took out some clean sheets, which smelt of the most amazing tropical fabric conditioner.

She knocked on Steve's bedroom door, and popped her head inside, and as there wasn't any sign of him, whatsoever, went straight in. She stripped the bedding from off his bed and put the fresh sheets on and walked through to the en-suite. She picked up a couple of dirty towels from off of the floor, which Steve had left lying around and thought him to be a *lazy* sod! As she walked back into the bedroom, she stopped in her tracks, as a rather wet and naked Steve was stood there, drying himself off with a towel. He looked totally shocked when he saw her, and rapidly wrapped his towel around himself. "Bloody hell Sarah, what are you doing in here," he asked her!

"Sorry, I thought you had gone downstairs."

"No, my power shower appears to have lost its power, so I used the one in the main bathroom!"

"Oh I see," Sarah said, barely containing her laughter. "What's so funny all of a sudden?"

"You, it's your face."

"Well, you took me by surprise, that's all."

"You really don't have to worry about your modesty, Steve, it's nothing that I haven't seen before, is it?" she blurted out. Where was her off button when she needed it, but it didn't stop her continuing? "So are you actually saying that I have embarrassed you?" Sarah asked him rather coyly. Steve noticed that Sarah's eyes had that same mischievous look, which he had seen once, before back in Florence and he instantly became aroused. Once again, their sexual chemistry was far too strong for either of them to resist. Steve's towel dropped onto the floor as they both fell backwards onto his bed. Soon they were both naked and Steve began to explore Sarah's body, kissing her breasts down to her belly button and beyond, as she moaned with pleasure. Suddenly he stopped and looked at her. "Hold on, isn't there something you're forgetting."

189

Sarah was breathless as she said, "What the heck do you mean?"

"You know, a thingy!"

"Oh my god, yes. Have you got any?" Sarah asked.

"Of course I have," he said, taking a condom out of his bedside drawer.

Sarah laughed and said teasingly, "I should give you a new name, Steve."

"Oh yes, and what might that be Sarah?"

"Ever Ready!" and Steve laughed.

"I always forget Sarah just how witty you are," he said as he pulled her into his arms once more and as they stared into each other's eyes, Steve asked her, "What are you doing to me Sarah, we weren't meant to do this again, were we?"

Sarah smiled and said, "Well, the same as what you are doing to me Steve, turning me on! Anyway, please," she said rather provocatively, "let's at least have the sex, before we do the whole recriminations thing."

Their lovemaking had been amazing yet again and it had taken Sarah off to somewhere that she didn't ever want to return from. When it was finally over, they both lay next to one another breathless. Sarah's heart was racing and her whole body was tingling, as it had when they had made love the last time. This time, however, Sarah sensed there was a slightly uncomfortable silence between them, which for some reason, made her feel awkward. She shut her eyes tight and wondered if Steve could possibly be having regrets about what had just happened. In case he was, she decided that she should get up out of bed and pulled the bed covers back, and quickly gathered up her clothes from off the floor. Without looking at Steve, she said in as bright and breezy manner as she could manage, "I don't know about you, Steve, but some of us have got work to do!"

Chapter 27

Steve thankfully had recently left for LA, once he was over his bout of man flu and would now be away for at least a couple of months whilst in negotiations with some important Hollywood producers. He would also spend some quality time with his family. Sarah felt relieved as it had become a little strained between them both of late. She realised that it would be sensible in future to keep their relationship purely about their work from now on. She had the feeling that it could all end up getting rather messy otherwise. She loved what she was doing so much and didn't want this particular phase of her life to end. Also, Sarah would be joining Steve in the middle of January and she was really excited about living in LA albeit, for a short time.

It was New Year's Eve and Sarah was happy to be spending it with Annabel and her baby bump and spend some quality time with her best friend. George had whisked Dotty away for the New Year to Bournemouth, staying in a five-star hotel and Dotty had been as pleased as punch at the prospect. Tony and Megan, along with the girls had surprised her by turning up on Boxing Day and they were all back on track once again. Sarah had always believed that this would be the case and was delighted for Dotty. Molly had also returned from Ireland and was cooking a meal for some of her friends later on. She'd told Sarah that she was happy to be back and naturally pleased because her mother had almost made a complete recovery, after her stroke. Sarah put her bags into her car and was almost ready to leave and just popped back into the house to say goodbye to Molly.

She found Molly in the dining room. "Oh Moll, the table looks resplendent, fit for a King or a Queen as always!"

"Oh, thank you Sarah, I appreciate that."

"So are you off now?"

"I am, indeed, and I cannot wait to spend New Year's Eve with Annabel, it's been far too long. I love having you back, Molly, I've really missed you. In fact we all have."

"It's grand being back at work, Sarah, and you know I have missed you all too, so I have."

"How did you find looking after himself?"

"Best you don't ask, but there is one word that springs to mind. Demanding!"

"That's for sure and I'm glad I wasn't here whilst he was unwell, I can tell you. He must have been a nightmare." Sarah laughed and agreed with her, but secretly thought to herself, *well not all of the time*. The two women kissed and wished each other a Happy New Year.

Sarah arrived at Annabel's apartment and quickly gave her friend a big hug and told her she was blooming, which was an understatement since the last time she'd seen her. It wasn't just the size of Annabel's tummy, that had changed either, because she no longer had her trademark red hair. It was still short, but now it was her natural colour of dark brown. "Oh my, look at you," Sarah cried. "Gorgeous!"

"Oh please, don't even kid me."

"You do, honestly Annabel, you look so well, motherhood must be agreeing with you."

"Well, I have to say, I feel really good, except that I am now the size of a house."

"No comment."

"Bitch," Annabel quipped.

"Only joking hun, you're only half the size of a house!" Annabel rolled her eyes at Sarah. "I also get very tired now, especially after a busy day at work."

"Still, not long to go, thank goodness."

"It must be awkward between you and Liam though."

"Yes, it can be and of course, we were as you know the subject of hot gossip around the office and the place was buzzing with it. Fortunately, things have settled down somewhat now and I guess it's yesterday's news!"

"Strictly business between the two of us now!" Sarah wasn't sure that she totally believed her friend.

"Really Annabel," Sarah said as she put her arm around her.

"Yes honestly I'm fine. It hasn't been easy for me, but even though Liam is an, well you know what he is, but I am not going to use that word anymore, as I

192

don't want to swear in front of my baby. Still he is the father of my baby and it wouldn't be good for me, or more importantly for the baby if I hate him."

"No, I agree."

"Does his wife know about the baby now?"

"Yep he told her and surprise, surprise, she is sticking by him."

"I know you and just about everyone else knew that he was never going to leave her."

"I am so sorry, Annabel."

"No, don't be. I was a fool to ever believe that he would. Still he is at least going to support me and our baby," she said looking down at her tummy and patting it.

"Anyhow, I certainly don't need him in my life and I can give this baby enough love for the both of us." The two women were emotional and hugged one another.

"Look at you," Sarah cried, "you've totally changed, there's a definite softness about you. I can tell you're going to be a brilliant mummy."

"Thanks Sarah, I hope so."

"I have to admit my mum has been unbelievably supportive too and we've been out shopping for baby bits together." Annabel looked at Sarah directly.

"I hope you don't mind, but I have asked her to be there at the birth along with you."

"Are you kidding me, that's the best news ever! Anyway, I'm going to spoil you whilst I'm here and the wonderful Molly has made us a lovely beef casserole for our meal tonight. She's having a dinner party for her friends, but she took the time to do something for us too. It smells amazing. All I have to do is make the starter and pud and don't worry as I have everything I need."

"You can just sit back and relax, Annabel!"

"Okay, thanks, you don't need to tell me twice."

Sarah and Annabel spent a quiet New Year's Eve, just enjoying each other's company as they saw the New Year in together, with non-alcoholic cocktails, certainly a first for Annabel and indoor fireworks, which had quite frankly been a bit of a let-down. They had chatted for hours and Annabel wanted to know all the gossip about what she called the exciting world of the film industry and how she'd found Florence.

Naturally she had quizzed her about Steve and eventually Sarah had told her that she had in fact slept with him, whilst in Tuscany. She kept quiet about the fact that it had happened again more recently. Sarah however, didn't quite get the response she thought she would. Annabel had been a little surprised exclaiming, "Oh my God, you didn't, did you?" and went on to warn her to be careful and not to get too involved with Steve. She thought Sarah could be playing with fire and she wouldn't want to see her bestie end up getting hurt. Sarah had promptly put her mind at rest by saying that she wasn't looking for any kind of a relationship, let alone with Steve Fountain. It had been just sex, pure and simple and she was after all, a single woman!

Annabel had laughed and called her a little hussy, which Sarah had thought was a bit harsh. Sarah knew she wasn't being entirely honest with her friend, but there had been some truth in what she'd told her. The sex between her and Steve had been like no other she'd ever experienced, not even with Richard, but she'd decided to keep that to herself. Maybe the newly sensible and wise Annabel would not have approved, who would ever have thought that. Impending motherhood had completely changed her best friend, which she found hard to get her head around, as Sarah had always been the more sensible one of the two. When Sarah had questioned Annabel about it, she'd laughed and blamed her hormones once more.

Whilst Sarah fully admitted to herself, that she could so easily fall for Steve's boyish charm, she should also be wary! In the past there had definitely been an ease between them, which although not necessarily tangible, she certainly felt its presence. Or was she in fact just fooling herself?

Chapter 28

Sarah had now been in LA for almost two weeks and she was certainly easing nicely into the way of life there. It was a wonderful place to be and she swam in the outside pool every morning. She was beginning to feel more relaxed as each day went by, as she found herself embracing the LA lifestyle, without too much effort. She also had regular workouts with Steve's trainer, Garth, who was an ex-marine and built like the size of a brick house and he definitely didn't pull any punches. It was relentless, and if she ever tried telling him she was tired, he would just shout at her to carry on and grow some balls. He wouldn't accept anything less than 100% commitment, which, if she was honest, was exactly what she needed. Everyone in LA was into the healthy lifestyle and although she already knew this, to see it at first-hand was something else. They all started the day with a healthy juice of some vile tasting, but healthy veggies and fruit juice which apparently were good for you and made your skin glow! The jury was still out on that one, but when in Rome! She'd also been to some very trendy Restaurants whilst there, where all the big Hollywood stars hung out and everyone liked to be seen. She had had a ball and was happy to people watch.

Steve certainly appeared happy and relaxed too, now that all of the post-production on (No Hiding Place) had been tied up and Tuscany now seemed like a distant dream. She also knew that he was buzzing about the idea of becoming involved in a new and exciting film, which was in the offing. The slight awkwardness that had continued briefly between them, had now passed and was back to a strictly working one only, and in fact if she wanted to continue working for Steve, it was going to be the only way. This time she was determined to do just that!

Before she'd left London, Sarah took Dotty on her surprise trip to the Palladium to see Cats. As a further surprise, Sarah had arranged for a couple of her old pals, who were part of her troupe, back in the day, to be there too. They had caused havoc whilst on the tour of the Palladium and were like cackling hens as they caught up with one another and reminisced about the good old days. It was clear for all to see, that they had all shared a special time together, being part of the infamous Tiller Girls. As a further surprise, Steve had joined them afterwards and treated everyone to Cocktails at the Shard and Dotty had been in her element. Sarah had been delighted to see her so happy and she had Steve to thank for that!

Steve had also kindly agreed to Sarah taking some time off in February to enable her to be at Annabel's side as her birthing partner, along with Julie, her mother. Poor Annabel was on tenterhooks as the birth drew ever closer. Sarah had only managed to go to one of her birthing classes, so she had bought herself a book to read on childbirth, just to be on the safe side. She'd watched endless episodes of 'One Born Every Minute' too! She just hoped that she would be able to keep her cool and stay strong throughout for Annabel, during the birth and she was extremely thankful that Julie was also going to be present.

Tonight, Steve was hosting a cocktail party and he had asked her to organise it, and to oversee the whole evening for him. He had invited some very important and influential people and Sarah understood that she would be present in a low-key working capacity. She would have to ensure it all went ahead, without any glitches. She'd been busy all day making sure that she delivered on what she'd promised Steve. She had hired a specialist catering company, who had come highly recommended, so hopefully it should all run like clockwork. Basically if any problems arose, she would have to deal with them and smooth things over. Vases full of wonderful exotic flowers filled the house with their amazing fragrance and the house sparkled from top to bottom.

She was still undecided as to what she should wear, as yet and she was running out of options, but thought it best not to go over the top, because after all she would essentially be working. After changing her clothes several times, Sarah had finally put on her faithful black halter neck cocktail dress, with its low back and thought it would have to do. Despite her saying she would never wear high heels ever again, she put on a pair of killer heels, which were bejewelled with rhinestones and sparkled like diamonds when they caught the light. She just hoped she wouldn't regret it later! She'd managed to put her hair up into a simple chignon which Sue, had shown her how to do whilst they were on set in Tuscany.

The party appeared to be going well and everyone looked as if they were having a great time, as plenty of chatter and laughter could be heard. So far, no major issues had occurred, like glasses being smashed or food ending up on the floor, but the evening wasn't over yet. Still it was highly unlikely to happen, she knew.

Sarah had personally greeted all the guests as they arrived and had made sure they were offered a drink straight away and made the introductions, where necessary.

She herself would not touch a single drop of alcohol during the evening, especially champagne, which always had an adverse effect upon her. Anyway, Garth had put her on a detox programme, and he'd made her promise that she would stick to it! Steve's mother Celia had been the first to arrive and she had surprisingly been in good spirits for once and greeted Sarah warmly and kissed her on both cheeks. She had brought her godchild, Vivien Hope with her, the daughter of an old family friend, who was staying with her from New York. She was a top criminal lawyer and currently taking a sabbatical, after working on a very high-profile case. Sarah had met her previously when she'd come over to the house for a BBQ. She had thought her to be a little bit too stuck up for her liking and it was clear that she viewed Sarah as the hired help, which had not gone down too well with her either. Sarah had not warmed to her one little bit!

To give credit where it was due however, she was an attractive and extremely confident woman and Sarah had to admit that she looked amazing in a Silver Lurex Jacquard cocktail dress. It was also crystal clear to Sarah, that Celia would like nothing more than if her darling son and Vivien were to get together.

Sarah had observed that the two women were similar and both, very driven individuals. However, she knew underneath her harsh exterior, Celia had a softer side, but she wasn't so sure about Vivien Hope. Celia had taken great pleasure in telling her that she was a top criminal lawyer and a highly respected one at that. In Sarah's opinion, you didn't get to where she had got to, by being meek and mild, or was she being unfair to the woman. However, she'd also noticed that Vivien had a totally different persona when she was around Steve. She found her unbelievably annoying, but questioned herself as to whether the real reason she had taken a dislike to Vivien Hope, was because she could actually be jealous of her? She quickly dismissed such a thought, after all why would she be jealous of Vivien Hope, it was ridiculous.

Steve had been the perfect host, paying attention to all of his guests. He was currently in deep conversation with a successful and rather influential producer in Hollywood, called Dan Rivers and his glamorous wife, Sienna Davies a well-known actress and boy, didn't she know it. Still she had at least been pleasant to

Sarah, even if it was slightly forced. Sarah was just about to go into the kitchen to check on how things were going behind the scenes, when Steve unexpectedly called her over. "Sarah, tell Dan and Sienna how good that script we have both recently read is."

Sarah thought about when she had returned the script to Steve, she had enthused about how good it was and that if Lucky Charm didn't get made into a film, it would be a travesty. Sarah had also been pleased when Steve had told her that he really valued her opinion and here he was kindly bringing her in on a discussion with the infamous Dan Rivers. "Yes, it's a brilliant script, Dan, it really is," she said enthusiastically, "and I found it captivating, I could barely put it down, it was so good."

"Well," Dan said in his soft Virginian drawl, "I think I would definitely like to hear more about it."

"I certainly don't think you will be disappointed Dan, it's a humbling story with several twists."

Dan nodded his head and then turned to Steve. "Okay, there's no time like the present. Are you free to meet tomorrow say, 3 p.m., Steve?"

"I will make sure I am, Dan," Steve said as he shook Dan's hand.

Steve looked pleased with himself as his eyes met Sarah's and he gave her a huge smile and his usual cheeky wink! She knew he was extremely passionate about this particular script, which he was hoping to get off the ground. It would be massively useful if he managed to get someone like Dan Rivers on board. Steve had mentioned to her previously that Dan, was as passionate about making films as he himself was, and was known in Tinsel town for taking the odd risk.

Sarah went to bed after seeing the last of the guests off and the catering team. She was exhausted and her feet ached. Steve was nowhere to be seen, so she made her way up to bed. She got into her PJ's and once she'd brushed her hair and cleaned her teeth, got straight into bed. It felt like bliss as she stretched out fully, but realised she had forgotten to bring her obligatory glass of water up to bed with her. She put her slippers back on and went down into the kitchen only to find Steve sipping a cup of coffee at the breakfast bar. "Hi, do you want to join me?"

"I'll sit with you for a while, but will pass on the coffee, thanks, as it will only keep me awake! I only popped down to get some water."

She went to the fridge and helped herself to some ice-cold water and joined Steve. "Were you pleased with the way it went tonight Steve?" she asked.

"Yes, very much so and I've made a few new contacts. It never hurts to network and it's brilliant that Dan could potentially be interested in getting on board with my latest project and hopefully getting Lucky Charm onto the big screen! It will take some doing, but I am determined to see this through, even if it kills me!"

"I'm sure you can do it Steve, and I am with you on that one, because it's a brilliant script and story."

"Thanks for keeping the party running smoothly tonight Sarah."

"No worries, that's what I'm here for."

Changing the subject Steve said, "What do you think of Vivien?" Steve had caught her somewhat off-guard and had well and truly put her on the spot. She also felt self-conscious, sitting there in her recently purchased black and white silk PJ's from a glossy LA boutique, and a pair of fluffy pink slippers. "I don't think I have an opinion on her Steve, because I don't really know her, do I?"

Steve looked at her in disbelief, shaking his head, but he had a smile on his face, which as always, lit up his blue eyes, and occasionally set her heart a flutter, as it was now. "Oh really, Sarah, I am not going to buy that one. Of course you've got an opinion on her. You have an opinion on everything and everyone!" Sarah tried to look offended at his remarks and shrugged her shoulders and wrinkled her nose as she did so!

"Well, if you insist then."

"Oh but I do, Sarah."

"How honest I mean, opinionated, do you want me to be?"

"Totally, of course. I will accept nothing less!"

"Okay, but just remember you asked for it!"

"I'm sure Vivien Hope is very nice, but I think she is also one very driven woman, who knows what she wants and I should think, she usually gets it."

"Is that it?" Steve asked.

Sarah paused slightly before going on to say. "I hope you don't mind me saying, Steve, but she does remind me a little of your mother, but to be fair your mother, deep down, is a real softie, especially where you're concerned." Sarah winced as she felt slightly uncomfortable about what she'd just said. Had she gone too far?

"Actually, that's very perceptive of you Sarah! Then you probably already know that my mother is trying to throw us both together!"

"Of course I do, but aren't you both a bit too long in the tooth for that? And for what it's worth, I don't think she's the right woman for you, Steve."

He looked at her directly and said. "Oh really and why is that then?"

"Steve, it's purely my opinion and I have nothing more to say on it." When would she learn to keep her mouth shut!

"Well, I don't think my mother will give up any time soon."

"She wants more grandchildren and according to her, Vivien comes from good stock, don't you know?" He didn't mention to Sarah that they also had a history together.

"Really, well it sounds to me as if she's talking about breeding horses, so good luck with that one. Anyway, I'm off to bed now, and I will see you in the morning, Steve."

"Hold on a second Sarah before you go. I've been thinking there isn't going to be much happening around here at the moment and I wondered if you would like to go back to the UK a bit earlier than planned."

"It would give you more time to spend with your friend Annabel, before her baby comes along. When is the baby due?"

"In just under two weeks." Sarah was surprised by his offer, but accepted gratefully. "That would be wonderful, Steve thank you and I know Annabel will appreciate it."

"No problem and of course you'll have to make up for it later by working extra-long hours, but I know that's never a problem with you, Sarah."

"No, I'm not one to shy away from hard work. Night Steve."

"Night, Sarah."

Once in bed, Sarah was feeling restless, as she lay there in the dark tossing and turning. She was pleased to be going back home and she couldn't wait to ring Annabel and tell her the good news. This would mean that she would be close by, should the baby decide to come into the world a little early. She also thought about Miss Vivien Hope and whether Steve could possibly see her in a romantic light! You could never tell with him, as he appeared to love all women. Anyway, fortunately she would be heading home shortly and all of her focus would be on Annabel, her best friend and new mum to be. However, her thoughts once again returned to Steve and she wondered if by sending her home, he was trying to get rid of her.

Perhaps he didn't want her around to cramp his style with the hard-nosed individual that was Vivien Hope. Sarah chastised herself for the umpteenth time, as she knew that she was being irrational, as always and perhaps overly harsh on Vivien.

Chapter 29

Sarah had been home almost a week, after she'd arrived back on a rather bleak February day, and there was absolutely no comparison, to waking up to the LA sunshine every day. Just to see a blue sky always lifted her spirits. She was staying with her mother for a couple of days, before going back up to stay with Annabel until her baby arrived. She'd already spent a few days helping her to make some final touches to the baby's room and other preparations, which needed to be done, before the baby came along.

Annabel had decorated it in soft neutral colours, along with her own personal artistic touches of Disney characters and it looked amazing. Sarah had bought Annabel a cosy rocking chair, which she hoped would come in handy for when she had to get up in the middle of the night to feed the baby and a soft cosy dressing gown. Sarah couldn't get her head around just how much her friend had changed. Sarah had always known that Annabel's brash exterior, which she displayed most of the time, was really to hide her own vulnerability. It was lovely to see the much softer side of Annabel shine through these days.

After a leisurely lunch and a catch up with Megan, Sarah dropped Dotty off at home, and then made her way to The Bake Stop. Iris had been pleased to see her and took her through to the back and insisted on hearing all the juicy gossip, which Sarah was more than happy to impart. The edited version of course! Naturally, she didn't tell her the best bits, some things that happen in Tuscany must stay in Tuscany. Iris once again repeated her and Dave's offer of first refusal on buying the shop. Sarah was happy to report to her that currently she was still having the best of times and she wasn't at all sure whether she could commit to such a project.

Iris had assured her that there was still a bit of time before they put the shop up for sale, and in her opinion Sarah could really make some brilliant changes to it, if she were to take it on, she was convinced of it. At that time Sarah once again, didn't want to contemplate even thinking about it!

Sarah returned to the cottage and found her mother surrounded by cruise ship brochures. "What's all this about, Mum?"

"George suggested that we should go on a cruise together."

"Oh really, that sounds like a great idea to me."

"Yes, that's what I thought and I've always wanted to go on one, remember, your dad always flatly refused to give it a try," she said with a wistful look on her face.

"Are you two getting serious, Mum?" Dotty shrugged her shoulders as she said:

"I wouldn't say that exactly and just so you know, we'd be having separate cabins. Treat them mean to keep them keen that's my motto," she said with a smile on her face.

"If you say so Mum, and anyhow that's on an as-and-when-need-to-know basis! As in, I really don't want to know."

"Fair enough," Dotty replied. "Anyway, how did you find Iris and Dave then?"

"Oh they're both well, and they send their love." Iris took me through to the back and grilled me on all my so-called gossip.

"Guess what, they still want me to buy The Bake Stop from them."

"Well, I think it would be a great idea if you bought the business Sarah, you've got all that money sitting in the bank, haven't you?"

That wasn't entirely true, as Sarah had invested some of the money, but her mother did have a point. "I know you're having a great time at the moment with this film stuff, but in the long term, what can it offer you? This is something you were born to do and you would have total control over what you did with it. You wouldn't have that ex-husband of yours interfering and taking all the glory from you either!"

"Oh I don't know Mum, maybe it's a bit too soon for me to embark on such a huge project."

"Or is it because you cannot bear the thought of tearing yourself away from that Steve Fountain?"

"Oh for goodness' sake Mum, give it a rest will you? My life does not revolve totally around Steve."

"Okay, have it your own way but there's no need to bite me head off," Dotty said, somewhat huffily!

"I'm sorry, Mum," Sarah said as she kissed her softly on the forehead.

"That's all right, I forgive you, love." Dotty knew she'd hit a raw nerve with Sarah, and any wise words of wisdom she had to say, as always would fall by the way side. Dotty didn't believe that Steve Fountain would be the right man for Sarah. Oh yes, he was a decent enough chap, but from the little she knew about him, he certainly didn't appear to be the kind of man to settle down any time soon. If he was anything like his father, Sarah should probably stay well clear of him. However, deep down Dotty believed that the horse had probably well and truly bolted by now and Sarah had fallen for him. Dotty was nobody's fool.

Sarah was packing her bags the following morning, ready to make the drive back up to London to stay with Annabel, when her mobile phone rang. On the other end was a very calm Annabel. "Hi hun, guess what, my waters have just broke and I have to make my way to the hospital." Sarah was surprised and taken aback, and also slightly panicked, as she wasn't expecting Annabel's baby to come early.

"Are you okay, as you sound remarkably calm Annabel?"

"Well, I'm not in any pain, at least not at the moment. Paul upstairs, my Knight in Shining Armour is going to take me to the hospital, and as we speak, is looking for some heavy-duty plastic to cover his seat with. He's got to take me in his little old MG, which is his pride and joy! I'm sitting here with a towel tucked between my legs right now. Oh bless you."

"Okay, well I'm on my way," Sarah said with some trepidation.

"Yes, but please don't panic Sarah, there's no rush as it is very unlikely that the baby will come just yet. At least I bloody well hope not," she said with a hint of panic in her voice. "So do I. Tell Paul to take good care of you and I will see you at the Hospital. I will. Love you, Annabel."

Chapter 30

Sarah picked up her bags and hurried downstairs. "I'm off Mum, Annabel's waters have broken."

"Oh have they, so junior is on his or her way then! How is she?"

"Amazingly calm at the moment."

"Well that won't last," Dotty said, with good humour. "Poor girl, she doesn't know what she's let herself in for. Still the end result is worth it. Give her my love and give me a ring as soon as you can when the baby is born, won't you?"

"Of course, I will," Sarah said as she kissed her mother.

"And you, young lady, mind how you go."

"I will Mum, don't worry about me."

As Dotty closed the door behind her daughter, she went back into the lounge and watched Sarah drive off, and she muttered to herself. "I will always worry about you Sarah, I'm your mother."

After her SatNav had taken her around the houses, Sarah eventually arrived at the Hospital, armed with lots of bags full of items which she hoped would help Annabel get through childbirth. She was beginning to feel a bit jittery herself, as she wasn't really sure what to expect, or how she would react. Okay she'd watched One Born Every Minute lots of times, but this was going to be a totally new experience for her. She was feeling nervous. One of the midwives kindly took her through to Annabel's room. She was relieved to see that Annabel was sitting calmly in an armchair flicking through some magazines and looked as cool as a cucumber. Sarah placed her bags onto the bed and hugged her friend. "So how are you feeling?"

"Quite frankly Sarah, not a lot is happening just now, apart from the odd little twinge and that could be wind, as I had a curry last night."

"That's way too much information, thank you Annabel."

"Anyway, I feel fine," she said taking a deep breath, before saying, "well, at least for now! No major panic apparently, on junior arriving any time soon, so the midwife has informed me."

"Oh poor you, Babes." Sarah knew her friend well enough to know that she was hiding the fact that she was nervous and who could blame her. "So, tell me what's in those bags, Sarah?"

"A survival kit for you, of course."

"There's plenty of chocolate and crisps! I also bought an aroma fan, with some essential oils to help keep you calm. I've got lavender, orange and vanilla. I have also downloaded some of your favourite music on my iPad and one really soft comfy pillow. Oh yes and I couldn't resist this," Sarah said as she pulled out a cute cuddly penguin and handed it to Annabel.

"Oh Sarah, I love him. He's mine though right?"

"Yes, of course he is!" Annabel adored Penguins.

"That's okay then. Right, pass me those choccies over!"

"Is your mum here yet?"

"Yes, she's just gone down to the cafeteria to get some coffee. Paul's only just left. Oh goodness, he is such a drama Queen and a complete nervous wreck. He actually thought I was going to give birth in his precious car. He made me sit on several layers of towels and black bin bags. It's a wonder I didn't slip off the seat!"

"More to the point, how the hell did you squeeze into his car?"

"With difficulty I can tell you," and they both laughed.

When Annabel's labour started, it began rather slowly, but by early evening, things were progressing somewhat, and Annabel appeared to be dealing with the pain fairly well, with the aid of gas and air. Both Julie and Sarah did what they could to help make her feel comfortable by rubbing her back and keeping her cool. More importantly, they tried to keep her spirits up. But by midnight, Annabel was experiencing more extreme contractions which were lasting longer each time and her legs were shaking uncontrollably with the pain.

She gripped both Julie and Sarah's hands like a viper and she also swore a couple of times and then unexpectedly shouted out at Sarah in a voice straight out of a horror movie, "Get rid of that bloody awful aroma fan, it's making me feel sick." Jane, the unflappable and brilliant midwife, told her to calm down as she was doing brilliantly and that she was almost there.

Sarah felt so sorry for her friend, whose face by now was very red and blotchy and her hair soaked in perspiration. She looked totally wiped out. The contractions were getting much shorter in between each one, and suddenly Annabel let out a piercing scream as they all encouraged her to do her breathing. But she kept saying over and over again that she had a strong urge to push, but the midwife told her to hang on, as she mustn't push just yet and told her to pant. Annabel looked up at them all with a sorrowful expression upon her face.

"Oh shit, fuck and balls. I cannot do this anymore, I'm really, really sorry," she said, tears running down her cheeks. Sarah looked across at Julie, who had a concerned look on her face and then she took Annabel's hand tightly into both of hers and said softly.

"You can do this babe, you most certainly can," and Annabel smiled weakly at her and began to sob, then her eyes widened as she said.

"Do you think so?" and Sarah nodded and smiled at her dearest friend. The midwife encouraged her too, and told her that she would soon be seeing her little baby and that he or she had lots of black hair. Annabel smiled. "I cannot wait to see my baby," she said with another sob.

The midwife looked up at her and smiled, "Well come on, just one more big push and baby will be here." Annabel began to push and as she did so, she let out an ear-piercing shriek, which Sarah would never ever forget, as her baby son came into the world at 12:45 a.m. and boy did he cry. Even the midwife commented that he had a healthy pair of lungs on him, as she passed him to his mother and Julie cut the umbilical cord. By then they were all crying and laughing at the same time. Sarah quickly got into photographer mode and took lots of pictures, before she and Julie finally left the hospital to let one very exhausted, but elated Mother and baby son get some well-earned rest.

It was almost 2:00 a.m. when Sarah eventually arrived at Annabel's apartment, and she felt completely shattered. It really had been an emotional roller coaster of a day and night, and it had also been hard to see her friend in such pain, but also amazing to then share in her joy, once baby Alfie came into the world.

Sarah got into her PJ's and made herself a cup of tea and some buttered toast, as she suddenly felt hungry.

All that she'd eaten throughout the day, was a chocolate bar and some crisps and copious amounts of coffee. Her head was still buzzing and she doubted very much that she would be able to sleep when she eventually fell into bed. She looked through the many photographs, which she'd taken of Annabel and gorgeous baby, Alfie. There was one in particular that had caught her eye, where he was yawning. He did in fact have masses of jet-black hair, just like Annabel when she was born, Julie had told them.

But her favourite had to be the one she'd taken of Julie, snuggled up on the bed with Annabel and Alfie in the middle of them both. Julie looked to be one very proud grandmother and you could clearly see the bond between mother and daughter, which had grown between them over the past months. It warmed her heart to see how happy Annabel was, and she became emotional all over again and she dabbed her eyes with a tissue. Without any warning, a feeling of sadness enveloped her and she began to cry. Perhaps it was a release from all of the tension she'd been through. But deep down she knew it was because she herself, would never have an opportunity to become a mother, like Annabel. So before she got too upset about it, she quickly got into bed and instantly fell asleep.

The next morning Sarah gave the apartment another clean, even though it didn't really need it and went shopping to make sure that there would be plenty of supplies in for when Annabel and Alfie came home. She'd received a call from Annabel to say that she hoped to be allowed to leave the Hospital later that day and she would let her know as soon as she found out what time. She had also bought lots of blue balloons with 'it's a boy' on them and a cute but overly large teddy bear balloon.

Once she returned to the apartment she set about making batches of food to put into the freezer for her friend, so that she had some decent meals on hand for when Sarah had to leave. She had spoken to Steve and told him about baby Alfie's arrival and he'd said that he would be staying on in LA for a little while longer so, there was no panic about her going back just yet. He would contact her once he knew when he would be returning to London.

Sarah was arranging some flowers to welcome Annabel home with, when her mobile pinged another message. She took out her mobile from the back pocket of her jeans and it was Annabel, asking her to collect her from the Hospital at 3:30 p.m.

It was after 5 p.m. when finally Annabel was allowed to leave the Hospital and once back home, Sarah carefully took young Alfie out of the car and carried him in his car seat into the apartment, followed by Annabel, who looked a little pale. Sarah placed a sleeping Alfie down and Annabel slumped down onto the sofa and yawned. She looked around the room and exclaimed. "Oh the balloons are lovely, thanks babe."

"You're welcome." Annabel yawned again and this time, Sarah suggested that she took a little nap.

"You look exhausted, Annabel."

"It would do you good and I can sort everything out, not that there's much to do really. I have made us a nice chicken casserole for later and your favourite pudding, buttery apple crumble and custard."

"Oh lovely, thank you. Maybe you're right, perhaps, I will take a little nap. I didn't get that much sleep last night," she said, looking lovingly at her baby son. "My little pickle kept crying on and off all night. Poor love, he's having trouble latching on at the moment, so I'm quite sore right now," she said looking down at her breasts, "and my milk is still coming in."

"Annabel, there is no perhaps about it, why don't you have a nice warm bath and a little sleep? It will do you good and I promise to look after Alfie, if he wakes up. I've made up some formula, just in case. Nappies, wipes, a change of baby grows, we're all good to go here."

"Thanks, you're a star."

"Don't be silly, that's what I am here for, so make the most of me. Anyway, you are one very clever girl," Sarah said as she sat down next to her best friend and put an arm around her. Over the years the two women had both had some highs and lows in their lives, but this was the best ever high. "I was so very proud of you last night Annabel, 8lb 10 oz, who'd have thought it?"

"Well not me, that's for sure," Annabel said wryly and pulling a face said, "it's not like shelling a pea you know."

"Yes, I think I got the gist of that last night! Poor you."

"Thanks, Sarah I couldn't have got through the birth without you and Mum."

"I wouldn't have missed it for the world and he was worth all the pain, wasn't he?" Annabel nodded and both of them had tears in their eyes again as Annabel struggled to say:

"Oh yes, you bet."

"Right, off you go to Bedfordshire and get some rest, before our little Prince awakes!"

Sarah had been with Annabel and Alfie for over a week when she finally received a call from Steve to say that he would be returning shortly and as usual gave her one of his long list of jobs which he wanted done, like yesterday. It had been very full on looking after both Annabel and Alfie, however Sarah had quipped to Annabel, that neither of them were thankfully as difficult to look after as Steve was. Alfie was now feeding better, although Annabel said her nipples were still sore. Fortunately, he did sleep for a couple of hours in between his feeds. Julie was going to be around for the next week and there had been a steady stream of family and friends visiting the apartment, all cooing over baby Alfie. He certainly was a cute baby, and everybody said so, including Liam who had visited once and Sarah had made herself scarce, before he arrived.

Annabel had told her that although he agreed he was a cute baby and commented on his dark hair, other than that, he hadn't shown a lot of interest in his son. She'd also said that she was perfectly fine and happy, as she knew that she had enough love for the both of them and could provide for Alfie. And for once Sarah believed her. As long as he paid his child support money on time, she didn't care. However, she didn't want young Alfie to grow up without knowing his father, so he wouldn't be getting away scot free, or that manipulative wife of his.

Annabel would make sure of it. Sarah had been surprised to find out that at the beginning of Annabel's pregnancy, Liam's wife had had the nerve to come round and try and convince Annabel not to have the baby. She had told Annabel that Liam would never leave her, or his family and Annabel had practically thrown her out of the apartment, but not before telling her that she and her weak, cheating husband deserved one another.

Chapter 31

Once again, Sarah was back to packing her bags, but it didn't bother her too much, as it had become second nature to her now, having spent the past eight and a half months doing it, on and off. Sarah had had an emotional farewell with Annabel and the adorable Alfie, who blew bubbles at her as she kissed him on his forehead.

She made her way back to North London and as soon as she entered the house, she really felt like she had returned home. Strange, because it wasn't her home. But she loved it. Buster came rushing up to greet her and went positively bananas as his tail wagged wildly. As always, he was trying to lick her face as she hugged him. Buster it's good to see you boy. "Well, someone is pleased to see you back," Molly commented, "and he's not the only one. Welcome home, stranger, it feels like ages since I've seen you."

"Likewise Molly, Sarah said giving her a hug."

"So come on, have you any pictures of this wonderful baby?"

"Well, how long have you got?"

"Why don't you go and get yourself unpacked and I will make us some lunch. I have some home-made tomato and basil soup, or is there anything else that you fancy?"

"Soup sounds great to me. I'll be back in a jiffy."

The two women sat down and had lunch together and once they had cleared away, Sarah showed Molly the photographs which she'd taken of Annabel and Alfie. "Oh he's gorgeous, and where did he get all that hair from?"

"Well, according to Julie, he takes after Annabel."

"Sarah, you're such an amazing photographer. I never knew that."

"Well, it's clear Molly, that we don't know everything about one another, do we?" Molly looked slightly nonplussed at Sarah's comment. Steve had told Sarah that Molly was in fact, the secret author of the Lucky Charm script and Sarah had been stunned, but this certainly explained why Molly was constantly on her laptop! "So, you're pretty good at keeping secrets yourself. I hear you wrote the Lucky Charm script. It's brilliant, Molly. I genuinely loved it and couldn't put it down after Steve gave it to me to read."

"Well thank you, Sarah. I used to write scripts in LA for some hit comedy shows a few years back. I don't know if Steve also told you," she said with a look of sadness on her face, "but my marriage also broke up whilst I was in LA."

"No he didn't actually, Molly, I'm so sorry to hear that."

"My husband was an alcoholic and I loved him fiercely at the time. However, he was a very abusive man. Finally, one night, I ended up in ER with a broken nose and that's when I came to the realisation that I simply couldn't take it anymore. My writing suffered and eventually one of the shows got cancelled by NBS. Anyway, I ended up having a nervous breakdown, and I was a complete wreck."

"I have known Steve for years, and he has always been such a good and supportive friend to me and he suggested that I come back here and be his housekeeper."

"It was just what I needed at the time, no pressure and I was able to leave my past behind me."

"It sounds to me as if you've been incredibly brave Molly and you should be proud of yourself. You have turned your life around and that couldn't have been easy."

"Not to start with, but that was 3 years ago and I have finally got my mojo back. I did some more studying and after several attempts of hard blood sweat and tears, I came up with what I believe to be the best bit of writing that I have ever done!"

"Well, it really deserves to be made into a film Molly."

"Oh let's hope so, it would be wonderful. I know if anyone can make it happen, Steve will, Molly," Sarah said enthusiastically.

"Yes I know, but it's not easy, so I'm keeping my feet firmly on the ground!" Molly got up from the table.

"Well, I have some chores to do, so I will see you later."

"Yes, and I had better get back to the office and do some work, as I've had my orders from Steve." Sarah went over to Molly and hugged her and said, "It sounds to me as if you thoroughly deserve some good luck."

Molly smiled, "thanks." She then looked directly at Sarah as she said, rather surprisingly, "you do know, don't you, that Steve's a wonderful man? He does however collect strays, of which I am one." Sarah was surprised at what Molly had just said, and wasn't really sure why she'd said it, but before she had a chance to respond, Molly left the kitchen. Sarah was left a bit confused by Molly's comment and wondered why she would say such a thing to her, she certainly didn't see herself as one of Steve's so-called strays! However, she didn't have time to think about that right now, as she had work to do.

After working solidly for quite a while, Sarah was just finishing off an email when Molly swept into the room and placed an open copy of Vanity Fair magazine in front of her. "Would you look at this, who's that woman with Steve?"

"Ah, that is Miss Vivien Hope, I met her whilst out in LA."

"She certainly looks like the cat whose got the cream, doesn't she?" Molly remarked. Sarah looked at the picture more closely and had to admit that she felt a pang of jealousy! She read the caption underneath the picture which said that it was Steve Fountain, who had a BAFTA and was a two-time Oscar-nominated British film director, with a mystery lady who were attending a Charity event for the homeless, which had been held at the Beverley Hills Hotel in Hollywood. "She really doesn't look the sort that Steve normally goes for, does she? And they look a bit odd, like with him being so tall!"

"She'd need a bloody ladder to kiss him!"

Sarah had to laugh. "Actually, she's a family friend and Celia is her godmother. She just happens to be a top criminal lawyer and an all-round, clever clogs from New York."

"I think Celia would like nothing more than if she and Steve were to get together. I know that's true, because Steve said as much to me," Molly took the magazine back from Sarah and stared at the photograph again!

"Oh my God, I recognise that name now."

"What do you mean?"

"Well, Steve went to live with his mother in LA, after his parents got divorced for a while and he had some of his schooling there. I think Vivien Hope was his beau back then, when they were at High School. I know I probably should keep me mouth shut, as he did tell me this in confidence."

"Well perhaps you shouldn't tell me then, Molly."

"No, no I know I can trust you, Sarah.

"You see he and Vivien were madly in love apparently, but they were both young, sixteen, I think when she got pregnant. Anyhow she didn't want to have the baby and neither did her parents, she was a very bright girl, destined for great things, which she's clearly achieved.

"So arrangements were made, you know Molly said raising her eyebrows, and she didn't have the baby. Steve was devastated at the time. Not long afterwards, they broke up.

"From what he said, she was rather ambitious even back then and that was far more important to her."

"That must have been awful for him, but I guess they were rather young. And by the way, you can trust me totally, I won't say a word, Molly."

"Do you think there's a chance they could get back together, Molly?"

"Well I wouldn't want to go back down that road meself, would you?" Sarah shrugged her shoulders, "probably not, but who knows what Steve will do, Molly. It's his life and none of our business."

"Okay, I guess you're right, Sarah. So, what is this Vivien woman actually like?" Molly asked. "Come on, you can dish the dirt," Molly asked inquisitively.

"Pretty as you can see, but I'm not really her biggest fan."

"Why is that then?"

"Put it this way, she treated me like the hired help, which I know I am, but she certainly didn't impress me that much! I'm probably being unfair to the woman, as I hardly know her, do I?"

"Well, she'll have her work cut out if she thinks she can snare our Steve again, he's much older and wiser and she hurt him badly before."

"Do you think Molly that Celia knew about her pregnancy?"

"Oh god no, she would have gone mad if she'd known about it, for sure. It was all kept hush-hush from her apparently."

"Right, changing the subject, how are the two love-birds getting on, Molly enquired?"

"If you mean George and my mother, they are having a marvellous time, or so my mother informs me. She rang me from the ship yesterday and they had just left St Lucia and by all accounts Dotty believes everyone should do a Caribbean Cruise. She said the food is out of this world and there is the non-stop sunshine."

"Also, she loves the entertainment, which is fantastic she says."

"And they're both learning to dance the Salsa, so Mum is well and truly in her element!"

"It's just as well there is no limit as to how much luggage you can take on board. I think she took her entire wardrobe and then some!"

"Oh, you should have seen George's little face when he left here, he looked like a dog who had two tails," Molly mused.

"It's good to see him so happy, it's been a while coming!"

"Yes, I agree and I am very happy for them both."

"Me too. Right, dinner will be ready in about half an hour, so turn off your computer, young lady."

"Yes, ma'am," Sarah said immediately closing down her laptop.

Chapter 32

Sarah had managed to fit in another quick visit with Annabel and Alfie, but just before she'd left Annabel's apartment, she had received an email from Steve to say that he was extending his stay in LA and that his mother and Vivien Hope would be coming over to visit at some point.

Sarah was surprised and realised that she wasn't overly happy about it, and she couldn't shake it off. What was wrong with her, after all she was only the hired help! When she got back home, Molly came to greet her. "Have you heard the news, Celia is coming over to stay and then this Vivien woman, that's all we bloody well need."

"Yes, that's exactly what I thought. Still this is Steve's home and we're mere menials."

"Oh come on Sarah, we're both more than that and you know it. So how are Annabel and little Alfie getting on?"

"Oh he's growing rapidly now and I am happy to report that both mother and baby are doing well and he is gorgeous."

"He has beautiful big eyes, deep brown like Annabel's and he is beginning to smile now, or maybe it's wind! I don't think Annabel is getting too much sleep, but she's loving every minute of it. She said to thank you for the shepherd's pie."

"Oh my pleasure. Well I'm going up to my room Molly, as I have a few things to do."

"Me too. Are you okay, you look a bit peaky, you're not sickening for something are you."

"I don't think so. I just feel a bit flat!"

"Well, Molly said with little enthusiasm, it's going to be all systems go here again, with Steve returning, whenever that might be. Then Celia and Vivien coming over, although I don't think we have to roll out the red carpet for them, like we did with Elenour. Of course, Celia can be a nightmare!"

"I can imagine, but I have to say, Elenour totally won me over whilst working with her. We certainly had a few ups and downs whilst in Tuscany, but I think she's just a bit misunderstood and I do know her a whole lot better now."

"Oh if you say so, I will just have to take your word on that Sarah."

Up in her room, Sarah began to feel rather irksome and fidgety and she once again reflected on what was happening in her life. Whilst Steve was away in LA she had been left feeling slightly redundant. Of course, she'd had work to do, but it had been on the whole, way too quiet for her. Without a doubt she loved the whole world of filmmaking and the excitement that it brought with it, but now in between projects it was hard to adapt to it not being so manic.

She also realised that she had been extremely naïve where Steve was concerned. What had taken place between them was sex pure and simple and he had never offered her anything else. Clearly, there wasn't any kind of a relationship or romance between them either. Every step of the way she'd told herself that she could handle it, but she now knew differently! She realised without a shadow of a doubt that she had developed much stronger feelings for him. She wasn't necessarily ashamed of what she'd done, but acknowledged that maybe she had been rather foolish. She so wasn't anywhere near as tough as she had thought she was going to be. She only had herself to blame for that. Having already had one man practically wreck her life, Sarah certainly wasn't prepared to allow herself to be hurt again, especially, as this time, it was totally self-inflicted. Then of course there was Vivien Hope, who knew what would develop between her and Steve, if anything!

Maybe now would be a good opportunity for her to move on and make her own way in life. She at least wouldn't have anyone else to answer to! She was confident that when it came to running a business, she had some good ideas and the business acumen to do it. Fortunately, she also had the money.

Sarah had always been impulsive, and suddenly she knew what she was going to do. She had literally made up her mind, there and then, that maybe this was the time for a change and she would definitely get in touch with Iris and Dave to test the waters about buying The Bake Stop.

Her mother was right, it had always been her passion to own a business and to use the skills which she'd learnt as a teenager. This would be going back to her first love and this time it would be entirely her own creation! She alone would make the decisions herself, and it would be all consuming like before, but this time she wouldn't have Richard taking most of the credit for everything, as he had been apt to do when they had ran their business together. More importantly, she would get right away from Steve, before her feelings for him became obvious!

Chapter 33

The days leading up to Steve's return had been hectic ones, but Sarah had managed to pop down and visit Iris and Dave at The Bake Stop and set the wheels in motion as to whether or not, it would be feasible for her to buy the business. Prior to that she had met up with her financial advisor and also her brother Tony! As a Corporate Lawyer, his knowledge and advice was invaluable. Iris and Dave had been over the moon when they knew that she was interested in buying the business and the plans which she had in mind for it. They were also honest enough to say, that her vision wasn't entirely what they had expected, but she had managed to win them over with some of her preliminary ideas and naturally, if she bought the business, it would be hers, to do whatsoever, she wished. Her mother was away on her cruise still, and she would save her news until she and George returned. For now, the fewer people who knew about what she was intending to do, the better because at the moment, it wasn't set in stone by any means.

Sarah was up extra early to do some lengths in the pool. She had recently got out of the habit of having a regular swim and now she was desperate to continue with her morning exercise and it was a great way to start the day. She was on her twentieth length and half-way down the pool when Steve called out to her, which took her by surprise! He had been due to arrive home the night before, but after waiting up until past midnight she had decided not to wait for him any longer and gone to bed. "Mind if I join you, Sarah?"

"Feel free, you don't really have to ask Steve, this is after all, your pool!"

He dived in at the deep end and made an almighty splash with water gushing over the edges! He soon caught up with her. "Ah, that's better," he said, "but not quite the same as out in LA with all that lovely sunshine."

"Oh rub it in, why don't you. What time did you get back last night?"

"My flight was late leaving, I think I got in around 1 a.m."

"You've not had a lot of sleep then."

"No, and I woke up early and felt restless and unable to get off into a deep sleep, hence the swimming."

"Welcome back to Blighty."

"Thanks, it's great to be back, but why don't we catch up over an early breakfast?"

"Yes okay, I've nearly finished my swim." Sarah carried on sedately swimming the breaststroke for a little while longer, until she got well and truly fed up with Steve continually splashing her as he thrashed his way through the water at 100 miles an hour!

Sarah got out of the pool, and as she did so, Steve watched her and as always, he was impressed by her fantastic figure! Oh God, women, he thought, they drove him crazy. Right now, he had enough on his plate, what with Vivien coming over to stay. His dear mother had convinced her to come over to visit the UK and had nominated him to look after her. He didn't really have the time, but no doubt he would have to spend some time with them both. Vivien's parents were long standing friends of his mother and as she would say, they were very well-connected people.

His mother was such a snob. He knew exactly what she was trying to do, as Steve and Vivien had been in love whilst in High School. Steve had been shocked when Vivien had told him that she was pregnant, and devastated when she'd said that she was having a termination. His mother knew none of this however. He was also slightly confused about his own feelings towards Vivien, but had to admit, rather surprisingly, that he was still fond of her. When Vivien had said she wasn't going to have their baby, he'd been heartbroken. He was young and madly in love with her back then.

Time as they say is a great healer, but he could still remember how much she'd hurt him. However, he had to acknowledge they were both extremely young and Vivien may not have become a top criminal lawyer, if she'd had a baby at that time. He also acknowledged that it was highly unlikely that they would have even stayed together! Steve knew he shouldn't touch Vivien with a barge pole and he didn't need any further complications in his life right now.

What with Sarah, who had somehow managed to make him feel guilty over their two highly sensual encounters. Okay she had always been quick enough to reassure him, that it was no big deal and that she didn't expect any commitment from him, but deep down did he really buy that? She'd got under his skin, that's for sure, but not for the first time, he forced himself not to think about her anymore, or Vivien for that matter, as he continued to swim at a mammoth rate in his pool.

Sarah showered and dressed in record time and pulled on her comfy pink jogging suit. She warmed some croissants through in the oven and prepared scrambled eggs. It was still early, and it would be a while, before even Molly surfaced. Steve walked in with his hair still wet and smoothed back and her heart skipped a beat. Oh how she wished it wouldn't! "Something smells nice, what are we having?"

"Scrambled eggs do you?" Sarah asked, taking the toast out from the toaster.

"Sounds good to me." She poured him a hot steaming mug of black coffee.

They sat down to eat breakfast together and Steve asked her what she'd been up to. "Well for one thing, trying to keep you happy, so do I get a tick on that front," she said looking him in the eye.

Steve hesitated slightly before he replied, "Yes, of course, big tick, as always."

"That's good."

"So what have you been up to?"

"Loads, but I have some very good news. It's looking more encouraging now, as there is a real chance that Molly's script will be made into a film, secret squirrel for now though as I haven't told her yet."

"Hopefully, when we get the green light, I will co-produce it and direct it. Still that's in the future, and before that, I am definitely going to direct that period piece set during World War II, which as you know is based on a true story."

"I just need to see if I can get Daniel Hudson to take on the lead male role and I already have someone in mind for the female Russian Spy. It would be ideal casting, perfect, but I know I will have my work cut out."

"Anyway, that won't begin until next year, but we will soon be very busy again."

"That's brilliant news Steve and I am over the moon about Molly. She will be so, so happy and no one is more deserving."

"And you, Sarah, are you happy?"

"Of course I am, why wouldn't I be?"

"I don't know, you seem unusually quiet."

"No, I'm fine."

"Okay, well, Sarah, there's something that I want to speak to you about."

"Jakey boy has asked me for some help, as he's about to direct a Pantomime, Peter Pan for his old drama group."

"What at this time of year?"

"Well, they are doing it as a Summer Panto."

"Oh good for him, I know how much Jake is committed to his old drama group and giving something back to the youth of Hackney."

"Here's the thing, unfortunately, I myself am going to be too busy, which is a shame as I would have liked to help him out. I will of course help out financially. I hope you don't mind, Sarah, but I have nominated you to help him!"

"I'm afraid it will probably involve a few weekends."

"No I guess that's okay, I definitely owe you one anyway. You've been more than generous with me of late, haven't you."

"Good, as he is going to pick you up later today, around 11 o'clock. Sorry there wasn't more warning!"

"What's new, I'm used to that Steve, but," Sarah paused slightly before asking, "why me?"

"That's not the reaction I thought I would get from you. I thought you would be pleased to spend some more time with Jake. Did I get that wrong?"

"No, we're really good friends."

"Just good friends eh," Steve said with a hint of sarcasm, which Sarah chose to ignore! "Are you sure that I will be of any use to him Steve, as I have no knowledge of staging a play, let alone a Pantomime."

"Of course you can, definitely! Anyway, it will be a great experience for you, Sarah. I cannot understand why you didn't go down the theatrical route, what with your dad's history and your clear love of films."

"Yeah, it would have made my dad really happy and looking back, maybe I should have. But, I was young at the time, so I took the cooking route instead. It seemed easier to me at the time!"

"Anyhow, you're way too good to stay working for me as just my PA, you know that don't you." Sarah shrugged her shoulders. "Well you are, and I am going to make sure that you get the opportunities you deserve, once we make a start on our next project together." Sarah smiled rather weakly and thanked Steve, before she left him to finish off his breakfast. His phone had been buzzing practically the whole time throughout their breakfast. He was clearly in demand, as usual.

Back in her room she changed into her jeans and a white T-shirt in readiness for when Jake picked her up and sorted out some of her paperwork. She felt a bit guilty from holding back and not telling Steve of her plans. So much had been going on in her life of late, which she wasn't quite ready to share with him just yet. She had put in an offer to purchase The Bake Stop and its premises, which Dave and Iris had accepted. She was extremely grateful to her brother Tony, who would be dealing with a lot of it on her behalf. She had so many plans for it and Geoff, one of her brother's friends was going to Project manage the job for her.

She didn't have any plans on leaving her job just yet, she most certainly wasn't ready at the moment. What she had in mind, would take some time anyhow and although she was excited, it was also tinged with sadness.

There was a loud toot from outside and she looked out of her bedroom window. It was Jake in a rather flashy red Mercedes car, and she laughed to herself. It was so typical of him, but she also knew that there was a lot more depth to Jake than that, because deep down he was an extremely generous and grounded person.

Jake was stood with the passenger door open waiting for her. "Morning Princess, your Chariot awaits!"

"I am not sure if I want to get in, as I hardly recognise you with that beard?"

She noticed a slight look of disappointment cross Jake's face. "Don't you like it?"

"Yes it's okay and I guess it does suit you," she said getting into the car and Jake shut the door behind her. "So what's with the beard Sarah asked as they began their journey."

"I'm in between parts at the moment, or resting as they say in the industry. I'm doing a couple of voice-overs here and there. I am also narrating a fantastic documentary about penguins living in Antarctica. It's been brilliantly shot and it follows this little chick called Percy, who has to survive in the worst weather conditions right up until adulthood. It's fascinating and I am loving it. You must watch it when it comes out on TV."

"I will definitely look out for it. Annabel, my best friend, adores penguins."

"Is that the one with the little baby."

"Yes it is."

"How are they getting on?"

"Alfie is thriving and so is Annabel and I have never seen such a change in someone as I have in Annabel."

"I bet you're a great auntie."

"Well, I try to be."

"Anyway, changing the subject what is going to happen today exactly."

"If I'm honest, it will be a bit of a muddle until they learn their lines and then of course, there's the set."

"I've already cast the actors, and typically as always, some are a bit disappointed, but they soon knuckle down and accept it. It can be challenging to begin with, but we just have to stick with it."

"How old are they?"

"About fourteen up to eighteen. They're a lively bunch, but it should be good fun. A mate of mine called Drew is a scriptwriter and has written the script for me, and it's hilarious. He will also help out today."

Jake had been right, it had been a challenging day, but the kids enthusiasm was uplifting. By the time they had left the Community Centre it was late and Jake suggested they made a stop and grabbed a burger at a drive-through, as they were both hungry. Afterwards, Jake dropped Sarah back at Steve's house and once again being a true gentleman, he got out of the car and opened the passenger door for her. "So Princess, are you ready to do this all over again next Saturday?"

"Yes of course I am, you bearded loon!"

"Hey, less of the bearded loon if you don't mind!" Jake put his arm around her waist and then tickled her cheek with his beard. "How's that?"

"Okay I guess, it's softer than I thought it would be."

"Oh really."

"You've been such a massive help today Sarah and I have really missed not being around you."

"Have you now?"

"Don't sound so surprised, because I have actually. It's a shame it didn't work out for us in Tuscany, as I think we could have made some sweet music together. I'm not giving up on you yet either!"

"Maybe you're right, but I think it would have only ever been a fling!"

"Is that all I am good enough for, a fling?" he said looking genuinely hurt. "Come on, Jake, you know deep down that is all it would have been." Jake raised his eyebrows and looked directly into her eyes and touched her face as he said, "Or is there someone else you're holding a candle for by any chance, not a million miles from here?"

Was she really that transparent, she thought and could feel her face burn, but hoped that Jake wouldn't notice under a moonlit sky. Feeling slightly flustered she said, "No, of course not." Jake shook his head as if to say he wasn't entirely convinced. There's still hope for me yet then, he said as he leaned towards her and gave her a gentle lingering kiss, which she enjoyed, just as Steve pulled up, blinding them with his headlights! "Right, I'm off, night, Jake, see you next Saturday."

"Night, Sarah." As she opened the front door, she could hear the two men chatting together, but she couldn't hear what they were saying. Sarah made her way up to her room, as she was exhausted and after a quick shower slipped into bed.

The day had been long and hard, but she had to admit, that it had also been a brilliant experience, even though being with so many teenagers, who were extremely boisterous was a bit hard going to say the least. Jake was like an excited puppy and the kids absolutely adored him and the atmosphere had been upbeat and infectious. It had totally recharged her batteries, which was what she'd needed. It would be a welcome distraction from all that was going on in her life at the moment and her eventual departure from Steve and everyone else who she had become so fond of. At least she would have George, around, that's, of course, if he and her mother hadn't fallen out on their cruise, but she didn't think that it was likely.

Chapter 34

Sarah was sitting in the office and was slightly flustered and sighed loudly, as she placed her mobile phone down onto the table.

She was going to have to fit in yet another visit to Biddenford, to meet with Geoff and the contractor, who according to Geoff was having a major strop over one of the changes she'd wanted to make. Trying to keep up with all that her job entailed and overseeing the work on The Bake Stop was harder than she'd envisaged. On the whole, things were progressing well, but occasionally, spanners appeared in the works, hence the visit to Biddenford would have to be made. Hopefully, if the refurbishment managed to keep on schedule, it should all be completed by early in the New Year and Sarah was happy with that. It had on occasion, been extremely stressful, but with her brother's help and Geoff as project manager, it had on the whole run fairly smoothly.

Steve suddenly burst into the office with Buster just behind him and flung an envelope down in front of her. "And when did you propose telling me about this then, Sarah," Steve enquired with a sardonic look upon his face! "By the way I should explain, that this was actually in with my post, so I opened it by mistake." Buster sat down next to her and placed his head onto her lap and looked up her, as if to say, don't worry I'm on your side! Sarah's hand shook slightly as she opened the envelope to reveal that it was in fact a letter from her solicitor, regarding the sale of The Bake Stop.

"I don't know what to say, Steve," Sarah said feeling very uncomfortable. "I never meant not to tell you, but I just kept putting it off."

"Oh really, and I guess that I am the last one to know around here, aren't I?" and Sarah nodded her head in answer. I feel so bad Steve and you certainly do deserve an explanation.

"Iris and Dave, who used to own The Bake Stop in Biddenford, mentioned about me buying it from them, before I started working for you. They had offered me first refusal on it, when they eventually retired. However, at that time I had

226

no desire to take it on, and that is the truth. The Bake Stop is an integral part of the village and I do have big plans for it."

"Oh, do you indeed!"

"Yes it's going to be a traditional bakery, with a coffee shop and in the extension, I am going to serve high end cream teas."

"My customers will get the London experience, but without having to leave the village."

"I am also aiming to run a teaching school upstairs and help some of the youngsters in the area and give them a head start."

"I see you certainly do have some rather ambitious plans don't you, Sarah. Who do you think you are, Jamie Oliver," Steve said with a hint of sarcasm.

"No of course not."

"You do realise that there are many risks with any new business! Are you sure you're doing the right thing?"

"Yes, of course I have to believe that I am Steve, but I have done some intense research and of course, I have taken financial advice too. I do have faith in this project, Steve. It's simply got to work."

"I am so very sorry that I didn't tell you earlier, it's inexcusable. I do, however, have to follow my own heart. But, you and Molly and George and everyone whom I've met along the way have helped me to get through, what had been an extremely dark period in my life."

"I am grateful to you all, and I will never ever forget any of you. Anyway, you won't be getting rid of me just yet. I won't be leaving you until the New Year and that will give you plenty of time to find a replacement for me won't it?"

"Well, I suppose so, he said rather brusquely. Anyway, what you do with your life, Sarah, is none of my business, but you should at least have had the decency to let me know." With that he left the office. Sarah knew she'd messed up big time, but there was nothing she could do about it now. She hadn't expected to have that rather awkward discussion with Steve today and she had been totally unprepared for it. Steve appeared to be seriously pissed about her decision. Even if he didn't understand the reasoning behind what she was doing, at least he knew now and it had been a relief to finally have told him.

She was still feeling unusually down and unsettled when Molly came into the office carrying a tray with a pot of tea and some biscuits. "Oh dear, you look like you've just lost a pound and found a penny! Are you okay, Sarah?"

"Well, the truthful answer is not really."

"Right, well why don't you have a break and have some tea!"

"That would be lovely, thank you Molly."

"So come on, I'm waiting." Molly was always so direct.

"Oh it's just that there is a further complication with the shop and I am going to have to make yet another visit down to Biddenford at the weekend. I didn't fully appreciate just how big this project was that I have undertaken, whilst also trying to hold down a very demanding job here."

"Oh it's not the job that's demanding, it's Steve," Molly said with good humour.

"The Bake Stop has been way more stressful than I had ever imagined, but at least Steve finally knows of my plans now."

"About time too, and that would explain his moody behaviour then."

"You two are a right pair."

"What do you mean?"

"Well, are you going to finally tell me what happened between yous both whilst you were in Tuscany, cos I feel sure something did!"

"Nothing much, just a little," Sarah was hesitant before she said, "well, you know!"

"Oh that kind of a nothing much eh! Oh sweet Jesus, you can tell me to mind me own business, but you should have known better, Sarah."

"Yes, you're right, but the trouble is, Molly, I had convinced myself that I could handle it, but the truth is," she said shrugging her shoulders, "I cannot and now," Sarah stopped.

Molly continued, "And now, Sarah, you're running away, is that what you're trying to say?"

"Well, not quite that, because I am passionate about what I am going to do, and it's made my mum so very happy. But I do need to get away from here, well to get away from Steve!"

Molly comforted Sarah and put her arm around her. "You poor wee girlie."

"It isn't Steve's fault, Molly, not entirely, I do only have myself to blame. I practically threw myself at him. There are some things that you cannot stop, like the tide from turning and for me, I was simply unable to stop myself from, well you know." Molly nodded her head.

"You love him, don't you?" Sarah became emotional as she shook her head. "I know how foolish I have been."

"Hush, don't go mithering yourself."

"Fortunately for me, I have never succumbed to Steve's charms and anyhow, I am way too old for him."

"Well I am hardly in the age bracket, he tends to go for either, am I."

"Back home he's what we call an ejeet."

"He just doesn't want to settle down and he thinks he is Peter Pan." Sarah sipped her tea and unconsciously dipped her biscuit into it. "I am okay, Molly, so please don't worry about me really, as you know I've been through a lot worse."

"I am going to miss you so much, Sarah, when you finally leave, for sure."

"I will miss you too and George, in fact everyone because living here has been like being part of a family."

"Well I'd better get on with the dinner, and you do know, Sarah, that you can always rely on me." The two women hugged.

"I appreciate that, thank you, Molly, you're such a good friend."

"No more than you have been to me!"

Chapter 35

The following morning Sarah made her way down to Biddenford and met up with Geoff and Rick, who was the building contractor, Rick had fortunately calmed down somewhat by now and they had come to a compromise over her plans. She was delighted to see that the extension was almost finished now, which would house the new bakery. There were a few issues she had to deal with and agree upon, but on the whole, she was pleasantly surprised. It was running to plan and she took some photographs of the work that had been done so far! There was much to do still, however.

Sarah had arranged to have brunch with her mother and she'd persuaded her to stay over for the night. As soon as she pulled up outside her mother's cottage, Dotty came out to greet her. "Hello love, come in, brunch is almost ready and the kettle is on." Sarah sat down at the kitchen table and Dotty brought over a pot of tea. "You're looking a bit peaky my girl," Dotty said as she poured their tea.

"Am I?"

"Well I think so, I expect you are working too hard."

"I've always done that, Mum."

"Yes but you've got a lot on your plate at the moment."

"Oh stop fussing Mum I am okay, really."

"Have it your own way," Dotty said somewhat tersely! "Anyway, how are things coming along then?"

"Not too bad, the extension is almost finished and I am getting a clearer view of things now."

"Well it's taking a while, isn't it."

"Yes, Mum, but quite a lot of alterations have been made, and there is always a hiccup or two, along the way! Have you heard from Iris and Dave at all?"

"Yes, I spoke to Iris the other day mum and she sends you her love."

"She asked how things were going and I told her the place still resembles a building site. Both are keen to be here for the Grand opening, but they are very happy to be spending more time out in Portugal."

"I bet they are," Dotty remarked, "who wouldn't want to be in all that lovely sunshine." Dotty looked at Sarah pensively, and said. "Actually, Sarah, I wanted to mention something to you."

"What's up, Mum?"

"Nothing, it's just well George and I have been thinking about taking another cruise, this time over Christmas. What do you think?"

"Mum, you're free to do whatever you like, go for it."

"Well, we had such a marvellous time on the cruise earlier in the year."

"I've already mentioned it to Tony and Megan and they are fine about it."

"Sounds a great idea, Mum. Is it getting serious between you two?"

"I couldn't possibly say, love, we are taking things slowly, you know one day at a time." Sarah wasn't sure if she believed her mother as when she'd stayed over last time with her, she'd noticed several man products dotted around in the bathroom. She would have loved to tease her mother, but thought better of it. "I asked George not to come down this weekend, because I wanted us to spend some girlie time together, just me and you, and have a good old catch up."

Sarah was in a better frame of mind by the time she returned back to London and more positive about The Bake Stop. Molly however was in a bit of a tissy, as Celia and Vivien Hope were due to arrive later that day after postponing their previous visit. She'd previously confided in Sarah that she was always on tenterhooks when she came to stay and therefore was unable to relax.

Molly had disappeared yet again, so Sarah went in search of her and found her in one of the guest rooms, which was the one Celia always used when she came to stay apparently. "For goodness' sake, Molly, what are you up to now. You should calm down and stop fussing. Surely nothing more needs doing in this room!"

"Easier said than done, Sarah, this woman will be looking for dust and anything else she can find wrong! She's like a Hotel Inspector I'm telling ya. I don't want to give her the opportunity to find fault."

"Yes, I can imagine, she could be hard to get it right for, as she is one demanding lady."

"Do you think those flowers look okay on that table, or shall I move them to the one nearer to the window."

"They're beautiful and they look fine where they are, Molly. Come on let me make you a nice calming cup of tea or something stronger," Sarah said winking at Molly.

"Oh God, let's make it something stronger, shall we!"

Chapter 36

Celia and Vivien's visit had been short and sweet and they had now returned to the States and fortunately for Sarah, she hadn't seen too much of them during their stay. They were out gallivanting somewhere most of the time. Her only involvement had been to ensure that all of their tickets were secured for the theatre and anywhere else they had requested to visit during their stay in the UK. George had always been on hand to chauffeur them around town. Whenever their paths did cross, Celia had been reasonably friendly towards Sarah, but when it came to Vivien, she herself had tried her hardest to be as pleasant as she possibly could be to the woman. She'd certainly brought enough luggage with her and all of it, was Louis Vuitton. Apart from that she'd managed to keep herself busy and dodged them as best she could. It soon became apparent, that Vivien was on a mission to see all of the sights of London, before returning home and she and Celia had been out early practically every day and most evenings. Steve had been the perfect host and of course, George had been in his element driving them both around London, sharing all of his knowledge.

Sarah had had to rely on any gossip from either him, or Molly. Vivien enthused to everyone that she had fallen in love with London, after visiting just about every touristy landmark in the Capital, but had particularly loved Buckingham Palace. Celia had also told Molly that Vivien had been so impressed with London, that she was actually considering a move across the Pond! She'd met up with an old friend, who was originally from New York, and had lived in London for ten years. He was now a Senior Partner in one of the most prestigious law firms in the Capital, and had told her that they would snap her up, and she only had to say the word!

Chapter 37

It was a bright sunny August day as Sarah made her way to the Hackney Royal Theatre. Finally, it was the big night for the Pantomime, which they had all been working so hard towards for weeks. It was show time and everyone was looking forward to it and buzzing with excitement. She was in no doubt that the youngsters were going to do a brilliant job, but she still felt a little nervous for them all.

Working closely alongside Jake, as she had been for the past weeks had been a real eye opener for her. Sarah had seen a completely different side to him and they had grown close. However, she'd kept him at bay, for now at least!

He was so popular with all of the kids and they absolutely idolised him and not only was he generous with his time, but also with his money and the Pantomime was going to be amazing. She'd enjoyed helping him immensely.

The day was full on and manic from the start, but after the final dress rehearsal, a few minor changes were made. There had been a glitch with Peter Pan's wire, but overall, Jake was confident, they were good to go. Jake had arranged for a catering company to bring in lunch and it had been superb and a very welcome break for everyone.

There was a lot of loud chatter in the girls' dressing room, as Sarah helped some of them get changed into their costumes, in readiness for their performance. The boys' dressing room was right next door. As you would expect, it was rather raucous, especially as many of them were playing the part of a pirate and it was hi jinx all round. Tinker Bell, or rather Polly, suddenly burst into their dressing room looking anxious and blurted out that Jack, aka, 'Captain Hook' had in fact lost his hook and was having a major melt down, which had now turned into a full on panic attack. Sarah had managed to calm him down, and his hook was eventually found in amongst a large box full of old props and fortunately a disaster had been averted and normality was resumed once more.

As the curtain came down, it was clear that the Pantomime had been a great success and the audience had been brilliant and so enthusiastic and had laughed at all the right times and luckily, no major hiccups. Having watched it a hundred times during rehearsals, it still made Sarah laugh and to see it in all its glory, in front of an audience was extremely fulfilling. The audience stood up and gave them a standing ovation. As the director and producer, Jake took a bow at the end and once the curtains came down, everybody went mad and the kids began jumping all over him and hi-fiving each other. They were all taking selfies on their phones and it was good fun! She herself was exhausted as she'd been running around backstage helping with props and costume changes, but it had all been worth it. A wonderful experience!

Jake walked Sarah over to her car and by now it was late, as she had helped to pack away all of the costumes and props and at one point had swept the stage. Luckily a lot of the kids' parents and friends had helped to take down the scenery, which would now have to be stored away. After the heat of the day earlier, a distinct chill was in the air and a high wind was blowing.

"You have been a star throughout all of this, Sarah, how can I ever thank you."

"You do constantly Jake, anyhow, I've had a ball, so I should be thanking you."

"Well, how about you let me take you out to dinner one night."

"Let me see, first, I will have to check my diary, of course!" Jake looked surprised. "I'm kidding, Jake. Give me a bell. You have been amazing too and the kids adore you."

"Yeah, I know it's me charisma, you cannot buy that you know."

"Definitely not," Sarah said laughing, "you big head!"

"Well, I prefer to call it confidence, but have it your own way!"

"I'm off now, Jake. I am bushed, good night."

"Okay, Sarah, I will speak to you soon." As he always did, he held her gently and kissed her softly on the lips. She gazed into his smoky brown eyes and had been sorely tempted to kiss him back, but thought better of it and quickly got behind the wheel of her car and headed off home.

Chapter 38

Jake and Sarah so far hadn't managed to get together for their night out. He was extremely busy working on stage, in a play at the Dominion Theatre in London's West End, but he'd promised to take her out on New Year's Eve and had told her it would be somewhere special. She'd been to see him in his play a couple of times. It was an intense thriller involving a love triangle and he had been brilliant in it and had received rave reviews.

Steve had kept her busy, as they were now in pre-production on his next film, the World War II drama, which he would be directing. What with fitting in her trips down to The Bake Stop, she was shattered every night and had little time for any nights out anyhow. Her relationship with Steve was a little frosty occasionally and sadly she thought, some of the warmth and friendship they had once shared, had gone.

In many ways she acknowledged, this was probably a good thing, as it would ultimately make her departure much easier to deal with somehow. She knew he was pleased that a new date had now been set for the Premiere of *"No Hiding Place"* after its postponement. It would now Premiere at the end of February. She had already told Steve she would be moving out on the 2nd of January. What better way to start a New Year, totally afresh and with a new beginning for her. If all went according to plan, the newly refurbished The Bake Stop, should open during March and she was looking forward to her vision and dream finally coming to fruition, but still had some reservations!

Sarah was busy typing some changes which had been made to the script yet again, and looked at her watch. She realised that Steve would be landing in LA in half an hour. She stopped what she was doing and sighed, as she was genuinely sad that she wouldn't be a part of Steve's next big production. It was going to be full on and exciting she was convinced of that.

George had left bright and early to go down to Biddenford to collect Dotty, as she was going to spend a few days with them in London and he could hardly wait, bless him. Sarah and her mother were going to do some retail therapy, before she and George set off on their cruise, which was fast approaching. Sarah planned to take them both out to dinner at Claridge's and as a surprise Annabel would be joining them too. Their Caribbean cruise would take them away for six weeks and Sarah was going to miss her mother over Christmas. But she would however be spending it with Annabel and Alfie and as it would be baby Alfie's first Christmas this was going to make it extra special.

She had just picked up the phone to make a call, when she heard the familiar voice of her mother and suddenly, Dotty burst into the room with George right behind her. "Oh hello, love, George said you'd probably be in here working." Sarah put the phone back down and got up from behind the desk and kissed and hugged her mother.

"Hi, Mum, did you have a good journey."

"Yes, fine, thanks."

"Right, you two girls, I will leave you to have a catch up and go and put the car in the garage."

"Okay, George, thank you and can you bring me case in love."

"Of course I will, Dorothy." It always made Sarah laugh when George called her mother Dorothy, he was certainly the only one who did and could get away with it too!

"Would you like a cup of tea, Mum?"

"I suppose it's too early for a G and T, isn't it?" Sarah gave her mother a disapproving look.

"Yes it is, Mum! Come through to the kitchen."

"Oh I must say, Sarah, this is a lovely house and what a gorgeous staircase, and this carpet, well it's so sumptuous me feet are disappearing into it, as it's so blooming thick!" Dotty followed Sarah into the kitchen and sat down at the table. Sarah began to fill the kettle at the kitchen sink, when Dotty asked. "Is his Lordship around?"

"Mum, please. One of these days, you will call him that to his face!"

"No I won't, don't be so silly. So is he here?"

"No, he should be landing in LA any minute."

"Oh I see, shame as I would have liked to have seen him again. Sarah, I think you'd better make my George a cup of tea too."

"Your George now is it, Mum?"

Her mother was flustered slightly, as she said, "Well no-no love, that was a slip of the tongue." Sarah didn't challenge her mother, but she smiled to herself. Her mother as always, was playing her cards close to her chest!

"Don't worry I was going to make him one anyway, and I know he likes it nice and strong." George came in and Sarah noticed the beaming smile he gave to her mother.

"So do you like the house, Dorothy, well, what you've seen so far?" he asked.

"It's lovely and I cannot wait for a guided tour later." The three of them were sat around chatting when Molly returned from her shopping trip. Sarah made the introductions and Dotty hit it off immediately with Molly and Sarah knew they were going to get along. They were like kindred spirits and both had tales to tell.

Sarah took Dotty upstairs and into the bedroom, which she'd been given to use, during her stay and it was clear she was impressed. George had already left her mother's case in the room. "Crikes this is lovely, Sarah," Dotty said, rubbing her hands on the silk bedspread. "It's a bit like Buckingham Palace in here isn't it," she said, laying out fully on the comfortable bed.

"Well not quite, Mum, but one could certainly become accustomed to it, don't you know."

"Not for much longer for you now though, is it?"

"Yes that's true, Mum," Sarah replied looking away from her mother as she did so. She was trying hard not to think about the day when she actually left.

"How's Steve? Is he getting used to the idea of you leaving?"

"Well, he doesn't say too much, but Maxine told me they are holding interviews next week."

"Well, no one will ever be as committed to the job as you have been."

"Thanks, Mum, I appreciate that, but I expect someone will be ready and waiting to take my place!"

It had been a whirlwind few days with her mother and an emotional goodbye as she wouldn't be seeing her now until after her cruise in the New Year. Although her mother's visit had been brief, they had certainly packed a lot into it. Plenty of retail therapy had taken place and Sarah had helped her mother choose a beautiful dazzling gold Lurex evening dress to wear to the Captain's Cocktail party. She had looked stunning in it and Dotty was so excited she could hardly wait to get away on their cruise. However, she had pointed out that she would naturally miss her family.

Sarah couldn't fail to notice how sparkly her mother's eyes were these days and she knew that George was responsible for that! George had joked that he would have a job keeping up with Dotty whilst on the cruise, because she would join in on all the fun and classes, especially dancing and cookery. Dotty was definitely hooked on cruising. Sarah couldn't be happier for her and she more than deserved to have a second bite at the cherry with George. Even if her mother wouldn't admit it as yet, Sarah knew she was very smitten with him.

Annabel had turned up at Claridge's as a surprise for Dotty, who had been over the moon to see her and Sarah had taken her over to meet little Alfie, who at eight and a half months old was changing every time Sarah saw him. He was on the verge of crawling and Dotty had commented to Annabel that she would get no peace then, as he would be into everything from now on. Sarah had never seen Annabel so contented and happy and she knew that she was dreading going back to work. Still she had a while yet, but Sarah had sympathy for her, and knew it was going to be a wrench. Julie was going to have Alfie for two days a week as she was working part time these days and on the other three, Alfie would be in a day care nursery.

Chapter 39

Sarah was in her bedroom packing, surrounded by suitcases and boxes which were full of her clothes and personal belongings. She had nearly cracked it all now and was ready for when she moved out. It was New Year's Eve and Christmas had come and gone in the blink of an eye, but it had been a wonderful time, spending it with Annabel and Alfie. Julie and John had joined them with Annabel's half brother and sister and their families on Boxing Day and they had all spent a lovely family day together.

It had been a joy being around little Alfie, who had typically been far more interested in playing with the discarded wrapping paper and empty boxes which his presents had come in. Sarah had bought Alfie a push along fire truck, with a rather loud siren, which he could also sit on, but he wasn't quite ready for it just yet, but it wouldn't be long, In fact he was a very contented baby and a joy to be around and he didn't cry often, except on the day when he was Christened. Sarah had been extremely proud of him, as she was now officially Alfie's godmother. He had cooed and smiled his way all through the ceremony, but as soon as the Vicar had poured water onto his head, he had howled and really let rip and it had taken ages before he calmed down once more.

Sarah looked at her watch and as it was almost 3.30, stopped what she was doing. Jake would be picking her up at 6 o'clock for their date. Dotty had rung her earlier to wish her a Happy New Year from her cruise, which was heading towards St Maarten, before the phone lines became impossible. She'd sounded so happy and had told her that she and George were both having a wonderful time. They still had a further three weeks cruising to do.

She would spend the rest of the afternoon pampering herself. She'd already had her hair and nails done earlier and intended to have a leisurely long soak in the bath. Frederick had coiffured her hair into a soft chignon, piled quite high, with lots of pins, and a ton of hairspray to keep it in place. She would have to be extra careful when in the bath. Frederick and Jean-Paul had been in fine fettle earlier. Once Frederick had finished her hair, he had exclaimed. "Oh my gawd, don't she look like Audrey Hepburn, you know when she was in *Breakfast at Tiffany's,*" he'd said to anyone who'd listen!

Their Salon had resembled a Santa's grotto. They did it every year throughout December for Charity, and it always raised a great deal of money. Today the pair had been dressed as Elves. Their Wedding had only taken place two weeks earlier and both were still blissfully happy and in high spirits. So far there hadn't been any of their infamous, full on major rows and fallouts, which they were well-known for! Still they always kissed and made up! As she had predicted the Wedding had been way over the top. Doves had been released after the ceremony in every direction and the venue had been themed as a Winter Wonderland, with more red hearts and flowers than she'd ever seen in her life. It had however, been an amazing day, full of emotion. Frederick's Ninety-year-old mother had clearly been moved, shedding a tear or two of happiness for her only son.

She was really looking forward to the night ahead and as yet, she still had no idea of where Jake would be taking her. Sarah had been unable to resist buying herself a new dress and she had splashed out on a very expensive black designer one for the occasion. It had a small ladylike fishtail, teamed with a chunky metallic belt and an alluring sweetheart neckline. Annabel had been with her when she'd bought it and had told her, she looked gorgeous in it. She trusted her friend's opinion, but in truth she hadn't needed any persuasion to buy it whatsoever, the dress fitted like a glove.

Sarah returned to her room, after quickly popping to show off her new look and dress to Molly who had given her the thumbs up. She too looked gorgeous, in a bright red cocktail dress, which Sarah had helped her choose. She hadn't been too sure about the colour, because she thought it may clash with her auburn hair. But Sarah had convinced her that it looked lovely on her! Molly's cheeks were flushed and she had admitted to Sarah, that she was so excited, but also rather nervous because, she hadn't been on a date in years. Callum had finally got around to asking her out, at long last! It was clear that they both fancied the pants off of one other.

Sarah was ready for the off now, and couldn't resist checking herself out one more time in the mirror, and realised she'd forgotten to put on her pearl necklace, which had once belonged to her Grandmother. It had three rows of pearls and finished off her look a treat! She picked up her overnight bag and made her way downstairs, taking her time as she did so, due to her long dress. Steve followed on behind her. He was clearly ready to go out too, dressed immaculately in his black tie and evening suit. "Hello, Sarah, and where are you off to looking so glam?"

"I don't know yet, it's a surprise! Jake is picking me up any minute now and I have absolutely no idea of where he is taking me." There was a loud toot from a car horn outside. "That sounds like him now," Sarah said as she walked towards the front door, but before she opened it, Steve called out to her and Sarah turned around to face him. "Yes, Steve?"

He glanced down at her overnight bag and then looked straight into her eyes which had a sparkle about them, and Sarah held his gaze momentarily before he said. "Happy New Year."

"Thanks, you too."

Jake was waiting for her outside and had the car door open in readiness for her as he let out a loud wolf whistle. He took her bag and placed it onto the back seat and then helped her get into the car. As he sat down in the driver's seat, he gave her a warm and gentle kiss on the lips. "God, you look amazing. Love your dress, Sarah, love it."

"Thank you and by the way you don't look so bad yourself." As always he smelt gorgeous too and it sent a shiver down her spine. She had always loved his aftershave, which she'd found out was Gucci Guilty. At last he had shaved off his beard and looked more like his old familiar self and of course, even more handsome in her eyes, in a smart black evening suit. "Thank you, Sarah."

"You know with that look, I think you could be the next James Bond, Jake."

"What a humble cockney East End boy like meself, I wish," he said with a huge grin!

"So where are we heading off to tonight, Jake?"

Jake revved the engine loudly and turned to her and said, "Tighten your seat belt little lady, and enjoy the ride because you're in for a great night."

Steve stood in the hallway after Sarah had left with a pensive look on his face. He had been sorely tempted to say something to Sarah, after seeing her overnight bag. But what could he say? Don't do anything I wouldn't do, or do you have a thingy with you? He almost laughed out loud at how ridiculous he was being. Sarah had looked beautiful tonight and he knew he was going to miss her after she left.

It looked as if she and Jake had reconnected and deep down, who could blame her! Jake was a decent enough guy and she deserved some fun, as long as he didn't hurt her. But that was none of his business, or was it!

No it wasn't, as she had pointed out to him, on more than one occasion, she was more than capable of making her own decisions, on who she should, or shouldn't be with. He truly hoped that he hadn't hurt her in any way.

He would be spending the evening with friends, including his new leading lady, Leoni Barton. Once again, she was young, feisty and gorgeous and just as problematic as Elenour ever was. Still that had worked out okay, at least he hoped so! Anyway, he was used to that particular type of woman, and as his mother liked to point out to him, he certainly knew how to pick them. He could see the raw talent, which Leoni clearly had, and of course she would be a challenge. He enjoyed taking risks and she undoubtedly would be just that. She may not have been the most obvious choice to play the part of his Russian spy, but his gut feeling was that she was the one. He had to trust his instincts, he always had. Okay, there could be fireworks ahead, but when had he ever taken the easy option! But, he believed with a great deal of effort, which he was fully prepared to give, he would push her to the limit and beyond, exactly as he had done with Elenour. He hoped Leoni wouldn't disappoint. He was banking on her working her backside off for him and that her talent would come across on the big screen! He didn't want to appear overly confident, but he wasn't usually wrong!

Thankfully, Vivien had postponed her move to the UK for the time being and he was relieved about that. He would always be fond of her, but he didn't want to open that particular can of worms, not now, or ever!

Sarah was on a high and full of anticipation as Jake pulled up outside the Shard. As soon they alighted from the car, their bags were immediately taken care of and Jake's car was driven off to be parked. "Oh, Jake, this is a lovely surprise." The Shard would be a fabulous place to see the New Year in and Sarah was genuinely excited. They walked into the foyer of the Shangri-La Hotel and checked in. The Receptionist gave them their room numbers and told them that their bags had already been taken to their respective rooms. Sarah looked at Jake with a smile on her face and said softly to him, "Two rooms!"

"Yes, Princess, you see before you, a true gentleman!"

"You're so modest, Jake," Sarah said with a sparkle in her eyes and she laughed. "Well, I am pleased to hear that, Jake," she said rather tongue in cheek.

In truth, Jake was hoping that they would only need the one room, but equally he clearly wasn't taking that for granted.

"Shall we get drinks before dinner, Sarah?"

"Sounds lovely but could I quickly pop up to my room first, to powder my nose."

"Yes of course, you can and I will see you in the bar of the restaurant, which is on the 32nd floor!"

Sarah wasn't disappointed with her room, which had been beautifully decorated in muted soft colours of blues and greys. Of course it had magnificent views over the City of London and as it was night time, it looked really spectacular with twinkling lights against a pitch-black sky! Jake was a very generous guy. She unzipped her case and hung up the few clothes, which she had brought with her and put her wash bag and make-up in the en-suite. This too had amazing views and a giant-sized free-standing bathtub and a state of the art shower.

She reapplied her lipstick and spritzed her perfume lightly all over and made her way down to the 32nd floor, where Jake was stood at the bar waiting for her. "You weren't long, Sarah!"

"No, just powdered my nose," she said, giving him a rather seductive smile.

"I have to say my room is gorgeous and the views are stunning, with the whole city lit up. It's so lovely, thank you so much, Jake."

"You're welcome and we're going to have a great night."

"Here, you are," Jake said as he handed her a glass of champagne. "I'm having a Vodka Martini Cocktail shaken, not stirred, Miss Moneypenny," he quipped in his best Sean Connery voice, which made Sarah laugh as she said:

"Ooh it's like having him in the room." They clinked their glasses together.

"Here's to a brilliant evening, Princess."

"First, we are going to have dinner, just you and me in the restaurant and later, we will be meeting up with some of my friends and yours!"

"Who?" Sarah enquired, curious to know. "You will just have to wait and see."

"You're spoiling me, Jake, and I want you to know that I'm absolutely loving it."

Jake kissed the back of her hand and said, "No problemo, you deserve it, Princess."

They ate in the Oblix Restaurant, which was extremely lively and it didn't disappoint with its; stunning views and the best of British and European food. It had been a leisurely meal, and the staff had been extremely attentive, and so had Jake! The atmosphere was buzzing with people having a good time. Some were in large parties, whilst others were in smaller groups or couples. There was an awful lot of chatter and laughter. Champagne was flowing, but Sarah was conscious that she shouldn't overdo it and had drunk mainly water. It was after all only 9.30 and the night was still young!

With their meal over, they took the lift and alighted at the 36th floor where Jake led her through to a private room. Sarah was surprised as she was greeted by a few familiar faces from Tuscany and the first one to rush over to greet her was Marie. "Oh, Cherie, there you are at last," she said throwing her arms around Sarah, and kissed her on both cheeks.

"Marie, oh how fantastic to see you," Sarah said giving her a warm smile and then mouthed a thank you to Jake. "This is such a lovely surprise and I see you're still with Dave then."

"Yes, and I have now moved to be with him in London. It's still full on, as we're both travelling loads but it seems to be working." It wasn't long before Sarah was given another glass of champagne which she was becoming so fond of!

The evening progressed and Jake and Sarah performed their rock and roll routine, as they had done once before, back in Tuscany and soon Sarah had quickly thrown her shoes into a corner of the room. She'd realised earlier her dress would be impossible to boogie in, and she'd quickly popped up to her room and changed into a chic little cocktail dress! Jake picked her up and threw her around like a rag doll and she didn't care, as by now she had consumed so much champagne, that any inhibitions she may have had, had gone right out the window.

It was fast approaching midnight and everyone was on the dance floor waiting in anticipation, ready for the count down. Five, four, three, two, one. Happy New Year was being shouted out all around the room, as they grouped together and sang their version of Auld Lang Syne! Balloons were unleashed as they slowly fell down from the ceiling and party poppers were being popped, as were the balloons! Jake took Sarah in his arms and kissed her long and hard, as he wished her a Happy New Year, which left her breathless!

It was 2.30 before Jake and Sarah finally made their way into the lift, with his arm firmly around her waist. Her once perfectly coiffured chignon had now started to fall down in an untidy mess, as her long mane had escaped some of the hundreds of pins Frederick had put in place earlier. Jake began kissing Sarah's neck and it was clear that both of them knew what each other was thinking. Although Sarah's head wasn't overly clear any more, but she felt happy and carefree and it didn't seem to matter that she was behaving a bit like a wanton woman.

The pair stepped out of the lift and made their way to Jake's room, and stopped briefly outside the door and kissed again, with Jake's hand firmly on her backside. Jake opened the door and scooped Sarah up into his arms and placed her down as soon as they were inside his suite.

Jake's Suite was pretty impressive as Sarah began to spin and dance around the room, shouting whoop-whoop at the top of her voice. "This is bloody amazing, Jake. It's huge in here and that bed, it's massive," she said, continuing to spin around the room until she almost fell over, but Jake caught her just in time.

"Come here, Princess, you're getting yourself all dizzy."

"No, no, Jake, please I'm all right, honestly. Ooh come on kiss me," she said, throwing her arms around his neck!

"You've had quite a lot to drink tonight, Sarah! How about I get you a nice glass of water, whilst you have a little sit down." Jake thought it might help to sober her up, but coffee would be better!

Sarah looked into his eyes and smiled sweetly at him. "Okay if you say so! You're soo, soo lovely to me, Jakey, and sexy," she said, trying to stifle a yawn. Jake steered a rather wobbly Sarah towards the sofa and walked across the room and grabbed a small bottle of still water from the fridge and took a glass from the top of the drinks cabinet. He poured the water into it and looked across at Sarah, who was by now sprawled right out on the sofa. She was fast asleep and all that could be heard was a short burst of a snuffling sound, followed by a puff, puff, escaping from her mouth. Jake looked up at the ceiling and rolled his eyes, as he rubbed his hand across his jaw and shook his head from side to side.

"Oh, Sarah. Fuck, not again! What are you doing to me?"

Chapter 40

Jake had dropped Sarah back home earlier at around mid-day, and they had both been relatively quiet throughout the journey, but to be fair she'd been feeling dreadful, with the thickest head she'd ever had. Maybe Jake was hung over too, but she didn't think he'd drunk that much. He had however, been nothing but kind to her, opening the car door as usual and carrying her bags, and his parting words were that he would call her later and urged Sarah to get herself off to bed.

She'd taken his advice on board and when she had eventually got up at 5 p.m., she took a shower to wake herself up. It didn't work unfortunately, as her head was still spinning slightly and she felt icky and groggy. She was also racking her brains as to what had happened between her and Jake the previous night! She vaguely remembered returning to his Suite, but after that it was a complete blur. However, she had woken up in his bed that morning alone, in just her panties. Her brain felt numb! It would be beyond embarrassing to ask Jake what had happened between them the night before! Oh lord, would she ever learn. Champagne and Sarah Carrington was not a good idea!

After her shower, she got dressed and put on her grey jogging bottoms and a white tee shirt and scraped her hair back into a ponytail and added a touch of blusher and lipstick as she still looked extremely pale. Thankfully, she had loaded up the Range Rover with most of her belongings the day before and she was ready for the off the following morning. George would return the Range Rover once he and Dotty came back from their cruise.

Sarah made her way downstairs and noticed how quiet it was in the house, until Buster jumped up at her as she entered the kitchen. "Oh hello, Buster, God you made me jump! Happy New Year, boy," she said kissing the top of his head. "Are you all on your own?"

A voice from behind her said, "No, he isn't!" It was Steve and he was giving her a disapproving look! "Heavy night, was it?"

"I think so, I must admit, I do feel a bit fragile."

"Well, you certainly look as if you are," Steve said rather unkindly.

"Thanks, Steve. Anyway, I was just about to make a cup of tea, would you like one?"

"No thanks, I am just about to go out."

"Oh, right okay, see you later," but there was no response, as he disappeared. Moments later, she heard the front door close behind him rather loudly.

Sarah sat down with her cup of tea, and Buster laid across her feet, looking up at her adoringly. Looks like it's just me and you then Buster she said, as she tickled him under his chin, which he loved and he wagged his tail furiously. Sarah placed her hands around her cup and hoped that after she'd drunk her tea she would feel better. After all, a cup of tea cured all ills, didn't it?

She spent some time sending texts to family and friends with good wishes for the New Year and caught up with Annabel, who was eager to know all the gossip on her night out with Jake. Sarah had told her it had been a fabulous evening. Annabel kept pumping her for more information, but Sarah had said that she would save it all for when they met up again. "Spoils sport" had been Annabel's only comment.

Sarah laid on the sofa flicking through the TV channels, and nothing took her fancy. She was feeling restless and irksome and thought about having an early night. As it was New Year's Day, you would have thought there would have been something decent on the box for goodness' sake. She did however have a change of heart and decided that she would go down to the Cinema room and watch a film. Buster stirred from his slumber and looked at her and then opened his mouth wide and let out a long yawn. As soon as she got up, he jumped up to follow her as always.

He would normally be banned from the cinema, but Sarah was feeling lonely and so for once she encouraged him to go with her. She was in need of some company and it was unlikely anyone would find out.

She'd had her fill of slushy Christmassy films and put on one of her all-time favourite films, Breakfast at Tiffany's and got herself a bag of sweets and sat down in the back row and looked up at the ceiling with its tiny lights twinkling away like shiny little stars. There were only three rows in the cinema, but you really did feel as if you were in a proper cinema. The rich red velvet seats were soft and comfortable and Buster laid down, resting his head on her pink fluffy rabbit slippers, which had been a present from little Alfie. Her mobile pinged and it was a message from Jake. It was relatively brief. It had simply said that his

Agent had been in touch and he would be flying out to LA early the following day, as he had an audition for a part in a new movie. He ended by saying he would be in touch once he returned home. He'd finished up with *Good Luck with The Bake Stop and take care of yourself Princess* with, just two kisses! He hadn't even bothered to ring her!

As soon as the film began for some reason, Sarah couldn't stop blubbing. She was feeling very emotional and overwrought and by the end of the film she was sobbing big time. Buster suddenly began to bark loudly and ran towards the door. Sarah got up tentatively. "What's up, boy?"

The door opened and Steve practically burst in. "Oh, Steve, you gave me such a fright. My heart is pounding."

"Oh sorry, I wondered where the hell Buster was and then I heard him barking and was concerned."

"Naughty boy, Buster you're not meant to be in here are you?!" Buster looked up at his master and jumped up excitedly and licked his face. "Okay, boy. Down you get."

"I'm afraid that's my fault. I brought him down here for some company."

Steve stared at Sarah, "Good God, woman, what the hell have you been up to?" he said, sitting down next to her.

"Watching *Breakfast at Tiffany's*! And I blubbed right from when I heard *Moon River* in fact I have sobbed on and off throughout the film and even more so at the end. You know, where Audrey Hepburn finds cat out in the pouring rain with George Peppard. That bit gets me every bloody time."

Pulling herself together somewhat, she said, "So what did you do New Year's Eve, Steve?"

"Me? I was out, schmoozing my new leading lady."

"Oh really, I'm sure if anyone can do that, it's you, Steve!"

"How you have to suffer for your art." Steve grinned at her and said, "I'll take that as a compliment!"

"You should," Sarah said wryly.

"So, do you normally cry that much when you watch *Breakfast at Tiffany's*?"

"No, to be honest I don't, but I am feeling so emotional," and suddenly, she burst into tears. "I'm freaking out here, Steve. What the hell am I doing? This new venture of mine. What if it fails? I'm so scared."

"It won't," he said firmly and reached for the box of tissues which were on the side and gave her a handful. "Come on, wipe your eyes! By the way, Sarah, I thought you looked gorgeous last night."

Sarah stopped blowing her nose and looked at Steve, surprised by what he'd just said. "Why thank you, flattery will get you everywhere she said in between sobbing. Actually, you didn't look half bad yourself!"

Sarah unashamedly had the urge to throw herself at Steve and kiss him, but thought that would be so wrong on many levels. However, he took her completely unaware by kissing her and it was a long and passionate one. Steve could taste Sarah's salty tears on his tongue and both were breathless when they finally stopped. "Oh, Steve, look at me. I'm a bloody wreck and I know I look awful in these old jogging bottoms." Steve ignoring her, took hold of her hand and gently pulled her up from her seat.

"Yep, you do look awful, but I'm trying to keep that lovely image of you from last night when you wore that sexy dress." Sarah looked visibly upset. "I'm only teasing you," Steve said as their eyes met, hers were slightly blood shot from all the crying she'd been doing.

"What are we up to here, Steve?"

"What do you think?" he said, kissing her once more as his hands explored her body.

"Well, we could always stop all this and have a cup of hot cocoa," Sarah said jokingly.

"Don't be ridiculous, woman. Come on, let's get thee up those stairs, because I'm not going to make love to you here in front of young Buster. I wouldn't be able to perform properly and anyhow, the poor boy's been done, it would be too cruel!"

The pair raced up the stairs and into Steve's room and very quickly jumped on to the bed and stripped off all of their clothes, which were quickly discarded onto the floor. They made love with every ounce of passion they had in them and lay quiet afterwards until Sarah got up and took a shower in the en-suite. Steve mulled over what had just taken place between them, yet again. It certainly hadn't been planned, but then it never had been with Sarah, and as before, he found it slightly unnerving. Sarah had a way of making him feel guilty about his actions at the best of times. For some reason, he had a strong urge to protect her, but for the life of him, he had no idea why. He wondered what had happened between Sarah and Jake on New Year's Eve, but didn't want to dwell on that right now.

When Sarah had first began working for him, it was obvious that she clearly had some battle scars, but Steve had always found her an extremely sensual and beautiful woman. The sex between them was amazing. She was also intelligent and smart and always had a calming influence on him, except for when they made love. In fact, she was the complete package. He'd relied on her more and more of late and she had never ever let him down, not once. He certainly didn't regret what had just happened between him and Sarah, how could he, but why did he feel so bad? He valued his freedom far too much to ever contemplate settling down and anyway Sarah knew the score didn't she?

He didn't want to commit wholly to anyone. His parents' bitter divorce had put pay to that and marriage was out of the question. It was fortunate that Sarah would be leaving the following morning and therefore would no longer be a temptation.

Sarah was on a high as she returned to the bedroom, and why wouldn't she be, after all she'd just had sex again with the man she loved. She'd put on one of Steve's white shirts, which had the faint smell of his aftershave and it clung to her body, which was still damp from taking her shower. Steve was observing Sarah as she walked back into the bedroom and he couldn't help but notice that Sarah's breasts were clearly visible through his shirt and she looked as sexy as hell. He was unable to take his eyes off of her slim, but curvaceous body. Her loose blonde hair was wet and make-up free in his opinion, she looked even more youthful and seductive and he instantly, became aroused. Sarah slid into the bed alongside Steve, and she quickly sensed this and her whole body ached for him once more. She turned onto her side and leant on her elbow to face him.

They gazed into each other's eyes and both giggled. Right now if Sarah had been a stick of rock, she would have *desire* running right through her whole body. This was the last chance saloon for her as she asked Steve, "How about you and me getting it on one more time, for old times' sake?" Steve laughed out loud and drew her into his arms as she wrapped her long legs around his body. He was completely powerless to resist her, as always. She began to kiss him with a sense of urgency, which had come from deep within. Soon they were writhing all over the bed together, as Steve kissed Sarah's breasts and instantly their longing and passion for one another overcame them and they made love once more.

It had all been a little frantic and afterwards they lay still, wet with perspiration and breathing heavily. She laid within Steve's arms as he stroked her hair.

Neither of them spoke for a long time. Sarah didn't want this night or rather morning to ever end. The sex between her and Steve was electric, but why oh why did she have to go and fall in love with him.

Meanwhile, as Steve lay next to Sarah, he reproached himself yet again. It was wrong of him to play with Sarah's emotions, but neither of them had put up much of a fight. Steve's head was all over the place and he had a real yearning for Sarah that went beyond the physical side. He tried to push such thoughts to the back of his mind. Sarah was the first to break the silence.

She looked at Steve and could see what she thought looked like panic in his sexy blue eyes. "Steve, for God's sake, don't look so worried."

"We both know what this is, it's just sex and this time it really won't be happening, ever again."

"I've had the most amazing time working for you. I have loved my job and it's taken me to places that I had never ever been to before, and I have now finally moved on with my life."

"Tomorrow," she said emphatically, "will be a new beginning for me and I am really looking forward to it." Once more Steve was stumped for something to say. Sarah always had a knack of doing that to him, but he had to say something.

He paused before he said, "I know one thing, Sarah, your business will be a great success with you at the helm and for what it's worth, I think you're very brave. I don't know of any other person who would be more committed than you." He meant it too. He had never had anyone work for him and give so much of themselves.

Sarah smiled. "Thanks, Steve, that means so much to me. Anyway, you've helped me too."

"I have?" Steve seemed surprised.

"Yes."

"How come?" he asked.

"Well, for one thing, you have given me a massive ego boost." Her voice cracked a little as she said. "Before I met you, I thought I'd lost my mojo, like *forever*."

Steve realised that Sarah was on the verge of breaking down.

"Are you really going to be okay, Sarah?"

She nodded and just about muttered, "Of course, I am," as she turned away. She was determined not to let her guard down in front of Steve. Tears threatened to fall and she was struggling to keep her emotions under control. If only she was able to tell him that she loved him and couldn't bear the thought of losing him. Why would she even have such a thought, when he had never been hers in the first place. He would definitely run a mile if he knew how she really felt about him. Sarah had always known the score with Steve. They had only ever been friends with benefits, and nothing more.

He didn't do commitment, but it still hurt her to the very core, she was an idiot. Thank goodness she would be leaving tomorrow. An exciting and new challenge awaited her and surely this would be enough to put Steve completely out of her mind. Fingers crossed this would be the case. Steve held her gently and kissed the nape of her neck, "Night, Sarah."

Sarah shut her eyes tightly, as tears rolled down her cheeks and onto the pillow, as she muttered, "Night." It wasn't long before both of them fell into a deep sleep.

The next morning, Sarah awoke with a bit of a jolt, and didn't feel that she'd had a peaceful night's sleep. She was also surprised to find that she was still in Steve's arms. Steve however was in a deep slumber. Only the odd snuffling sound could be heard coming from him, as he slept peacefully. Sarah looked at her watch, it was 7 a.m. Today was going to be a difficult one for her what with moving out and she would rather have done it without a raging headache. It must be due to the tension that she was feeling. Yesterday she'd woken up with a bad headache but that had been down to the champagne! Still it had been New Year's Eve! She pulled the bed covers back and as gently as she could, slid out of the bed, and managed not to disturb Steve.

Sarah looked down as he slept peacefully, and with his messed up hair, he looked quite boyish, well he would have, if he didn't have such a heavy stubble. Molly was right, he was just like Peter Pan and he didn't want to grow up and take on responsibilities. He didn't look his age either, which she had found out was forty-two. She also had a mad desire to jump right back into bed and snuggle up with him again, but that would have been the wrong thing to do.

Back in her own room, she ran the shower for a while to get it to the right temperature and stood under its large shower head, allowing the water to cascade over her body. This would be the last time she would ever take a shower here. Suddenly, she began to cry quietly, her body shaking as the water washed away her tears. Every day working for Steve had been exciting, uplifting and exactly what she had needed. But it was time for her to get on with the rest of her life. Once The Bake Stop was up and running, surely this would keep her busy and there wouldn't be enough time to think about Steve. She was definitely in a much stronger place than she had been in a long time. But she had to acknowledge too, that there was an empty feeling, which gnawed away inside of her. She knew however, that giving into this was something she had no intention of doing. As her mother would often say, what doesn't kill you makes you stronger. She just hoped that her mother was right.

Chapter 41

After dressing in her jeans, hoody and flat shoes, Sarah made her way down to the kitchen and was greeted by Buster. As usual, he was pleased to see her and his tail wagged furiously from side to side, knocking loudly against the table leg and Sarah bent down to hug him. Oh I am going to miss you so much boy. She took a treat from the cupboard, and he ate it gratefully and woofed it down as always. Tears smarted once again in her eyes as the reality of leaving fully hit her. As she stood up, she was surprised to be greeted by Molly, as she came into the kitchen.

"Morning, Sarah, you're up early!"

"Morning, Molly."

"Happy New Year, Sarah."

Sarah kissed Molly and wished her a Happy New Year too. "So where did you come from."

"Oh, I got back late last night."

"I didn't hear you."

"Well, I was as quiet as a Church mouse."

"So did you have a good time with Callum?"

"I most certainly did."

"Is that all I'm going to get?"

"For now," Molly said, laughing.

"I'll put the kettle on."

"Anyway, how are you, did you have a good time with Jake on New Year's Eve,"

Sarah hesitated before saying, "Yes, lovely, he took me to the Shard and it was fabulous."

"Marie, my good friend, who I met whilst in Tuscany, was there and a few others. It was lovely to spend time with them all and Marie has now moved to London to be with Dave, her boyfriend."

The two sat down at the table. "Are you going to be okay, Sarah? If you don't mind me saying, you're looking awfully sad."

"Well, I hope so, but I am sad to be leaving and getting a bit nervous about The Bake Stop."

"I'm going to miss you, Sarah, we all will and it's going to be so quiet around here once you've gone."

Molly had become very fond of Sarah, and she was such a kind and generous person. She also doubted very much, that Steve would be lucky enough to find such a good PA again. Sarah would be a hard act to follow.

Molly could tell that Sarah was a little distracted and the sadness in her eyes was clearly evident for anyone to see and she looked so pale, as if she hadn't slept at all. It was a shame that Steve was too dumb to have noticed how much Sarah cared for him. It was in every look and gesture she made. The man was a fool, but she wasn't paid to give him advice, not in the love department at least. Anyhow, Molly knew he wouldn't have listened to her anyway! However, he should never have messed with Sarah's emotions, because she was a decent woman. Molly placed an arm around Sarah's shoulder. "How about some coffee?"

"Yes please, Molly and I need to take a paracetamol. My head is thumping and you'd better make that coffee strong too please."

"Will do."

"Thank goodness I packed up the car the other day, I don't think I could have faced doing it now."

"So have you any gossip for me, like what went on with you and Jake?" Sarah's mind was more on her night of passion with Steve. No wonder her head hurt! "We'll have to save that for another time," Sarah said, thus avoiding the question yet again.

"Oh, I see, like that is it."

"I know that I drunk too much and I'm still paying for it."

"Would you like some breakfast, Sarah?"

"No thank you, Molly. I am going to get myself ready for the off. The sooner I get away the better. I've lots to do once I get back to Biddenford!"

"Oh come here you," Molly said, hugging Sarah before she went upstairs with tears smarting in her eyes.

Chapter 42

Sarah had put the last of her bags into the Range Rover and was ready to say her goodbye to Molly and Buster. So far there had been no sign of Steve and Sarah was relieved about that. She found Molly in the kitchen and Buster was laying on his comfy bed, but came over and sat down looking up at her and then looked towards his lead. "Oh sorry my boy, I cannot take you out today." Sarah would miss him so much.

"Do you know what, I think he loves you nearly as much as he loves Steve," Molly said.

"The feeling's mutual, isn't it Buster?" Sarah said, hugging him.

"Right, that's me done, Molly."

"Okay, girlie. Promise me that you will keep in touch."

"Of course I bloody well will, and thank you Molly, you've been brilliant and I really mean that."

"You too. Here, I have a present for you," Molly said, as she presented Sarah with a small box containing some essential food items and then gave her a massive bouquet of flowers!

"Oh, Molly, you're a star, thank you so much."

"It will save you having to stop off somewhere."

"Come on, and I will walk you to the car." The two said their goodbyes and kissed one another. Molly hugged and kissed Sarah once more, and then went and stood at the front door with tears in her eyes, as she waved Sarah off.

Chapter 43

Sarah walked into her mother's cottage and the first thing she did was to fill the kettle up and place it onto the Aga and make herself a lovely cup of tea. There was always something comforting about her mother's kitchen. She sat down at the kitchen table and gave Annabel a call. "Well, I'm back home, I feel like I have come full circle!"

"Well, you have, but look what you've been up to whilst you have been away!"

"Yeah, it's been amazing. But I certainly have my work cut out now. The shop fitters will be making a start on Wednesday," she hesitated slightly before saying, "and I am really excited!"

"Mind you if I have to look through another catalogue or at swatches of materials and paint pots, it won't be too soon."

"By the way, thank you for all your input, hun, it's been invaluable."

"You're welcome."

"Ooh, I cannot wait to see it, Sarah. When do you think you will have the Grand Opening of the most fabulous The Bake Stop?"

"Oh give over, but if all goes according to plan, I'm going to try and push for early March, Geoff thinks it's fairly feasible. I guess I will just have to wait and see."

"Oh brilliant."

"You and Alfie will come, won't you?"

"You try and keep us away!" Sarah could hear Alfie crying in the background. "Oh his Highness has just woken up, better go!"

"Okay, give Alfie a kiss from his favourite Auntie Sarah."

"Will do, bye."

Sarah had spent most of the day sorting out emails and focusing for once totally on The Bake Stop, which made a nice change. She'd been juggling two jobs for such a long time, and it felt liberating that she was free to concentrate on her very own project. She hadn't realised how much of a strain she'd been under, especially over the past few months.

She went up to her old bedroom and began to sort out her things and to put her clothes away. She'd certainly returned with more clothes than before she'd left. She would have to have another clear out and take some of it down to the Charity shop.

There was a knock at the front door. Sarah wasn't expecting anyone, so she quickly looked out of the window and her heart began to pound as she recognised Steve's four by four outside. She ran down the stairs and she knew her face was flushed. She opened the door and received a surprise as it wasn't Steve, but Callum who was standing at the door. "Oh hello, Callum, I didn't expect to see you, come in."

"No, I won't thanks, Sarah, I'm here on a mission from Steve and I have to get back."

"Where's Steve?"

"Oh you know him, the usual off to meetings, etc."

"Yes, as always."

"Right, stay there and hold on one moment as I have got something for you from Steve. Now, I know this sounds a bit weird, but Steve said you have to close your eyes."

"Okay," Sarah said, wondering what the hell was going on!

"Yeah, it's a surprise you see. You won't open them, will you?"

"No, I promise!" Sarah squeezed her eyes shut and she heard Callum run back towards the car and return almost immediately.

"You can open your eyes now, Sarah."

When she opened her eyes again, Callum was holding the cutest little Labradoodle puppy she'd ever seen. It was the colour of a milky latte. "Oh my God, it's gorgeous."

"It's a little boy and he's all yours, Sarah. Steve said he knew how much you'd miss Buster, but he couldn't possibly part with him. Here, you take hold of him, I've got all the gear that you're going to need, I can promise you that." Callum wasn't wrong, as Steve had thought of everything, including several books on raising a puppy. Her mother's lounge was filled with boxes of doggy bits!

"Look, I hope you don't mind, Sarah, but I have to dash."

"No, of course, thank you, Callum."

"He's a lovely little fella, Sarah."

"Yes, adorable."

"Must go. Bye, Sarah."

"Bye, Callum." Sarah watched Callum drive away and then went back into the lounge and sat down with her new little bundle of joy on her lap. "Oh gosh, you are a little sweetie," she said, kissing the little pup on his head.

A short time later, her mobile rang and Sarah answered it. "Hello, I hear you've got your little pressy. What do you think of him?"

Sarah had quickly realised that the puppy which Callum had delivered, was in fact a little girl, but for now, she would keep quiet about it! "Oh he's gorgeous," she said with a smirk on her face, "but I am not sure what Mum will have to say when she finds out!"

"Oh, she'll be all right. I thought you would love him. What are you going to call him because I think he looks like a Rex," Steve suggested.

"You've seen him then."

"Of course I have, I chose him for you, from four puppies."

"Oh I see, well, he's extremely cute!"

"I had hoped to give him to you myself, but I have to be in Manchester today."

"Well, he's the best gift ever, thank you."

There was an awkward silence, before Steve said. "Right I have to be in a meeting in five minutes. Look after yourself, Sarah, and good luck!"

"You too," Sarah replied as she switched off her mobile phone and let out a loud sigh. However, after one look at her darling puppy, who was curled up on her lap and yawning her head off, suddenly her own mood changed completely. She definitely felt happier now. She forced any thoughts of Steve Fountain completely out of her mind. They were clearly done and dusted. She placed her little bundle of joy back into her cosy wicker bed, which housed a soft squidgy cushion and went back into the kitchen. She was feeling hungry by now and heated up Molly's chicken casserole with veggies. As always it was delicious, Molly was a fine cook. Oh dear she would miss her and everyone else too. Still, this was home for her once again, at least until she could move into the apartment above the shop.

Sarah turned the TV off, cleared up in the kitchen, and decided that she would have an early night, she was exhausted. She looked at her little puppy who was sleeping peacefully and picked up the wicker basket and carried it up to her bedroom. She fully expected some whimpering during the night from Roxy, as poor baby this would be the first time away from her mother. Anyhow, she couldn't bear to be parted from her. Sarah took a bath and afterwards jumped straight into bed and began to read one of the many books she'd been given on bringing up a puppy. She'd had no idea of how much was involved in raising a puppy. Sarah would have to learn fast on her feet and when Roxy was old enough, would book up some puppy training classes for her. It was going to be awkward, what with Dotty not being around to help her at the moment. Oh dear, she was not really sure what Dotty would have to say about their latest addition to the family! Hopefully, she would fall in love with her, as she herself had already done.

Chapter 44

Sarah sat down on the sofa and sipped her tea, after yet another stressful and busy day, which she had spent mostly on site at The Bake Stop. However, it had really begun to come on in leaps and bounds over the past few weeks. All the commercial equipment had now been installed in the bakery and she was quietly confident that the opening would indeed take place, as she hoped in March. Annabel had once again given her some invaluable help in choosing the furniture.

Dotty and George would be arriving home later, and she was really looking forward to seeing both of them, as she'd missed her mother, especially over Christmas. They had been away for six weeks and living back at the Cottage this past few weeks, even with her being so busy, was quite lonely at times. Somehow, she had become used to living with several other people in Steve's large house, but overall, she was happy, especially with how The Bake Stop was progressing. Thankfully, she had Roxy to keep her company now, and it could be hard work training her sometimes! It was like having a baby, and she had been flabbergasted at just how many puppy gizmos were now available to buy. She'd even got an adaptable seat belt so that she could take her out safely in the car. Sarah had decided to call her Roxy, as this was as close as she could get to Rex, which was Steve's original choice, had she not turned out to be a girl. How that had happened was still a mystery, but she didn't care. She had fallen deeply, madly in love with her.

Dotty hadn't been overly impressed when Sarah had told her about the latest addition to the family, exclaiming that it was typical of Steve to give her a gift, without giving too much thought as to the impact it would have on everyone else.

Sarah set about preparing a light supper for her mother and George, as they were due to arrive home at around 9 o'clock and had made a Macaroni Cheese, with salad which was a favourite with George!

There was a knock at the door and it was Peggy with an overly excited Roxy. Sarah made a fuss of her before she darted over to her food bowl. "Come in Peggy, so how has my baby been today then?"

"She's been as good a gold as always, Sarah."

"Blimey can she eat though."

"I know, but she can only have what she's allowed."

"Oh yes, and I've only given her a couple of treats when she's been a very good girl."

"Do I need to buy some more food for you yet?"

"No, you've given me more than enough and I will let you know when I do, don't worry."

"You're a star Peggy, and I don't know what I would do without you."

"Oh I love looking after Roxy, mind you my Mr Pickles isn't too keen on her, but at least he's stopped hissing at her now."

"Would you like a cuppa, Peggy?"

"No, I'd best be off, it's me bingo night and it's about time I bloody well won too," she said somewhat disgruntled.

"I've got my granddaughter and little Isabelle descending on me tomorrow. Chloe's finally left her partner, and I know I shouldn't say it, but it's about time too. Connor is a complete toe rag and she's better off without him."

"Oh dear, I suppose from what you've told me it's no surprise."

"No, not really, it's a brave thing for her to do and I am proud of her. Unfortunately, there's no room for them at my daughter's house, but I'm more than happy to have them."

"Will you be okay to look after Roxy, won't you be a bit too busy now?"

"No of course, not. No problem at all."

"Well, I will be home all day tomorrow, as Mum and George are back tonight, so I will see you Wednesday."

"All right love, bye."

"Bye Peggy, and thanks once again!"

Roxy began to get excited and jumped up around where her lead was kept, so Sarah put it on her and they went down to the local park. Roxy was still too young to be let off her lead, but she was growing fast and would soon be attending her puppy training classes. It was fairly quiet but it wasn't long before they bumped into Jane, who used to attend Sarah's cake class and was a regular in the park with Billy, her Jack Russell who Roxy adored. Roxy, immediately began to get excited and rolled over onto the grass and inevitably, a lot of sniffing went on. They walked slowly around the park together before Sarah took Roxy home.

After wiping Roxy's paws, she settled down in her basket and fell asleep instantly. She still slept rather a lot, which was only to be expected. She'd taken loads of photographs of her and there wasn't a bad one amongst them. She'd also taken lots of photographs during the alterations at The Bake Stop, step by step and she would put them all into an album, once she got them developed. She couldn't wait to show Dotty the shop now, as it had certainly progressed somewhat since her mother last saw it.

Sarah went upstairs to put some towels away into the airing cupboard, when she heard her mother call out. Sarah, we're home. Sarah ran down the stairs and hugged her mother and then hugged George. "Well, you two both look well."

"Oh, Sarah, we've had the most amazing time, haven't we George?"

"We certainly have, Dorothy." At this point Roxy began to bark, it was as if she was saying, hey don't leave me out.

"Oh is this our new lodger then," Dotty said and walked over and tickled Roxy's tummy, whilst Roxy lapped up the attention. "You're certainly a little cutey, aren't you," Dotty said as she picked her up.

"I hope she hasn't chewed any of me furniture up."

"No Mum, she hasn't, she's been a good girl."

"Peggy has been looking after her for me, whilst I've been at work and is happy to continue doing so. She adores her, so you don't have to worry."

"I didn't say I wouldn't look after her did I," Dotty said rather gruffly.

"No, Mum, but you didn't seem too keen when I told you about her."

"Oh you know me love, and if you will pardon the pun, me bark is worse than me bite."

"I guess I could look after her for you if you like."

"Thanks, Mum, you can share her with Peggy."

The three sat down and ate heartily. "I have to say George said, this macaroni cheese is lovely, Sarah. The food has been amazing aboard ship, but it's nice to have something simple for a change."

"Well, I think there was a compliment in there somewhere, George," Sarah said, laughing at George's comment.

"Oh well, you know what I mean!"

Sarah gave George a beguiling smile and said, "Of course, I do."

Chapter 45

Sarah, Dotty along with Annabel, returned to the cottage, after being shown around, the almost finished The Bake Stop. Its opening day had been set for the 21st of March and the next job would be to send out the personal invitations.

"Right, I don't know about you two girlies, but I've had enough tea to last me a lifetime," Dotty said. "I'm going to have something stronger now, care to join me."

"Oh no thanks, Dotty D," Annabel said, "I've got to drive home."

"What about you, Sarah?"

"No thanks, Mum, I actually feel sick from trying out too many cream teas."

"Perhaps, you hadn't better let anyone hear you say that Sarah, it's definitely not a good PR move, take it from me," Annabel said.

Sarah laughed, "You know what I mean, I am stuffed."

"Okay, so it's just me then for drinky poos," Dotty said going into the kitchen. Mum still thinks she's on her cruise, not that she needs an excuse!

"Are you feeling okay Sarah, you do look a bit peaky and I know your mum thinks you've been working way too hard lately."

"I know she does, but I have to push on now, time is money."

"Promise me you will have an early night."

"I will."

"Anyhow babe, I can honestly say your pastry skills are second to none, and the bread was amazing."

"Yes, Jack is a clever fellow, and fortunately for me, very talented with dough too. The Art Deco lights in the restaurant look amazing! Yes, and I have you to thank for that, they were a real find Annabel and under budget, for a change."

"My pleasure, babe, and that gramophone gives it all a touch of authenticity, brilliant, Sarah."

"Thank goodness Dave managed to coax Jack to come and work for me and Dave's help has been a godsend."

"So what happened with Jack's job in London?"

"I don't think he was happy with all the travelling and more importantly, he wasn't spending as much time with his young family as he would have liked."

"Lucky for you then."

"It's cost me a bit obviously because he can earn way more in London, but I couldn't do without him. I know I can trust him totally.

"I have been extremely lucky with my staff so far. I really, really hope that this is all going to turn out to be as good as it's been playing out in my head, Annabel."

"It will, Sarah, and I've always believed in you and it's going to be a huge success, trust me."

"Thanks, hun."

"Right I'd better make a move, I promised Mum that I wouldn't be too late."

"Sure, thanks for everything, Annabel."

"Me, I've done nothing."

"Yes, you have."

"Give hugs and kisses to Alfie and say 'Hi' to your mum."

"Will do."

"I cannot believe, my baby is going to turn one next week. Oh my how time flies. And I cannot wait to see his cake, Sarah, are you sure you've enough time to make it?"

"For my favourite little boy? Of course."

Dotty came through with her Gin and Tonic in her hand.

"Cheers girlies."

"I'm off now Dotty D."

"Okay, love."

"Lovely to see you."

"You too, see you both next week at Alfie's party."

Chapter 46

"How much longer are you going to stare at that bloody invitation, Sarah?"

"Sorry, Mum, what did you say?"

"Oh, Sarah, what's up with you? Are you going to his Lordship's Premiere or not?"

"Oh I don't think so, Mum, I really do have too much on here at the moment."

"Well, it might do you good to get away for the night love, not to mention you gave your heart and soul to everyone on that film set." Somewhat more softly, Dotty said, "You deserve it love. Also, a free overnight stay for two at the Dorchester. I could have been your plus one!"

Sarah was a little short with her mother when she said, "Yes I know, Mum, I am sorry, but my new business is more important to me right now."

"Oh well pardon me for interfering."

"No you're not, Mum. Ignore me, I'm just tired."

"When aren't you, love."

"I'm going to make a fish pie for tea, that all right with you?"

"I'm not that hungry, Mum, an omelette will do. I will do it myself later if that's okay?"

"No, I can make it for you. I might as well have one too, as there's no point in me doing fish pie for one."

"Okay thanks, Mum, I have a few things to see to before dinner."

Up in her room, Sarah flopped down onto her bed. Fish pie, yuck the thought of it made her stomach flip somersaults. Thank goodness Dotty had decided against it. She looked in the mirror and thought how washed out she looked, with dark circles under her eyes. There was no way she was going to go to the premiere of *No Hiding Place*. She felt and looked dreadful, but it hurt her deeply.

To stand on the same red carpet alongside the stars of *No Hiding Place*, who she was extremely proud and fortunate to call her friends, would have been a night to remember. But, she had to think of herself now. She knew it was tough on Dotty, as she was so disappointed with her decision, but it couldn't be helped.

Sarah was still in shock. Yesterday, her doctor had dropped the biggest bombshell ever. He'd told her that she was pregnant. Her mother had been nagging her for a couple of weeks to book an appointment and finally she did. Even now, she just couldn't believe it. She hadn't even told Dotty yet. What would she say? No doubt she would be as surprised as she herself was! Sarah would have to tell her tonight. It wouldn't be fair to withhold this most joyous of surprises, and yes she was in shock, but she was also over the moon. However, tired and feeling nauseous.

Dotty called up the stairs, "Sarah, your tea's ready."

"Okay, Mum, I'm coming." Sarah wasn't sure if she felt sick because of her pregnancy or due to the nerves she had due to the news she was about to impart to her mother!

"Oh there you are, love, cheese and ham okay for you."

Sarah's stomach flipped once more. "I'm so sorry, Mum, but I don't actually feel I could eat it right now."

"What's up with you, Sarah? Come on, tell me. I know something is wrong!"

"Sit down, Mum." Dotty did as she was told. "I'm pregnant, Mum."

"What pregnant, but how?"

"Well, the usual way, of course, but like you I was equally as surprised when Doctor Harrison told me."

"OMG, Sarah, this is BLOODY WONDERFUL news, isn't it?"

"Yes of course it is." Dotty got up and hugged Sarah tightly to her. "You've been nagging me to make an appointment at the doctors, so I did. I asked Dr Harrison the same thing as you Mum, as in how, with all the IVF that I've had before and I didn't get pregnant. He said there could be many explanations, one of which may be that me and Richard were incompatible."

"Oh I always knew that, Sarah, and it was him that had the problem," Dotty said harshly, "not you."

Dotty had the biggest smile on her face when she said, "So when is my little grandchild due then?"

"September 12th, Mum."

"This explains why you've been looking so peaky of late, which has clearly not all been down to the hard work which you have been doing. Thank goodness,

Sarah," Dotty said, becoming emotional. "I've been really worried about you, you know."

"Yes, I know Mum."

"I'm going to take extra good care of you from now on," Dotty said, blowing her nose onto a tissue and passed one to Sarah, who was also crying by now.

"You always have, Mum." Dotty looked at her, with raised eyebrows, and as always didn't hold back. "So who is the father?"

Sarah cast her eyes down and said, "Well…"

"What do you mean, well? I'm assuming it's his Lordship." Sarah was still quiet. "Isn't it?"

"I think so, Mum."

"You think so? Sarah Margaret Louise Carrington, what have you been up to exactly?"

Chapter 47

Dotty was sitting in the lounge having her usual pre-dinner gin and tonic and had herself a crafty cigarette, she only had the occasional one now. She'd promised Sarah she would give them up, but was finding it tough on occasion. She didn't like those e-cigarette thingies. The doorbell rang and Roxy barked loudly. Dotty peered out of the window and noticed a rather flash car parked outside. "Who on earth could that be Roxy? If there is any trouble girl, go straight for the ankles or even higher if you have to." Roxy bounded up towards the door wagging her tail excitedly, but at least she was still barking. Dotty opened the door, but was totally unprepared to see Steve standing in front of her, and was rather taken aback.

"Hello, Dotty, nice to see you. Can I come in?" Dotty hesitated briefly and then ushered Steve through. He stepped inside and made a big fuss of Roxy. "You've certainly grown boy since I last saw you." Roxy was in her seventh heaven, rolling onto her back, whilst Steve rubbed her tummy.

"Well, of course she has. She was only a tiny pup last time you saw her," Dotty remarked rather acidly.

"Is he behaving himself?"

"No, of course not, she's chewed up a few things I can tell you. I'm on me third pair of slippers, but she's a lovely girl aren't you, Roxy."

"Hold on a minute, how come you keep saying she and calling Rex, Roxy; what's that all about?"

"Yes, Steve, that's right because when Callum brought down what we were led to believe was a little boy, *he* turned out to be a little girl."

"How on earth did that happen?"

"Well, Steve, I would have thought, you of all people should know the difference, with your wealth of experience with the ladies," Dotty said with more than a hint of sarcasm. "I swear when I went down to the breeder's home, that the puppy I picked out for Sarah was a boy."

270

"That may be so, Steve, but Callum brought Roxy to us, and Sarah is very fond of her, so it doesn't matter now," Dotty said, petting Roxy and giving her a treat.

"And I see she's not the only one by the looks of it," Steve remarked.

Dotty chuckled, "Is it that obvious?"

"'Fraid so!"

"Wouldn't be without her now, would we darling."

"Be a good girl and go sit in your basket," and Roxy did as she was told, but she did have a woeful look in her eyes and made a whimpering sound as she did so.

"You'd better sit down, Steve."

"Can I get you a drink or anything? I'm just having my G and T."

"No thanks, Dotty, better not as I'm driving."

"Have you heard from George?"

"Oh yes, he's having a lovely time catching up with his family. They're all coming over here in the summer, so I will get to meet them then."

"I think it's great, that you are both hitting it off by the way."

"You are certainly very well suited."

"He's a very nice man and we enjoy doing the same things that's all Dotty said a little haughtily, there's nothing more to it!"

"Okay, Dotty, there is no need to be so defensive!"

"I'm not," Dotty said giving Steve a stern look.

"What's up, Dotty, you're not your usual effervescent self today."

"I am perfectly fine thank you," Dotty said huffily. "Well, I seem to be getting the cold shoulder somewhat."

"Don't know what you mean, Steve."

"I see you are still smoking," Steve remarked. "Is Sarah still nagging you?"

"Of course she is, I hardly smoke these days and certainly not around Sarah, I've promised to give them up completely."

"Why might that be?"

Keen to change the conversation Dotty said, "How about, I make you a nice cup of tea."

"All right if it makes you happy, Dotty."

"How about a slice of your delicious fruit cake that I've heard so much about. That's if you've made one?"

"Of course I have." Steve followed Dotty through to the kitchen. Dotty's cottage was not only homely, but also warm and cosy. However, it was rather too hot in the kitchen for Steve's liking, which was probably due to the Aga. He pulled himself a chair out, from under the large oak table, which practically filled the room. It was all so very different to his own contemporary homes. This had real charm. He sat down. "So, Dotty, why are you giving up the cigarettes then?"

"I just am, I promised Sarah that's all."

"Oh I see." Dotty filled the kettle and placed it onto the Aga and brought the cake tin down from the cupboard. Steve had a lot of respect for Dotty. She was a tough individual and she didn't suffer fools gladly. He sensed there was something wrong, but what at this precise moment, he had no idea. With the kettle boiled, Dotty made Steve's tea. "There you go," Dotty said as she placed his tea and cake down onto the table.

"Thank you, Dotty."

"My pleasure, you're very welcome."

"This cake is delicious, Dotty. Is Sarah selling it in her shop?"

"Of course she is. It's one of her best sellers."

"How's it all going?"

"Very well indeed."

"Where is Sarah, I thought she would be home by now?"

"Steve, she worked for you for well over a year. You of all people should know she is a workaholic and this is her own business now."

"Yes, I know. Unfortunately, her replacement wasn't so committed. I had to let her go, she spent far too much time on her mobile and she was a terrible gossip."

"You must have known it would be hard to replace Sarah."

"Yes you're right, Dotty, it was."

"Was she young, your last assistant?"

"Why do you ask?"

"Well, I've read you like your women young."

"Oh really." Steve laughed, "You shouldn't believe all you read about me, Dotty. I see you're razor sharp as always."

"Well, I won't be changing now, will I," Dotty replied looking at Steve directly.

"I don't expect you will and I wouldn't want you to," was Steve's response. "Anyway, I will finish my tea and pop down to the tea room. It's not far away is it?"

"Well if you'd bothered to turn up for the opening, you would have known wouldn't you? I had to be in LA at the time Dotty and Sarah understood."

"Yes, that's the trouble with my daughter she is far too understanding for her own good."

"Actually Steve, before you go, I need to have a word with you, if you don't mind. Although I have to say, Sarah would probably kill me if she knew I was interfering."

"I knew there was something wrong. Come on, Dotty, fill me in."

"You're sitting down, so that is a good start."

"Oh it's that bad, is it?"

"Well, it depends on how you react once I tell you."

"Just get on with it, please Dotty."

"You know, Steve, I shoot straight from the hip, always have. But in the long run, you're going to find out one way or another and I would like to have my say first." Steve looked at Dotty impatiently.

"Okay," Dotty blurted out, "Sarah is pregnant. Three and a half months to be precise and I believe you're the daddy. Although Sarah hasn't said as much to me, as yet! She's still taking being pregnant in, bless her. Anyway, against my advice, the silly girl is totally besotted with you. Sorry no offence meant, Steve, as I know you're a nice guy, but Sarah's been through so much." Steve couldn't take in what Dotty was saying, as he was completely taken aback and lost for words. "I'm sorry, Steve, I thought that would probably be a shock for you," Dotty said a little more kindly.

"Why didn't Sarah tell me?"

"I think you must know why, Steve. I am not sure as to what went on between the pair of you, but Sarah gave me the impression that it wasn't anything serious. In fact, she has said very little!"

Steve still looked surprised, as he shook his head. "But Sarah told me that she was unable to have children. In fact, we spoke about it once and she said that she and her ex-husband had tried for years to have children and that she'd even had IVF. She also said she thought that it was one of the reasons why their marriage broke down."

"No, no, it broke down, because he was a complete arse hole, if you'll pardon me French. He was a lying, cheating toad and clearly to be crude, he was firing blanks. Richard used to blame Sarah all the time, especially when he'd been drinking. They did try IVF a few times, but after it didn't work out, they made the decision that it wasn't meant to be and that was that." Dotty stopped briefly. "Steve the only reason I'm telling you all of this now, is because I have never seen my Sarah so happy. She'll be nearly 40 when this little baby," Dotty's voice cracked slightly as she became emotional, "our little miracle baby comes along. It's all she has ever wanted. She's totally self-sufficient, she has money and what looks to be a successful business, which is going from strength to strength. On top of that, she has the love and support of her family. Anyhow, you have both come from two different worlds."

"Dotty, I don't think you should presume to know everything about me, or even Sarah."

"Steve, your lifestyle and playing around is all well documented."

"In my defence, it's not all true, you have to believe me. It sells newspapers and magazines."

"Whatever, but if you haven't realised it yet, my daughter is a pretty special woman. I doubt that you even have an inkling that she is in love with you, do you?" Steve smiled at Dotty, but made no comment on the news that Dotty had just told him. "Have you anything to say at all, Steve?"

"Yes, lots but I've got to go, Dotty, I have to see Sarah."

"Steve, please think this through before you go and see her. Like I said, she is so happy and if you are not able to commit to her, and then again," Dotty paused, "I'm not even sure if you're the father. Best I don't say another word." Dotty sighed, who was she kidding, of course Steve was the father!

"Bit late for that, but I do have a lot of respect for you, Dotty, but this really is between Sarah and me."

Dotty looked apologetic. "I know, Steve, and I do understand that, but Sarah has been through hell and back in the past. I couldn't bear to see her get hurt again. Believe me Steve, if you hurt her, when it's my time to leave this mortal earth, I swear, I will come back and haunt you."

"Oh don't worry, I believe you actually would, there's no doubt about that, Dotty."

Steve got up and kissed Dotty. "I have to go now and I really do have immense respect for you. You're a pretty special woman yourself, you know, Dotty, thanks."

"What for, Steve?"

"I haven't got the time to explain it to you right now."

Dotty smiled and kissed him on the cheek. "Good luck, Steve, I think you'll need it."

"Thanks, bye, Dotty." He disappeared like lightening and Dotty was left pondering whether she would regret opening what some would term her big mouth! Still it was done now and that was that as they say! She hoped her instincts were right and that she wouldn't regret her meddling!

Chapter 48

The Bake Stop had only been open a month, but it had all taken off in a big way and every day was full on. The opening had been what her nieces would say, awesome. James Hunter had surprised her by agreeing to come down to officially re-open the newly refurbished, The Bake Stop. This had to be kept top secret, otherwise it would have all kicked off and caused mayhem. It did the trick though, as it had gone viral and it had been in all of the local newspapers, and the Daily Mail, without costing her a penny, brilliant free advertisement! She would be forever grateful, as the Restaurant was full right up until August for cream teas every weekend. The bakery and coffee house were equally as busy, and it was great to see so many of the locals, who were coming in early every morning to get their fresh bread and croissants and appeared to be happy with new style, The Bake Stop.

Sarah and Sophie had nearly finished for the day. The kitchen and tables were clean and set ready for customers the following morning. Sarah was beginning to feel tired, as it had been hectic and she'd been on her feet for most of the day. Sophie tried to ensure that she took time out as much as possible. This however wasn't proving easy, as Sarah didn't know the meaning of slowing down one little bit. Sophie was like a mother hen towards her. She had proved herself to be invaluable to Sarah, not just as her assistant, but as a friend too. "Right Sarah, we're done here. I'm off, but promise me that you will go straight home."

Sarah looked at her. "Oh stop worrying, you're as bad as my mother."

Sophie looked at her sternly.

"Okay I promise, sergeant major. Anyway, if I don't, my mother will be on the phone. You know what she's like."

"I certainly do."

"Well, I will see you tomorrow," Sophie said and kissed Sarah on the cheek. Yes see you tomorrow, bye. "Thanks for everything, Soph."

"My pleasure."

Steve sat in his car trying to work out how he should play this. He was still reeling after his conversation with Dotty. He was shocked to hear he was going to be a father and even more shocked that Sarah wasn't apparently sure whether to tell him. On reflection, maybe he deserved it. After all, he had always been honest with her. She knew the score with him, most women did. The experience between his parents when they had divorced, had done enough to put him off commitment and marriage forever, or so he'd thought. He wasn't entirely sure of what Sarah's reaction would be when she saw him.

He could see Sarah and another woman working together, setting the tables in the restaurant. She had her hair tied back in a ponytail as she always did whilst working. She looked happy and had a white chef's jacket on. From where he was sat, he couldn't tell if there was a baby bump or not yet. Steve began to feel uncomfortable about spying on Sarah and he decided it was time he got a grip of himself. He suddenly got out of his car and walked towards The Bake Stop. He hesitated briefly, by the shop door before it suddenly opened. This took him by surprise and Sophie nearly jumped out of her skin. Sophie stared at him blankly, before she realised who he was. She smiled and raised her eyebrows at him and took a backwards glance towards Sarah. What was she to do. Steve looked imploringly at her, as he said shoosh and put his fingers to his lips, indicating for her to be quiet. Sophie wasn't sure whether it was wise to let Steve into the shop. Perhaps she ought to at least forewarn Sarah. However, with her fingers crossed and her heart in her mouth, she let Steve through into the shop and took her leave. She took another glance over at Sarah and just hoped she had done the right thing!

Sarah was still tidying up behind the counter with her back to Steve. She took off her chef's jacket and was just about to turn off the lights when she saw him. Her jaw dropped and she felt weak at the knees. Steve walked over to her and apologised. "I'm so sorry, Sarah. I didn't mean to shock you." Sarah's heart was racing. Typically, as always, Steve was dressed immaculately in his casual clothes, namely one of his expensive white shirts, and jeans and as always, with not a hair out of place. She was struck by just how devilishly handsome and fresh faced he was and her heart skipped a beat. She managed to regain her composure.

"Well, you're the last person I expected to see, Steve."

"Yes, I can imagine. I'm sorry that I wasn't around for the opening of The Bake Stop."

"That's okay," she said rather coolly, masking how she really felt, as that wasn't how she was actually feeling inside, far from it.

"I love the décor by the way. Art Deco, it's very you."

"Thanks."

"How's the business going?"

"Very well, thank you. Booming, in fact. Hard work, but as you know I'm not afraid of that!"

"I don't doubt that because you were definitely the hardest working PA I've ever had, by miles. Just as you told me you would be, when I first met you at my house that day." There was an awkward silence between them before Sarah asked

"So what have you been up to?"

"Do you mean to say you don't bother to check anymore?"

"I'm busy, Steve, but I did hear that *No Hiding Place* has been a huge hit at the box office. You must have been relieved."

"Definitely, although I had a few sleepless nights I can tell you." Sarah wasn't about to admit that she'd followed everything he did. Not to mention that George and Molly kept her up-to-date on every aspect of Steve's life. "I was really sorry you didn't come to the premiere."

"Me too, but it was extremely full on here to get the place open on time."

"You should have been there, Sarah, as some of your input which you gave to me was invaluable."

"That's a kind and generous thing to say Steve, thanks."

As usual whenever Steve was around Sarah, he struggled to find the right thing to say. "So have you missed me?" he said with a cheeky grin on his face.

"Well, I haven't exactly had the time Steve, as it's been all consuming here."

Steve knew he had to bite the bullet. It was now or never! "I popped round to see you at your mum's cottage earlier and Dotty told me you were still here."

"Oh did she?"

"Yes, and she's as feisty as ever, I see!"

"You know my mother, she tells it exactly how it is."

"Yes, she certainly does. Sarah come and sit down."

"No, I'm perfectly okay, thank you."

"Please sit, I want to talk to you." He pulled a chair out from behind one of the tables and Sarah sat down. Steve sat opposite and looked directly at her. "I know about the baby Sarah."

Sarah exclaimed, "Oh my God!"

"I told Dotty not to say anything, not to you or anyone yet. Did she ask you to come down here? Wait until I get home."

"Stop it, Sarah, calm down for goodness' sake! She didn't contact me at all. I knew nothing about any baby. But there is something, however, that I would like to ask you!"

"Oh yes." Sarah's heart began to beat faster again. "I think I can guess what that is."

"You can?" Steve said, sounding surprised.

"Oh yes, I can and to answer your question, Steve, you are the daddy, and just so as you know," she continued looking rather sheepish. "I didn't sleep with Jake on New Year's Eve!"

"Well, that wasn't what I was going to ask you, but I already knew that, Sarah."

"You did, how?"

"Jake told me."

"Oh he did, did he?"

"Yes."

"How come?"

"Jake came around to see me and pointed out a few facts."

"So what are these facts," Sarah asked, trying to hold back a smile!

"Mainly that I have been very stupid to let you slip through my fingers."

"Really?"

"Yes really, he does care about you, Sarah."

"Yes, I guess I knew that already, and he is the most charming and kind guy I've ever met and such a hunk too."

"Steady on," Steve said, "you're hurting my feelings, now, Sarah!" Steve cleared his throat. "When were you actually going to tell me about the baby, by the way?" he asked with a serious look on his face.

"Well, knowing Dotty, she's probably already told you that I wasn't going to tell you, not just yet anyhow. Who needs any gossip magazines with my mother around. She's a proper busy body," Sarah said, sounding exasperated. Sarah was aware that she needed to handle this carefully. Steve had well and truly put her on the spot. She hesitated for a moment before saying, "Steve, we didn't ever have a proper relationship, did we? We were more like friends with benefits," she said and her face flushed slightly. "I'd convinced myself you didn't want to be with me. I believed that I was perfectly capable of raising a baby on my own if that's what I had do!"

"Could you really do that to me?"

Sarah looked full of remorse and answered as honestly as she could. "I don't know if I can explain it to you properly, Steve."

Steve smoothed his hair back, as he was apt to do when he was feeling stressed. "Please try, Sarah, as I want to try and make sense of all of this."

"The only explanation I can think of, is that I've kind of been in shock myself, but also in this most wonderful baby bubble. The real reason I didn't come to your premiere was because I was feeling sick all the time and I looked awful! Perhaps, I haven't been thinking clearly at all." Sarah's eyes lit up and then filled with tears and her voice cracked just as Dotty's had. "I never ever thought I would be in this position. Me, having a baby, it's a shock, but a wonderful one at that!"

Steve took hold of her hand as he said gently, "I know that, Sarah."

She was on the verge of breaking down completely as she said, "Can you ever forgive me, Steve, please?"

Steve took his time in answering her, and Sarah's heart began pounding once again.

"I guess I can, but only because I love you." Sarah sat motionless for a while and was stunned into silence.

Suddenly, she burst into tears, sobbing uncontrollably. It was a release from all the tension which she had held back during the past weeks, which she'd been trying so hard to ignore. Since becoming pregnant, her hormones had been all over the place. Steve passed her a napkin from the table and she blew her nose onto it. With red eyes and a runny nose and still crying she asked. "Sorry, but did you just tell me that you love me?"

"Yes, you and the baby. Who's the lucky guy eh? Two for the price of one and actually, I did think you'd take this news a bit better somehow! We were both rather remiss the last time we made love and forgot to use a thingy!" Steve said, teasing her.

Sarah laughed out loud. "Oh God yes, but I am extremely happy about that," she said as she dried her eyes.

"That makes two of us then, doesn't it!" Steve couldn't contain himself any longer. He took Sarah into his arms and kissed her softly at length. As was the way between them both, they couldn't keep their hands off one another. Sarah looked at Steve and her green eyes predictably had a look of mischief in them. Steve had always found her totally irresistible. She was indeed his one weakness in life and he was putty in her hands and yet, undoubtedly she was the best thing that had ever happened to him.

Sarah grabbed hold of his hand and led him up the stairs into her apartment. "You've worked your magic up here too I see, Sarah."

"Yes, and it's been hard work. The only room that isn't finished yet, is the baby's room. I've also got a workstation for my cake classes. Do you want to have a look?"

"What do you think?" They both laughed as Sarah took Steve through to the bedroom. "You're a wicked woman, Sarah Carrington," and for an instant they just stared into each other's eyes and Steve stroked her face tenderly. He slowly undressed her and placed his hand onto her tiny baby bump, looking at her with love and pride. "You know, Sarah, you look amazing you're barely showing he said lifting her up and laying her gently onto the bed."

Steve then laid down beside her and wrapped his arms around her and they immediately began kissing and soon their passion overtook them both and she felt a hunger for Steve that was so familiar to her. Their lovemaking was certainly more gentler than in the past and calmer than on previous occasions. It did however, have a much more meaningful effect upon both of them. They were a couple, united as never before.

Afterwards, Sarah laid in Steve's arms. Both were slightly out of breath. Steve stroked Sarah's face and said, "I really missed you after you left, you know. I hadn't realised what an impact you'd made on my life and I tried so hard to ignore it for a while at least. It was a bit like losing my right arm."

"Really?" Sarah asked.

"Yes, you made yourself indispensable. Oh and by the way I must tell you, that we have finally got the go ahead to make Molly's film, so I have spent a lot of time in Ireland, checking out locations."

"Oh that's brilliant news."

"We all miss you, Sarah, that's Molly, George and Buster, but I have missed you the most," he said kissing her once more. "We all want you to come home!"

"Is it because I was always there to run your little errands for you?"

"No, of course not. Anyhow, I thought I irritated the hell out of you most of the time. I seem to remember something about me being bossy!"

"Well that's true, Sarah. Your mother is right though, you are very special."

"My mother. What did she say to you exactly?"

"Don't worry, Dotty is only looking out for you. It made no difference, pregnant or otherwise, my reason for coming here today, was to tell you that I love you. Clearly, I certainly didn't know about junior," he said, kissing her tummy gently. That was a total surprise! "Anyway, you know your mother, she never minces her words and I admire her for that."

"You're being way too polite, Steve, some would say she was a bit gobby, but I love her to bits."

"I know you do. I just hope our baby doesn't take after her." Sarah laughed.

"Well, we will just have to wait and see. How do you really feel about becoming a daddy?"

"I won't lie to you, Sarah, I am nervously excited and I'm not sure if I'm grown up enough to become a dad and as you know, I'm as selfish as hell!! But if I'm honest, I'm over the moon. A little mini me."

"What if it's a little girl?"

"Then it will be a mini you." He placed his hand over her naked body once again to stroke her stomach.

"Steve, I cannot even begin go tell you how nervous I was at first, and it never even entered my head that I could ever be pregnant. After all the heartache with Richard and the IVF and the years of utter disappointment. Sarah almost broke down. I am so lucky, so very lucky, Steve."

"We both are, Sarah, and I can see that you are positively glowing and you look like you're on cloud nine."

"I am, especially now. I have only just got used to the idea of becoming a mummy she said bursting with happiness. I guess I was scared, but now I cannot wait for junior to come along."

"Do you know the sex of baby Fountain yet," Steve asked.

Sarah said emphatically, "NO, it's too soon and anyway, I don't want to know either."

"All right, I get the picture! I will go along with whatever you decide, correction have already decided." Sarah slapped him gently on the arm.

"Cheeky. We could find out I suppose."

"No, let's have a surprise." Steve pulled Sarah into his arms and kissed her on the forehead.

"Steve, did you know that I practically fell for you right from the outset. Fool that I am."

"That's one thing, Sarah, you're definitely nobody's fool. Not only are you beautiful, but you're a very wise woman."

"Thank you, Steve."

"Oh and by the way, what was it that you came here to ask me?"

"Do you know," Steve said looking puzzled, "I have forgotten! Let me see, oh yes, will you marry me?" Sarah was stunned into silence. "Well," Steve asked, "what's your answer?"

"You're not kidding me, are you?"

"Of course not, you idiot." Sarah flung her arms around Steve's neck.

"Do you really need to ask. It's a big YES from me," she said, trembling with excitement.

In a short space of time, she'd just found out that the man she loved with all her heart, not only loved her, but had just proposed. Her head was spinning. They kissed once more, passionately, but suddenly Sarah pulled away from Steve. "Oh my god I'd better phone up my mum and let her know I am not coming home tonight."

"What are we," Steve laughed, "a couple of teenagers?"

"Well, she worries about me. I haven't ever slept here as yet. I've become so used to being around company, that I find it quite lonely when I am on my own."

"Well, you aren't going to be on your own anymore, are you?" Steve said kissing her again. Sarah didn't want the kiss to end, but pulled away from Steve once more, breathless. "Please, I want to tell her our good news."

"Dotty's not stupid, she'll have guessed what's happening, but go on. I'm a patient man."

"Oh yes and who told you that," Sarah laughed as she grabbed hold of her mobile phone and rung her mother. "Hi, Mum, it's me."

Dotty was as sarcastic as ever. "Oh you're still alive then."

"Yes sorry, Mum, I forgot the time."

"I'm only joking, love. I'd have been very (and she emphasised the word very) upset if you had have come home tonight. I wasn't sure if you were still speaking to me after my chat with Steve."

"Of course, I am silly."

"Oh that's good."

"Anyway, I just rung to tell you that Steve has asked me to marry him and I've said yes."

"Oh tell me something I don't know. Anyone can see he's crazy about you."

Steve was listening to their conversation and took the phone from Sarah. "I told her you'd know Dotty."

"I guess I can put the shotgun away now then can I," Dotty said and Steve laughed.

"Always the joker, eh Dotty?" Steve said handing the phone back to Sarah and began to kiss the nape of Sarah's neck and she was immediately turned on. "Got to go, Mum, speak to you tomorrow."

"Okay, love."

"Night and I am so pleased for you Sarah, well, in fact, the both of you."

"Thanks, Mum, love you."

"Love you back," and as Dotty put the phone down, tears smarted in her eyes and she had a huge smile on her face. Steve made love to Sarah once again and afterwards they lay together, both happy and contented.

Chapter 49

In just over a month, a hastily put together wedding was about to take place, as Sarah stood in her wedding dress and Dotty looked on at her daughter. "I'm speechless, Sarah." Dotty's eyes filled with tears, which threatened to fall onto her cheeks and Annabel quickly passed her a tissue.

"Well, that's a first, Mum," Sarah said, kissing and hugging her mother gently.

"You look absolutely gorgeous, love," Dotty managed to mutter. "It's a shame your dad's not here to see you," Dotty said, and Sarah also became emotional, as Annabel gave her a tissue as well.

"Your mum's right, you do look gorgeous, well, beautiful in fact." Sarah was wearing an A-line ivory dress which was elegant, yet simple in soft chiffon and lace, and it hid her baby bump well. Her mother had given her a pretty single strand pearl necklace, which complemented her dress perfectly.

And the diamond and pearl earrings that Elenour had given to her matched it perfectly. Earlier, Frederick and Jean-Paul had styled her hair into an up-do, as it was a very hot day and they had all agreed, it would be the best option. Otherwise, the heat could possibly turn her hair into a frizz ball, which is certainly not a good look for any bride. The pair of them had been faffing around her all morning, but she knew it was only because they cared about her, and wanted her to look her best. They both had tears in their eyes too. Jean-Paul had said that she was one hot Momma and Frederick dramatically chirped in that it reminded him of his and Jean-Paul's big day and he too became emotional. Sarah's eyes sparkled and she exuded radiance. It was clear to all, who were close to her, just how happy she was. Annabel and Molly both looked lovely too as her Maids of Honour, with Sarah's two older nieces, Amee and Mya as her bridesmaids and little Sacha who at five years old was so cute, as her flower girl. Their dresses were in the palest shade of pink and Amee wore the same dress as Annabel and Molly, which was very sophisticated and made her look older than her 17 years. They all looked gorgeous and Sarah thought Annabel looked hot too.

Sarah knew she shouldn't meddle in other people's lives, but Steve's best friend, Daniel was the kindest man ever. He was a rugged but good-looking man too, which also helped and more importantly, he was available. Sarah thought how great it would be if he hooked up with Annabel! He was such a brilliant friend to Steve and now also to her. However, naturally Annabel's number one priority was Alfie, but it would be so nice were it ever to happen. Oh dear, she knew she really shouldn't interfere and with every passing day she realised she was turning into her mother. Now there was a thought!

It was Daniel who had suggested that they should get married at his vineyard. It was the most perfect setting, and they would have complete privacy. Set in the heart of Provence, it was a beautiful and rustic location, miles from anywhere. Surrounded by stunning scenery, as far as the eye could see, with fields full of lavender and sunflowers.

There was a light tap on the bedroom door, before Tony came in. "Come on, Sis, are you ready yet?"

"They're all waiting for you outside you know." He stopped suddenly and said, "I must say you've scrubbed up. Okay!"

"Oh cheers, bruv!" Sarah said looking slightly hurt.

"Only kidding, you look lovely, Sis," he said squeezing her hand tightly.

"That's better, I thank you kind, sir," Sarah took an intake of breath and looked at her brother. "Phew, I think I'm as ready as I ever will be."

"Mum, what about you?"

"I'm ready and I promise not to blub the whole way through the ceremony love."

"You do look totes amaze yourself, Mum, lilac really suits you, you know."

"Thanks, love and I always knew there was bit of an Essex girl lurking in you somewhere."

"Yes I agree, lilac does look great on you, Mum," Tony said, "but we'd better keep an eye on her later, eh Sis!"

"Why is that?"

"Well, what would happen if Mum had a few too many champagnes and goes wandering off into one of those lavender fields, we would lose her forever."

"You can be quiet, Tony, there's no need to take the mickey."

"I shall behave meself, don't you worry." The three of them laughed and linked arms and made their way slowly down towards the Vineyard, whilst Sacha gently dropped pink rose petals in front of them, exactly how she'd rehearsed it and a backup basket was also on hand in case they run out!

As Sarah stood alongside Steve, they stared into each other's eyes, he whispered that she looked beautiful. Sarah took an intake of breath once more, and looked around at all of their family and close friends and had a warm and fuzzy feeling inside of her and the best was yet to come when the baby arrived. Her mother she knew was doing her best to stay in control of her emotions. She also noticed George and Dotty exchange a loving look and he had his arm protectively around her. Even Celia was dabbing her eyes, and was being supported by Steve's sisters. Steve's dad, Eddie, was there too with his wife and Steve's half-sister, and although she hadn't got to know him well as yet, he seemed a kind and generous man.

Sarah and her mother had cried a lot in the past, but this time, she knew her mother's tears were of happiness. The ceremony was simple and as they were pronounced man and wife, Steve took Sarah gently into his arms and kissed her warmly and called her wifey. Just at that moment, the baby began kicking and Sarah laughed.

"What's so funny then?" Steve asked her.

"Well, junior is having a good kick around."

"Is he now," Steve said, as he placed his hand on her bump. "I reckon that's a little footballer in there and it's probably because he doesn't want to be left out of the celebrations."

"Hold on, Mr Fountain, you keep referring to our baby as a he and it could be a she," Sarah interjected. They were both getting very excited about the arrival of their baby, as it was only four months away, until Sarah's due date. They had argued a little as Steve still desperately wanted to know the baby's sex. He believed it would be better to find out beforehand, so that they could decorate the nursery in the appropriate baby colours! He said it would save time in the long run and was totally convinced the baby was going to be a boy and had already mentioned that he would like to name the baby Eddie, after his father. But as far as Sarah was concerned, the jury was still out on that one and definitely subject to negotiation. Sarah was still adamant that she didn't want to know the sex of their unborn baby. Steve had said tongue in cheek that if it was a boy, they could always try again for a baby girl. Sarah had laughed and said that they would just have to wait and see. She was certainly happier and more content than she could ever have imagined would be possible. Taking on the job with Steve Fountain had definitely been the best decision, Sarah had ever made.